A ROMAN RANSOM

ROSEMARY ROWE

A ROMAN RANSOM

headline

First published in 2006 by
HEADLINE BOOK PUBLISHING

2

Cataloguing in Publication Data is available from the British Library

ISBN 0 7553 2741 1

Typeset in Plantin by Avon DataSet Ltd,
Bidford-on-Avon, Warwickshire

Printed and bound in Great Britain by
Mackays of Chatham plc, Chatham, Kent

HEADLINE BOOK PUBLISHING
A division of Hodder Headline
338 Euston Road
London NW1 3BH

www.headline.co.uk
www.hodderheadline.com

Foreword

A Roman Ransom is set in AD 188, at a time when a large part of Britain had been for almost two hundred years the most northerly outpost of the hugely successful Roman Empire: occupied by Roman legions, criss-crossed by Roman roads, subject to Roman laws, and administered by a single governorship answerable directly to Rome. The increasingly unbalanced Emperor Commodus still wore the imperial purple and had recently declared himself a god, while his continued excesses, lascivious lifestyle and capricious cruelties continued to be a legend throughout the Empire.

Of course, for most inhabitants of Britannia such political considerations were remote, and they were content to live their lives in the relative obscurity of provincial towns and villages. Celtic traditions, settlements and languages remained, especially in the countryside, but most townspeople had adopted Roman habits. Latin was the language of the educated, and Roman citizenship – with its legal, commercial and social benefits – the ambition of all. Citizenship was not at this time automatic, even for freemen, but a privilege to be earned – by those not fortunate enough to be born to it – by service to the army or the Emperor, though it was possible for a slave of an important man to be bequeathed the coveted status, together with his freedom, on his master's death. (To impersonate a citizen, when one was not, was still a capital offence.)

For some, however, the rank was theirs at birth. Children of citizens were citizens themselves, and by this date any child born of free parents within the walls of a *colonia* – the prestigious Roman towns originally founded for retired veterans – was also a citizen by right (though doubtless older established families looked down a little on such parvenus). Even then the privilege of citizenship did not automatically extend to other family members who did not qualify: it seems they simply enjoyed a kind of reflected glory – enhanced social status without full legal rights – unless they could achieve the honour by some other means. (Glevum, modern Gloucester, was a *colonia* and one such family features in this tale.)

None the less most ordinary people were not citizens at all. Some were freemen or freed men, scratching a precarious living from trade or farm: thousands more were slaves, mere chattels of their masters, with no more status than any other domestic animal. Some slaves led pitiful lives, though others were highly regarded by their owners and might be treated well. Indeed, a slave in a kindly household, certain of food and clothing in a comfortable home, might have a more enviable lot than many a poor freeman struggling to eke out an existence in a squalid hut.

Power, needless to say, was vested almost entirely in men. Though individual women might wield considerable influence, and even own and manage large estates, females were excluded from civic office, and a woman – of whatever age – remained a child in law, under the tutelage first of her father, and then of any husband she might have. Marriage officially required her consent (indeed she was entitled to leave a marriage if it displeased her, and take her dowry with her), but in practice many girls became pawns in a kind of property game. There were few other occupations open to a wealthy woman, and daughters were often married off to men they scarcely knew, for the sake of political or financial expedience.

Poorer women worked beside their men, often in dreadful conditions. For a woman alone, the range of possible occupations was far more limited, unless she sold herself to slavery, as many did. Some widows learned the secrets of herbal remedies, and acted as midwives attending local births. Since it was unfashionable at this period for Roman matrons to suckle their own children, there was also a call for wet nurses to serve in wealthy homes. Lucky women managed to fulfil both roles at different times.

Many wet nurses were slaves, bought for the purpose, and living in their owner's household: but there is evidence of both free-born women and freed women too working in this capacity. They often cared for their charges in their homes – sometimes looking after more than one at once – and were generally respected by the community. It was considered important for a wet nurse to be 'of good character', since it was assumed that virtue or vice could be ingested with the milk, and a good wet nurse could command a higher wage than most other women of her rank. Children were commonly suckled till they were two or three years old, sometimes even more, and the nurse was often kept on in the household afterwards as a continuing attendant for the child.

After a Roman baby was born, a number of rituals had to be performed. First the father had to 'pick it up' – literally to raise it from the floor – as a sign that he accepted paternity, and received the child as his. The legal power of 'life and death' which had been vested in the *paterfamilias* in ancient Rome had lapsed by now in everything but name, and a father could kill his children with impunity only if he could show sufficient cause in law – a daughter caught in adultery, for instance, or a son suspected of a plot against his life. However, until a child was 'lifted up', it had no existence under law at all, and the *paterfamilias* could still decide to throw it to the dogs, or sell it as a slave. It could even be buried in the house – as many courtyard infant burials attest.

Once the acceptance had been made, there was still another ritual to perform. At the age of nine days for a boy (eight for a girl) a naming ceremony was held at which the child was 'purified' and showered with tiny metal gifts (which seem to have been threaded on cords round arms and feet, perhaps like little rattles), and a lucky charm or *bulla* was hung round its neck. This potent token was regarded as a most important symbol, representing protection for the child's soul, and to lose it was a dreadful tragedy. A boy would wear his till he came of age, traditionally at fourteen years, a girl would usually keep hers till she wed – which might be longer by a year or two; in both cases it would then be ritually removed, in a ceremony where childish toys and clothes were placed upon the household altar and solemnly sacrificed.

Roman children were still swaddled in the early weeks – wrapped in tight bandages to restrict movement – since it was generally believed the limbs were weak and in need of support. This does not seem to have been a custom with the Celts, and there was already a school of thought which held that babies should be allowed to move their arms and legs, and that fresh air was beneficial to the health. As soon as they were old enough to crawl, they were generally dressed much as their parents were, though there is evidence of knitted bonnets and 'leg-coverings', which I have interpreted in the story as a sort of elongated sock.

Such fashions, both in child-rearing and in general health, were not uncommon in the ancient world. There was a long tradition of discussion on such things, and the medical diet of Celsus, mentioned in the text, was only one of a dozen theories about patient care, painstakingly copied on to scrolls and circulated through the Empire.

The medical profession was an established one, although (with the exception of midwifery and other specifically 'female concerns') the practice was generally confined to men. Greeks were the most highly respected doctors at the time – well trained, sometimes at considerable expense, and generally well educated and well paid. The Greek physician Galen had served at the court of Marcus Aurelius, and his fame had spread throughout the Empire. After that every seriously wealthy household aspired to have a private physician of its own, preferably a Greek one – though not every *medicus* was a Greek, by any means. (The army, for instance, had produced its doctors too, experts in surgery and herbs for treating wounds, some of whom worked in private households after their military service was complete.) Some of these physicians were slaves, but many more were not. Some were even Roman citizens, but were retained by the household for a monthly fee. There were, however, also doctors licensed by the state or by the local council, which generally provided them with premises and a small remuneration for their work. Their patients usually came to them, and didn't pay a fee, so public doctors were much more poorly paid – and often poorly trained.

Of course, treatments were largely herbal, although – as mentioned earlier – diet and exercise did play a part. The 'rocking therapy' and 'cabbage diets' mentioned in the text were both popular techniques, and there was also a belief in bloodletting and cupping as a cure for many things. Other cures depended on the use of amulets and charms. Superstition still played a major part in Roman life: every Roman householder began his day with proper oblations to the household gods, and any serious problem would require a sacrifice, as in the story.

Even the law courts operated on a system of *fas* and *nefas* days: dates that were propitious or otherwise. A morning when the proper rituals were not observed might cause the whole day's business to be void, and if an accuser could not bring the offender into court there was no case to answer anyway. The laws and law courts mentioned in the text are, of course, those relating to Roman citizens – non-citizens received much rougher justice, often in courts presided over by harassed officials in open places, which meted out far harsher sentences. What might be exile for a citizen might well be execution for a lesser man.

No wonder the Apostle Paul once made his famous claim, '*Civis Romanus sum.*' (I am a Roman citizen.)

The Romano-British background in this book has been derived from a wide variety of (sometimes contradictory) written and pictorial sources. However, although I have done my best to create an accurate picture, this remains a work of fiction and there is no claim to total academic authenticity.

Relata refero. Ne Iupiter quidem omnibus placet. (I only tell you what I heard. Jove himself can't please everybody.)

Chapter One

I had been ill. That was the only thing I knew – and it was the first real thing I'd been aware of for a long, long time.

There had been fevered dreams. A slave-ship. Beatings. Thirst. I was tossing, chained and shivering, in that filthy hold again, hearing my young wife calling out my name as the pirates tore us from our home and carried us apart. Then these tortured images of my past would pass and instead I was sweltering and helpless in a fiery cave; or my mosaic workshop was consumed in flames, while mocking demons forced hot liquids down my throat.

Now, though, as I forced open an exploratory eye, those nightmare visions seemed to have dispersed. I appeared to be lying in a sort of bed of reeds in a little roundhouse which I vaguely recognised as mine – although I could not for the moment make any sense of this. Yet the place was so familiar: the central fire, the wooden stools, the cooking pots – even the Celtic weaving loom set up against the wall. If this was a dream, I thought, I was content with it. I could almost feel the warm glow from the fire, and feel the smart of wood-smoke in my eyes.

I almost feared to blink in case this cheerful scene proved to be a mere illusion too and – like the rest – would shimmer and vanish into mist. I closed my eyes experimentally but, though I did so several times, my surroundings remained as solid as before. For a moment it was too much for my addled brain to solve.

Then I heard a voice from somewhere near at hand and I was aware of someone bending over me. I smiled, expecting it to be my wife, but as I came to fuller consciousness I saw that it was not Gwellia at all. It was an old, skinny, wrinkled man with a bony nose and pointed chin, dressed in a tattered toga with wine stains on the front and a circlet of fresh flowers on his balding head. I shut my eyes again. This was obviously another nightmare.

But he didn't go away.

'He was ill for almost a whole moon, of course, before you sent for me.' He had a high cracked voice, and spoke Latin with the careful diction of the Greek. 'It would have been much better if I'd seen him earlier, so I could have contrived to have him purged. But I have done a great deal in the last two days. Obviously recovery will not be swift, but I believe he is past the crisis now. Drinking bad water, that is my surmise. Vomiting, fever and delusive dreams – this is the course of the disease and there have been other cases in the town. And the insides of his lids are red. I have seen this kind of thing before.' He moved the oil light closer to my face, until I could almost feel my lashes singe.

I flinched.

He was not apologetic. Quite the contrary – although he did withdraw the light and I realised that he'd sat back on his heels. 'He feels the heat. That's good!' There was evident satisfaction in his tone. 'That shows that he is partly conscious now, and that is promising. I doubted for a long time that he would survive, even with all the herbs and potions I prepared. But at least that dreadful raging fever has gone.'

A second shadow loomed up on the wall and I was aware

of another figure by the bed. However, the medicus clearly disapproved. He stood up suddenly and there was a warning in his voice. 'Forgive me, honoured citizen, for instructing you, but perhaps you should not approach him any closer. I believe this is the foul-water sickness, as I said before, but I cannot be quite certain. It may yet be the plague. We can only watch the pattern of disease. You know that there is a murrain raging presently in Rome and it is not impossible that it might travel here – these things spread with fearful rapidity. I would not have you catch the seeds of pestilence. They rise in the miasma of the patient's breath, and can take root in your own. Remember, Excellence, I did advise you not to come at all.'

Excellence? I was so startled that I almost raised my head. Marcus Aurelius Septimus, my patron, here?

This dwelling might be built on his estate – indeed he'd granted it to me as a reward for work I'd done for him – but it was the first time to my knowledge that he had ever crossed the door. Patrician citizens of his exalted rank do not often come visiting in lowly roundhouses. But one glimpse of that patrician form – tousled blond curls around the still-youthful face, the broad purple band along the toga edge, and the heavy seal ring on the hand – was enough to convince me that he was truly here. The personal representative of the outgoing governor and the most important man in all Britannia – at the bedside of a humble one-time slave? No matter that I was a freeman now, his client and a Roman citizen – it was incredible that he should visit me like this.

Perhaps I was still dreaming after all.

Another figure loomed up with a lamp, and this time it really was my wife. 'Believe me, medicus,' she began. Her tone was courteous but firm. I smiled a little to myself. We had been torn apart when we were first enslaved and reunited only recently, but, though the years of slavery had aged us both, in many ways she remains unchanged. My Gwellia could always be forceful when she chose. 'It was not my wish to put His Excellence in danger of the plague. I did not for a moment think that he would come himself. I should not have sent to him tonight at all, if he had not specifically commanded it. "If your Libertus starts to come to consciousness, you are to send up to the villa instantly – no matter whether it is day or night." That's what he said – and praise be to all the gods, it's happening at last, thanks to the potion you mixed for him. I'm only sorry that my messenger seems to have disturbed you at your meal.'

Of course, when I turned my mind to think of it, I realised she was right. Marcus was not in formal banquet wear, but he too had a wreath round his head. The two men had obviously been interrupted at some private dinner. Certainly this place was only minutes, on a horse, from the door of Marcus's country house, but of all the improbable things which greeted me, the fact that my patron and his guest had left their meal to come to me was the most surprising of all. Marcus was a stickler for social niceties, and was famously devoted to his food.

I began to wonder just how ill I'd been.

Ill enough to warrant a physician, it appeared. It was a luxury I'd rarely known and certainly would never have dreamed of for myself.

I might possibly have called in the state physician, once, if things were desperate. There had been a well-trained medicus in Glevum at one time, working on a licence from the town council, which also provided him with premises and paid him a retainer for his services. Such men are not permitted to demand a fee, but if they treat you successfully it costs you all the same, as you are naturally expected to 'show your gratitude'. However, he was dead, and now his two ex-slaves, who had been bequeathed their freedom on his death, had applied for licences themselves and set up in his place, though their only training was assisting him. I knew them well: a pair of cheerful rogues, chiefly famed for drinking too much wine and prescribing cabbage diets as a cure for everything. In general I preferred to heal myself.

This medicus was obviously a different breed of man. He was wearing a toga, for one thing, which meant that he was a full Roman citizen, and he was clearly educated and successful, since he was sufficiently eminent to be invited to Marcus's country house to dine. A high-paid private medicus, perhaps, retained by some wealthy family in the town? Probably. The best physicians in the world are Greek. There is a proper training school for them and they have been feted by high society ever since the late emperor received Galen at his court. By his diction this man was clearly Greek. His fees would be enormous.

And Marcus was providing him for me! I felt my eyes mist up with gratitude.

'Well, is he well enough to talk?' My patron's question cut across my thoughts. He took another step towards the bed, shaking off the physician's warning hand.

'But Excellence . . .' that hapless man began.

'Oh, don't fuss so, Philades! I've taken the precautions you asked me to. Breathed in and spat out as I came into the room, to send back the infection, and washed my hands with ashes from the altar of the household gods. I even put on that stupid amulet you told me I should wear. If all that won't protect me, I don't know what will. Besides, I've been here twice before, and I haven't caught it yet.'

'That may be the protection of the amulet, of course. Real ivory, worked into a pattern of the sun and containing a fresh piece of dragon-herb. It's a signal charm against attack by snakes, but it can save you from the pestilence as well. All the same, Excellence, I must advise you to move back. An evil pneuma rises from a man when he is ill.'

'Philades, it is important that I talk to him as soon as possible. Every hour that passes makes things worse. Why do you suppose I brought you here?'

'But, Excellence, I have explained all this to you. This man is very ill. It is doubtful that he would hear you, even if you spoke, and certainly he couldn't answer you, though he is clearly better than he was. Even if he comes back to total consciousness he may never be the man that once he was. It is possible his wits will be disordered, or he'll remain very weak. It will be a moon, at least, before we can be sure. I know you feel that you must speak to him, but surely there are other advisers to whom you can turn?'

'Don't you suppose that I've done everything I can?' Marcus sounded grim. 'I've told everyone I can think of who might be of use. The army, the town watch, the council – everyone! I've even had the passers-by brought in and questioned them for hours, in case they'd seen anything that might help us. But none of it has done the slightest good. It has been almost three days now, and there is still no news. I'm getting desperate. If anyone can help me, it is Libertus here. He sees things that other people don't. He has a pattern-maker's mind.'

So, this visit was not purely out of sympathy for me. Marcus had a problem, and that was why he'd come. I might have guessed as much, if I had not been thinking stupidly. It must be something serious, as well, for him to call in this expensive medicus.

They were still talking as if I wasn't there. 'But Excellence, even if he does come to himself, after this he will almost certainly need to rest in bed. A half a moon or more, at his age, probably. How can he do anything to help?'

'I don't expect him to *do* anything – I just want to hear his thoughts. I've exhausted every other possibility. So get him back to consciousness as soon as possible. That's what I undertook to pay you for.'

My brain was working slowly, but I could think of nothing in the whole Roman world which was important enough to make him act like this. Curiosity did more for me than any potion could. I forced my eyelids open and half raised my head. 'I am awake,' I murmured, though it came out as a croak. 'What is it, Excellence?'

He pushed past the medicus at once and came up to the bed. If I was carrying the seeds of plague he didn't seem to care. He bent towards me, and I saw his face. It was as drawn and anxious as I'd ever known it. 'Old friend, can you hear me? I am desperate. Talk to me, Libertus. You have got to help. It's my wife, Julia, and my little son. They were with the wet nurse in the courtyard of the house the other day, while I was at an *ordo* meeting in the town. The nurse was sent into the kitchen for some cooked fruit for the boy, and when she came back with it she found they'd disappeared. Julia's cloak and the child's toy were lying on the ground, as if they'd been abandoned there in haste, but there was no message and none of the other slaves had seen them go. You must help me, Libertus. This was three days ago and no one's seen them since.'

Chapter Two

If it had been possible for me to sit bolt upright, I'm sure I would have done – if only out of sheer astonishment. 'Disappeared? But that's impossible!' It came out as a cross between a croak and groan but at least it showed that I had understood and my patron was clearly gratified by this.

'I know it is impossible, old friend,' he said, moving closer to my side and speaking with careful emphasis, as though to a small child. Obviously he felt that in my current state of health I might have difficulty following what he said to me. 'My house is full of slaves and door-keepers – who could get in unobserved, and how could they get out? And even if they managed that, wherever could they go? The house is in the open countryside and there were no unexpected visitors or passers-by all afternoon. Yet it seems that the impossible occurred. One minute Julia and the boy were sitting there, and the next they weren't. I don't know if it is sorcery or what – but there is no solution I can find. I've even been to see the augurers.'

Marcus had dealings with the omen-readers from the temple court as part of his public duties in the town, and this remark was rather a surprise. My patron was not in general a superstitious man: he made the proper sacrifices to the gods, of course, but he was no more likely than I am to base his hopes upon the shape of clouds or the flight of a flock of winter birds. It was an indication of how desperate he was.

'And?' I said.

He shrugged. 'They were no help at all. Except that the chief priest did suggest that Jupiter might possibly have turned himself into a swan again and carried her away.'

'You don't believe that?' I said cautiously. I was born a Celt and I have no special reverence for Roman gods, preferring the older deities of stone and hill, but it is not wise to be dismissive of their powers. One can never be too careful with divinities.

Marcus was clearly thinking something similar. 'It seems so inexplicable in normal terms that I'm almost ready to suspect the gods. I've made propitiation, just in case. But on the whole, Libertus, I think there is a human hand at work.'

'You've questioned everyone?'

He nodded. 'I brought in everyone who visited the house that day, even people who were passing on the road, and of course I've questioned all the slaves. I even offered a reward for any information that would help. But – though I threatened my servants with a visit to the torturers if they lied – the story that I got from all of them was the same. No one had seen or noticed anything.' He paused and cleared his throat. 'It's my wife and son, Libertus. You must help.'

To my alarm I realised that his voice was trembling, and for a moment I feared that he might forget himself and weep. That would have cost us both embarrassment. Roman patricians pride themselves on perfect self-control. If Marcus had broken down in front of me, he would later have been furious with us both.

'I know you've got your villa slaves arranged in matching pairs,' I said, as briskly as I could, hoping to divert his thoughts to practical matters. 'I suppose you split them up to talk to them?'

'Of course I did. It took me two full days.' My patron had mastered his emotion now, and he used his ordinary tone. There was even a touch of his usual impatience, I was glad to note.

'Two days?' I echoed, more to give myself space to think than because I was surprised. In fact it was a wonder it was done so soon. Every Roman villa has a household full of slaves, and Marcus has got even more than most because of his system of arranging servants in neatly matching 'pairs' – similar in height, age and colouring.

It was a relatively new whim on Marcus's part. Julia's now-dead second husband had first adopted it in the big house in Corinium, which she had brought to my patron as a dowry when she wed. Marcus had been enormously impressed and had immediately begun to introduce it to his own establishments. So now almost all the villa staff were paired: not the garden and kitchen slaves, of course, nor the individuals with special expertise, like the secretary and the chief steward – but all the ordinary servants that visitors might see.

The system was an ostentatiously wasteful one, of course – that was the point of it – but it had advantages. It meant that no slave was ever likely to be on his own. Marcus was a fair master, and his slaves respected him – and they positively adored their mistress – but in any household, when a slave is unobserved, there are always temptations to idleness and even petty theft – a date, a fig, a sweetmeat or a sip of wine. But now there was always a watching pair of eyes and a potential wagging tongue: and because every servant had a witness as to where he'd been and what he'd said and done, it was easy to cross-check his movements.

'You spoke to the gate-keepers, I suppose?' I asked. 'In case she went out of her own accord?' There were several exits from the villa, through the orchard and the *nymphaeum*, as well as the main gates at the front and rear, but Marcus had guards on all of them these days.

'Especially the gate-keepers. They have nothing to report. They would not have questioned it, of course, if they had seen their mistress pass – she is their owner, after all, and has a right to come and go. In fact, she often does command a carriage to go out visiting, and to give the child an airing too. The nurse advises it. Now that he is out of swaddling clothes and can move his limbs, she encourages fresh air and exercise. She even has a little cart for him – she says it hardens him and makes him strong. But they weren't using it that afternoon – they had already been out in the morning, visiting a friend. Julia had an attendant with her and they came back as usual. After that they did not leave again. The gate-keepers are quite adamant on that.'

'And none of them left his post? Not even for a moment?'

'They swear that they did not. Even when I gave each of them a small . . . encouragement.' He gave a short, embarrassed laugh. 'Although you won't approve of that, I know.'

I sighed. I knew what form such encouragement would take, and he was right – I was not in favour of such things. In my experience, a man who is under torture will often obligingly remember things that did not occur, merely in order to make the anguish stop. Useful for extorting false confessions, possibly, but not much help if one required the truth.

Marcus must have sensed what I was thinking, because he hurried on. 'They were able to give me a full list of everyone who came and went that afternoon. There were not many visitors and they were just what you'd expect: a group of my *clientes*, seeking me, a cart bringing a delivery of olive oil, and an old woman who comes round selling herbs. But that was all.'

'A cartload of olive oil?' I said. I was envisaging how it might be possible to conceal a woman and child among the large amphorae on the cart. Particularly – though I did not voice the thought aloud – if the pair were conveniently rendered silent, limp and still. Drugged with poppy juice, for instance. Or dead.

The same thought had obviously struck my patron too. He shook his head. 'The cart came to the rear gate as usual, and was unloaded by my own kitchen slaves – the oil was carried into the courtyard and poured into the storage vats.' Like many country houses, Marcus's villa had large amphorae set into the ground to store such things as oil and grain; the great pots kept them cool and safe from pests. 'It was a dealer we have used for years, but I had him arrested yesterday, and they searched his yard and cart. There was absolutely nothing to be found. Of course, he protests his innocence – and anyway he was under observation all the time with my household servants coming in and out, taking linen to the fullers or fetching chickens from the farm. In the end we had to let him go. Of course, I had the oil vats searched at home.' His voice was shaking with emotion again. 'And the cesspits and the pond. In case.'

'Nothing?'

'Nothing.' He paused. 'Libertus, they were flesh and blood. They can't have vanished. They must be somewhere. Even if I am too late and they are . . .' he couldn't bring himself to say the word, and went on, 'if they are not alive, I still want them found, so that I can give them proper burial. That's why I need your help.'

'And your *clientes*? You have questioned them?'

'Of course. But they arrived together, and they stayed together in the ante-room. My slaves confirm it. And before you ask, they were escorted to the gate. It's impossible to imagine how anyone could get in unobserved, let alone get out again, at the same time abducting Julia and the child.' Marcus was getting heated, but then his manner changed. 'But you are right, of course. It seems that somehow, someone has. I can only pray to all the gods my family are not suffering now.'

Any father would do his best, of course, in circumstances like this, but Marcus was unfashionably devoted to his wife and son. Most wealthy Romans saw their ladies as mere accoutrements, bringing wealth or power to the house, and of use for providing sons, as recommended by the state. But Marcus wore a lock of Julia's hair inside a pocket pouch against his heart, even when he visited the baths. Citizens who did not know him well were sometimes tempted to murmur sniggering remarks behind their hands – though generally they did so only once, if Marcus ever got to hear of it.

Of course, he was more than usually fortunate in his choice. His marriage to the lovely Julia had been every Roman's dream: a wealthy widow, accomplished, charming, beautiful, and – as it turned out – fertile as well. The baby, Marcellinus, was a healthy, sturdy lad. I have no children of my own and am no expert on such things, but Gwellia assures me that he has his father's eyes, is already making sounds that might be words, can crawl prodigiously and is generally a miracle of forwardness. Marcus, of course, is sure that he has spawned a future senator at least, if not an emperor.

Never mind coming to a humble roundhouse to seek help
– he would have gone to Dis and back for his wife and boy.
And now not one, but both of them were gone. Marcus
could have lost a limb with less regret.

'Libertus, are you hearing me?' My patron's urgent voice
recalled me to myself. I had allowed my thoughts to drift. I
tried to haul myself upright and look awake, but the sudden
effort was too much for me and I sank back on my pillows
with a groan.

I could hear the sharp concern in Marcus's voice.
'Medicus, he's drifting back to sleep. I cannot lose him now.
Do something. Another clystering or bloodletting perhaps?'

That brought me back to consciousness at once. I've been
subjected to cupping once or twice, and I am not an
enthusiast for the experience. In my current weakened state,
I felt, such procedures would finish me. I forced open my
unwilling eyes again. 'No need for that. I'm resting, that's all.
I can hear you, Excellence.' I searched for some other, more
intelligent remark to convince him that my mind was functioning, but all that came out was a burbling sound.

'Excellence!' It was the physician's sing-song voice. 'With
due respect, you must not tire him out. The old man is
clearly tougher than I thought he was, but you can see that
he has had enough. If you weary him too much he will
relapse, and I cannot answer for what might happen then.
What this man needs is rest and nourishment. I will prepare
some medicine for him. Sleep herbs perhaps to help him
through the night, a compress of sweet cecily to hold the
fever down, and feverfew to keep the sweats at bay. That way
there is more chance that he'll recuperate and be able to
assist Your Excellence again.'

I felt a rush of helpless gratitude. I was aware of being

extremely tired, and the effort of concentration was draining me. However, far from leaving me alone, Marcus was moving to kneel down by the bed. That was so amazing that it made me smile. I have never known my patron bend the knee to any man, even the provincial governor himself, yet here he was grovelling on my roundhouse floor. It was a sign, I thought vaguely, of how distraught he was and possibly of how unwell I'd been.

'Libertus,' he was saying urgently, 'don't you slip away as well.'

'Don't touch him, Excellence.' The physician's voice was sharp. 'Forgive me, but you are getting far too close. There is still a chance of plague. I would be failing in my duties as a medicus if I did not beg you – require you – to move back.'

Even in my drowsy state I understood how dangerously daring that remark had been. I heard my patron give a shocked intake of breath, but – unwillingly – he did get to his feet. However, he could not let the matter pass without rebuke.

'Medicus, you overstep the mark. You only came into my employ a couple of days ago,' he grumbled. 'The fact that I paid you handsomely to leave the service of the household where you were before does not give you the authority to speak to me like that. If there are orders to be given, I will issue them. Is that understood?'

A lesser man might have retreated and apologised, but the medicus was made of stronger stuff. 'You have given me authority to protect your well-being,' he said. 'If you set a man to guard a town, you would call him a traitor if he failed to warn you of danger on his watch. I am merely doing the same thing for your health.'

Marcus snorted and I held my breath, expecting an

outraged outburst, but there was none. My patron simply did what he was told and retreated to the safety of the fire.

'I am grateful to you for your understanding, Excellence,' the medicus was saying in that high-pitched voice of his. 'What would the province do if you fell ill yourself? Now, you engaged me to bring the pavement-maker to himself again, and I have done so with some success so far. But, if you wish me to continue with the task, then we should leave him now. Not only for his own sake, but for yours as well. This roundhouse is a draughty, smoky place – and whereas he, as a Celt, is doubtless used to it, you, Excellence, are manifestly not. You have been continually coughing and your eyes are red. I recommend that you return at once to the comfort and warmth of your own home. I will keep my litter here, and follow you as soon as possible.'

Marcus grunted briefly in consent, and turned to Gwellia. I was drifting softly, but I heard him murmuring, 'Would it be a good idea, do you suppose, to transfer him to the villa when he is well enough? It would be much easier for you to care for him – we could put him in a proper Roman bed, in one of the heated rooms, perhaps, where there is a hypocaust underneath the floor. My kitchens could try to tempt his appetite. I am sure that he would recover far more quickly there, and the medicus would be on the spot.'

What the physician might have thought of that, I do not know. I simply heard my wife begin to say 'You are most thoughtful, Excellence . . .' and then stop as there came the sound of running footsteps at the door.

'Excellence!' It was the voice of Junio, my curly-headed slave. Usually he slept beside my bed, saw to my needs and acted as assistant-cum-companion in my workshop in the town, but in my illness he'd been banished from my side and it seemed that he'd been keeping watch outdoors. Now he sounded breathless and upset. 'Excellence, forgive my interrupting here. There is a messenger at the gate for you. One of the servants from your country house. I am to bring you this at once.'

'What is it?' Marcus said.

'This letter, Excellence. It was delivered to your villa a little while ago – though no one quite knows when. One of the gate-keepers found it left inside the porch – it seems it had been thrown there by a passer-by.'

'What does it say?' Marcus's voice was strained.

'They have not opened it. It is a makeshift thing – simply a piece of folded bark, addressed to you in charcoal on the front. The lettering is poor – it might be anything. But it is tied up with a strip of lilac cloth – it seems to have been torn from something, by the ragged edge, but – see – it is embroidered with gold thread. Your servants thought that you should see it as it is. The handmaidens are sure that it's your wife's. She was wearing a lilac *stola* the day she disappeared.'

'Let me see it. More lights here.' I could almost hear my patron trembling. He moved towards the fire, where the light was best. The medicus and Gwellia both went to him, taking the oil lamp and the candle to assist. There was a silence. I tried to raise myself up on my arm again, and this time I succeeded, more or less.

'It's from her hem. I've seen her wear the garment many times. And look, there is a lock of hair inside the cloth. That is hers too, if I am any judge. And this small downy lock is from the child.' He wrapped the curls inside the cloth again, and placed it reverently inside his toga, beside the other in

18

the pocket pouch he wore. Then he unfolded the piece of tattered bark.

'What does it say, Excellence?' I asked him quietly.

He turned to me, and even in the firelight I could see that he was close to tears.

'It says, "If you wish to see your wife and son again, ensure that Lallius Tiberius is set free." '

Chapter Three

At these astounding words there was a little hush, during which I found that I was – for the first time – wide awake, but before I could say anything at all, the doctor asked the question that was on all our lips.

'Who is Lallius Tiberius?' he said.

'Obviously some criminal who is in custody and now awaiting trial.' My patron was struggling to keep his voice under control. 'In fact, now I come to think of it I seem to know the name – though not in connection with any case of mine.' As representative of the outgoing governor, Marcus was the senior judicial figure in this whole area of Britannia. Only the most important cases – or those involving the most wealthy citizens – were tried by him, although of course he could be called upon to arbitrate if the need arose.

The medicus was making himself busy as my patron spoke, officiously moving a little table which I kept in the hut and placing it at the bottom of my bed. 'I too have heard the name – or something very like it, anyway. But for the moment I can't think in what connection it arose.' He turned to Gwellia. 'A bowl and water, here.'

Marcus ignored him and pursued his train of thought. 'I remember! I've seen it on the lists for civil trial in one of the minor courts. But I did not preside at the introductory plea. One of my junior magistrates must have heard the accusation

21

and ruled that there's a case, and it will come before the appointed judge on whatever the temple tells us is the next propitious day. After the ides, I expect. It won't come before me, even then – merely some elder citizen agreed on by plaintiff and defendant, with a legal officer to see fair play.'

'But surely it must be something serious,' the doctor said, taking the basin which Gwellia brought to him. 'For his supporters to have taken such a desperate step.'

Marcus was staring at the piece of bark, turning it over in his hands. He sounded mystified. 'Yet I'm quite sure it's not. I can't remember what the charges are. Some question about money, I believe – setting on someone in the street and robbing him. Enough to bring him up before the courts. I doubt if I should have noticed his name at all, except that he attempted to escape during the preliminary hearing – the one to establish that there was a case to answer – and there was an application that he should be held in custody until the proper trial could be heard. At his accuser's own expense, of course.' He frowned. 'I don't know who is at the bottom of all this, and who could have sent the note. Clearly it wasn't Lallius himself, since he is presumably still locked up in the cells. It must be his supporters, as the doctor says. But what do they think it has to do with me?'

'You are the most senior magistrate in the province,' I reminded him. 'They presumably suppose that you can bring pressure on the court, and have the case dismissed.'

'Well, this message seems to solve one mystery, at least.' The medicus spoke cheerfully, as if there was no longer any reason for alarm. 'It is clear now what has happened to your wife and son. Someone has abducted them to force your hand in this – and these people will have to keep them safe and well, otherwise they have nothing they can bargain with.'

22

As he spoke, he stooped, picked up a small, carved wooden chest from somewhere on the floor, and placed it on the table he'd prepared. I had seen such things before, and knew what it was likely to contain – a selection of dried herbs, each in its own built-in compartment in the box, with differently sized horn scoops suspended from the lid.

'Bring me warm water from the pot beside the fire,' he said to Gwellia, 'and a drinking cup. I'll make a little potion for our friend,' and with that he began to measure out ingredients, for all the world as though our problems were suddenly resolved. 'There,' he went on in his creaking voice, adding the hot water to the mixture he had made, 'I think that this should send him back to sleep. And once he has finished drinking it, Excellence, I advise you once again that we should go back to the villa and you should try to rest.'

'Philades, be silent!' Marcus's voice was sharp. 'You are quite absurd. How can you suggest I rest tonight?'

'I will make a sedative for you as well,' the man said, nodding his bony face importantly. 'There is clearly nothing you can do for now. But first thing in the morning you can make enquiries, and when you find out where this Lallius lives you can send the town guard down there to storm the house. Of course,' he added, in a judicial tone, 'I suppose – as you say – he did not do the deed himself, so the captives may not actually be there, but once you've made a few arrests the torturers will get the truth from somebody. You'll soon discover where your wife and son are being held and be able to bring them safely home.'

Marcus had lost patience. 'Storm the house? And have these abductors kill their prisoners at once? Of course I shall do nothing of the kind.' He gave a bitter little laugh. 'I imagine that's what they're relying on. And as to taking sedatives, the thought is quite absurd. How can I rest when I have evidence that they have laid hands on my wife – torn her robe and cut bits from her hair? You expect me to take a draught to make me sleep, when she is lying terrified somewhere? I just thank the gods the child is too young to understand.'

Marcus pushed past the physician and came close to me, ignoring Philades' protesting cry of 'Excellence! I beg of you! The seeds . . .'

I had managed to raise myself a little more by now and my patron came to kneel beside the bed and handed me the folded piece of bark. 'Look at it, Libertus. What do you make of it?'

It was impossible for me to read it properly but Gwellia brought the oil light so I took the bark and turned the message this way and then that, as if by peering at it I could persuade it to tell me something more. My patron looked so stricken that I longed to help, but it was hard to concentrate and I could determine nothing except that the letters were so badly scrawled that they could have been written by a child. Probably deliberate, I thought. This was an adult's message – short, simple and brutally direct. I passed the letter back.

'Well . . .' I began, trying to think of something sensible to say.

'Please, Excellence!' The medicus had come hurrying across with the cup, and now placed himself firmly between my patron and myself. 'I beg that at least you will stand a little further off. It is said that smoke destroys the evil with its breath. You would be safer over there, beyond the fire.' Marcus ignored him. I was obliged to do the same.

24

'This does seem an extraordinary affair,' I said. 'You're sure this Lallius is not wanted on a capital offence?'

Marcus moved his head to look at me, past his human shield. 'Not if I recall the details correctly, though he won't have full Roman rights, of course. I'm pretty sure this Lallius is only a citizen through his colonial birth.'

I nodded. Glevum was founded for army veterans, a city-republic within the Empire, and has the status of colonia. That means that any townsman born free within the walls is automatically a citizen by right – whatever lineage he may have had. That would explain why Lallius had the full protection of the court, and was not merely tried before some lowly official in a yard somewhere, but obviously he had no serious standing in the town.

'Legally a citizen!' I said. 'So he won't be subject to the harshest punishments. How extraordinary that he ran away.' I am no expert on the civil law, but I knew that the accuser is required to bring his man to court, using his own guards and at his own expense. It often isn't easy, but unless it's done the case will fail. It's most unusual to lock a wealthy prisoner up, unless it is a really serious affair or he is charged with some criminal offence against the state. Lallius seemed to have brought his incarceration on himself.

'Excellence . . .' Philades began again.

Marcus waved him impatiently aside and addressed himself exclusively to me. 'A stupid business really. It's coming back to me now. Lallius is obviously very anxious not to come to court. Since his attempted escape he has tried every legal trick that he could find. It took hours to agree the formula for trial – you know that if there is irregularity in that, the case can be dismissed – and even now he hasn't given up. I understand he's hired an advocate to try to find a flaw in the proceedings, something technical which would get them nullified. It all takes time, and you know what lawyers charge – he must be running up enormous bills.'

'It must be the punishment that frightens him,' I said. Thinking pained and wearied me, but I did my best.

Marcus looked surprised at that idea. 'If he was not a citizen, perhaps that would be understandable. For the lower orders it can be crucifixion for violence and robbery on the public road – though even then the penalty is hardly used these days. But Lallius would be facing exile at most, even if he'd killed the man he robbed – and obviously he has not done that, since his victim is the one who brought the case.'

'And who is this victim?'

Marcus shrugged. 'Not anyone of note. Someone called Cassius as I understand, and anyway he wasn't badly hurt – just pushed roughly to the ground, and punched a bit. It's possible the judge might call for *talio*, and rule for some physical revenge – but it's more likely Lallius will be faced with restitution and a fine.'

'And that might ruin him?' This wasn't making any sense to my poor addled brain. 'You'd hardly think so, if the man can afford a legal advocate!'

Marcus said thoughtfully, 'You're right, of course. It should not cause him any real distress. Fourfold damages, that's what the law allows – and even that will not be very much. The sum concerned was not a great one, as I understand. A few hundred *denarii*, no more.'

I thought privately this might depend on how you looked at it. 'A few hundred *denarii*' seemed an enormous sum to me. And it was clearly significant to the victim too, I thought, since he had taken the trouble to have Lallius arrested at his own expense and then confined to jail. Marcus was the richest man for miles – though he was famously careful with his cash.

Aloud I said, 'So there is no question of Lallius being sentenced to the mines, or being forced to sell himself to slavery to pay the fine?'

'Unless some other charge emerges, I doubt it very much.'

'Then, Excellence, does it not occur to you that this is very odd? The penalties for kidnapping are terribly severe – especially when the victim is someone like your wife – and those for attempting to corrupt a magistrate are sterner still. Surely it would make more sense for Lallius to simply face the charge, and pay whatever fine the court awards.' I was getting animated as I spoke and tried to sit upright, but the doctor prevented me by coming to my side and handing me the cup he had prepared.

There was no escape. I drank my herbal brew. It tasted horrible.

Marcus had remained kneeling on the floor beside the bed till now, but it seemed my words had struck home and he leaped up all at once. 'Odd? Of course it's odd. It's worse than odd. It's unforgivable. My precious wife and child. And when I find the men who did this, I swear by all the gods . . .'

He seized the lamp from Gwellia, who was still standing by, and deliberately dangled the piece of bark into the flame. We watched in silence as it curled and blackened in the heat, flaring up until at last he dropped it on the floor and ground it with his heel into the beaten earth – as if he was grinding the writer underfoot.

I waited for another outburst, but he'd regained his self-control. His face was a masterpiece of calm. Only his hands betrayed his state of mind. He fingered the pouch that hung round his neck, stroking it as tenderly as though it was part of his missing family. When he spoke again his voice was harsh. 'I've destroyed their cursed letter, and it's what I'll do to them, as well. And I have legal grounds. They've attempted to corrupt me! Me – an imperial magistrate, the outgoing governor's chosen deputy! It's an insult to the majesty of Rome – and that is a capital offence. Wait till I get these villains to the courts.'

There was a startled hush. This was no idle threat. Marcus was famously an expert in the law. He prided himself on his reputation in the courts for being strictly fair and equally unmoved by tears or bribes, but he also knew what penalties he might exact. I have known him pass harsh sentence on a former friend. What he would do to the abductors of his family I did not dare to think.

'Excellence . . .' The doctor was still trying to interpose.

Marcus rounded on him. 'What is it, Philades? Surely you're not about to warn me, yet again, that I might catch the plague? I tell you, it hardly matters to me now. Besides, I don't believe a word of it. I have seen men who were struck down by the plague. Believe me, I'd know it soon enough.'

Besides, I thought, you would face greater risks than plague if that would help to bring your family back. But even as I framed the thought, Philades was speaking, with a surprising dignity that belied his stained toga and dishevelled air.

'Excellence, you pay me for advice, and I have given it. Now it is up to you. If you catch the sickness I shall do my best to treat you – but as you know, there is no certain cure. However, that wasn't what I wished to say to you. It was about the family of this Lallius. It occurs to me that I might know who they are.'

'Then why did you not mention it before?' Marcus demanded snappishly. But he had taken heed. Having ignored all previous warnings from the medicus, he now perversely seemed to take the threat to heart. He moved away and went to stand beside the door, where he was at the greatest distance from the central hearth. Junio, who had been standing there, was now obliged to move.

Marcus ostentatiously arranged himself in the place where the smoke curled up between us to form the thickest screen, and then he spoke again. 'Very well, Philades, I've done as you command. Now what have you to say?'

'With respect, Excellence, I did attempt to tell you, some little time ago – but you refused to let me speak. I fear it took me a while to make the association with the name. The point is, I don't know the man himself, but I think I might have met the father once – he visited the house where I was formerly employed. Numidius Tiberius, the old man was called – if, indeed, it is the same Tiberius family.'

Marcus was obviously startled by the name. 'Numidius? But he's a well-respected man. Even I have heard of him. He's on every board and body in the town which does not actually require a man to be a citizen – and I'm sure he'll get that status in the end. A few benefactions to the *civitas* – paying for some games or public works perhaps – and he would be certain to be recognised. No doubt he can afford it. Isn't he some kind of weights and measures officer?'

Philades was packing his herbs away again. He nodded. 'Chief coin and weigh to inspector in the town. That's lucrative enough. And he married well. His wife brought a large estate with her as a dowry, too.'

I found that I was grinning. Everyone knew the ageing, grim-faced officer who sat each day in a little niche inside the forum wall, with his steelyard and his weights and balances, ready to deal with any coins not issued by the state.

The idea of his expending money on public spectacles was so incongruous it made me smile. Numidius was a very careful man.

Of course, he had to be. It was a post of honour. There were often foreign-minted coins around, and some old tribal ones, but the coin officer would weigh them, determine the amount of gold or silver used and so assess the value there and then, so that traders, even from outside the Empire, could buy and sell with ease. I have used his services in that regard myself.

But that was not the lucrative aspect of the job – that came from settling marketplace disputes. Roman gold currency itself was often brought to him by suspicious stall-holders, and weighed to ensure that no rogue had filed the edges off and kept the precious metal for himself. Conversely, if a buyer of dry goods believed that he'd not received full measure from a certain stall, his purchase could be checked against a volume-stone: a large block of stone with a series of variously sized holes in it. All for an unofficial fee, of course. The coin inspector gets a small retainer from the state, but it is important for local traders to have him firmly on their side. No wonder that Numidius Tiberius was rich.

'But surely,' Marcus said, voicing my own thoughts, 'Numidius is not the sort of man to have a son in jail, especially not on a charge of robbery like this? Dozens of people in the town are named Tiberius. What makes you suppose that there might be any connection here?'

He sounded irritated and dismissive, but the wizened old physician stood his ground. 'Excellence, I might be wrong, of course, but I rather think it might be the self-same family, because the story fits. Numidius's wife was called Lallia – I heard him mention it – and there was a son, named for his mother because she died in giving birth to him. You recall there was a fashion a few years ago for calling sons some version of the mother's name – so Lallius Tiberius would make sense.'

Marcus hurrumphed. 'A tribute to his wife? It sounds uncharacteristically sentimental of the man, from what I know of him: but it is possible, I suppose, since she brought such a dowry with her. And her child would have been born within the walls, and so been a citizen although his parents weren't. That also fits. How do you come to know all this, in any case?'

'Numidius was calling at the house – paying court to my employer's niece. As I say, this Lallia was dead. Numidius had lived alone for many years, but had decided it was time to wed again. And provide himself with another heir, I rather think. I was asked to check that the girl had no disease. Her father thought it would be a splendid match for her, although there is a difference in age, of course. The coin inspector is a wealthy man.' He closed the lid and swept the table clean with his toga sleeve. 'Numidius did speak about his son, as I recall – though not with great affection. The lad was causing trouble even then.'

Marcus was nodding thoughtfully. 'And now he is bringing shame on the household once again. Yet it seems that they planned all this to ensure his release.'

I thought about what Philades had said. My brain was working only sluggishly, but something had at last occurred to me. 'We can't know that,' I objected. 'If the doctor's right, this family seem unlikely candidates to plan a ransom note.'

My patron stared at me. 'Well, who else could it have been?'

My inspiration failed me and I shook my head. 'Perhaps

the young man has associates, and wrote to them from jail? I don't know. It's just that, given the background of the family, it seems a most peculiar thing for them to do. You would expect them to take the legal route. Indeed, it seems they have – you said that Lallius had an advocate. Or simply pay the fine. But putting themselves beyond the law like this? When the father hopes to be a citizen one day? I can't imagine what they'd hope to gain.'

Behind the pall of intervening smoke I saw Marcus shrug. 'Isn't it obvious what they hope to gain? Of course his family have arranged all this. Who else would take such risks? Numidius has money and thanks to that dowry he probably owns property elsewhere. Perhaps he simply planned to run away once Lallius was free. But they will not escape, you can be sure of that. I'll put a watch on all the roads. There's nowhere they can hide.'

'So will you send down at first light and storm the house?' The medicus had closed his box by now, and was wrapping it in a cloth with special care. 'It is no secret where the coin inspector lives – indeed, I could take you there myself.'

'Of course I shall do nothing of the kind! You can imagine what would happen to Julia and Marcellinus if I did.' He paused, then went on in an altered tone, 'But there is nothing to prevent my sending in the guards once Julia and the boy are safely home. Indeed, presumably she will be able to say where she has been and identify her captors afterwards.'

I said nothing. The more I considered the situation, the less I liked it. What Marcus had said was obviously true – his wife would be able to identify her kidnappers – but that only made the whole affair seem more sinister to me. I could see no way that Julia could be forced to hold her tongue once she was free – unless she'd been blindfolded throughout.

However, I didn't wish to mention that aloud. Marcus had quite enough to worry him.

It was the medicus who asked the question that was in all our minds. 'So, Excellence, what do you intend to do?'

Marcus made a gesture of despair. 'I don't know. I'll sleep on it. I imagine that in the end I'll have to do as they demand. They've got Julia and the boy – what else can I do?'

I roused myself. 'Be careful, Excellence, before you do anything at all. There may be other ways. If you give in to them it sets a precedent and they may make more demands. There are still some days, you say, before he comes to trial. Give yourself at least some time to think.'

He snorted. 'And leave my wife and child in jeopardy? I can't take the risk. But never fear. These scoundrels won't make a mockery of me. Come, Philades. You have been telling me for hours that I should leave this man to rest. Junio, go to the gate and tell my litter-bearers that I'm on my way.' He turned to me. 'Goodnight, old friend. Sleep well, and mend your health. Gwellia, take good care of him.' And he turned and disappeared into the night.

The medicus gave me a helpless look, then shrugged. 'Try to rest,' he murmured, then snatched up his box of herbs and scurried after him.

Chapter Four

I do not know if it was the effect of the potion that the medicus had given me, or merely the shock and strain of the foregoing events, but I remember nothing more that night. I must have slid into unconsciousness and slept for many hours, because when I opened my eyes again the day was well advanced. Thin winter sunlight was streaming into the roundhouse through the door; there was the smell of warm oatcakes coming from the hearth and Junio was squatting by the fire.

I turned to look at him. That was a mistake. I groaned. My head felt like a cavern filled with aching stones.

Junio was quickly on his feet. 'Master, at last you are awake?'

I nodded. Another error. He grinned down at me.

'It's good to see you back with us again. Would you like some breakfast? Are you well enough to eat?'

'Perhaps one of those small oatcakes,' I replied. 'I see that they are hot.' I smiled to myself, knowing that Gwellia would have made them to tempt my appetite. They are my favourites, as she is well aware.

He shook his head. 'I'm sorry, master. My mistress did make them especially for you, but the medicus has been here and says that you must not have them after all. Only some thin gruel or broth at first, he says, because the seeds of poisoning are in you still and liquid food will help to wash them out. He's left another of his potions for you, too.' He crossed to the table by my bed and picked up a drinking cup. 'He said you'd have a headache when you woke.'

'He was right,' I said, but I submitted to the drink. This one was cold and yellowish and thick and tasted just as dreadful as the last, but to do Philades justice, I did feel a little better afterwards. My brain was still full of those confounded rocks, but at least they didn't clash together every time I moved my head.

I propped myself up a little more. Gingerly. My head did not fall off. 'Surely one little oatcake wouldn't hurt?'

Junio grinned. 'What, waste this barley gruel your wife has made? And after all the pains I've taken to keep it warm for you?' He gestured to the little pot on the hearth beside the fire, just visible where he'd heaped the embers up round the sides of it. 'Besides, I told you what the doctor said. I would not dare to cross his will. My mistress thinks he's halfway magical, because of what he's done for you. Though if you ask me, I think the potions that she made herself had started the cure before he came along. You were already beginning to sleep sound again, and be less raging hot.' As he spoke he squatted down and raked the ashes from round the pot. Then he hooked the lid off neatly with a handy stick and, using a beaker as a dipper, began to serve up the steaming contents into a wooden bowl.

'Gwellia was making herbal draughts for me?' I said, warmed by the thought of her concern, and watching all this in a kind of daze.

'Master, she has done little else since you were taken ill. She must have brewed a hundred recipes. All the ancient Celtic remedies – and some Roman ones as well – but of course you couldn't eat or drink. All we could do was bathe your lips from time to time and try to force some drips into your mouth. It was not until that physician came and showed her how to press your tongue down with a spoon that she was sure you'd swallowed anything. He got a cup of potion down you then.'

'A hot one?' I enquired, suddenly making sense of all those fiery demons in my dreams. Poor Gwellia!

He had filled the bowl of gruel by now and was getting to his feet. 'Up till then, every time we put water in your mouth you struggled like a landed fish and dribbled it all out. But of course once you began to drink you started to improve. So now she thinks the medicus has saved your life, and his every word must be obeyed. He said you needed gruel, and so she made you some.' He took down a glazed pot from the shelf, and added a little honey from it to my breakfast dish. He waved the spoon at me. 'Marcus sent this for you as well – a present from his bees.'

He brought the spoon and basin over to the bed. I expected him to hand them both to me but he did nothing of the kind. Instead he got to his knees beside me and prepared to feed me as though I were a child.

'Junio!' I protested. But he ignored my pleas.

'Doctor's orders.' He grinned up at me. 'You are not permitted to exert yourself today, not even so much as to raise a spoon. I am to get you to eat as much as possible and report it to the physician afterwards. Open wide.'

Perhaps my patron and his medicus were right. It was exhausting swallowing the food, without attempting to hold the bowl and feed myself as well. I could manage only tiny sips, although – for some reason – it tasted quite ambrosial today. In general I'm not very fond of gruel.

'Tell your mistress this was very good,' I said, after a few minutes, leaning back to pant and rest my spinning head. 'Or, better, I will tell her so myself. Where is she now?'

'She has gone to have a rest.' Junio held another spoonful of warm gruel to my lips. 'The poor lady has scarcely slept since you fell ill. She has hardly left your side except occasionally to snatch an hour or two of sleep – and even then she always made sure that there was someone here.'

'You?'

He grinned again. 'Who else could be trusted to keep an eye on you?' A shadow crossed his face and he looked serious suddenly. 'Though it was worrying. You were hot and cold and shivering by turns, talking in your sleep – thinking that you were back in slavery again and that your wife was lost. You threshed about a lot as well – shouting out her name and struggling.'

I shuddered at the memory. 'I kept dreaming that the pirate boat had come and the slavers were snatching us apart.'

He made a sympathetic face. 'We tried to comfort you. Many an hour she has stood here by your side, whispering that you'd found her now, and everything was well – but you didn't even know her when she spoke to you.'

'Poor Gwellia.' This time I said the words aloud.

He gave the grin once more. 'Poor all of us,' he said. 'We servants had to sleep in the dye-house first of all – since it was obviously impossible to stay in here – but then Marcus sent down his slaves to help us build another sleeping room, next door to this. Kurso and I did most of it, but Cilla helped – once she had got the idea of how to weave the walls from osiers, and daub them with manure and clay to keep the water out. It's very snug, with a hearth, a wooden bench and everything, so that those who were not watching you could sleep, or work or cook without disturbing you.'

Kurso and Cilla! I had half forgotten them. I was so accustomed to my little threesome here – myself, my wife and Junio – that for a moment I'd failed to remember that I now had other slaves. Of course, I had acquired them in the last few months, much to Gwellia's delight – though both times it had been more or less by accident, as a kind of payment for my services. 'How are they both?'

'Much as usual. They'll come and see you, now you are awake. When they come in, that is. Kurso is out with the chickens now and Cilla is gathering kindling for the fire. They have been a great help while you've been ill – Kurso hasn't broken anything for days.'

I grinned. Poor Kurso had been a kitchen boy before, but he had been so ill treated by his former owners that he was really too nervous to work in the house. He could still run faster backwards than forwards, and jumped every time you spoke to him – usually dropping any dish he held – but he had found a kind of contentment in tending our chickens, goats and kitchen crops, and helping in the workshop now and then. Cilla, on the other hand, was skilled. She was a gift from Marcus's house, a plump, bright, cheerful little maidservant who helped with household chores and generally waited on my wife – when Junio wasn't making eyes at her.

If they hadn't been in servitude, there might have been a real romance between those two, I thought – but of course liaisons were forbidden between slaves. I had once or twice considered the idea of rewarding Junio with his freedom in the end, but when I had discussed it with the boy he had sworn that he would publicly refuse – which would make him my bondsman in perpetuity. Anyway, he was too young to manumit. That was a problem for another day.

I said now, 'I shall look forward to seeing both the others soon, and my new sleeping hut as well. Marcus has been very good, it seems. You know he was even talking yesterday of having me moved up to his house? It's almost a pity I've recovered quite so well. I might have enjoyed a day or two of luxury – Marcus's slaves take splendid care of his guests – and the under-floor heating would have been a treat. But now I suppose he will not need my help.'

Junio stabbed another spoon of gruel at me. 'You are a cynic, master. Your patron was genuinely concerned about your health. He would have had you up there two days ago and more, but the medicus arrived and said that you could not be moved. But I expect you're right. Now that he's let this Lallius fellow go, presumably he'll get his wife and infant back, so you have lost your chance.'

This time I did sit bolt upright. 'He's let Lallius go? Already? Dear gods! I thought at least he'd talk to me again before he rushed into anything like that. Junio, I'm afraid I fear the worst. He does not even know who he is dealing with. There could be more demands. He has no guarantee of anything, not even a firm promise of how and when they will be returned. Or has he had some message that I haven't heard about?'

'I don't believe so, master.' Junio looked instantly penitent. 'I should have woken you. I wanted to – I know he really came here to try to talk to you – but when he heard that you were still asleep he changed his mind and insisted that I should leave you undisturbed.'

'Marcus has been here again? Today?'

'He looked in with the medicus a little while ago – on his

way to the basilica, he said. Poor man. He looked as if he hadn't slept at all. He'd had the high priest of Jupiter up there half the night, and between them they've found a way to handle the matter. I was to tell you that. He'd decided to do what the abductors said, without appearing to. He was pretty shaken and extremely grim. I think he was unhappy at trifling with the law. You know how he always prides himself on being strictly just.'

'So he is proposing to overrule the magistrate who presided at the preliminary court?' I could hardly believe it. Junio was right. Marcus would have cut his own hand off rather than betray his role of trust – in any other circumstances but these.

Junio shrugged. 'Not that exactly. They've hit on some legal quibble which will allow him to dismiss the case. It is only a pretext. Something about the official sacrifice and the magistrate in question coming late and failing to observe some minor rite – crossing the threshold with his left foot first, or something of the kind. It's the sort of thing that these days would ordinarily be ignored, but once the high priest has identified the lapse, it is enough to throw question on all proceedings for that day by making the magistrate unpropitious – "nefas", as they say.'

'So any decisions that he made that day can be annulled, without making Marcus seem to be personally involved, or drawing attention to any accused person in particular? I hope it works. It's so unusual for courts to be annulled that people are bound to wonder why. If news of Julia's abduction has already reached the town – as almost certainly it has, since Marcus had all the passers-by brought in and questioned – someone is certain to put two and two together in the end.'

Junio clearly did not share my reservations. 'Even if they do,' he said, 'they won't be able to prove anything, not even who he wanted to set free. It isn't fair, of course, because other offenders will get off as well and the magistrate will have to pay a fine. However, you must admit it does what was required. Not only will Lallius – among others – be released, but, because the formula itself has failed, he will be free from any legal charge, at least until Julia and Marcellinus are returned. Then, Marcus says, he'll bring him in again, and those who helped him, too – on charges of conspiracy if nothing else – and Dis knows there'll be no mercy for any of them then. Marcus will conduct the case himself.'

'That is exactly what worries me,' I said. 'It doesn't take a rune-reader to see that's what he'd do. And that he'll make the punishment as harsh as possible. So, is it likely that these people will simply let their victims go? Julia knows who they are.'

'You think so, master?' He was still attempting to spoon gruel into me.

I was getting tired of eating it by now and I dodged his ministrations long enough to say, 'She must do, don't you see? It's not as if they were a band of unknown brigands who had burst into the villa with their faces covered and their daggers drawn. There was no disturbance of any kind at all. There were lots of slaves about and the door-keepers say there were no strangers in the house, and all visitors have been accounted for. But someone must have seen these people come or go. And that suggests . . . ?'

'That the kidnappers were people who often came and went!' He was delighted with his reasoning. I had a mouthful of cold gruel by now, but I nodded my approval. I have long encouraged Junio to work things out like this – just as I have taught him how to work with stone. 'So you think it's somebody the household knows?' he went on. 'Or several somebodies – whose faces are familiar to the gate-keepers? I see. That does explain how they got in, at least – though how they managed to smuggle Julia and the child out is another matter. There was no sound or sign of any struggle in the court. They must have been abducted by a trick.'

'I think that's possible. It would obviously be much easier to get Julia past the gate if she was somehow persuaded to co-operate.'

Junio was slowly following my train of thought. 'I still can't understand it. The gates are always guarded. You don't think she might be hidden in the house, or grounds?'

'Not if Marcus searched it fully, which I'm sure he did. Or unless she and the child are already dead, of course. Bodies might be hidden easily enough.' I saw the look of horror on his face, and wished I hadn't voiced my thought. I added, for myself as much as Junio, 'But we can take some comfort from the note. That wasn't from the villa, and it had pieces of Julia's hair and gown on it. It seems more likely she's being held elsewhere.'

He nodded doubtfully. 'Let's hope that you are right – that she was lured out by an urgent message, or something of the kind. In fact, if Julia was somehow persuaded to go out willingly, she might even have evaded the door-keeper of her own accord. Though, obviously, she is a prisoner now.'

'Exactly.' I remembered this time not to nod myself. The rocks inside my head were clattering again, probably in protest against all this thought. 'But you do see that once Lallius is free, she has no further value to the kidnappers? Quite the opposite. She is a threat, since she can presumably tell Marcus who they are. So it might actually be dangerous to let Lallius go.'

'But what else can Marcus do?' Junio was so desolate he let his spoon relax. 'Julia and the child are in danger anyway. And if he had refused to comply with these demands, what do you suppose would happen to them then? These people have already torn pieces from her dress and hair. They obviously aren't treating her with very much respect. And as for that poor child . . .'

I opened my mouth to say that as long as Lallius remained in custody, at least we had something we could bargain with, but Junio, recovering, was too quick for me and before the words got out the gruel got in. I was still spluttering and swallowing when Kurso darted into the room.

He always was a nervous, edgy child but now, standing there with his cheeks flushed and his fingers tugging at his tunic hem, he was positively quivering with suppressed anxiety. 'M-m-master?' he stammered.

'What is it, Kurso?' I spoke as gently as I could, but he was evading my eyes as usual.

'Master, there is a c-c-carriage at the gate. Your p-p-patron's here. I am sent to see if you are s-s-still asleep.'

'Which you are obviously not!' broke in a familiar voice. All eyes turned to the doorway and there was the man himself. He was in full regalia, dressed for his attendance at the court: his snowy linen toga was banded with wide stripes of purple and a wreath of laurel, signifying justice, was set upon his curls, giving him a solemn dignity. His handsome cloak was fastened by a gem-encrusted brooch; he had a heavy gold torc round his neck – a tribute present from some Celtic chief – and he had his favourite baton in his hand. He looked the personification of a magistrate, a walking symbol of Roman legal power. He was attended by his favourite page, a slim, good-looking youth with sleek black hair and darting eyes, in the ostentatious uniform of all Marcus's messengers – a short-cut crimson tunic edged with gold, and a striking cape to match. And lurking behind them was the medicus.

If I was Lallius, I thought, I would be awed.

However, there was a smile on my patron's face, and the haunted look of yesterday had gone. He bounded over to my bed at once, ignoring my servants and their rather less-than-graceful bows.

'Good morning, my old friend – almost good afternoon, in fact. I am sorry to disturb your meal but glad to find that you're awake and in good health.' He extended a hand for me to kiss, and I raised myself and touched my lips to the heavy seal ring on the finger.

'Good morning, Excellence. I see from your manner that the news is good. I hear you found a way to meet the kidnappers' demands.'

He laughed 'Am I so transparent? Well, it's true. And I've received a promise of my family's release.' He spoke with confidence, but he was anxious all the same: I could tell from the way he moved around the room, fiddling with the weaving loom hanging on the wall and tapping his baton on his hand – a sure sign that he was inwardly disturbed.

I said carefully, 'Well, I am very pleased to hear it. I was afraid that you would not. So Julia and the child are safe. I can understand why you're relieved.'

The page, who was standing close to me, put on a pious face and flashed me a warning glance. 'Citizen, this matter is surely a confidential one. Your slaves . . . ?'

It was impudent. I stared at him. My patron always chose

his personal messengers for their striking looks, and this boy was no exception. I had encountered him before. He was called Pulcrus, 'the good-looking one', and he deserved the name. The trouble was, he was aware of it, which made him – as now – depressingly self-confident and self-satisfied.

'We may speak quite freely in front of both my slaves,' I said. With Marcus there I did not dare deliver a more overt rebuke. 'They have my confidence, and His Excellence himself was here last night, talking quite openly about the affair.'

The page turned pinker than his tunic, but it was impossible to deflate his self-conceit for long. 'One cannot be too cautious, citizen,' he said.

I looked at Marcus, but he was ignoring us and fingering the weaving on the loom 'I presume, Excellence, that you've had instructions of some kind,' I said.

His forced, cheerful air was back again. 'I have only to go back to the villa, and when it gets dark, leave the outer gate ajar with no one guarding it. "Then what you have lost will be returned to you." That's what the message said.'

'What sort of message?'

'Another scribbled note on a strip of bark. Much like the first. I found it waiting for me in the council room, a moment after the announcement had been made. I had my page make the proclamation in the forum, publicly, from the steps of the basilica so that all the crowd could hear. Did Junio tell you what we had decided we were going to say?'

I nodded. 'More or less.'

'I did not altogether know what to expect, or how the kidnappers would contact me, but I went back into the council room, and there it was – a guard had found it on the floor and handed it to me. My name was written on the outside of the scroll. It was tied up with another section of Julia's dress, and sealed with her ring. I knew immediately what it was.'

'He didn't see who left it?'

He made a little face. 'No chance of that. The forum was as crowded as it always is, and there were hordes of people on the steps as well – there is a lot of business in the court today.'

'But who could have got into the council room?'

'Well, almost anyone. The councillors, of course. The slaves who clean the place. The guards. Or almost anyone with business in the court – and there were enough of those today.' He looked embarrassed.

It was the medicus who hastened to explain. 'There were several bakers there, presenting a complaint. We've had a lot of rain these last few months, and the standard of the grain ration is poor. It's begun to sprout, they say, and is turning sour, so it is impossible to use. They want the corn officer dismissed and forced to pay.'

Marcus shrugged. 'The town has brought in grain from warehouses elsewhere, but that has proved expensive and it hasn't helped. These bakers get their friends and families to come into the forum and demand a trial by popular acclaim – like the old "people's court" there used to be. And other people come to urge them on and bring petitions to the council room. It's quite impossible to keep them out. Any of them could have left the note.'

I gazed at him. 'So you will leave the gates of your villa open and unguarded in the dark, and hope your wife and baby are returned?'

I had put it very bluntly and it appeared to sober him. The falsely cheerful smile faded. 'There will be no further danger to the house. All the inside servants will be armed. I shall have secret watchers put in place, of course.'

'And you don't think the kidnappers will be expecting that? And be ready to take action if you do?'

The hunted look had come back to his face. 'The hidden guards will make no move until my family is returned. That's obvious. I can't endanger them.'

'So you'll have to let the abductors think they've got away? Get clear of the villa grounds, in fact? Suppose that they disappear into the woods? It would not be difficult – the area around the house is forest everywhere.'

He shrugged. At that moment he looked an aged man. 'That is just a risk I have to take. But what else can I do? Julia is in danger of her life, and Marcellinus too. But the kidnappers won't get away. I'll see to that. And you, my friend, are going to come up to the villa as my guest and help make sure they don't. Provided that the medicus agrees.'

Chapter Five

Only a little while earlier I had been joking that I would enjoy the luxury of staying in the villa for a day or two, but suddenly I didn't want to go.

This was not mere contrariness. Now that Marcus had let Lallius go, I feared the worst. Political ransoms of this sort are rare but they are always difficult to deal with, and this one seemed particularly so. The abduction had obviously been carried out with considerable care and cunning, and the kidnappers had won resoundingly. Marcus had no guarantee of any kind that his wife and child would really be released – in fact he did not even know for sure who he was dealing with: I was convinced we hadn't heard the end of it, and that there would be new and more extreme demands.

However, if my fears were proved correct – or even if they weren't – I knew how my patron would react. Torn between love and duty he'd be beside himself. He'd ask for my advice at every turn – and very likely ignore it anyway – but if anything went wrong it would always be my fault, for not counselling him to do things differently. Since he had already involved the high priest of Jupiter in this, I would much prefer that he continued to seek sacerdotal help: then, no matter what counsel he received or what the outcome was, it could all be blamed upon the gods.

However, I could not refuse outright to help, and once

Marcus had decided on a course it was extremely difficult to change his mind. In vain I pleaded that I was happy where I was, and that I would make a swifter recovery in my own domain, surrounded by my loving wife and slaves.

Marcus dismissed my protestations with a lofty wave. His house was warmer, it was free of draughts and smoke, the food was plentiful and better quality, and the medicus would be at hand to keep an eye on me. As to my household, they could come as well, if I so desired, although any of his servants would be at my beck and call. Indeed, since I was obviously still feeling delicate, he would order his cook to make special food for me and provide a slave to taste it before I ate, to make sure that I didn't swallow the seeds of any more disease.

'In fact, old friend,' he finished cheerfully, 'you could come with us now. I have a carriage standing at the door. Philades can walk back to the house.'

At this point, however, the doctor intervened. 'Your pardon, Excellence. The patient is not well enough for that,' he said, and I wondered again at the privilege of contradiction his job afforded him. 'It is possible that he could be transferred this afternoon, but proper preparations must be made. The bedding must be put into the sun to air, and the room warmed up before he comes – an extra brazier in addition to the under-floor hypocaust. And jolting in a carriage is not a good idea. He would be better on a covered litter, where he can be transported lying down, and wrapped in blankets to prevent a chill. After the sun has passed its height, perhaps, to take advantage of what warmth there is. I will accompany him, of course, and give him a potion to help him sleep through the ordeal. Under those conditions, I would be prepared to countenance the move – though necessarily there is a risk. Although I do not think he is infectious now.'

Marcus is not accustomed to taking orders, and I expected an outburst at this high-handed tone, but my patron merely nodded meekly. 'As you say.'

Of course, Marcus would hardly be the first to forgive a gifted doctor for failures of respect. There is the famous story about Thersis, a young medicus in Rome, who – having bought himself too many expensive hand-copied books – was forced to sell himself into slavery to pay his debts. He too gave orders to his owners all the time, but he was so skilled at healing that they put up with it: so much so that when he later tried to buy his freedom back, they set such a high value on him that he could not afford the price and he ended as a runaway with a bounty on his head. All this was more than twenty years ago, but the attitude of doctors had obviously not changed.

Nevertheless, I hadn't expected my patron to show such tolerance. He was almost deferential as he said, 'Everything shall be arranged exactly as the doctor recommends. So, Libertus, that is settled then.'

I tried to protest that Gwellia must be consulted before decisions could be made, but Junio had already gone to waken her. She came in looking tousled and rather bleary-eyed but she was quite alert, and to my dismay – once she had heard the old physician's view – decided that this was a good idea. In fact I think that she was secretly delighted by the whole prospect.

With very little further reference to me, it was agreed that a litter would be sent and I would be transported to the villa sometime after noon. The medicus would come back to accompany me, with Junio, and Gwellia would follow a little later on. Cilla and Kurso would stay here and mind the house, but would be available if called upon.

'It's all very fine for you,' I muttered to my wife, after our distinguished visitors had gone. 'Marcus will expect me to help him catch these men, and I think he's made the task impossible. Everything that he has done so far is absolutely the reverse of what I would advise. He's given in to their demands, without making the least attempt to find out who they are, and he has no guarantee that they will do anything they promise. We don't even know how the kidnapping was done. He has consulted the chief priest of Jupiter, whom I can hardly contradict, and I don't see how I can help at all. And my head is aching dreadfully, as well.'

'My poor husband.' She came over and patted my pillows with her hands. 'It is time for you to rest. Don't concern yourself too much. You just do what you can. Marcus cannot overtire you with his demands while Philades is on hand to take your part. And a few days up at the villa can only help your health. Philades as good as told us so.'

'If that doctor had told you that it would improve my health to be dangled from the ankles in a stream, I believe that you would have it done at once,' I grumbled. 'I would rather do my resting here, with you and Junio to look after me.'

'It will be a rest for me, as well,' she said, and that so shamed me with my thoughtlessness that I made no more objections to the move. When the litter came (a substantial affair, a sort of bed suspended on a frame, with leather curtains all round it to exclude the draught), they brought it right up to the roundhouse door. I submitted to being bundled on to it – carried by four of Marcus's slaves as though I were a sack of hay or corn – and wrapped in blankets like a newborn child. It was a lengthy business even then. The medicus fussed around me with his herbs, and I was forced to drink another horrid draught before I left. I did, however, score one little victory.

'If I am well enough to leave the house,' I whispered to Junio, as they prepared to lurch me to the door, 'then I am well enough to have an oatcake. Give me one, and never mind what the medicus might think. I'm supposed to be your master, after all.'

He vacillated for a moment, but then he grinned. He gave me a ferocious wink and as he tucked the blankets round me on the litter, he slipped a little oatcake into my hand and pulled the outer covers over it.

'Don't choke yourself,' he whispered, as he dropped the curtain and gave the signal for the bearer-slaves to move.

It is not more than a mile from my roundhouse to the villa, a pleasant enough walk on a summer day with the forest stretching round on every side, but this afternoon the journey seemed to take an age. A carried litter is a bumpy ride, even when the bearers are taking all the care they can. Today each rock and pothole and tree root in the path seemed to send a fresh shock through me, and even with my blankets I was shivering and cold. I was glad when we reached the junction where our little lane meets the main military road, and the worst of the swaying and the jolting ceased. We settled to a rhythmic steady bounce.

After that it was just a question of enduring it. The doctor's potion had numbed me to a dream-like state, but I did just manage to keep awake enough to work my right hand free and nibble at my oatcake till I'd finished it. I was not really hungry in the least and I hardly did it justice, but it was a gesture of defiance and somehow it made me feel a little more myself. Though a little queasy, too, in truth.

I shut my eyes.

At last the bouncing stopped. I felt a sudden draught and was aware of someone lifting the curtain, but by the time I opened my eyes again, the curtain had fallen back into place. I was in a semi-stupor by this time but I could hear voices some way off, and I assumed that we had halted at the villa gates. The impression was strengthened, a moment afterwards, when I felt the litter being lowered to the ground. I lay back, waiting for someone to come and lift me out.

Nothing happened. More voices. I used my free hand gingerly, and lifted up the curtain at my side to see what was delaying us.

We were still outside the villa. Very close – I could see the wall and the leafless fruit trees of the orchard on the other side – but the gate was not yet in view and there was nothing on the left-hand side but woods. So what had halted us? A bear or wolf, perhaps? There were rumoured to be such animals still living in the forest hereabouts, and bands of brigands too, though I had never set eyes on any of these things. I lifted back the curtain even more, and – with due caution – craned my head to see.

No snarling beasts confronted me, but there was something in the middle of the road. The litter-bearers had put down the chair, and gone to see what the obstruction was.

I struggled up a bit and craned a little more. It looked for all the world like a pile of logs, just dumped in the middle of the road, as if someone had come here with a cart and simply unloaded it where it was most in the way.

I had to lean a long way out to see, but when I did I saw that I was right. It was a pile of wood, and it completely

54

blocked the route. The bearer-slaves were starting to haul parts of it away under the supervision of the medicus, but it was too big a pile for them to move with any ease. Junio, I saw, was clambering round the side and was obviously on the way to the villa to get help.

But help was on the way. A donkey cart had reached the other side and the driver was getting down to see what was afoot. He was a big man and he was furious. I could hear a stream of oaths and curses even from where I lay, but he joined in the job of clearing up the road, lifting huge tree trunks in his burly arms and dragging them aside in a way which made the bearer-slaves look ineffectual, although they were used to lifting things, of course, and were strong lads themselves.

I was so busy watching what was going on that I'd abandoned all pretence of lying still and was propped up on my arm, leaning halfway out of the litter on one side, with the right-hand curtain pulled completely back. Therefore, when somebody lifted the leather curtain behind me, and pushed something hard and bulky in against my legs, it took me a moment to realise that it was happening.

I turned my head as quickly as I could, but already the leather screen had fallen back, and I could not swivel round at first because the object – whatever it might be – was pinning down my feet. I had to make an effort before I freed myself, and by the time I'd rolled across and lifted the other curtain up again, there was nothing to be seen. My visitor – whoever it was – had already disappeared into the trees. However, I could now see what they'd left behind: something large and hard and wicker-basket-like.

Despite my aching head I sat upright to get a better view. A basket, certainly, but of unusual size – the kind of basket people use for storing foodstuffs. It had a sort of cover made of woven reeds and I stretched out an exploring hand to lift the lid. And then I stopped. There was a distinct sensation reaching me, a sort of rocking, as if something inside the basket had begun to move.

I had meant to lift it closer so that I could examine it more carefully, but it was too heavy for me to move one-handed in my state of health, and I could not move without upsetting it – and I wasn't at all anxious to do that. I was not at my most quick-witted, I suppose, but it was coming to me what other things are kept in woven baskets of this type.

Snakes, I thought, feeling an unpleasant little chill run down my back. Or some other animal. In fact, I was becoming sure of it. The whole thing was wiggling by now, and there was a sort of muted sound that might have been a hiss.

And then I lost my nerve. I did what anyone in their senses would have done before. I let out a roar. 'Junio!' I bellowed. 'Philades! Somebody! Come here!'

But my cry must have disturbed the basket's occupant. There was a last convulsive wiggle and the whole thing toppled on its side. Before any of my travelling companions could hurry to my aid, the lid fell off, the basket rolled, and I found myself staring with horrified fascination at what came half slithering and half crawling out of it.

Chapter Six

It was not, after all, a snake – though it was almost as slippery as one. This was a child – a small, filthy and bedraggled child, coated from head to foot in grease. It was naked, apart from a piece of ragged cloth round its loins, and another stuffed into its mouth and tied securely round the lower face as if to prevent the infant from crying out – and the whole body, from the shoulders downwards, was covered in that shocking film of yellow grease, which gave off a strong and strangely pungent smell.

'Who in the name of all the gods are you?' I said aloud. I had heard of changelings – left among mortals by the gods – but I have never really believed in such things. Some pauper's child, perhaps, thrown into the litter in the hope that someone would take pity on him and raise him as a household slave? Whoever he was, my heart went out to him. (It was a 'him', I saw. He was crawling rather listlessly about, and as he did so the tattered cloth round the lower limbs fell free, and put the matter of sex beyond doubt.)

Despite the stench which emanated from every part of him, I stretched forward to take him in my arms. My whole intention was to comfort him. I tried to free the bond round the face but to my alarm he tried to flinch away. His eyes grew wide. He stared at me, then all at once he screwed them up again. His face got very red and I guessed that without the cloth round his mouth, he would be screaming now.

All the same, I could not bear to see him gagged. I undid the tie as gently as I could and eased it from his mouth, but far from soothing him, my action seemed to enrage him even more. He took a shuddering long breath and let out a mighty howl.

'Hush!' I muttered, rather helplessly, holding him awkwardly and attempting to rock him in my arms. I was just wondering what on earth to do when the curtain of the litter was pulled aside and I saw the medicus looking in on me.

'Libertus! I heard you call. What is it? Are you ill? I thought you were asleep . . .' He stopped, staring at the little bundle in my arms. 'What in Hermes' name have you got there?' He came and knelt down beside me, letting the leather curtain strips fall round us as a screen.

For answer, I handed him the infant, which promptly kicked, arched itself into a rigid line, and launched into another fit of screaming howls. I had never realised how lustily a small child can bawl.

Philades held the wriggling apparition at arms' length. He looked at it a moment and then stared from it to me. 'Dear Zeus, it's Marcellinus! How did you manage this?'

I was so startled that I almost leaped upright. 'Marcellinus? Surely not? The kidnappers have already arranged for his return, and for his mother's too – tonight when the villa gates are to be left "open and unguarded", wasn't that the phrase? Anyway, this isn't Marcus's child. Remember, I have seen him, medicus, and you have not. This child is far too big.' Admittedly small children look much the same to me, but there was nothing about this one that I recognised at all.

The doctor looked long and hard at me. 'You have seen

the boy, you say? And how long ago was that? Before you were taken ill? That must be a moon ago at least – and children of this age grow very fast. Come, pavement-maker, don't play games with me. This is Marcellinus – and we both know it is. Look, there is the tell-tale birthmark on his leg.'

I gawped. I remembered, vaguely, that there had been talk of such a mark – shaped like an eagle, a symbol of good luck – but I had never seen it, since the babe was always swaddled when I looked at it. But on this child's thigh, beyond a doubt, was a purple stain which might (with imagination) look something like a bird.

I shook my head again. There was no sign of a bulla – the lucky charm that every Roman child is given a few days after birth, and never leaves off again until he comes of age. 'But he has no bulla. Marcellinus had a gold one round his neck. I was at the naming ceremony when it was put on him.'

'So I am led to understand. But in the circumstances I would almost be surprised to find it, wouldn't you? Any thief would be delighted by the opportunity. No doubt it has been removed and sold by now.'

I murmured doubtfully. Of course the medicus was right in principle, but it was hard to imagine even the most hardened kidnapper deliberately snatching such a precious object from a child. To lose a bulla was to invite appallingly bad luck – to a Roman it is almost like losing one's contract with the gods – and it would require the most extensive sacrifice and ritual to expiate the loss and create another one. I began to argue the point, but then I trailed off. I had to admit that the medicus was right – I had been ill for many days and a bulla is easily removed.

I stared at the greasy little form again. It was hard to

reconcile this ragged, smelly apparition with the cosseted, perfumed and pretty little boy who had so often been held up for my admiration in the past. Yet, the more I looked, the more I realised that it was genuinely possible. Indeed, now I began to admit it to myself, I could see that there was an undoubted resemblance to my patron in this child: the same nose, the same colouring, the same fair, curling hair – though that was new to me! When I'd last seen Marcellinus he had been nearly bald! And there was undoubtedly the birthmark. Even to my weary half-drugged mind, it was clear that this was indeed the missing boy.

But I was not too drowsy to have a sudden thought. I had not recognised the child, although I'd seen him several times before, so how had Philades, who by all accounts had never met the boy, worked out so quickly who it was?

I was too tired and sick to play at guessing games, and I confronted the physician openly. 'I accept that you are right. It is the missing child. But tell me, Philades, how did you know? About the birthmark, in particular? Marcus didn't mention it to people, generally, and I thought that you had never seen the child.'

The doctor gave me a grim little smile. 'Did you think you were the only one who knew that little secret, pavement-maker? I'm sorry to disappoint you, in that case. Marcus has been describing it to everyone, so that they could identify the boy if he were found.'

Of course! I should have thought of that myself. I nodded. 'And you are in his confidence, I know – in fact you have become a regular Thersis, haven't you?' It was an attempt at flippancy, I know, a joking reference to that affair in Rome – but levity was obviously not Philades' style. There was not the vestige of a smile: in fact if anything he looked grimmer than before, and I rather wished I'd left the words unsaid. 'Well, thank Jupiter the child has been returned to us,' I said, in the hope of covering the moment's frostiness. 'Though Marcus will be furious when he sees what they have done.'

I meant it. What Marcus would say when he found that his precious son and heir had not only been stripped of his fine clothes and golden bulla, but smeared with stinking grease and shut up in the dark like an animal in that basket, I did not care to think. I even feared he'd vent his rage on me, for bringing the child back to him like this: my patron has always had a tendency to blame the messenger for unwelcome news.

The doctor said nothing, but the boy squirmed sideways and began to squeal again. Philades expertly scooped him up against his shoulder and began to pat him firmly on the back.

At least, I thought – watching this procedure helplessly – my worst fears had not been realised. We'd received no word of Julia, but at least the boy had been returned to us alive. I'd feared that they were both dead, but the boy seemed generally none the worse for his terrible ordeal. Indeed, the medicus had performed a sort of miracle. Marcellinus had been red-faced and fretting visibly, but now he stopped howling, burped once, and then relaxed. The sobs subsided first to gulping gasps, and then to contented little bubbling sounds. Though these were muffled against the toga cloth, I recognised the hissing noises which had alarmed me so. I felt a little stupid recalling my earlier fears.

'You are skilled with children,' I mumbled awkwardly. 'Do they teach you that in Greece? Or did you learn it somewhere, afterwards?' Most Roman-trained physicians I had met, including the state-licensed ones in town, had learned what they knew either from army doctors or from people trained by them, and were more comfortable with wounds and fevers than with children's maladies.

If Philades heard this feeble flattery he ignored it utterly. 'There!' he said, with brisk efficiency. 'That was the problem. Digestive vapours. He's obviously more comfortable now, and fortunately he seems to be more or less unharmed.' He flashed me a swift, appraising look. 'I'll hand it to you, pavement-maker – you may be sick, but you are still cleverer than I gave you credit for. How in the name of Jupiter did you bring this about?'

At first I didn't understand what he was driving at. 'What do you mean?'

'The boy's return. I presume you did arrange it, somehow, with the kidnappers?'

I stared at him. If he had suggested that I'd had dealings with Hercules himself, I could scarcely have been more taken aback. I shook my head. 'He was pushed into the litter in that container there. It was a surprise to me.'

'But you must know who brought him here?' He was watchful and suspicious, suddenly. 'You saw the man?'

'I don't know any more than you do. Someone pushed him in against my back, and ran away into the woods. Or I presume he did. Odd, since there was already an arrangement for the child's safe return. But that's all I can tell you. I swear on the gods.'

Philades paused in the act of patting Marcellinus, as if some passing deity had turned him into stone. 'Surely you must have caught a glimpse, at least? Since you were un-accountably awake?' He was avoiding my eyes, I realised.

'I saw nobody,' I said. 'I was lying on my side and looking

62

out the other way. By the time I'd turned round it was too late.'

He was still gazing elsewhere with exaggerated care. 'So you couldn't identify the person even from the back? That's most unfortunate.'

'I was watching you dealing with the logs,' I said. All this emotion was exhausting me. 'You know I was. Besides, I'm ill. I don't know why you – of all people – should expect me to be alert. It's only chance I wasn't fast asleep.'

He grunted. 'If you say so, citizen.' This time he sounded frankly sceptical. Did he suppose that I had chosen not to look, because I was sick, exhausted and preferred not to incur the troubles that witnesses invite?

'I'm sure the litter slaves would bear me out on this,' I went on grumpily. 'They must have seen me leaning out to look.'

'I doubt it, citizen. I instructed them to keep their attention on the task. We heard your cry, of course – but we all assumed that you were just shouting in your sleep again.'

I frowned. 'But you came back?'

'Of course. I was about to wake you from your troubled dreams and give you something to ensure that you relaxed. I have some dried herbs, ready mixed, here in my pouch.' He gave me that appraising look again. 'Which, after all this shock, you should have in any case.'

So he had genuinely expected me to be asleep, I thought. Or drugged into unconsciousness, perhaps. I was suddenly overwhelmed by a strong desire to avoid his sleeping mixtures at all costs.

I changed the subject with forced cheerfulness. 'Why don't we tell the bearers that the boy is found?' I said. 'They are still working on the logs, and we are inside the curtain, so they won't have seen – they must be wondering why you have been so long.'

He wouldn't look at me. Instead he examined the now-sleeping child with care: moving the limbs, and opening the eyes and mouth and staring into them. 'Leave that to me. I'll tell them presently. If I announce it to the servants now, they will come rushing back, and that will lead to even more delays. If you are right, the kidnappers must be still nearby in the woods. They may have other plans to slow us down.'

'Other plans?' I echoed, stupidly.

'Of course. Who do you suppose arranged this blockage in the road? It must have been to ensure that they could hand him back.'

I was feeling worn and wretched, but I could see that he was right. If someone wanted to stop a conveyance which was on its way to the villa, this was the perfect method. A roadblock made a litter, in particular, extremely easy to approach. Any other sort of carriage would require some kind of constant attendance by a slave, if only to stand by and hold the horse, but litter-bearers would put their burden down and go to clear the road. So the kidnappers could put the basket in unobserved . . .

Unobserved? I brought myself up short. Only if the occupant was more or less asleep! Most litter-riders would be wide awake while travelling – only an ill man would doze, as I had done. And in that case – I felt a little prickle of unease run down my spine – it was likely that the kidnappers knew exactly who I was, when I was coming, and what means were being used to convey me here.

And then it dawned on me. I must have been affected by those sleeping drugs or surely the idea would have come to me before.

Who had known that I was coming here this afternoon – and insisted on a litter as the vehicle? Who had decided to accompany me himself, and made no secret of the fact that he would give me a draught to make me sleep? Who – when the litter halted at the logs – was perfectly placed to push the basket in, while everyone's attention was on something else? The answer was Philades, in every case! A newcomer to the household, skilled with herbs and drugs, who had turned up – as if by accident – immediately after the child and its mother had disappeared.

I shook my head. It was absurd. Why should the doctor be involved in anything like that? I must be rambling. I had no earthly proof that he was involved – and there were surely things my newly thought-of theory did not explain. For instance, he could clearly not have brought the basket here.

Though – I thought, uneasily – he could easily have picked it up from some appointed place, or given a signal to an accomplice in the woods. And he had expected me to be asleep – indeed, if I had not been nibbling at my forbidden oatcake and thus kept myself awake, it is almost certain that I would have been. Was that why he had questioned me so closely about what I might have seen – and why his manner had so abruptly changed? This road-block was a bold and daring plan, but he had the intelligence to have thought it up. I stole a glance at him, and found that he was looking appraisingly at me, although he dropped his eyes at once and went on ostentatiously examining the child.

I felt a cold stab of alarm. We were outside the villa and I was in the doctor's hands – a situation that I didn't like at all. I was not at my most capable, I knew. My reasoning was slow. Junio was gone, and the bearer-slaves were under

65

Philades' command. My best defence was to get into Marcus's house as soon as possible.

'We must tell His Excellency the news at once,' I said, emphasising the honorific title to remind Philades that I had powerful patronage. 'It's obvious the kidnappers have had a change of plan, though I shouldn't be surprised if there were more demands to meet before there is a chance of Julia's release. Poor Marcus. I know how I should feel, if it were Gwellia. I wonder what he will do now about the villa gates?' I tried to keep my manner as calm as possible, but I was aware that I was wittering.

The look the doctor gave me would have withered iron. 'You can give your version of events to Marcus very soon. I'm sure he will be as totally amazed as you and I. As to additional demands, was there any message in the basket with the boy? About how we are to ransom Julia, perhaps?'

I hadn't thought of that. 'I haven't looked.'

The medicus gave me another of his looks. He said nothing, but stretched past me and with his free hand tipped the basket out on top of me. As he did so I saw what I had not taken in before, that there were cloths inside – not very clean or lovely cloths, but enough to form a sort of cushion between the child and the bottom of the container. I rummaged through them, not very expertly, realising how weak I had become.

'Nothing there.' I lay back, exhausted by my efforts.

'Pity,' he said tersely. 'But it is good to know that someone has been caring for the child. He's been kept moderately clean, at least.'

I forced my addled brain to work this out. Marcellinus was hardly what I'd describe as clean, but it was true that he had been snatched away without a change of clothes, and – as I understand it – with children of such a tender age these things are pretty frequently required. 'Except for that stinking grease, of course,' I added.

Philades glanced at me. 'The hog's grease, you mean, to keep off the cold? Don't worry, pavement-maker, I had noticed that. I shall mention it to Marcus, never fear. A poor man's remedy, but sound enough. Mixed with the warming herbs of Mercury: garlic, lavender and rue, if I am any judge. And he has obviously been fed, and recently. Is that a fair assessment, do you think?'

'I don't know,' I muttered, feeling thoroughly confused. I could vaguely remember being greased myself when I was small, though I was sure that it hadn't stunk like this. However, the memory prompted me to ask, 'Did his mother do all this for him, do you suppose? The food and everything?'

He swept my words aside. 'Oh, Julia couldn't suckle him herself. I doubt she ever did. More likely she gave him to the wet nurse as soon as he was born – most wealthy matrons do – and then of course her milk would cease to come.'

I was too embarrassed by this mental picture to say anything beyond, 'I knew he had a wet nurse, naturally. But I thought that he was suffering from hunger pangs. There was a piece of cloth bound round his face when he arrived. A twist of it was stuck into his mouth. He seemed to have been gnawing at it. I supposed . . .'

The medicus said impatiently, 'A comforter. Dipped in milk and poppy juice, no doubt, and given to the child to suck – since clearly he's been drugged.'

'Drugged?' I was genuinely horrified. 'Of course some Roman parents give their children sips of poppy juice to make them sleep – for instance when new teeth are breaking through – but I know that Julia did not approve of that. Marcus will be furious.'

I meant it. However, I could see now why Marcellinus had been so sluggish earlier, and why he had crawled so listlessly about. Even now, as the medicus examined him, I could see that the eyeballs were rolling back into the head: and as soon as the eyelids were released they drooped, and the child was ready to slide back into the arms of Morpheus.

'Well, someone has been giving this infant poppy juice,' Philades said, as if he had scored a point at my expense, 'and much more of it than could be administered on that scrap of cloth. Possibly the drug was mixed with something soft to eat. It would have to be something sweet. Poppy milk is very bitter on its own.' He had lifted the boy into the air and was smacking his face, quite sharply. 'Come on, young fellow, we must wake you up.'

Marcellinus stirred and began to fret again.

'So he was taking solid food?' I said. Of course I should have known that for myself. Wasn't the servant sent to get cooked fruit for him, the afternoon that he and his mother disappeared? 'Why did he need a wet nurse, in that case?'

Philades looked incredulous. 'Surely you know that children often go on suckling long after they are eating other food as well: sometimes until they're almost three or four, when they can start to drink a little watered wine? But whether he's been suckled while he's been away, who knows? Of course, anyone can hire a wet nurse, at a price – but the watered milk of cows or goats would do if the child can manage through a piece of straw.' He turned back to Marcellinus. 'Just one burp more, I think!'

Philades put the child back against his shoulder – irrespective of the stinking grease which was leaving smears against his toga – and began patting him firmly between the shoulder blades. 'There, that should answer your question, citizen. This boy has obviously been drinking milk, judging by the posset that he's produced.' He gestured to a mouthful of pre-digested goo, which the child had just deposited on his shoulder folds. 'That's better, little man.'

'I see.' I tried to look intelligently at the stain. It did not seem to worry him at all. Admittedly the toga was already none too clean.

Philades swung the boy down from his perch. 'But enough of this. The lad is getting cold. Hog's grease alone cannot protect a child from chilly winds. And you yourself should rest. Whatever else, you are my patient still.' He was wrapping the now-gurgling Marcellinus in one of the cloths from the basket as he spoke. 'Here! You take him in the litter with you and try to keep him warm. I'll go and organise those lazy slaves.' He handed the half-sleeping infant back to me, and moved the curtain strips as if to rise and leave.

All at once he seemed to change his mind. He turned back, opened up the pouch he'd mentioned earlier and poured a little of the dried mixture out into his hand. I had just opened my mouth to say something in farewell, when I found that he had deftly placed the herbs in it.

'Chew these,' he said. 'They'll help you sleep again. You're looking pale. I'll see you at the house.' He stood up and raised his voice again. 'Slaves, what are you doing there? Are you not finished yet? This man is sick. It is imperative we get the litter into the villa soon.'

There was a muffled answering shout from further up the track, but the medicus had already let the leather curtain fall back into its place. It screened the child from outside view,

Chapter Seven

After what seemed like an eternity, but was in fact probably only a very little while, something did happen.

First there was a great deal of shouting further up the road, from where the logpile had been lying in the way. Then I could hear the snort of oxen and the crack of whips and I guessed that, in answer to Junio's request for help, a party of land slaves from the villa farm had been sent out with some animals to move the logs. My suspicions were confirmed when a moment later there was first a pause and then a mighty clatter, followed by the sound of splintering and cheers.

Almost at once I was aware of running feet, and a good deal of hasty whispering nearby. I heard Philades' voice: he had obviously come up beside the litter and was giving some order to the bearer-slaves, but he had dropped his tone so I could not catch exactly what it was. Then, without further warning, the litter lurched into the air again, and I resumed my jolting progress down the lane.

I closed my eyes and lay back in relief. Probably my fears had been irrational. Once inside the villa, I was safe. I cradled Marcellinus in my arms and permitted myself to drift into a doze, dreaming of the Roman comforts which Marcus had promised me.

A moment later, though, I started up again. Something

about the motion was somehow different. The jerking, rhythmic rise and fall had ceased, and instead I was subject to a creaking roll, interspersed with sudden jolts and shocks. It took me a moment to work out what it meant, but then it came to me. I was no longer being carried by the litter-bearers. I had been put on to some kind of vehicle.

I raised a tiny corner of the curtain and looked out. I was right: the litter had been lifted on to a cart.

I was thoroughly disturbed by now. I struggled up to get a better view, though I took care not to waken the sleeping child in my arms. With the curtain wholly lifted I could glimpse the road below me through the wooden boards, and the back of the wagon-driver's head. But otherwise the cart was empty. I was on my own. The medicus and the bearer-slaves were nowhere to be seen, and there was no sign at all of Junio.

Worse, we were not on the proper lane any longer. The ground that bumped beneath the wheels was not a track at all, but simply flattened soil – humped here and there in ridges as if it had been tilled. Somehow we had left the road and were jolting now across an open field.

I tried desperately to work out how this had been achieved, and only one explanation was possible. There is a little lane on Marcus's estate, which meets the main road just before the gates, and leads round to the back entrance and the farm. The cart-driver must have turned that way and then branched out across the farm on this rutted trail which was not a route at all. I felt cold shivers running down my back. Where were they taking me?

I threw caution to the winds and thrust the curtain back. 'Where are you going?' I shouted to the man. 'Take me to the villa, instantly.'

No answer.

I called to him again. 'If you don't, there will be serious trouble, I can promise you. His Excellence is expecting me. And don't think you can hide what you have done. The cart is leaving tracks across this ground. My slave will have them looking for me very soon.'

He did not deign to turn his head, but the mention of Marcus did spark a response. 'Just doing what I'm told!'

'By whom? Where are you taking me?'

This time he made no reply at all, not so much as a grunt, but a moment later we turned sharply through a gate and bumped back on to a track. I was about to expostulate again when I saw a group of land slaves working in the field opposite. One of them was pushing on a breast plough to make furrows in the ground, while the others were following with buckets – planting beans, by the look of it. The planters stopped to watch us pass and one ran ahead to swing a gate for us. As he did so, I saw the villa straight in front of me.

The driver had turned the cart towards the house. Was it because I'd called to him? Had the doctor ordered him to come this way? And why? It was not possible that the rear lane was also blocked by logs, so there must have been some other reason for this unlikely route. To prevent me from speaking to the gate-keeper in front? Or had it been intended to take me somewhere else, until the driver realised that I was still awake?

'Be sure that I shall tell your master about this. And where's my slave?' I called. Once again, the driver made no reply at all.

However, we were now visibly headed towards the back entrance of the house, so I dropped the curtain to exclude the draught – for the sleeping child's sake, if not my own. Shortly afterwards we rumbled to a stop.

'Hello, Malodius, what have we here?' A burly gate-keeper pulled back the curtain-flap. I recognised the man from earlier visits to the house and I smiled with relief.

'Greetings,' I murmured, with heartfelt gratitude.

This man had let me into the villa more than once and I expected him to greet me with proper deference, but now he barely glanced at me before he burst out in a braying laugh. 'A new kind of lying-in, is it, with an old grandfather instead of a mother, and a grubby child?' He addressed himself to the driver as if I wasn't there at all. 'Surely you aren't going to take this lot inside? Whatever's the master going to say to that?'

The cart-driver had got down from his perch and come round to look. It was obvious, even from where I was lying, how he had got his name: Malodius means 'the evil-smelling one', or 'stinky' if you like. He was a man of middle years: a small, fat, scowling, hairy creature with a tattered tunic and bad teeth, and he gave off a strong scent of oxen and manure, and an odour of bad cheese that seemed to be his own. His impact was out of all proportion to his size.

He gave the door-keeper a bad-tempered scowl, deepening the creases in his face. He shrugged. 'Don't ask me. I just do as I'm told. First I have to take the ox cart out and use the beasts to move a pile of logs that some confounded idiot contrived to leave right in the middle of the lane outside – well, I don't mind that so much, it's what the beasts are for – but then I have to bring this wretched litter in, as though I were a blooming carriage-driver if you please. And not even on the proper cart track either, but bumping all the back way through the fields. That's the doctor's orders – and he has to be obeyed. You know what Master has been like the last few days: anything the medicus decides is to be done at once, if not a little sooner. And all this while there were proper litter-bearers standing by. Don't ask me why, 'cause I don't know myself. I don't even know who's in the blessed thing.'

So my surmise was right. It was Philades who'd ordered him to take that most unlikely route. Yet only hours ago the doctor had been arguing against my travelling. Had he sent me along this rutted track, used only by the ox cart and the land slaves for their work, in the hope that, in my weakened state, it would be too much for me? Well, I was not submitting to any more of this. It was time to make my presence felt.

'Don't worry, gate-keeper,' I said. I tried to sound as stern as possible, but instead of sounding masterful, my voice came out as a sort of feeble bleat. 'I am a client of His Excellence. You've let me in before. I think you'll find that he's expecting me and has a room prepared. And this child in my arms is my patron's missing heir. I assure you that your master will be best pleased with you if you permit me to take his son inside as soon as possible and get him warm and washed.'

'Great Minerva!' The gate-keeper came close and stared at me. 'I know that voice. It is the pavement-maker, isn't it? I'm sorry, citizen, you are so thin and pale I did not recognise you for a moment there. Malodius, what are you thinking of? This is the master's client and – dear Mercury! – the master's son as well – what are they doing on the oxen cart? There will be trouble when he hears of this. Citizen, I apologise a thousand times. I'll send for some slaves at once, and have you carried in. Wait here, Malodius. I'll go for help myself.' He dropped the litter curtain and I heard him running off.

He had been positively grovelling, but the cart-driver was

clearly not impressed. I heard him muttering to the ox as he unhitched it from the shafts. 'Well, they can't blame me,' he grumbled. 'I just do as I'm required. If they wanted a proper carriage for the job, they should have sent for it. It's not as though there isn't one to hand. Ready and waiting, too – I have to clean and polish it for hours every day. And what for, I'd like to know? It hasn't been out since the mistress went missing. But do they think of that? Of course they don't. They just put the litter on my cart and tell me to take it the back way through the fields to the gates – so that is precisely what I did. How was I supposed to know it was the master's son aboard? Nobody ever tells me anything – and then it's always my fault if anything goes wrong.'

How long he might have stood there muttering like that I cannot guess, but at that moment a whole troupe of Marcus's slaves arrived, all matched and uniformed, and suddenly there were more people to assist than there were jobs to do. Eager hands seized the child, wrapped him in scented blankets and bore him tenderly away. Others were on hand to help me down. I too was swathed in blankets and half carried, half supported through the gate, across the outer court and peristyle, and into the inner garden and the back wing of the house.

It was the first time that I'd been fully on my feet since I fell ill, and though they asked about my welfare at almost every step, I found I was too weary and light-headed to say anything at all. I was content to go where they were leading me. It was obvious that they had their instructions on that score. Marcus has a pleasant inner garden, full of statues, fountains, flowers and herbs, quartered by paths and fringed by a verandaed colonnade that links the main block of the house with the sleeping rooms on either wing, and with the kitchen and storerooms at the back. The door to one guest apartment was ajar, and we paused outside it. I recognised the second-best bedroom in this whole part of the house: Julia herself had slept here until recently, when Marcus built a separate wing with new apartments for all three of them, set round a little courtyard of its own.

The room was waiting for me, with a proper Roman bed – a stretched goatskin suspended on a frame which gently bore one's weight. I was lowered on to it, tucked into the finest woollen coverings, and piled around with soft pillows to support my head. The floor was heated by the hypocaust beneath, as it was in all the public areas, but the room had been made additionally snug on my account. A cheerful brazier stood by, exuding warmth, and a bowl of something steaming awaited me on the wooden cabinet beside the bed, and another on the table by the door. An emperor could not have asked for more.

Almost before I was properly ensconced, my patron came rushing in to me. As well as the usual retinue of slaves, including the young page whom I'd seen earlier, he was accompanied by a portly man in a flowing robe – whom I recognized as the high priest of Jupiter himself. Not only was I immersed in luxury, I seemed to be holding a sort of court as well.

'Libertus, my old friend. What joyful news. The boy is back – and you, it seems, were there to rescue him.' Marcus came right up to my bedside and held out his hand.

My fears about my welcome were unfounded, it appeared. I struggled up and kissed his seal ring, then sank back again. 'I was in the litter . . .' I began.

His free hand waved me into silence. 'The medicus has told me what occurred. Do not distress yourself. I'll hear it all from your lips a little later on – for now it is enough that you are safe, and that the boy is too.'

'He's well?' I was still ready for an outburst at the indignities which had been visited upon the child, but Marcus merely gave a nod.

'He has been washed and cleaned and Philades is with him even now. Jupiter greatest and best be praised, it seems he's taken no harm.'

'Though he's lost his bulla – don't overlook that fact,' the chief priest put in, self-importantly, as if the very mention of the god required him to speak. He was newly appointed to the post, after the death of the previous high priest, but – being florid, short and plump – he did not have his predecessor's natural air of gravitas and authority.

Marcus looked more serious at once. 'That is true, of course. I'd not forgotten it.' He turned to me and smiled. 'It means that I must leave you for a little while. My friend the pontifex' – he indicated the priest – 'instructs me that we must go to the main temple in the town and sacrifice a pure white calf at once.'

I was surprised into a whistle and an irreverent remark. 'A pure white calf? Without any kind of mark? That will cost you a *denarius* or two. At such short notice, in particular.'

Far from upbraiding me for my impertinence, Marcus said gravely, 'True, but it must be done as soon as possible. The pontifex knows where I can find one, at a price.'

The high priest must have read my doubts, because he hurried to explain. 'It is quite essential, I assure you, Excellence. Both to give thanks for your son's return and also to expiate the bulla's loss – and then with the ashes we can reconsecrate the boy, give him a new neck charm and begin again. We'll have a ritual at the altar here, on the first auspicious day. Tomorrow, if you can get a new bulla made in time.'

Marcus nodded. 'I will try. I want it done as soon as possible.'

The high priest looked at me. 'You were at the boy's first naming ceremony, I understand? Perhaps you will be well enough to attend the second one. The ritual will be more pleasing to the gods if we can duplicate the first as closely as possible.'

I was about to answer, but Marcus shook his head. 'We have the chief priest of Jupiter to officiate – that is sufficient to ensure success.'

The chief priest looked as if he were unsure whether to plump up with importance at this compliment or to be affronted by the way his words were swept aside. Eventually he settled for the preen. 'All the same . . .' he ventured.

My patron said firmly, 'Libertus has been ill; he must be left to rest. The medicus was emphatic on that point. In fact, it is against advice that I have come to see him now – but I felt I had to thank him for everything he's done and assure him that everything is well. But now we must leave him to his well-earned sleep. Philades has left a soothing draught for him somewhere.'

'But it's on the tabletop!' the pontifex exclaimed, following the direction of his glance. 'Your friend cannot drink that! Have it disposed of instantly! Surely even a Greek physician is aware that leaving a remedy on a table is a dreadful augury for anyone who takes it afterwards?'

'I'm sure he intended nothing of the kind,' my patron said soothingly. 'It is a purely Roman superstition, I am sure. All the same, I'll have it moved at once. Page, see to it.' The pretty young man did so immediately, and Marcus went on

79

with a smile, 'We'll have another one made up for you. I don't imagine there is any curse, but we won't take any chances – there has been enough misfortune in this house already. And, speaking of propitiating fate, we must go at once and make that sacrifice. We will be back this evening, before – I hope and pray – Julia is returned to us as well. I have ordered my slaves to leave the gate open and unguarded, as I was told to do.'

I doubted that his wife's return would be so easy, but he was optimistic and since I feared to cross his mood I contented myself with murmuring, 'And Lallius?'

He smiled grimly. 'I shall leave instructions with the garrison while I am in the town. Lallius will be arrested at his house, just as soon as I am certain that Julia is safe and send the word to them. I'll have the guards round up all his associates and bring them in for questioning as well. Don't worry, I have it all in hand. Now, try to get some sleep.' He turned to his retinue. 'Slaves, Libertus is to have anything he wants – subject to the doctor's views, of course. But first he needs to rest. See that a watch is kept outside his door and that he's not disturbed. Come, pontifex.'

And with that he gestured to the priest to follow him, and left the room with his servants obediently at his heels.

Chapter Eight

To my immense delight, when the crowd of other servants had retired, I looked up to find Junio standing at the door holding a steaming basin in his hands. He came over, grinning, to my side, and put it down.

'Well, master,' he said cheerfully. 'I'm glad to have you to myself at last. I hear that you have brought Marcellinus home – but without his bulla, I believe. That will cost Marcus a cow or two at least!'

I nodded. 'My patron's gone to Glevum with the priest to find one now and make a propitiation sacrifice.'

He grinned. 'And to present a *defixio* against the kid-nappers, so the servants say. He's going to nail it to the temple doorpost while the chief priest himself stands by. It's the gossip of the villa, as you might suppose. Everyone is trying to guess what curses he will choose.'

I gave a feeble smile. It made a kind of sense. Marcus was not usually a superstitious man – his religious observances were of the public kind, required of all important magistrates. Drawing down curses was not his general style. But there were always metalworkers outside the temple doors offering to make a *defixio* for you – a beaten tablet to be nailed up on the wall, consigning your enemies to ruin and calling down the vengeance of the gods – sometimes with appalling details of what you wished to happen to the victim's vital parts. 'It will help him vent his feelings, I suppose. He must feel pretty powerless, otherwise.'

Junio grinned. 'I gather the chief priest himself suggested it – and there's to be a special blessing prayer for you. Does that not delight you?' He winked. 'Of course, you might have preferred a monetary reward, but . . .' He trailed off, but I knew what he meant.

I nodded ruefully. My patron always declined to 'insult me', as he said, by offering money for my services – an insult I could easily have borne. However, I was now his guest and I defended him. 'Marcus has been very good to me – he's seen to it that I have slaves, and property.'

Junio laughed. 'Which cost him next to nothing! I think the medicus was genuinely shocked when Cilla told him how she came to you as a reward for something really important that you did! However, if praise is what you want, you must be satisfied. Marcus has told everyone in the household how clever you have been in bringing Marcellinus home again.'

'That's another thing that worries me.' I was happy to be able to confide my doubts. 'I did nothing. I was simply there, and the child was put into my carrying bed on top of me.'

'I heard that you'd claimed it was just a lucky chance. The household don't believe it, on the whole, and I suppose it must sound a bit unlikely if you didn't know all the facts. But I tried to convince them that you couldn't possibly have arranged for it – that you have been far too ill to do anything of the kind, and I have been with you all the time. The chief priest seemed to accept my word for it – said that, in that case, you were clearly the instrument of the gods. But Marcus still suspects that you contrived it in some way and is hoping that you'll do the same for Julia very soon.'

'Oh, dear gods. And I had no chance to speak to him alone and persuade him otherwise! I'll have to try again when he comes home.' I remembered my suspicions of the medicus, and added, 'I'd like to talk to Marcus about all this in any case, before Philades does.'

Junio made a doubtful face. 'In that case, master, I'm afraid you've lost your chance. The medicus is going to Glevum too – I've heard the servants say – though he's left the strictest orders for your care. However, Marcus has said you can have anything you need – so I thought you might be glad of a restorative. I have one ready that I've prepared for you.' He picked up the still steaming basin from the cabinet and lifted it gently to my lips.

I drew my head back, ready to refuse, but then I caught the scent. It was not, as I had feared, another of the doctor's brews. It was a bowl of mead, hot and mixed with spice, which my slave had obviously prepared for me himself. It has always been a favourite drink of mine, and today it tasted like the nectar of the gods. I took it from his hands and drained the bowl.

Junio gave me another of his conspiratorial grins. 'Don't let Philades see you drinking that. You're fortunate that he's allowed you gruel. His patients are usually given oxymel, he says. Nothing but mixed vinegar and honey for days and days if they awake from fever. Apparently he was holding forth about his methods at the feast the other night. But obviously you were progressing well enough to make him change his mind, and you are to be moved on to a light food diet, with hydromel to drink. But I don't think that he would approve of mead.'

I had already made a mental resolution not to swallow anything further that the doctor made for me, unless it had been tested by a poison-taster first. Marcus had promised me one, after all. However, I did not say that to Junio. He would have volunteered his services at once – and his life was as precious to me as my own.

'Hydromel is not too bad,' I said. 'Honey and water mixtures I can stand. But a light food diet!' I feigned a playful groan. 'Snails, green vegetables and vinegar? How could anyone get well on that?'

Junio took the bowl away and laughed. 'Well, you can have some fruit and seafood too. That's what Celsus recommends, apparently, and Philades is a follower of his. He's got all his prescriptions written in a scroll and he has been into the kitchens to instruct the cooks. But there is a long list of forbidden foods, I fear. No cheese, bread, poultry, meat or roots until you are safely on the mend.'

I looked at Junio. I wondered about voicing my uneasiness to him. 'I don't altogether trust that medicus,' I said.

Junio clearly thought I was referring to the food. 'I'm not surprised. I know that you hate snails. But don't despair. There are other recommended remedies which he has in store as well, some of them a bit more interesting. He is talking about visits to the steam room here, when you are well enough. Marcus has the bath-house furnace stoked in readiness. To cleanse the blood, apparently. And even carriage rides are good, it seems. I heard him telling Marcus that it's "passive exercise". A little rocking will improve your health, he said, that's why he decided to put you on the cart this afternoon and give you a little outing through the fields.'

I felt that stirring of alarm again. I had intended to complain to my patron about that uncomfortable ride, but clever Philades had got ahead of me. Of course, it was still possible that what he said was true – even I had heard of 'rocking therapy' – but earlier that very day he'd been concerned that I should avoid the jolt of carriages in my weakened state. I did not think he'd simply changed his mind. However, I did not wish to cause Junio alarm.

'Well, I hope there are not too many treatments of that sort,' I muttered. 'That journey almost killed me. I confess that I prefer your remedy.' I gestured to the bowl. 'That mead has done me good. I feel stronger than I've done for days. And more clear-headed too. Though I don't think our physician would much approve of it.'

Junio gave me a look of wide-eyed innocence. 'There was no mention of spiced mead on his forbidden list, so I did as I thought fit and made you some.' He winked at me. 'He didn't mention oatcakes either, I recall. Not specifically. So if I should happen to find one in my pouch . . .' He produced one, as he spoke, and handed it to me with a grin. 'The one you had before has clearly done no harm, and I know how much you like them. Indeed, I think my mistress plans to bring some when she comes – she says that Roman kitchens never make them properly.'

The oatcake was delicious, if a little crushed. I relished every crumb. 'Thank you, Junio.'

He smoothed my pillows, took the bowl and moved towards the door. 'I'm glad I pleased you, master. However, I am told that now I must go away and let you rest. I'll wait outside the door. Unless there's some further service that you'd like me to perform?'

There was. The hot mead did seem to have revived my brain. I pulled myself a little more upright. 'In fact, Junio, there is something you can do,' I said, dropping my voice so we could not be heard. I know, from my own experience, how whispers travel in a house full of slaves. 'If you can find any of the household slaves who saw Julia and the child that afternoon, before they disappeared, I would like to have a word with them as soon as possible.'

He shook his head. 'Marcus has left instructions that you're not to be disturbed. And he has already questioned all the slaves himself.'

'I know,' I said. 'And he discovered nothing. But that does not mean that there is nothing to be learned.' I glanced at the doorway to ensure that we were not being overheard. 'I am sure that someone inside the villa is involved in this affair.'

Junio looked horrified. 'Someone inside the villa! Not just a trusted visitor? Dear gods!' He came back to me and gazed into my face. 'I know you, master. It is more than that. You are thinking of someone in particular. Whom do you suspect?'

He spoke too loudly, and I shook my head. If there were any listeners in the court they would be straining now to capture every word – and in any household there are always spies. Besides, I still had no proof at all against the medicus – and naming him might do more harm than good. I decided I would try another ploy: laying the facts before my slave and seeing if he would come up with the same conclusion for himself. He has been following my methods for a long time now, and prides himself upon his reasoning.

'I believe that someone knew our plans today.' Quickly, I outlined my thoughts about the blockage on the road, and the way the child had been returned to us.

'Too convenient to be an accident?' Junio nodded. 'You know, exactly the same thought occurred to me – and to the doctor, too. He said as much to Marcus. That's why His Excellence is half convinced that you arranged this with the kidnappers.'

'Which you know that I did not.' I looked at him.

'Of course not . . .' He broke off. 'Great Minerva! But I do see what you mean. If you didn't tell the kidnappers, who did? Only our household and the villa staff had any notion that you were coming here – and even that was not until today. So it must be someone in this house. That would fit with what we thought before.' He paused and shook his head. 'But what have any of them to do with Lallius?'

I had not even thought of that myself. I'd been so caught up with thoughts of Philades I had quite forgotten the coin official's son. 'A shrewd question, Junio,' I said.

He flushed with pleasure. 'And another thing. Why did the kidnappers change their minds like that, about returning Julia and the child tonight? They'd already left instructions about the gate. Why stick the boy into your litter, anyway?' He frowned. 'Maybe the child was crying and proving difficult to hide and they were eager to get rid of it, do you think?'

'It's possible. They gave him poppy juice to keep him quiet.'

'Well, in any case it doesn't matter now. He's been returned to us unharmed, and Julia is likely to be free tonight as well. Then all we shall have to do is catch the kidnappers.'

I shook my head. 'I wish it was as easy as you say. I've always thought she wouldn't be released – not without further payment, anyway.' I paused. 'Perhaps not even then.'

He caught his breath. 'You think it's possible? Even now that the child has been returned?'

'Julia was always under greatest threat. You work it out. Marcellinus hasn't learned to talk, so it's obviously safe to let him go. But Julia . . .'

That seemed to startle Junio. 'Great Jupiter, that's true.

You said before it would be dangerous for them to set her free. And she's a clever lady. She will have worked that out. She must be terrified, especially now she's been separated from the child.'

There was a silence. I think both of us were fearing that Julia might be already dead.

Then Junio spoke again. 'So it looks as if someone in the household has been involved in this – by passing information to the kidnappers? It might have been by accident, of course. She was very much beloved.'

'You see why it is necessary for me to talk to Julia's slaves?'

Junio nodded. 'Of course. I'll see what I can do to find those girls and you can question them as soon as you have slept. Though, master, I'm afraid that you will have to wait till then. Marcus has left the strictest instructions with the staff that no one but myself is to come into your room till he gets back. His servants will not disobey his explicit command, and we can't expect them to.'

'So this room is out of bounds to everyone? No doubt the medicus suggested that as well?'

Junio laughed. 'Well, something clearly needed to be done. The slaves were all crowding round the door when you arrived, all buzzing to hear your story for themselves, till Marcus barked at them to keep away. They tried to ask me questions in the kitchen, when I went to get your mead, but of course I didn't tell them anything – I didn't know exactly what had happened anyway. I'm sure they'd all love to talk to you, but just for now they can't. However, I'll see what I can do. I might even try to win their confidence and have a word with them myself.'

And before I could summon the effort to protest, he'd tiptoed from the room.

It was irksome to be lying helplessly in bed, unable to do anything to solve this mystery; and it was worrying to know that I was in the doctor's hands. I have rarely felt so powerless and so trapped.

I controlled my panic. Philades had gone to Glevum, so I was safe for now. I was still struggling with the effects of my previous sleeping draught and that jolting journey had exhausted me, so – even without the doctor's suspect bowl of herbs – I was already drifting into sleep. I tried to fight it, but the bed was luxurious and warm. I felt my eyelids close.

When I opened them again it was to realise that it was already getting dark and someone had lit an oil lamp in the room.

Chapter Nine

It was Marcus's voice which brought me to myself. 'You are awake, Libertus?' I looked up and found that he was standing at my bedside, with the pageboy and Junio attending him. No medicus, I thought. That was good. Now, perhaps, I would have a chance to talk in confidence.

I smiled and tried to clear my pounding head. I tried a foolish little pleasantry. 'I am now, Excellence,' I said.

There was no vestige of an answering smile. 'Then I would like to ask your counsel, if you are well enough.' He was dressed in his official robes after visiting the shrine. The distinctive smell of the thanksgiving sacrifice – smoke, incense, and burnt feathers – still clung to him, but there was no hint of his earlier rejoicing manner now. His face was stern and sombre and he sounded drawn and strained.

I half sat up at once. 'What is it, Excellence?' I was alarmed. What had the physician been telling him? Or was there something the matter with the child, after all? Or bad news of Julia? I seized on the least worrying possibility. 'Is Marcellinus well?'

'Excellence!' The voice came from the door and I saw Philades, who had been standing round the corner in the court. I felt my spirits sink.

My patron seemed about to reply to what I'd said, but the doctor came pattering forward to his side and whispered in that high-pitched voice of his, 'Allow me, Excellence. Better if I handle this for you – I can assess the patient, and decide if he is well enough to stand up to questioning.'

Marcus nodded, glanced towards me, and said nothing more. This was not like my patron. He never allowed others to tell him what to do and usually he confided everything to me.

I did not know what Philades was up to, but I did not trust the man – and judging by the look he was giving me, dislike was mutual. And yet my life and health were in his hands: that was inescapable, as long as I was here. I would have to be doubly on my guard, I thought.

The doctor made no move to approach the bed and he kept his hands uncomfortably behind him all the time. His manner and his cracked careful Latin suggested that he was giving evidence in court, rather than replying to an innocent enquiry. 'The child is well enough. Indeed, he seems surprisingly unscathed. Not even particularly disturbed by his ordeal – too young, I suppose, to really comprehend. Unfortunately, he is also too young to tell us what occurred – which, as I am sure you would agree, is fortunate for the conspirators.' He aimed a short, grim smile at me, as if he had scored some point at my expense, and then retired to resume his glowering behind my patron's back.

Marcus was still frowning. He had pushed back his ceremonial wreath and was raking his fingers repeatedly through his curls – a sure sign that he was seriously agitated and disturbed. Then he said, in a flat voice, 'I should thank you once again for your part in bringing my son home. And it is true. He seems to be in splendid health. It's only a pity that his mother isn't here as well, to care for him properly.'

He glanced at me. 'I will do anything to ensure her safe return.'

So he was still hoping that I could somehow help in this. I wanted to disabuse him of that idea as soon as possible. 'I don't know what to advise, Excellence,' I said. 'Do you propose to do as the kidnappers suggest?'

He looked at Philades, and Philades looked at me. 'What do you mean by that?' the doctor snapped.

'Leaving the gate open and unguarded,' I answered in surprise. Surely they had not forgotten that?

A look of what might have been relief crossed Marcus's strained face. 'So you don't know what has been happening, old friend! I was almost sure that you did not, though some people have tried to convince me otherwise.' He turned to the medicus, a measure of impatience in his tone. 'Well, come on. Show him, Philades.' He waved the doctor forward.

Philades sidled to the bed and most unwillingly handed me the object which up to now he had been keeping carefully concealed behind his back.

It was a writing block.

Not the kind of writing block which I'd expect to find here in the villa, but the simplest kind, the sort that schoolboys use. No fancy carvings or delicate ivory here: simply a wax tablet in a crude hinged wooden frame, though this one had been roughly daubed on either side with some kind of reddish pigment. The original ties to fasten it had long since broken off and there was no sign of a seal, but it had been bound shut with a length of leather cord, which was wrapped round it twice and knotted very tight.

I looked at Marcus, but he simply gave a nod as though I should carry on. Not knowing what else to do, I began to pick at the leather fastening, but my fingers seemed peculiarly inept and in the end I had to pass it on to Junio, who took it from me and began to work it free.

While he struggled with the knots I voiced the obvious. 'Another message from the kidnappers? With more demands, no doubt?'

The doctor interrupted. 'How could you know that? The tablet's sealed.' He glanced at Marcus. 'I tied it up again myself. He can't have seen inside. He must have been expecting something of the kind.'

Marcus, still silent, looked enquiringly at me.

'I thought it was inevitable that there would be more,' I said. 'I said as much to several people earlier. This tablet has arrived quite recently?'

Marcus confirmed as much in a weary tone. 'It was found in the orchard, where the watch-geese are, while we were away in Glevum performing the sacrifice. One of the servants discovered it, beside the wall, when she went out to feed the geese. It was brought to us as soon as we returned.'

'The orchard?' I looked at him sharply. 'The orchard is within the villa walls, so no casual visitor could reach it. And anyway, it is extremely odd. Surely the watch-geese would have hissed if any stranger approached, or indeed if anything had startled them at all?'

Before Marcus had a chance to answer, Philades broke in. 'Oh, but they did hiss, citizen. There are witnesses to that. There were land slaves working in the orchard earlier, and at one point the geese were certainly disturbed – so much so that one man climbed a tree beside the wall to see what was going on. He found there was a commotion outside in the lane. I imagine you can work out what that was?'

Thank all the gods for Junio and his mead! My mind was a little clearer now and I saw where this was leading. 'I suppose it was the litter and the pile of logs?' I had noticed the leafless fruit trees at the time.

'Exactly, citizen.' That grim, tight smile again. 'Of course, they concluded that the noise was what alarmed the geese, so they thought no more about it and went back to work – as no doubt the conspirators intended them to do.'

That was aimed at me, I realised. Yet he had been out there in the lane himself. If attack was the best form of defence, I thought, he was a master at it. But I was too weak to get involved in challenges like that. 'And the writing block? The slaves did not notice that?'

'Not at that moment, surprisingly enough. But it was certain that someone would see it in the end: that scarlet paint would make it stand out against the grass. There are always land slaves passing that way – leaf-sweepers, gardeners, and the man who tends the bees – and there are household slaves who go there every night to feed the chickens and the geese. As anyone who knew the house would know.'

I made a sound that might have been a 'Hmmm'.

'I see that you agree,' the doctor said. 'Somebody who knew the household, and who'd stopped outside. You are clever at deductions, pavement-maker – who answers that description, would you say?'

I met his eyes. 'Either of us two, I suppose. Although . . .' I was about to add that any suspicion which attached to me could equally apply to Philades as well – more so, since I had been lying in the litter and he had been standing in the lane, and had personally ordered the bearers to go and work elsewhere. Marcus, however, was too quick for me.

'Libertus, do not be absurd,' my patron said. 'Of course it was neither of you. I said as much to Philades before. Let's have no more of this. I want to make it clear, to both of you, that I will not tolerate accusations of that kind, unless you have some kind of solid evidence. So, unless one of you saw the other with a writing block, or with a basket concealed beneath his skirts, please turn your attention to the problem facing us, and think who else was passing in the lane.'

So the medicus had voiced suspicions about me – though Marcus was clearly not impressed by them. And he had made it clear that he would not countenance any doubts I might express about Philades. I would have to bide my time, and wait for evidence to present itself. However, another thought occurred to me. 'The man in the donkey cart might have had the opportunity, perhaps,' I ventured.

Marcus turned to Philades. 'What donkey cart? You did not mention this.'

The doctor looked momentarily nonplussed, then flashed a poisonous look in my direction. 'There was a carter held up by the logs. He'd obviously been delivering something further down the lane. He helped to clear the road. But he cannot have played any part in these events. His vehicle was on the other side, beyond the block.'

'All the same,' Marcus said firmly, 'we will have him found. Page, see to it. Have a message sent to Glevum, that they are to watch the gates for any empty donkey carts arriving at the town.' He sighed. 'And tell them they are not to pick up Lallius as yet, but continue to keep a close watch on his father's premises. We will send word as soon as Julia is safe. He must not be permitted to escape.'

The pageboy bowed and seemed about to take his leave but Marcus made a gesture which prevented him. 'If he is taking a message to the town,' he said, 'perhaps he should take the money too. What do you think, Libertus? Should he take the gold or not?'

He was asking me for my advice again, and it was hard to give. If Gwellia had been snatched away from me, I would have given her abductors anything they asked. And yet I was convinced that it was wrong. 'So it is gold they want?' I said. 'I'd been expecting worse. More political demands or something of the kind.'

'Of course, he hasn't seen the message yet,' my patron said. 'Give it to him, Junio.' And my slave, who had managed to untie the knot at last, handed the tablet back to me.

I took it and unfolded it with care. This time the writing was not so badly formed, but it was blurred and irregular as if someone had used a rough stick to scratch the wax, instead of a proper stylus. There was nothing imprecise about the message, though.

You have followed our instructions. That is good. We have returned the boy to you as proof that we are not bluffing. However, if you hope to see your wife again alive, it will cost you rather more. You will leave a basket in the lane tonight, at the corner by the hollow oak, containing two hundred *denarii*. You will put it there at dusk and leave the place unwatched. No tricks. If our messenger picks it up safely, you will receive your orders for delivering the rest of the money later on. Otherwise, light candles for your wife. You have been warned.

I looked at Marcus. 'You intend to pay the ransom?' I enquired. It was a pointless question. I was certain he would pay, just as he'd fulfilled their earlier demands. I imagined that the kidnappers had reasoned the same way. But he had asked for my advice, and I would give it, though it would be unwelcome, I was sure. 'You realise that even if you do, this won't be the end?'

'I know. They say so in the note. But what option do I have? Whoever they are, they still have my wife. I have enough money in the house for this. Two hundred *denarii* is not a massive sum.'

I found myself nodding. It seemed an enormous sum to me, but I knew that Marcus had several hiding places for his treasure underneath the floor – I had helped design the pavements which concealed some of them. 'It is obvious that you have money in the house,' I said. 'Only yesterday you told me that you were offering a reward for information which might lead to Julia and Marcellinus's safe return. Doubtless the kidnappers have heard that too.'

Marcus brushed the thought aside. 'All the more reason why I have to act. Time is getting short. Any minute it will be getting dark and they will be looking for the money in the lane. Philades thinks that I should send a decoy out to seem to leave the bag, but keep a lookout from inside the walls and try to rush them when they come for it. But I can't put Julia's life at stake. Libertus, what do you think I should do?'

I glanced at Philades. What was he up to now? Why did he think a decoy was a good idea? 'Could we gain ourselves a little time?' I said. 'Leave a message where they want the money left, perhaps, saying that you are prepared to pay, but that you must have proof that Julia is safe before you part with anything at all.'

Marcus looked brighter suddenly. 'Perhaps. And I could set someone in the lane to watch the man who picks it up, and follow him back to where he goes. Maybe he will lead us to where Julia is.'

'How can you possibly post watchers in the lane so they

will not be seen?' Philades did not even pretend to be polite. 'It is the very thing the conspirators will expect. No doubt they have eyes already in the wood, watching the villa precisely to make sure you don't set spies on them. Besides, what would happen to Julia if you do?'

'An ambush would be even worse,' I snapped. I was tired, but at least my brain was functioning again. 'It's always possible that it will fail. We don't know how many people are in the wood and how well they are armed. And you would not catch the real conspirators. There is mention of a messenger picking up the cash: no doubt a slave or some hapless beggar simply doing what they're told – at one or two removes, if the kidnappers have any sense at all. The messenger will know nothing of any consequence, except that he is to hand over the bag at some appointed place, which – thanks to the watchers in the woods – will be deserted when you get to it. Meanwhile the real culprits will be far away with Julia still in their hands. And they will know that you tried to double-cross them, too. Certainly, I cannot counsel such a course.'

It was a long speech in my current state of health, and I paused to rest. I was still debating what else I could advise when Marcus said, in a determined tone, 'Well, I must do something. I will use my page to drop the ransom money. He can ride out to Glevum with the message for the watch, and do it on the way. I'll send a letter with him asking if he can stay in the gatehouse overnight.'

The medicus said grimly, 'I still think you should send a decoy out. I am prepared to go myself . . .'

So that was his little game, I thought. Go out with the money and disappear with it? I almost voiced my thoughts aloud, but my patron intervened.

'Philades, there is no help for it, I fear. Having permitted them to blackmail me over Lallius's release, I am in a weak position now. They still have Julia. I can't afford to let anything go wrong. I'll have to pay the full amount and let them walk away. But I'll make sure they suffer for it later on.'

'It is a pity that there is so little time.' I was still fretting at the thought. 'Otherwise we might have contrived a more inconspicuous spy. The road is used by people living round about: one of them might walk along the lane – to pick up firewood, for instance – and that would seem entirely natural. If we had somebody like that to watch on our behalf . . .'

Philades interrupted me, his voice a sneer. 'One of your slaves, for instance? Or your wife?'

I had not thought of that, but I rather wished I had. I pulled myself a little more upright.

'Why not?' I said. 'After all, she is coming here tonight.' The thought was cheering. 'She is resourceful and intelligent. If we could send a message with your page, she could keep an unobtrusive watch as she comes along the lane and tell us if she sees anything unusual at all.'

Marcus shook his head. 'If there are watchers in the lane, they'll see the pageboy stop outside your house, and if she comes here afterwards they'll guess at once she is working as a spy. She will be lucky to escape their hands herself.'

He was right, of course. My thinking was confused, or I'd have seen that straight away. I said, 'I'm foolish, Excellence. Of course you're right, and I would not put Gwellia at any kind of risk. In fact, on second thoughts, it occurs to me that she might be in danger anyway. These people clearly know a great deal about us all: they may well know that Gwellia is my wife. If they see her walking all alone along the lane they'll capture her – two wives to ransom are worth more than one. Yet we've agreed that she won't bring any slaves with her. Could someone escort her here, perhaps? Not an armed guard – obviously that would alarm the kidnappers – but at least attendants to keep an eye on her. Junio himself could go, perhaps?'

'But surely, pavement-maker, that is dangerous as well?' The medicus looked triumphantly at me. 'Better to prevent her coming here at all – at least until the morning. The page could safely tell her on his way to town: there is no problem in her receiving a messenger from here, provided she doesn't leave the house. In fact, I will go with the boy to Glevum, if you wish. I could ride behind him on the horse, and ensure he's not attacked and robbed before he leaves the coins, and see that the woman understands the risk. Two people would be safer in the lane than one.'

It may have sounded rational enough, but I didn't trust the doctor a thumb's-breadth by this time and I especially didn't want him calling at my house. 'I don't think so, Excellence,' I said urgently. 'If one of these conspirators knows the business of this house, they will know that Philades enjoys your confidence. I can't think of anyone who would look more like a spy.'

Marcus paused in the doorway. 'You're right, the pair of you,' he said. 'I'll send the message to Gwellia with the man who brings the oil. He's here again today. He can stop his cart at your house on his way back to the town – no one looks twice at a delivery cart.' He turned towards the page. 'Page, you can take the money out, as I said before, and go straight on to Glevum with my messages. You understand? Then on your way back tomorrow you will call at the roundhouse and accompany Libertus's lady to the villa here.

101

It should be safe enough by then, but we will take no risks. She can still have an escort in the lane.'

The young man preened, obviously delighted to be going alone. 'As you command, master.'

Marcus gave a grunt of satisfaction. 'Then come with me. There's no time to be lost. We'll get this ransom counted out, before it is too late. Julia's safety may depend on it. You too, Philades.' He left the room, gesturing for the medicus to follow him.

But before he left the doctor came over to my bed. 'You consider yourself very clever, mosaic-maker,' he whispered, 'but I'll outwit you yet. I was talking to that female servant at your house today, and I know more of your little secrets than you think. Remember that.'

I seemed to have made myself an enemy.

Chapter Ten

When he was sure that they were safely gone Junio came over to the bed and murmured, so quietly that I could barely hear his words, 'Well, there's a sudden change of atmosphere! That sounded like a threat! What have you done to upset the medicus?' He was straightening up my bedcovers as he spoke: not that there was anything at all amiss with them – they were soft wool and sublimely comfortable – but he obviously felt the need to busy himself on my account somehow. Here, with all Marcus's establishment, there wasn't very much for him to do. 'And,' he raised my head and plumped my pillows up, 'what does his meeting Cilla have to do with anything?'

I shrugged back into the cushions. 'I don't know. He's up to something, but I don't know what.'

'There's something odd about it, certainly. This morning at the roundhouse he was all concern for you, but suddenly there's quite a different mood. When I was waiting at the door I overheard him on his way here through the court tonight, asking Marcus if he'd known you long, and – when your patron said he had – muttering that high fever can affect the mind and make people act in unexpected ways.'

So I hadn't been imagining it. 'What did Marcus say to that?'

'Not much!' Junio gave a little laugh. 'Told him not to be a fool and to concentrate on doing what he was paid to do, and getting you well as soon as possible. I was surprised he spoke so firmly, and so was Philades – Marcus is usually in awe of him, and I think the physician's accustomed to being listened to. He was clearly not best pleased – he turned a shade of puce – though he could not say anything, of course.' He had turned his attention to the pretty shoe-shaped lamp and was refilling it from the little flask of oil. 'He seemed to want to keep His Excellence away from you, I thought. Said you were still weak, and needed time to rest. But Marcus wouldn't listen to a word. Told the medicus to send some herbs to the kitchen and have them make another of his clever brews for you . . . Ah, and here it is!'

A pair of red-haired serving boys – so alike they almost looked like brothers – had suddenly appeared together at the door. They had divided the labour of carrying a small bowl by dint of putting it on a largish tray and taking one end each. When they spoke it was a kind of duologue, with each boy finishing what the other said. The effect was a sort of curious sing-song chant.

'Please, citizen. We are sent to bring you this . . .'

'It's from the medicus . . .'

'And we're to wait outside . . .'

'And take away the bowl . . .'

'It's a replacement for the other one he sent,' the slightly skinnier of the two finished, with a triumphant air. He was a little younger than his companion, I realised, though he was if anything the taller of the two.

I grinned. Marcus's careful matched-pair policy was going to be strained to breaking point as these two young lads grew up.

The slave-boy took my grin as an invitation to say something else. He looked at me, and blurted suddenly, 'We're not to put it on the tabletop this time!'

The other servant nudged him warningly. Obviously he had spoken out of turn.

This time my smile was really meant for him. 'You heard about that little incident?'

A shy grin. 'Everyone in the villa must have heard by now. Pulcrus was sent to throw it all away.'

'And naturally he told everybody in the servants' room?' I said.

The boy gave an enthusiastic nod. 'He thinks he's really somebody, that page: the master takes him everywhere so he's always boasting about the special jobs he's asked to do. You can get tired of listening to him sometimes, talking about where he's been and how he's in the master's confidence, especially when you've been stuck inside the house all day.' It came out in a rush and earned him an even harder nudge.

Junio came to his rescue by picking up the bowl. 'Anyway, master, here's your sleeping draught.' He wrinkled up his nose and gave an exploratory sniff. 'It looks a bit dispiriting, but it doesn't smell too bad.' He brought it over and handed it to me. The two boys watched me, unwinking, from the door.

'Dispiriting' was a hopeful word for it, I thought. It was a darkish liquid, with dank herbs floating in its depths – and despite my slave's assurance, it smelt like rotting grass. 'I don't think I shall be drinking it,' I said.

He glanced at me sharply. 'Oh, come, master. If it will do you good . . .'

'That's just the point,' I said. 'I'm not convinced that it will do me good at all.'

105

The startled glance became an outright stare. 'But why? His other potions have restored you wonderfully – my mistress is convinced he saved your . . .' He broke off, and a look of comprehension crossed his face. 'I see,' he said. 'The medicus? You think . . . But surely . . .'

I shook my head at him, to warn him to be careful what he said, but the talkative young slave-boy caught me in the act. Fortunately he misinterpreted my gesture. 'I'm sure the doctor didn't mean to bring bad luck,' he burbled. 'I expect he just put the potion on the tabletop by accident. He isn't very Roman in his ways. But he is awfully clever with his cures. The best for miles around. That's why the master bribed him to come here. I heard him say so to the pontifex.'

This was too much for the other serving boy. 'Hush, Minimus! Can't you learn to hold your tongue? Slaves are expected to speak when spoken to, not start conversations with the master's guests.' He turned to me. 'I'm sorry, citizen. This boy is only new, and he has much to learn. He gets us into trouble all the time.'

'Don't worry,' I said gently. 'I'm interested in what he has to say. In fact your friend – Minimus, is it? – can tell me more. Philades is famous for his potions, then? Do you know him well?'

Minimus had been silenced by his friend's rebuke. He had turned scarlet and was gazing at the floor. He shook his head. 'Hardly at all,' he mumbled. 'I never heard of him until he turned up here. The day after the mistress disappeared, it must have been. Maximus will bear me out. We were sent to let him in when he arrived.'

'That's right,' the other boy confirmed.

I looked at him. 'You're Maximus? So you two are called

Biggest and Littlest? But why are the names the other way about?'

He didn't smile at all. 'I was called Maximus before he came. He was bought to match me so they named him Minimus – partly because it seemed to fit my name, and partly because he was the youngest slave of all. But he's grown a lot and now it's turned into a sort of joke, you see. But Minimus is right. We had never set eyes on the medicus before that day – and we greet all the guests. Even Marcus did not seem to know him very well.'

'Though he thinks most highly of him,' I observed. 'How did Marcus find him, anyway? He must have met him somewhere.'

Minimus appointed himself spokesman once again. He laughed. 'Oh, we can tell you that, though the master would not like it advertised. Philades was working for a friend of his – someone on the *ordo*, the council in the town. Marcus was often invited there to dine – in fact he was there the day the mistress disappeared.'

I looked at him. 'How do you know all this? From the page again?'

He nodded. 'He was with Marcus at the time, of course. Half of the *ordo* had been invited there to dine – mostly on purpose to meet the doctor. You know what these Roman feasts are like – you show off the clever men in your employ to impress your guests. Philades was asked to join the diners over wine to talk about his wretched Celsus scroll and generally show how intelligent he was. Marcus was rather laughing at it, on the journey home, but when he found out what had happened here he quickly changed his mind. He wanted you to help him, so he needed help for you. He went back to see the councillor . . . and that was that.'

I nodded. 'More or less suggested that he made a gift of him?' I've known Marcus use that strategy before.

'He expressed an interest in the doctor, certainly,' Maximus said carefully. 'Of course, the councillor could not easily refuse.'

I grinned. 'Nor Philades, I suppose? Not with a person of His Exellence's rank?'

Maximus looked surprised. 'I hadn't thought of that. After all, although he's just a Greek, the doctor is a proper citizen. I suppose he could have decided that he didn't want to come – though I can't imagine anybody daring to say that.' He saw my grin and he was tempted to a sudden confidence. 'Anyway, I think Philades himself was offered a lot of money, too. More than he was getting in the other house. That is what the page said, at any rate. The doctor never talks about himself. Even the master can't persuade him to say much about his life – except the cases he's been called upon to cure.'

Minimus made an affronted sniffing noise. 'Now who's making conversation to the guests?' he muttered sullenly. 'And, speaking of His Excellence, he'll be expecting us. We were just to bring the potion in and take the bowl back to the kitchens afterwards. Then we were supposed to go and wait on him.' He ran a nervous tongue round his lips.

I looked at the steaming bowl which Junio had placed carefully on the stool beside my bed. 'It's far too hot for me, in any case,' I said. 'You two run along. My slave will take the tray back. It will be all right.'

They looked at each other doubtfully, then Maximus said, 'If you are quite sure, citizen . . . ?'

'Quite sure,' I said. 'And thank you for your help.'

Minimus flashed me another of his grins. 'If you want anything at all, just send for us.'

Junio escorted them to the door, and shut it after them. He turned to me.

'Well,' I said. 'What do you make of that?'

He moved the bowl and came to perch beside me on the stool. 'One thing is certain, master,' he said earnestly. 'You must be wrong about this kidnapping. It's clear that Philades can't be involved. We agreed that those responsible were well known in the house – otherwise their arrival would have caused a stir and the gate-keepers would have remembered them. That obviously does not describe the medicus. He'd never been inside the villa till Julia was gone.'

I frowned, reluctant to give up my suspicions. 'He might have planned it, all the same,' I said.

'When he was working in the town for someone else? It seems improbable. How could he know anything about the place? You heard what the pages said. His employer was treating him as a novelty – inviting people in to show him off – so he obviously hadn't been in Glevum very long. Not even long enough to learn Roman superstitions, it appears.'

'Perhaps.' I wouldn't drink his potions, anyway, I thought – not because of where he'd put the cup, but because of what he might have put inside.

Junio had been following another train of thought. 'Marcus seems to make a habit of acquiring staff by admiring other people's servants and offering them a higher wage to come to him. The privilege of being rich and powerful, I suppose. I gather – from the maidservants that I was talking to – that's how he acquired the wet nurse, too. Though not from the same councillor, of course.'

'Ah,' I said. 'The wet nurse. She interests me a lot. What do you know of her?'

Junio shot me a triumphant look and began to reel off a

list of facts, as if to prove that he was just as good a source of information as the red-haired boys. 'Firstly, she is a freewoman, not a slave, it seems. Second . . .'

I interrupted him. 'She's not a household slave? You are quite sure of that? You'd expect that somebody of Marcus's rank would have a wet nurse of his own. In fact, don't I vaguely remember seeing such a girl? Before this fever struck? I'm sure there was a little slave who was the wet nurse then.' I tried to recollect, but I had only glimpsed her once or twice. Wet nurses do not generally mix with visitors – especially males.

Junio grinned. 'You are quite right, master. Marcus did buy one from the slave market at first, but Julia didn't find her satisfactory. The girl did not give sufficient milk, she said, and had no experience of caring for a child. Apparently she wasn't much more than a child herself. Some of the other servants thought it pitiful.'

I nodded. I had heard of this before – young women deliberately got with child by the slave-master, so that they could be put on the market as a nurse. There was always a demand for wet nurses, and, provided the girl had good teeth and no disease, there would soon be a willing customer prepared to pay a handsome price for her – though generally he would not take the child. The slave-trader would have to rear that at his own expense for sale, or else get rid of it. It seemed a vaguely unpleasant trade to me – quite different from the older women who offered their nursing services of their own accord. 'So Julia had that slave sold on, and they engaged this other girl instead?'

'That's right. Myrna is not the class of girl they'd usually employ, but she came highly recommended by a friend. Well, more than that. As I was telling you, she worked for one of the councillors in town, a certain Grappius, and the family thought her indispensable. Marcus had to drop a lot of hints, and offer quite a bribe, before Grappius would agree to part with her. She's a little older, obviously – seventeen or so – but otherwise she's everything the experts recommend. "Good health, good habits, and good *habitas*" – a sturdy frame – that's what they always say. And copious milk as well. Julia was very particular about that. Grappius's wife was a friend of Julia's, and has several children of her own. Fortunately the youngest is now old enough to wean.'

I remembered what the medicus had said about all that. 'Surely Myrna can't have been wet nurse to them all? If she is seventeen . . . ?'

'The elder sister served the household in the same role. A family tradition, it appears – the mother was also a wet nurse in her day and still acts as a midwife now and then. So there was plenty of experience to draw upon. Just what Julia wanted. Myrna has grown up with nurslings all her life. The family have nurtured children in their house for years.'

'But Marcus did not send Marcellinus to her home so she could nurse him there?' I knew that many wealthy Romans did farm infants out like this.

Junio made a face. 'Marcus obviously prefers to have his servants come to him – whatever other people choose to do. Anyway, I gather that Julia would never have agreed to let the baby go. She's rather . . . well . . .'

'Protective of the boy?' I could understand it if she were, I thought. I knew that she had lost a child years before, when she was married to a former husband, and for a long time Marcus had believed that she would never breed again. This son was a precious gift to both of them.

Junio nodded. 'That was the real trouble with the earlier

girl, they say – she was getting too fond of Marcellinus and of course she was with him all the time. So Julia got rid of her and took Myrna on instead. She wanted Marcellinus to herself.'

'But doesn't Myrna live here?'

'Not any more. She did at first, just for a week or two, but once the boy was sleeping through the night Julia preferred her to go home at night and just come in by day to feed and care for him. It suited Myrna too.'

I tried to imagine Julia rising in the night to soothe a fretful infant, but I failed. Presumably there was always a handmaiden close by to lend a hand if Myrna wasn't there.

Junio saw my look. 'I think there was a touch of jealousy again. Myrna was getting too fond of Marcellinus, it appears, and Julia insisted on looking after him herself as much as possible. She did much more than many wealthy Roman mothers do – stayed while he was being fed, and supervised while he was being washed and changed. She even played with him. As long as Marcus wasn't here, of course – in that case her duty was naturally to her husband first.'

'So Myrna was not wholly a success?'

'Strangely it seems that in some ways she was. Julia did rely on her advice and took her everywhere she went. She is an anxious mother in a lot of ways, and was always asking questions, so they say – about fresh air and teeth and exercise and when to let him cry. And she acted on the answers, too.'

I frowned. 'So where is Myrna now? Gone home for the night?'

He shook his head. 'She's not been here at all for several days. Marcus couldn't bear to have her in the house after Marcellinus had been snatched away – and there wasn't any job for her to do. He sent her home. She has got her little daughter to care for, anyway. That's why it suited her to live at home again.'

'Of course!' I said. I had forgotten that the wet nurse must have had a child herself – otherwise she would not have had the milk. However, another thought had just occurred to me. Children of that age are dying all the time, and I have heard that sometimes such a loss can drive a woman mad and even make her try to steal a substitute. I wondered if something of the kind had happened here. I was about to ask 'And is the daughter well?', but Junio's next words disposed of that idea.

'Not a strapping child like Marcellinus by all accounts, but the villa servants say she is a lovely little girl – just a moon or so older than the boy. Her aunt or grandmother used to bring her here each day – especially when the lad was small – and Myrna used to suckle her as well. Apparently there was sufficient milk for two. But now the older sister mostly nurses her – though they still bring her here from time to time.'

I raised my eyebrows. 'Abundance runs in the family, it seems.'

'One of the recommendations for a wet nurse, so I hear. And Myrna seems to be a splendid nurse. She could not have been more loving to the boy if he had been her own, they say – as far as Julia would let her be. The day he disappeared Myrna was terribly upset. Blamed herself for the abduction, everybody says – because she was not in the courtyard at the time.'

'The child was officially in her care, I suppose.'

'That's just what Marcus said when he came home. He was half crazed with it, of course – threatened to have her flogged and dragged before the courts for negligence and endangering the safety of a Roman citizen. Jove alone knows what would have happened to her then. The poor girl was trembling so that she could hardly speak. They had to burn feathers underneath her nose to stop her fainting dead away. But of course he didn't do it in the end. As several of the household pointed out, it would have been unjust. Julia was with the child herself – and she was the one who sent the girl away.'

'Fetching something for the child to eat? Isn't that what I was told?'

He nodded. 'A little stewed and sweetened fruit. Myrna was in the kitchens at the time, watching as they put the honey in and stirred it up. There are plenty of witnesses to that.'

'And Julia's other slaves?'

'All busy doing chores elsewhere. That was not uncommon after lunch, I understand. Julia liked to spend time with the child on her own – apart from Myrna, obviously. Sitting in the courtyard, or in the orchard looking at the geese. Even the garden and kitchen slaves knew better than to intrude.'

I looked at him. That was interesting, if it was the case. 'I would like to speak to Myrna.'

'That can be arranged. Marcus has sent for her again, now that the child is back. She should be here tomorrow. The page took a message to her house today, as soon as Marcellinus was returned, but Myrna had gone into Glevum for the day with a basket of her mother's croup remedy to sell, and there was only the sister in the house.'

I raised a brow at him. 'You seem to know a lot about it. From the page again?'

Junio laughed. 'Maximus is right. That Pulcrus is so full of vanity, he'll tell you anything – especially if you flatter him a bit. He thinks he's Dionysius where females are concerned – and Myrna is a pretty girl by all accounts. It would make you laugh to hear him sum her up – as though she was a cow he hoped to buy. "A bit on the plumpish side, perhaps, but well enough. She'll be a catch for somebody one day. She has an occupation and her mother has a house so probably she'll never have to beg." That's what he said. Perhaps he hopes that he'll be lucky there, and Myrna will contrive to buy him free.'

I ignored this fantasy on Junio's part. I had more pressing matters on my mind. 'There were no other nurslings at the house that day? I thought the family had a string of them.'

'Marcus insisted on exclusive rights. That was Julia's doing, so I hear – afraid of Marcellinus's catching some childhood disease. It was a condition that, while Myrna suckled him, the family had no other fostered nurslings in the house, in case of bringing illness in. Marcus paid her handsomely, of course, and the household weren't sorry to agree. But for the last few days the boy has not been here, so Myrna's not been earning anything. That's why they were selling the mother's remedy, I suppose. Had to do something to bring some money in.'

'Well, it would earn a few brass coins, I suppose.'

He shrugged. 'You'd be surprised. It might do more than that. It's famous – everybody says so. Even Julia used to buy it now and then.'

'Everybody? So you've talked to several people, not only to the page.'

Junio flashed me an embarrassed grin. 'Oh, I've had a little chat. To some of Julia's personal handmaidens at least, while you were fast asleep. In fact . . .' He raised his fingers

Chapter Eleven

'Come in!' I called, and at once a plump young face peered round the entrance door, followed an instant later by the owner of the face – a little freckled dumpling of a girl. She might have been perhaps thirteen, and even without the pink uniform tunic I would have known that it was one of Julia's maids, simply because her face was rather plain. It was one of Julia's more unappealing little vanities – surrounding herself with handmaidens who were less than beautiful, so that she looked more handsome by comparison. (It was not a necessary strategy: Julia was lovely in any company.)

This dumpling gave a sketchy little bob.

'You wanted something?' I enquired from my bed, in what I hoped was my most paternal tone.

The girl, though, had no eyes for me at all. She looked at Junio and her cheeks turned even more pink and mottled than before. 'I heard your signal, Junio. At least I thought I did. Did you want me now?'

I found that I was grinning inwardly. I find it hard to picture Junio as a heart-breaker, though no doubt the cheerful smile and tumbled curls do have a boyish charm. But the dumpling was clearly quite enamoured of him. And, of course, the boy is growing up; almost sixteen, we think, although – since he was born in slavery and no record of his birth was ever made – that is an estimate. He does not know how old he was when I acquired him, and he was so undernourished at the time that I can only guess. But somehow the frightened scrap that I took pity on and bought, all those years ago, had become the strapping fellow who was before me now, blushing to the roots of his unruly hair.

I gave him a knowing wink, which made him pinker still. I had no qualms about teasing him a bit, because of course there was no chance of any serious romance. The law forbade slaves to form personal attachments of that kind, and these two belonged to different households anyway. Besides, I was aware that, even if he had the chance, Junio would bestow his affections nearer home – on plump, dark-haired little Cilla, my Gwellia's serving maid.

None the less, he'd clearly made another conquest here – and probably without intending to. So I could not resist a touch of banter in my tone. 'And who is this young person?' I enquired

'She is called . . . um . . .' He hesitated. I was right. Though he had fluttered her a little, he didn't know her name.

'I am Porphyllia, citizen,' she supplied. 'One of the handmaids to the mistress here. Not an important one, you understand. Mostly I work where I am out of sight, though I sometimes do assist the mistress with her wigs.'

I nodded. Another of Julia's little vanities. Like many Roman matrons she has several wigs, and has been known to buy a fair-headed slave especially for her hair, shave her and then sell her on again. 'So what are your duties?' I enquired.

'Fetching and carrying for the mistress when she's here, and cleaning her apartment when she's out. Mixing up her perfumes and her beauty creams. My special responsibility is for her clothes, mending them, or sponging muddy hems – if it is a garment that she wants to wear again – or sorting things out for the fuller's man. I bring the washing water from the well, and stand by while they help her wash and dress. I'm not one of those who accompanies her about.' She dipped another little curtsey in my direction, for politeness's sake, and went on staring straight at Junio. 'At least until I'm older, anyway. Anyway, she always takes the wet nurse with her now.'

'There's four of them like her,' Junio said. 'I thought you'd like to speak to them yourself. Porphyllia has no other duties to perform just now, so I asked her to wait out in the court till she was called. I assured her that it was quite permissible to come and talk to you, now that her master's back. He only said that no one was to come while he was gone. I found her in the servants' waiting room.'

I nodded. Every Roman house of any size has an anteroom where waiting slaves can sit until their services are next required.

The girl, however, was alarmed by Junio's words and anxious to assure me that she was no idler. 'There isn't a great deal of work for any of us, now that the mistress isn't here,' she blurted. 'I wanted to help with looking after Marcellinus – feeding him goat's milk in a cup like the other girls – but they wouldn't hear of it. Said I was too little and I didn't know enough. Well, possibly they're right, but I would like to learn. He's . . .' She was obviously a girl who liked to talk a lot.

Junio cut across all this to say to me, 'Porphyllia was attending Julia on the day she disappeared.'

The freckled face turned still more scarlet underneath the telltale dots. 'Well, not attending her exactly. I was to sponge the dress that she'd been wearing earlier, and grind some chalk and arsenic for her face. I took them to our room – the sleeping quarters for the female slaves. And not just me. She sent us all away.'

That was just what Junio had said. 'Was that unusual?' I urged.

Porphyllia refused to look me in the face. 'Not really. She often did that in the afternoon. She liked to have Marcellinus to herself – she even found other errands for Myrna when she could. But it's nonsense what they say. I don't think the mistress was jealous of the wet nurse in the least – it was just that she preferred to tend the child herself.'

There it was again: the suggestion that Julia had become possessive of the child, because the nurse had become too fond of him. 'Myrna was too affectionate to the boy, perhaps?' I said gently.

She avoided my eyes again. 'I'm not claiming that. Julia is my mistress, and it isn't up to me to say anything at all. But if she was as jealous of the wet nurse as the others say, she wouldn't have kept her on – she got rid of the other poor girl, after all. But she took Myrna with her as an attendant almost everywhere – anywhere that she could take the boy, at least. Even that morning, before she disappeared, she had Myrna to attend her when she went out visiting. And she always turned to Myrna for advice – even if some people think she shouldn't have and that if she'd kept him swaddled up properly and indoors in his crib, instead of letting him crawl round the courtyard with his wooden dog, none of this would have happened.'

'You don't agree with air and exercise?'

She avoided that one. 'It wasn't his mother's fault if he was taken away – and don't you listen if they tell you otherwise. She never took her eyes off him, that day, from the moment they came home. Even when he was being fed, she wouldn't go and eat – she had her own lunch sent in to her room and stayed with him right through, till was time for him to have his daily airing in the court.'

'She was more watchful than usual? Almost as if she was concerned for him? Fearful that something might happen to the boy?'

She looked thoughtful suddenly. 'Well, I suppose so.'

'You noticed she was anxious at the time?'

Her face turned pink. 'Well, not exactly that. I wasn't really there. I didn't see her when she came back from her drive – not properly, I mean. I had my duties, and I got on with them. But since you mention it, perhaps there was a wariness about her, as if she wanted to keep watch on Marcellinus by herself. Mind, she often did send everyone away. There was a lot to do. She liked her things kept nice. If it was not to sponge her hems and clean her perfume box, it was to air the clothes or find the jewels she wanted for that night.'

I interrupted before she gave me a full account of every job she'd ever been called upon to do. 'So she shooed everyone away that afternoon?'

'Everyone except the wet nurse, certainly. I know what you are thinking, citizen. Of course, some people say it is bad luck for a lady of quality to have no maids at hand, and therefore she brought her troubles on herself, but it was by her own command. We were just doing what we'd been told to do, and whoever kidnapped the mistress and the child, it obviously wasn't one of us. I hope you'll point out to the master, citizen, that none of the handmaidens can possibly be blamed.'

Behind her, Junio pulled a face at me. Now that she had started she was like an undammed brook, and would babble on till I stopped her.

'Well, you have been most forthcoming, and I'll tell Marcus what you've said. Is there anything else of interest that you can helpfully recall?' I murmured.

The gentle irony was lost on her. She took a deep breath and lunged on again. 'Oh, lots of things. I told your man-servant. In fact, when you come to think about it, you realise there were a whole host of omens of bad luck that day – though, funnily enough, we didn't notice at the time. But afterwards, when we were talking in the sleeping room, we all remembered just how bad it was. I told your slave.' She gave Junio a flirtatious look. 'I tried to tell my own master about it too, but he wasn't interested.'

'My master is!' Junio said, but she really needed no encouragement. She was already launched upon the list of evil auguries.

'To start with that morning, the butter wouldn't set – you know what an awful sign that's supposed to be. Then the master stumbled on the threshold when he left the house – left foot, too, so it would have been safer not to go out at all. Then Julia's hem got hitched above her feet so that her ankles and her sandals showed – I saw her like that in the court myself – and for any matron that's an omen of bad luck. The perfume oils refused to mix, as well, and then – about mid-afternoon – the gate-keeper saw a flock of wild birds flying overhead and they circled round the house from left to right. Well! You know what a dreadful portent that is, if the proper sacrifices don't get made – and of course they didn't, 'cause the master wasn't here. And when he came in, he didn't seem to care. He was too worried about where his wife and child were gone. But you know what they say: "When the geese fly sinister, there's trouble for the house." The gate-keeper was grumbling at the time.' She flashed a winning smile at Junio. 'Was that the bit you wanted me to tell?'

I glanced at my slave, who grinned back at me, in a way which suggested that his heart was safe. He nodded. 'I thought the gate-keeper was interesting. That is why I called her in,' he said.

'Which gate-keeper was that?' I prompted.

'Aulus, his name is. He's an awful man. Smells of onions, and tries to put his hands on you when you aren't looking. But I believe his tale about the birds. It fits in with all the other omens, too. He tried to tell the master, I know that. Not that the master took any heed of it. Aulus has been complaining bitterly for days that he offered information, but was given no reward. Anyone in the servants' room will vouch for that.' She glanced at me underneath her lids. 'Will I be getting anything for this?'

'I told you,' Junio said promptly, 'I'll see what I can do. It all depends on what Aulus has to add. When he's off duty, we will have him in.'

She tossed her head. 'Well, he's off duty now. He must have been relieved, for a little while at least. I saw him going into the kitchens earlier. Looking for more onions, I shouldn't be surprised.'

I was about to ask about the rota for the watch – whether Marcus had left the gates unguarded, after all, and at what hour the relief arrived and how long he'd be on guard – when I decided I could derive the information with more certainty from the door-keeper himself. I beckoned Junio.

'Perhaps we should speak to Aulus.'

He had read my thoughts. 'I'll go and summon him.'

'I'll show you where the kitchens are!' That was Porphyllia. I was about to urge that there was no need for this as

Junio knew the house but I realised that I'd disappoint the girl, and – more – that if she didn't go with him, she'd stay with me, and after all her burbling I was worn out as it was.

'Do that,' I said, leaning back upon my pillows with a sense of luxury. 'Oh, and Junio – while you're there, tip out that goblet in the gardens as you pass. I don't care to offend the medicus.'

He picked up the offending cup and went to the door with it. Porphyllia was already waiting for him there, and as they went out into the court I heard her asking, 'Here, what's that? A potion from the medicus? They say it's almost magic, what he does. Would he make me a love draught, do you think? There's a boy I'm rather fond of, but he doesn't notice me. I've got a few sesterces which I've managed to put by and if I asked the doctor . . .'

Their voices faded into silence and I leaned back on my bed. I was thinking about Aulus. If I was right, I'd met the man before.

Chapter Twelve

It was the same Aulus, though I was surprised to find him here again. Marcus had transferred him to the Corinium house last year. I had suspected it was the man I remembered as soon as Porphyllia mentioned onions, and when he came into the room there was no mistaking him: a great coarse lumbering bear of a man with a leering manner, shifting eyes and a habit of flicking his tongue out nervously and moistening his thin lips when he spoke.

He did it now. 'Ah, citizen, it's you. What do you want with me?' He eyed me warily. Unlike most other people in the house, I knew about his past. He had been gate-keeper here long before Marcus had acquired the house, and in those days Aulus had combined his duties at the gatehouse with the more profitable business of spying for the state – informing on his previous owner to the authorities. True, the man in question was a most unpleasant person – but the chief authority in this area, then as now, was Marcus Aurelius Septimus himself.

So Aulus had always been Marcus's private spy, trained to keep an observant watch and doubtless duly rewarded for his services. It was not an arrangement I cared for even then, especially since Aulus was not over-blessed with brains – but he'd fulfilled his double role with a certain cunning relish, and Marcus had used him quite a lot. I'd even had some useful leads from him myself, though I'd had to bribe him for the privilege. So it was particularly interesting now to hear that he was publicly grumbling that he had given information to His Excellence, and had not been paid for it.

'What do you want, citizen?' he said again. 'I've got to be back on duty very soon.'

I looked at him. He really hadn't changed. He had swapped his former ugly cudgel for a more formal sword, and he now sported Marcus's scarlet uniform and a handsome heavy cloak, but apart from that he was the same old Aulus still, right down to the stench of onions and stale beer. He was born to be brutish and rather underhand, and there was a hint of menace in the way he looked at me. There was no room for subtlety. I tackled him outright.

'Porphyllia says you have been cheated of your just rewards,' I said, trying to sound as sympathetic as I could. Aulus was always on the lookout for a *denarius* or two, and I thought this was the best way to gain his confidence.

Aulus was not so easily cajoled. He looked at me with distrust. 'I'm sure you've heard. There was a flock of birds,' he muttered. 'Flying left to right. Got to be an omen of bad luck, that has.'

I hauled myself a little more upright. 'Aulus,' I said, 'don't waste my time like this. There's something else. Of course there is. Marcus didn't employ you all those years to have you tell him nonsense about flocks of birds.'

He turned a sullen red. 'Well,' he said, 'there was another thing. I've told His Excellence – but he's not interested. Said it was not significant, since it was not that afternoon.' He licked his lips again. 'Of course, if you could see your way . . .'

I ignored the blatant hint. 'What was not significant?' I said.

126

He hesitated, obviously still hoping for a bribe.

'His Excellence will tell me, if you do not,' I said. 'Save yourself a whipping, and tell me what it was.'

He breathed stale onions at me. 'The fact that there were people lurking in the woods,' he said at last. 'At least, I think there were. Julia said she saw them, and she's no idiot. But when I went to look, there was nobody in sight. I suppose they slipped away into the trees.'

The way he spoke about the mistress of the house was over-familiar from a household slave, but I ignored it. 'When was this?'

'That morning, when she came back in the carriage from visiting her friends.' He hawked and spat, leaving a damp patch on the floor beside his feet. 'Might have been the kidnappers spying out the house, I thought.'

'It's possible, I suppose. Have you told Marcus that?'

He shrugged. 'I tried to. But His Excellence would hardly hear me out. Said that when it came right down to it, I hadn't seen anything at all. Me, who was his eyes and ears for years! And he refused to pay a single *quadrans* for my help. I think that he actually believes . . .' He broke off.

'What?'

'Nothing.'

'He thought you made it up, to earn a share of that reward?' I said, and was answered by his shifty, red-faced scowl. I nodded. I would not have put it past the man, myself. 'I'm surprised that you did not suggest he checked the facts. Other people must have seen them.'

'I did suggest it, but who was there he could ask?' Aulus retorted gloomily. 'The carriage-driver might have noticed, I suppose. But it was not our private coachman. Marcus had our carriage out himself, and Julia had arranged to hire one for an hour or two, so that she could go out when she wanted to.'

I pricked up my ears. 'Was that unusual?'

He shook his head. 'She's used the man before: she books him when Marcus has appointments in the town. Fellow's got a little business on the Glevum road: a coach, half a dozen horses and a cart or two. I think he has a stable lad, and another man who drives for him as well, but he mostly makes a living hiring himself out. Next time I saw him I asked him if he had noticed anyone in the woods, but he swears he didn't hear or see a thing. He doesn't want trouble with his wealthy customers, that's the truth of it, and of course I can't force the man to talk. And then I got annoyed and did a stupid thing. I said it was a pity the mistress wasn't here herself to tell him what was what, but His Excellence got to hear about that and he was furious. He lost his temper, roared at me and refused to pay me anything at all. I've even had my duty shifts increased – I'm sure the master had a hand in that.' He had turned pink and shifty.

I was thinking that in the circumstances it was a wonder that his remark had not earned worse, when Junio (who had been standing by so quietly that I'd half forgotten him) asked the obvious question. 'What about Julia's attendant?' he enquired. 'The wet nurse accompanied Julia that morning, didn't she? Surely she could speak up on your behalf?'

I turned to Aulus. 'By Bacchus, so she did. That's right, isn't it?'

He made a scornful face. 'Of course she could, if only she was here. It was her who got out of the carriage at the gate to tell me what Julia had seen. I didn't think of that at first – it was only after the master had been quizzing everyone that I remembered it.' He caught my eye and flushed. 'All right, so by then he was offering rewards. What difference does it make? By the time I thought of getting the wet nurse to vouch for me, they'd sent her home again. I can't leave my post and go off to look for her. And Marcus wouldn't listen when I tried to talk to him.'

'Well then, I'll talk to her myself as soon as possible,' I said. 'If she bears out what you say, I'll tell His Excellence myself. She'll be here in the morning, I believe.'

'So they've arranged to have her back, have they? I wondered if they would.' Aulus's ugly face turned pinker yet. 'She generally gets here about the second hour,' he went on. 'You do that. Talk to her. You'll see. She'll tell you that what I said is true – in general terms at least.'

So he was already starting to retract his words! I turned to Junio. 'You can watch out for Myrna when she comes. Make sure she doesn't speak to Aulus at the gate. I don't want him coaching her in what she has to say.'

The gate-keeper sneered. 'Don't worry about that. I'll be off duty and asleep by then. She usually uses the back gate anyway – after all, she's not a visitor. Myrna only came the front way if she was accompanying the mistress anywhere.'

I looked at him suspiciously. Of course Myrna was likely to go round to the back – like any other tradesman visiting the house. But all the same . . .

Junio, however, was ahead of me. 'Master, I knew you'd want to see her,' he said. 'I've left instructions with all the gate-keepers that they are to let us know as soon as she arrives tomorrow. Whichever gate she uses.'

I nodded. 'Well done, Junio. I'm sure that Marcus won't object if we have a word with her first thing – though obviously we'll have to keep it brief. Marcellinus will pre-sumably need feeding by that time and she will have other urgent duties to perform. But it won't take long to discover if what Aulus says is true.'

Aulus grunted. 'You'll find out,' he said. 'Now, was there anything else, or can I go back to the kitchen and find something to eat? They had a bit of bread and soup for me, but no doubt it's cold by now, and anyway I'll be lucky if I've time to eat at all. I told you, they've increased my duties at the gate, and there'll be trouble if I'm not back double-quick. I'm on an extra half-shift as it is.'

'Very well, Aulus, you may go,' I said, and he stumped out without another word.

'So,' Junio said, 'we'll see what Myrna says?'

I nodded. 'I was anxious to talk to her in any case. It seems she was the only slave about that afternoon – even if she was in the kitchens at the time – and I want to hear her version of events.'

In fact, the more I thought of it, the keener to speak to her I was. If we were looking for somebody with links inside the house, but who had the opportunity to come and go at will, Myrna was obviously a candidate. Furthermore, Marcellinus had been cared for, after a fashion, while he was missing from his home. Someone had fed him, kept him clean and rubbed him in hog's grease as a protection from the cold. Someone who knew about young children, by the look of it. And Myrna might have done that – she had been absent from the house. But why? And what had she to do with Lallius?

I shook my head. It was hard to imagine why the child's own nurse, who clearly loved him well, should tear off his precious bulla and his clothes, give him poppy juice to keep him quiet and pack him inside a basket in the dark. And what of Philades? Did he somehow know the girl? Had they met before, in Glevum? After all, they had both worked for councillors. Had she somehow been instrumental in the doctor's being here?

I was anxious to question Myrna as soon as possible.

I got my chance to talk to Marcus about it a little later. He came to see me – dressed for dinner now – and still with the medicus a step or two behind.

He seemed depressed and sober. 'Porphyllia told me that you weren't asleep. I've come to tell you that we've put the ransom money out. The page took it, left it where they said and then went on to Glevum. I don't know if they've picked it up yet, but I assume they have. I sent the oil-seller out a little afterwards, and told him that if he sees anybody in the lane he is to send me word. I didn't tell him why, of course – the fewer people in the area who know that I've agreed to pay the kidnappers, the better, or we shall have this kind of thing again. But there's been no word. I'm sure these villains are far too clever to be conspicuous. In the morning, when it's light and my page comes back again, I'll send him to discover if the money's gone.'

'And Gwellia?' I said.

'I asked the oil-seller to call in and tell her not to come tonight, on the medicus's orders, because you had to rest.' He caught my glance. 'I had to tell her something – I did not want her to worry unnecessarily, and I couldn't tell the oil man about the ransom note. So,' he forced a joyless smile, 'if you have everything you need, I think that's all we can do tonight.'

I assured him that I was entirely comfortable. It was true – I am not accustomed to such luxury.

He nodded. 'You are looking more like your usual self. No doubt the draught the doctor left for you has helped.'

131

'You did take all of it?' the doctor asked. 'The second time?'

That was a tricky question. 'Every drop has gone,' I answered truthfully, and saw the doctor's small, triumphant smile.

'Then we will say goodnight,' my patron said. 'The kitchens have some soup for Junio and there is some hydromel for you. I must go to dinner and attend my guests – though I don't feel much like eating anything. However, the chief priest of Jupiter can't be made to wait. He is staying at the villa overnight again, and will conduct the reconsecration ceremony for my son at dawn.' The chief priest has his own house in the temple court and has public duties almost every day, but when you are rich and powerful, it seems, even the gods must wait from time to time.

I seized my moment. 'Speaking of the morning, Excellence, may I have a word with Myrna as soon as she arrives? There are several things I really want to ask her to explain. I think her testimony may be of vital help.'

Marcus nodded vaguely. 'As you wish – though I don't know what you hope to get from her. I'm sure that when I questioned her she told me everything she had to tell.'

'With respect, Excellence,' I said, 'there may be things she doesn't know she knows.'

'Your pardon, Marcus Septimus.' The medicus almost sounded humble for a change. 'Allow me to make a small suggestion here. By all means allow him to interrogate the girl, but perhaps we two should be present when he questions her? You can ensure that she gives the same account, and I can keep a professional eye on poor Libertus here, and make sure that he does not exhaust himself.'

The 'poor Libertus' had a mocking tone, but my patron

seemed oblivious of any irony. He nodded. 'Anything you say, of course. Just as long as we get Julia safely back.' He gestured to the doctor. 'Come! We must cleanse our hands and make libations to the family gods before we eat. Libertus, we shall see you in the morning. After the bulla rituals, of course. The priest assures me that for the best results we should begin those at first light: we have consulted all the calendars and tomorrow is fortunately a propitious day. I wish that you were well enough to attend yourself. However, we shall see you afterwards and you can talk to Myrna then. In the meantime, try to get some sleep.'

Chapter Thirteen

I did not trust anything the doctor offered me, so I ignored his honey and water mix and had a sip or two of Junio's soup instead. It had been an enormously long day for me, and I was tired after all the exertions of the questioning. In fact I was surprised to find how very weak I felt. I lay back on my luxurious pillows in the comfort of the bed, and – knowing that Junio was nearby on guard – permitted myself to close my eyes again.

My sleep was fitful, though, and full of dreams. Several times I jerked back into wakefulness, worrying over the problems of the day, and wishing that Gwellia was safely by my side. I felt as if I'd scarcely slept at all, but I must have done, because before I knew it the first light of morning had crept across the court and was throwing a soft glimmer in through the window bars.

At the same time I was aware of movement in the colonnade outside. I raised myself on my elbow and saw that the door was slightly open and two garden slaves were already busy on the path outside sweeping the leaves and dust away with brooms of bundled sticks.

I raised myself a little higher still. 'Master?' That was Junio, already up and moving, although I had not heard him stir from the sleeping mat which had been placed beside my bed. 'You are awake, then? Do you wish to rise? They are making preparations for the bulla ritual.'

He pushed the door a little more ajar, and I could see that the court was full of industry – slaves with water jars were sprinkling drops to keep the dust at bay, others were scuttling about with coal and kindling wood, or carrying perfumed water to the master's suite. Two maidservants were moving among the flower beds, selecting the most aromatic herbs and leaves.

'They will put them on the altar to the household gods,' Junio told me in a whisper. Though himself a Celt, he was raised in a Roman household as a slave and delights to tell me of the customs he saw then, as though I had never encountered them myself. 'Now, I have brought an extra tunic and I've found a cloak – a warm one with a hood. Do you want me to help you into them? Even if you merely sit there on the bed, it will give you more authority when you interrogate the nurse.'

I nodded. I had thought the same – although when he came to offer me his arm, it took a surprising effort to stagger to my feet, and I had to sit down again quite heavily. By degrees, though, he slipped the tunic over me and strapped my sandals on. With the woollen cloak around me I felt warm and cosseted – but more like a man again; after a few moments I gave a sign and, with his help, I contrived to stand and take a few tottering steps towards the door.

I stood at the door of the sleeping room and felt the morning air against my face. It was cool and misty, but the freshness of the day – after the stuffy smokiness of the heated room – was as sweet as Junio's hot mead had been. I gulped a few, intoxicating breaths.

The doors were open all round the colonnade – all the rooms in the court led off it, as they generally do in houses of this type – and from where I was standing I could see into the main block of the house, the central area where the atrium was and where the altar to the household gods was kept. The niche itself was hidden from my sight, but I could see that the chief priest and Marcus were already in the hall, together with the medicus and the senior slave of the house, who was holding out a phial (obviously the ashes from the temple yesterday) and preparing to pour the contents on to the altar. Servants were scurrying around with trays of sacrificial food, and lurking in the shadows was a man I recognised, with some surprise, as a silversmith whose Glevum workshop was not very far from mine.

'He brought the bulla, then?' I said to Junio.

'A little earlier, while you were still asleep. He did well to get it here in time. Look, here is Marcellinus – with the handmaidens. And the servants have brought a burning brand to light the altar fire. The rituals are about to begin.' He looked at me. 'You're not proposing to attend yourself?'

I shook my head. 'Not this time. It will be a drawn-out affair if I am any judge. And anyway, without my toga, I am not dressed for it.'

I remembered the first ceremony very well – the naming day is a great occasion in a Roman child's life. I was one of the invited guests, and thus had been privileged to bring a metal trinket (bought at some expense) to add to the chains of tinkling charms which are traditionally placed round the baby's wrists and legs to entertain him as a kind of rattle during the ritual. Marcellinus was then only nine days old (as custom dictated boys should be), but he was very good and hardly cried at all – even when a strange man in incense-perfumed clothes (the high priest, who had been called in to officiate) took him from his father's arms and muttered over him, before slipping the gold bulla round his neck and then seeking an extra benediction from the gods by passing the new-named infant through the sacrificial smoke.

There had been copious sacrifice, of course, and a sumptuous feast afterwards for all the witnesses, with baby and parents dressed in splendid robes throughout. This hurried substitute, without his mother present and with no important visitors, seemed a sad affair by comparison. Apart from the medicus and the silversmith, only the household slaves were there to witness the event – and not even all of them, since some still had duties to perform elsewhere.

I moved back to the shelter of the entrance to my room, where I was out of sight, before anybody glanced up and spotted me. In my state of health I did not welcome the idea of standing shivering in the atrium while lengthy prayers and blessings were tunelessly intoned – even if the chief priest of Jupiter himself was chanting them.

'Bring me that stool from beside my bed,' I said to Junio, 'and I will wait here in the doorway for Myrna when she comes.'

But Myrna didn't come. Most of the household servants were in the atrium, and it was very quiet in the garden now, except for the chanting from the atrium, and the pungent smell of burning sacrifice. Eventually it was Porphyllia who appeared, hurrying from the kitchens with a tray on which were a bowl of cold cooked apple and piece of bread, and a cup of the dreaded oxymel. This, evidently, had been prepared for me.

'Would you like some breakfast, citizen? I was told to bring you some since you were clearly up. The doctor has said that you can have this today.' She offered me the tray. 'Go on,' she urged, as I showed signs of pushing it away.

'Marcellinus had some of the fruit earlier. It's perfectly delicious . . . that is . . .' She turned scarlet and clapped her fingers to her lips.

'You tasted it yourself?' I said.

She nodded ruefully. 'Only a tiny little bit. I spilt it on the way. I know I shouldn't – but it looks so good . . . Don't be angry with me, citizen.'

'On the contrary,' I said. 'If you recommend it, I will have it too. In fact, you have given me an idea. There are not many of your normal jobs to do at the moment, I think you said, while Julia isn't here?'

She nodded doubtfully.

'Then you can be my food-taster,' I said. It was quite safe, of course. Once it was known that one of Julia's slaves had been appointed to the task, it would be pointless to try to poison me. 'Marcus promised I should have one, and you'll do very well. I'll ask him about it when he comes.'

'Oh, citizen. Would you really? That's wonderful.' She was gazing at Junio with sparkling eyes. The poor lad would not thank me for employing her, I thought, but I did have other reasons of my own. Porphyllia was a natural chatterbox, and I was certain that I could learn a great deal about the house from her.

I sent her off, delighted. I shared the bowl of fruit with Junio, and – when she was safely out of sight – he slipped out and made a private oblation of the honeyed vinegar on the garden beds.

I became aware that the chanting from within the house had stopped, and the smell of charred herbs and feathers was beginning to disperse. The winter sun was well into the sky by now, and it must have been at least the second hour, but there was no sign of Myrna. Nor – for a long time – of anybody else.

At last Marcus, resplendent in his finest toga, and weighed down with jewels – obviously put on for the bulla rites – emerged into the courtyard with a worried air. Two of his house slaves were escorting him, but he brushed past them and came straight across to me. I struggled to my feet and would have knelt as usual to kiss his hand, if he had not motioned me to sit.

'So the wet nurse hasn't yet arrived,' he said, by way of greeting. 'I'll send somebody to the house for her. You shall see her immediately she comes.' He sounded grim. I would not care to be Myrna when she turned up, I thought. 'You slept all right, I trust?' he added.

I nodded awkwardly and pressed my lips against the outstretched hand. 'I have been waiting for her here. The bulla ceremony went off without a hitch?'

He frowned, as if he had to recollect, and then said wearily. 'There was one moment when we were alarmed: the chief priest almost dropped the flask of oil before the sacrifice. That would have been serious, of course – we should have had to start the rituals again – but fortunately he recovered and we avoided that.' He was answering my question but there was something wrong. I could tell it by his face.

I tried to think of something bright and comforting to say. 'So Marcellinus has a bulla round his neck again?'

A nod. 'This time I hope it will remain there until he turns fourteen and is old enough to be a man!' He was talking too quickly, and his tone was forced. I noticed he refused to meet my eyes.

'Is there some new problem, Excellence?' I ventured.

He turned and looked at me. He had been moving restlessly up and down the colonnade, but now he halted at my bedroom door. 'Libertus, come inside. I need to talk to you.'

I was alarmed. Marcus wished to speak to me alone, and it was clearly something very serious. I feared the medicus had done his worst.

However, it was not an invitation that I could easily refuse. With Junio's help I limped into the room again, while Marcus left his other servants just outside the door. That made me feel uneasy, but my patron made me more uneasy still by motioning me to sit down on the bed, while he sent Junio outside for the stool – a most unusual happening indeed. It is one thing for Marcus to squat down on a stool when the man he is talking to is ill; quite another when that man is dressed and seated like an equal. My patron is a stickler for proper protocol.

But today he was more concerned with other things – and this interview was not the doctor's doing, it appeared. 'Libertus,' Marcus burst out, 'I have news for you. My page has just returned. You remember that he went to Glevum overnight?'

I nodded, wondering what this was leading to.

'Then you will remember what else he was to do this morning on his way?'

I did, of course. 'Call at my roundhouse and accompany my wife?' I looked round, feeling a broad smile crease my face. 'She's here, then? Where is she? Can I talk to her?'

Marcus carefully avoided looking at my face. 'That is just the problem. There was no one at the house.'

Despite my heavy woollen coverings I felt a tide of coldness running over me, starting at my feet and rising to my hair. Gwellia, missing! Whatever I'd imagined, I had not expected that.

Marcus cleared his throat. 'Try not to be alarmed. It may be nothing, after all. She did not know the page was going to come, and she might have set off to come here on her own . . .' He trailed off.

'In that case she would have been overtaken on the road.' My lips framed the words, but little sound came out. My throat was suddenly constricted and my heart beat fast. 'Where is the page?' I said.

'He's waiting in the ante-room. I'll have him brought to you.' Marcus nodded towards Junio, who disappeared to fetch the page at once. My patron turned to me, making a helpless little gesture with his hands. 'Libertus, we don't know that anything is wrong. She may have gone off to pick up kindling – or anything at all. She had her slaves with her. That is encouraging. A woman attended by her slaves is much safer from' – I was sure that he was going to say 'attack', but he changed it hastily – 'anything at all that might befall.'

'You know the slaves are with her?' I was almost sharp. I was beginning to understand how Marcus must have felt when he found that his wife and child had disappeared.

His Excellence looked sheepish. 'Well, that's what we presume. At all events there was no one in the house. But here's the page. He'll tell you about it. Pulcrus, tell the citizen what you found.'

The young man ran a hand across his hair, adjusted his tunic at the neck and seams and gave a self-important little cough before he spoke. I'd many times smiled at his vanity before, but this morning I could have shaken him. All this preening self-conceit when my poor Gwellia was missing! I strove for self-control.

'Well?' I prompted. 'What have you to report? You rode up

to my house and found the lady wasn't there – and then what did you do?'

Pulcrus looked aggrieved. 'Nothing. What was there to do? The place was clearly empty. The fire was out, the floor was swept and everything was neatly put away. I went up to the door and called, but no one came. I stuck my head round the other doors – there was a dyeing house and some sort of sleeping space – but there was nobody there either so I came away.'

'There was no one in the garden or with the animals?' I said.

He shrugged. 'Not that I could see. Or if they were, they must have been completely deaf. I shouted loud enough, but there was not a sound, except the chickens squawking in the coop.'

'Pulcrus, be less insolent to the citizen, or I shall have you whipped.' Marcus's voice was cold.

But I was trying to visualise the scene. 'So there was no sign of any struggle in the house?' I said. 'And she didn't leave a note of any kind?'

'Not as far as I could see.' Pulcrus was looking sulky now.

'And the fire was completely out, you say?' That was unusual; it took a long time to create a spark to light another one. 'And yet the chickens had been shut up for the night? That's what you're telling me?'

'It seems so – and that's really all there is to tell.' Pulcrus turned towards his master with a smirk. 'Except that the ransom bag had vanished from the tree – I did stop and check for that.'

'Then go! Wait in the servants' room again – I may have need of you.' Pulcrus flounced off, and Marcus turned to me. 'What do you make of it? Like Julia, it's almost as if she left the place by choice. Only my wife disappeared alone and Gwellia took the slaves.'

When I recalled it afterwards, I realised that this was the first time I had heard my patron admit that Julia might have left the villa of her own accord; but I was too wrapped up in my own concerns to register it then.

I shook my head. 'But if Kurso left the chickens in the coop, it sounds as if he expected to be back. He would not leave them without food for long.'

My patron was standing close to me, and to my surprise he reached across and patted my shoulder with his jewelled hand. It was an awkward, fleeting gesture which came uneasily to him – Romans are not given to contact as a rule – but I understood that he meant to signal sympathy.

'Well,' he said, 'there is nothing we can do for now but wait.' He looked at me. 'What do you think, Libertus? Have you any theories at all? Do you suspect this is connected to the kidnapping?'

I was too deep in misery to think at all. I said, 'I suppose it must be.'

'Old friend, you don't know anything that you're not telling me?'

I raised my head, which had been in my hands, and stared at him. 'Of course not, Excellence.'

'The doctor thinks you do. And certainly the situation's odd.'

I didn't follow him. I was only thinking about Gwellia. 'Odd, Excellence?'

'Why should the kidnappers change their methods, suddenly? Writing on a tablet instead of bits of bark?'

I shrugged. 'Ran out of bits of bark, perhaps? Who knows?'

He shook his head. 'I'm sure it's more than that. Philades

is right. That last message was completely different. It ignored the arrangements that had been asked for earlier, and, though it was scrawled untidily, it was better written too. You think that someone different may have written it? Or dictated it, perhaps? And why have they suddenly seized Gwellia – if they have? Libertus, think! This may affect you, too.'

'I don't know,' I said unhappily. 'One of the problems with this whole affair is that it seems to have been cleverly executed – the abduction is still a mystery to me – and the plans meticulously laid. Then suddenly everything is changed – the child's return, the note thrown over the wall with new demands. And why should they want Gwellia? I can't be blackmailed for a ransom price.' I sighed. 'I don't understand. Perhaps it is intended to make us more confused.'

Marcus was on his feet again by now and running restless fingers through his hair. I knew just how he felt. I could feel the cold despair run up my spine every time I thought about my wife. If the kidnappers were hoping to create anxiety, I thought, they could not have done it more successfully.

I was about to say so to my patron when there was a tap upon the door.

'Master?' It was Pulcrus, all self-conceit again. He bowed. After that earlier reproof for insolence, he was especially pompous now. 'Forgive me for intruding. A mounted messenger has come here, from the garrison . . . Something that occurred just after I had left.'

'Well, show him in then.' Marcus looked at me. 'It might be some news of Lallius at last. According to my page, a guard was posted in the street all day, keeping a discreet watch on his house. But Lallius has not been seen at all since his release.'

Pulcrus was at the door again, accompanied by an imperial

messenger, resplendent in his purple-edged cape and uniform. Even Pulcrus must have felt a little drab.

The newcomer came to kneel at Marcus's feet. He'd learned his speech by heart. 'The commander tenders his respects to your most gracious Excellence and begs to offer his report.' He glanced warily at me and Junio.

'You may speak freely,' Marcus said. 'The residence of Lallius is still under constant watch?'

'Indeed, Excellence. It is his father's house, in fact – the coin inspector, old Numidius. Lallius did not return last night – it's possible that he has fled the town – and we have seen no one come or go except the household slaves. However, a young woman was discovered shortly after dawn, loitering around the entrance to the house. She was dressed in servant's clothing, but she is not part of the coin inspector's household – we know all of them.'

Marcus exchanged a look with me, then barked, 'I trust that you arrested her at once? She may have information. Most probably she is a messenger.'

'Naturally, Excellence!' The man looked affronted that my patron should ask. 'They took her to the cells and questioned her.'

'And?'

'And she denies that she has ever met the family.' The soldier permitted himself the suspicion of a smile. 'But we know better. She was talking to a servant from the household in the street – one of our spies was watching all the time. And she was seen in the same area last night at dusk, as well. There was an older woman with her then. She won't say who it was – or admit to anything. The commander was about to have her stripped and scourged, to find out what she knew, but suddenly she claimed your protection, Excellence.'

'What?'

'Claims that she was recently a servant to your wife, and says she would account for herself to you and you alone. Well, of course, when the commander heard that, he did not proceed. He said that you had asked to have all suspects brought to you, in any case, so he had her put in chains and he'll be sending her to you as soon as an escort and transport cart can be arranged. That is what I am sent to report. In the name of his most serene and divine imperial majesty the Emp—'

Marcus interrupted. 'Never mind all that. You are dismissed. Pulcrus, bring him refreshment in the servants' waiting room.' The two went out and Marcus looked at me. 'Myrna – do you think?'

My thoughts had been following exactly the same track. 'And her mother, by the sound of it. They went to Glevum yesterday. And if she's been arrested, we know why she has not come here today.'

'It seems she did have some connection with Lallius, then.' Marcus was looking seriously upset that someone in his household might betray him in this way.

It was my turn to comfort him. 'Unless she was just calling at his house to bargain for your family's release? She was fond of Marcellinus, I believe.'

Marcus brightened for a moment and then shook his head. 'If she was innocent she couldn't know about the kidnappers' demands. She wasn't here. How could she have guessed that Lallius was involved? I have told nobody except yourselves – apart from the chief priest.'

He had forgotten that the page had ears, I thought. It was likely that the whole household knew by now. But even that would not explain the facts. Pulcrus had not seen Myrna since the ransom note arrived.

'So it seems that she knew Lallius after all,' I said.

'But how? How does a wet nurse meet a man like that? And how could she possibly have abducted Julia? Myrna was here inside the villa all along.'

'She might have helped the kidnappers,' I pointed out. 'Or laid a trap for Julia, to entice her to go out of her own accord. She was the only servant near her at the time.'

Marcus sighed. 'Well, we have ways of finding out. Even if you don't approve of them. And this time, Libertus, I shan't hesitate to use them. The wretched girl will tell us everything she knows. To think we trusted her! Jove give me strength. The sooner they get her here the better, though it will take an hour or so. Then perhaps we'll find out something significant at last. In the meantime, I suppose, we shall just have to beg for patience from the gods.'

Chapter Fourteen

Gods or not, I knew at once it was impossible for me to simply wait and see. I wanted to do something – anything! – which might help to resolve this mystery. Gwellia was gone! Marcus had been living with this sort of strain for days, and I began to see why he had been rushing to and fro, content to drive to Glevum twice in a single day. When you are consumed with worry, sitting still leaves too much time for thought. Action, of any sort, is comforting.

Yet what was there to do? I had planned to question Myrna, and that was not possible – not until she got here, anyway. I might have brought the other villa servants in and talked to them, perhaps, but it seemed that there was little they could add. Anyway, I was not convinced that I could concentrate.

I needed to do something physical – to be out beyond the walls, looking for some trace of Gwellia. I was desperate to visit the empty roundhouse, too, in case there was something that the page had missed – anything at all that might bring me closer to finding my missing wife. Yet clearly I was in no state to walk anywhere at all. And then a stratagem occurred to me.

'If Myrna has had dealings with Lallius before, it's probable her family would know. I wonder, Excellence, if it would be wise to go down there and round up the sister and the child, so we can question them. If you would give me transport, I could go down myself.' He looked a little doubtful, and I added hastily, 'I could look in at the round-house on the way, as well, in case there's anything the page has overlooked.'

Marcus was still running his fingers through his hair. He looked at me sadly. 'It might be useful to do as you suggest. I might come with you, too. Anything is better than simply waiting here.'

'Then I may use the carriage, or a cart at least?' I was glad of his suggestion that he'd accompany me. I am no rider, and I did not want a horse.

I rather expected him to agree at once, but all he answered was, 'We'll see what the doctor has to say.'

I thought I knew what Philades would say, and I was not mistaken. When he was summoned and his opinion asked, he was quick to declare that such an outing was not wise at all. 'In the patient's current state of health, it might even be dangerous,' he finished, screwing his wrinkled face into a sneer.

'Come now, medicus,' I countered. 'Only yesterday, as I understand, you were actually prescribing carriage rides. And it seems that you were right. That little journey in the cart has clearly done me good.' In fact I was feeling as flimsy as a flower, but I was determined not to show it. I would investigate my wife's disappearance if it took all the strength I had.

Before he could say another word, I had risen unsteadily to my feet and taken a faltering step towards the door. (I had to flash a warning glance at Junio, otherwise I knew he'd try to help, but I wanted to make my point and stand un-aided.) When I had reached the safety of the wall, and could lean on it for support, I turned back to Philades. 'You see?'

The doctor was still trying to frustrate my plan. 'Libertus is still very weak,' he said. 'If he goes for a rocking trip, he should not go alone. I could accompany him, perhaps.'

I could think of nothing I would welcome less, but I need not have worried. 'I'll go with him myself,' my patron said. 'If Myrna has dealings with the coin inspector's son it's possible she knew about the kidnapping.'

'Libertus suggested that to you?' The doctor gave me another poisonous look.

Marcus ignored him. 'It's hard to credit it. We have been generous to that household. Apart from paying Myrna a very handsome sum, Julia used to buy the mother's teething remedies, and sometimes other things as well. We always gave an extra *as* or two. And whenever she used to come here, bringing that little girl up to be fed, we never sent her home without some food. Even the day Julia went, they turned up here a little later on – the old woman had a basket of herbs and things to sell – and the steward gave them something even then, although of course he had to send them home.'

'Myrna still had milk enough for two?' I said.

'Just as the mother once did and the sister too. It's one of the recommendations for the job. I'm very keen to talk to the family, in fact, since there is nothing else that I can usefully do here, at least until this escort party comes. We'll take a cart and bring them back with us. It isn't far to go. A mile or two towards the town, I understand. My page will know exactly where to find the house; he's been there several times. He can accompany us and show us where it is.'

'And Junio?' I ventured. The page would ride beside us, but Junio was on foot.

My patron almost smiled. 'And Junio, of course, since you

151

wish it. He can travel on the cart. It will save him squatting on the carriage floor, though Julia and I have often travelled with a slave like that.'

I saw Philades frown. I think he had been planning to invite himself along, but not at the price of riding on a cart.

Marcus in any case had other plans for him. 'Philades, I'm leaving you in charge, in case the kidnappers attempt to be in touch again. If there is any message, you know where I have gone. Send one of the servants after me at once. I don't expect the party from Glevum will arrive before we're back, but if they do, see that the girl is securely locked up. There's a room upstairs we sometimes use for slaves who are awaiting punishment. Put her in there, and put a guard on her, but make sure she doesn't speak to any of the staff. I don't want her concocting any further lies with them.'

It was almost comical to see the doctor's face. He clearly wanted to come out with us, but he could hardly turn down Marcus's request. 'I am honoured, Excellence,' he managed finally.

Once the decision had been made, our preparations did not take long. The carriage – as Malodius had said yesterday – was polished and ready, and only required a horse between the shafts. In no time at all it was waiting in the lane with Malodius grumbling in his cart behind.

With Junio's help I struggled out, and was duly ensconced with pillows and a rug, though it cost me more effort than I wanted to admit.

I don't know if rocking therapy is genuinely beneficial, but the motion of the carriage was not disagreeable. Marcus had pulled the leather curtain aside, and I leaned back on my cushions and looked out at the lane. There was not much to see. Damp trees, ragged with winter. A wretched, wandering dog. A peasant bent double under a pile of sticks. An arrogant young horseman who stopped to watch us pass. No sign of Gwellia, however hard I looked.

'Nothing to see here, my old friend,' my patron said. 'It was a vain hope anyway.' He looked pale and tense, and after that he said nothing more at all until we reached the enclosure where my roundhouse was.

Junio was already off the cart and opening the gate. He came to help me down, and at Marcus's suggestion the page accompanied us. My heart was thumping as we went into the house – I was still hoping against hope that Gwellia might be there, or at least have left some message that only I would recognise. But there was nothing of the kind. Everything was exactly as the page had said – neat, tidied, empty, with the fire damped and cold. That was somehow more troubling than a fight-scene might have been: the embers are never usually permitted to go out. It is a tedious matter to make fire, and without it the house seemed dark, impersonal and chill. In any case I was half numb with grief.

I sent Junio on a scouting mission, but he soon returned. Nothing in the dye house either, or in the servants' new sleeping room next door. Nothing in the well or in the food storage pits. (That was a small comfort, anway. We'd once discovered a dismembered corpse in there.) No one with the animals in the shelter at the back – all clamouring as if they had been shut up for the night. I instructed the two boys to take them food, but not to let them out.

I sat on my own stool and looked helplessly around. My wife had not taken any clothes with her, as far as I could see, or anything else except an ancient leather bag which was missing from its usual hook beside the door. Where was she? I dared not allow myself to think of what might be happening to her at this very hour. I would have done anything at all to bring her back, but I was powerless. I felt very old and lost. However, there was clearly nothing to be gained from sitting here, so when Junio and the page came back they helped me out to the carriage once again.

Marcus was not accustomed to being made to wait. He was peculiarly unsmiling and abrupt when we returned and I could see he was impatient to be off. 'We must be on our way to Myrna's if we're going to go at all. I want to be back at the villa before the escort party comes. Very well, Pulcrus – ride on and lead the way.'

This time our progress was slower, though considerably more jolting and uncomfortable. We were no longer on the wide gravelled lane that leads to Marcus's villa from the military road, but on the ancient, narrow, muddy track which is the old way into town. It is a shorter route, used by pedestrians and mules, but it was not designed for carriage wheels. It is narrow, full of rocks and roots, with muddy corners and vertiginous descents, and only negotiable by carriages with care. However, it was soon clear why we had come this way. The road wound past several isolated farms and little homesteads nestling by the lane. One of these was Myrna's, by the look of it.

The building was rather a surprise. It was made of stone and square-built, like a Roman house, though it was low and squat and rather rambling. It was set back a little from the road, and as we came closer I could see that one end of it was sorely in decay. Part of the roof had fallen in, and grass and weeds were growing through the walls of what had obviously once been a stable.

Marcus looked at me and raised his brows. 'Not the sort of place I expected at all,' he said. It was the first thing he had said since I got back in the carriage. 'Quite a substantial dwelling, in its day.' He nodded to the page. 'Well, go and fetch them out.'

The page swung obediently from his horse, gave Malodius the reins, and swaggered up the path towards the door. He peered inside, then raised his hand to knock. 'Is anybody there?' we heard him call.

As if in answer a ragged woman appeared from round the side. She trailed one grimy infant by the hand, and carried a second on her hip, while another was clearly on the way. She was thin, and had that worn and haggard look that many peasant mothers have. She stopped to speak to Pulcrus, and we heard her murmuring, and then he escorted her to us.

She sketched a clumsy bob, and launched into speech at once. Her Latin was fluent, if ungrammatical. 'Pardon me, your mightiness, but I've been saying to your page it's no good him hollering 'cause there's no one there. I can't account for it. Promised she'd have a remedy for me today, she did, for little Aldo here.' She indicated the infant at her side. 'See how his nose is running?'

Indeed it would have been difficult to miss. There was a slick of mucus extending to his chin and dribbling down on to his tunic-front. The child put his grimy thumb into his mouth and went on gazing solemnly at us.

Marcus dragged his eyes away from this wretched spectacle. 'You don't know where they've gone?'

'I don't know no more than you do. She said that she'd be here. Walked miles to get here, I have, and all to find her gone. Now what am I to do? I'll have all five of them with snivels next, and I've got no clean tunics for them as it is.'

The idea of another three at home was frightening. 'You

could rub some hog's grease on his chest,' I ventured, remembering what the medicus had said.

Her look was pitying. 'I might do if I had a hog,' she said. 'But where am I to find that sort of thing? I was hoping that the woman here might give me some – she's not cheap, but she'll help you now and then if you're really short of money.' She seemed to realise that this was hardly a concern to wealthy men like Marcus, and she added hastily, 'Begging your pardon, mightiness, that is.'

However, her little outburst had given me a thought. I leaned as close to Marcus as I could and murmured in his ear, 'You might offer her a few sesterces, Excellence, if she can tell us anything of use. I can speak to her in Celtic if you wish?'

Not soft enough! She heard me. 'That would be much easier for me,' she said, lapsing into the local dialect. It was not identical to mine, but I could understand it well enough. 'Of course, I'll tell you anything I can. What do you want to know?'

I passed this on to Marcus, who took out a silver coin and held it up between his finger and thumb so that she could see it. 'About this family . . . ?' he said, keeping his Latin very slow and clear. 'A mother and two daughters, I believe?'

She nodded. 'And the little granddaughters, of course. Myrna's got one and Secunda has the twins – I don't know how they manage to limit it to that. Perhaps it's being a wet nurse does it, like they used to say.'

This rather puzzled me, and I asked her to explain, though when she did I rather wished that I had held my tongue.

'Feeding a child is supposed to prevent you falling for another one – I thought everyone knew that – though Jove knows it didn't work for me. Course, Myrna hasn't got a husband now – he drowned down at the ford, poor thing, before the child was born.'

'Myrna had a husband?' I exclaimed. Of course, I should have thought of it before – where there are children there must have been a man – but all the same it came as a surprise.

She gave me a pitying look. 'Well, naturally she did – those two girls may not be citizens, but they're respectable. Their mother saw to that. Not that she had an easy time herself. Widowed twice, poor woman, but she managed to survive. Of course she was always handy with herbs, and she used to help women when they came to birth – I believe her mother used to do the same. First husband was a proper brute, from what I hear of him, but he fell down a well one night and left her penniless. But she wouldn't be defeated – went as midwife to a family in the town, and when the mother died in childbirth she stayed on as wet nurse to the babe. They didn't pay her much, I understand, but at least it kept a roof over her head.'

'Quite a substantial roof, by the look of it.' I gestured to the house.

'Oh, that was her second husband. He was a cart-maker, and pretty well-to-do – you can tell that from the house – but then he cut his hand. Got poison in it, and wouldn't heal. He was doing less and less, but it killed him in the end and after that she was on her own. Brought up the two girls, though – and taught them a trade. Said the world would always be in want of nurses.'

Marcus was looking enquiringly at me, so I gave him the gist of it. He frowned and said in Latin, 'I thought that she took nurslings in?'

157

The woman understood him, and turned back to me. 'Oh, that was later, when the girls were growing up. She did try taking passing travellers in – the house was big enough – but it wasn't very safe with only women in the house, so she started taking children in instead. Paid a farmer's wife to wet-nurse them till Secunda was old enough to wed – since then of course they've done it all themselves. Mind you,' she added, looking at the coin, 'I'm only telling you what people say. I've only known her for the last few years.'

'And how exactly did you come to meet her?' I enquired. She gave me that pitying look again. 'She still helps at birthings, and she helped at mine. My eldest would have killed me else, I think, and it looks as if I'll need her help again.' She hitched up the squirming child at her hip and looked despairingly at her bulging waist. 'And I buy her remedies. Magical, they are. Croup, colic, teething pains, you name it, she's got a cure for it. And she's reliable.' She looked behind her at the empty house. 'Usually she is, at any rate. But this morning, it seems, she isn't here. It's very strange. There's usually somebody about – if only the elder sister and her two little ones, come to mind the baby. But I can't wait any longer; I shall have to go. I've left the other four youngsters in the roundhouse on their own and I'm afraid that they'll fall into the fire.'

I relayed all this to Marcus, who held up the coin again, saying as he did so, 'You've looked round the back?'

This time she seemed uneasy, but she answered him direct. 'There's nobody about. There is a little courtyard behind the house. I heard a noise and thought they might be there, but there was no one to be seen. I was just giving up and deciding that I'd go home again when you came. That's all I know, I swear by all the gods. I didn't go inside.' She tugged at her son, who was pulling at her skirts, 'Don't fidget, Aldo. We'll be going home soon.'

She reached for the *sestertius*, but I prevented her. 'A noise? What sort of noise?' I said, using Latin too so that my patron understood.

She looked away and shrugged. 'A sort of squeak,' she said. 'Rats, probably. Most likely from the stable end they never use. I didn't go to look. Obviously they wouldn't be in there. The place is dangerous. The son-in-law has taken all the carts – they were given as a dowry when Secunda wed, because her husband's got a little business on this side of town. Then there was a storm and half the roof fell down. They keep odd sacks of corn and things in there, but otherwise they haven't used the place for years.'

I was thinking furiously. It occurred to me that a space like that would make a splendid prison, if it could be secured. I could think of no reason why the missing women should be here, but I could not overlook the possibility. I turned to Marcus.

'All the same,' I said, 'I think it would be worth our while to look. It's possible there might be something there.'

I didn't say that it might be our wives, but perhaps he had worked out something of the kind himself, because he said very quickly, 'Junio, go and search. You too, Pulcrus. And Malodius – you go the other way. If anyone is there you can cut off their escape.'

Malodius got down, glowering, from his perch, and went to guard the path on which the woman had appeared. Junio went round the other way towards the ruined block, while Pulcrus – at my suggestion – went into the house.

'See if there's another exit to the rear,' I said. 'We don't want anyone escaping by that route.' Then I got down from the carriage and painfully took up a position at the gate: I was a deterrent there, I told myself, although I should have been little use if anyone had actually tried to vie with me. The woman glanced nervously at me.

Aldo was snivelling again. 'Saving your presence, mightiness,' the mother said, addressing herself to Marcus and ignoring me, 'if you have no further use for me, can I take the children home? Aldo's getting fretful and the baby needs a feed, and there are the other four to think about as well. You can find me at my roundhouse if you want me any more.'

Marcus nodded, and tossed the *sestertius* to the ground. Aldo was on it like a flash, and she was obliged to prise it from his hand. 'We're grateful, mightiness,' she said, dropping it into a patently light purse. 'Aldo, say thank you to the gentlemen.'

The suggestion sent him huddling to her skirts, but at least it stopped his tears, and with hasty apologies she led him off and we saw them disappearing through the trees.

They were hardly out of sight, however, before Junio came running back to us. His face was ashen and he was breathing hard.

'Excellence! Master!' His shout brought Pulcrus rushing from the house. 'There's someone here all right. She . . . they . . .' He shook his head. 'I think perhaps you'd better come and see.'

Chapter Fifteen

It had not been an easy death, that much was evident. The young woman was lying peacefully enough now, but there were ugly bruises on her face and body as though someone had beaten her before she died. There was a lot of blood. Not only from the deep wound beneath her heart but also from slashes on her legs and arms. She had not been able to defend herself, because her hands were tied behind her back, so tightly that the cords were cutting into her flesh.

She was lying huddled on the flagstone floor of what might once have been a sort of workshop for the cart-maker. The roof here had somehow survived the collapse that had destroyed the remainder of this part of the house, but the area was not much used, and had been allowed to fall into neglect. It was cut off from the inhabited wing, in any case, by piles of fallen debris from the collapse, and only approachable through thorny weeds – though there was a trace of what might have been a path. It was clear what had made the squeaking sound – the rusty door was swinging in the wind, although it was evident there was an outside bolt.

Inside, however, the room was surprisingly intact. There was a narrow window space that gave a little light. A solid wooden wheel still stood against one wall, and a pile of axle timbers lay on a dusty bench, together with a row of open pots holding what looked like the remains of ancient grease or paint. Apart from that the place had obviously been cleared. There were no tools on the workbench (though fresh patches showed where they might have been) and the floor showed signs of having recently been swept, but it was covered in dark splatters now and a pool of drying blood. The place smelt horribly of death.

It was a moment before anybody spoke. This unexpected encounter with murder had shocked us all.

Then Pulcrus cried, 'By all the gods! It's Myrna. What have they done to her?' He bolted for the garden, and was copiously sick.

It broke the silence. Marcus walked slowly over to the corpse. 'He's right. There's so much damage to her face, I wasn't absolutely sure at first, but now I've looked closer there can be no doubt. I thought it might have been her sister – Secunda, or whatever she is called. They are – were! – quite alike, although Secunda was a little taller – taller than Julia, I think. But this is clearly Myrna.' He looked at the pathetic form on the floor. 'At least it used to be. Poor girl. I fear that it is her association with us that brought this fate on her.' He turned towards my slave. 'Junio. Fetch my page and get her covered up. In fact, you can find Malodius and get her on the cart. We'll take her to the villa – we can't leave her here.'

'At once, Excellence.' Junio bowed and disappeared.

Marcus seemed surprisingly stricken by the death. He avoided my gaze and spoke aloud, but as though he were talking to himself. 'We'll give her some sort of funeral and put her ashes in the servants' grave – unless her family turn up again and want to perform the rituals for themselves. We can't allow her to be simply thrown into a common pit, as if she was a pauper or a criminal. She was working for our household, after all, and I don't imagine she belonged to any guild.'

'You are generous, Excellence,' I said. I meant it. He was offering to do this at his own expense. Most slaves are paid up members of a funeral guild (though Marcus, like many owners, pays the fee on their behalf) precisely to ensure a fitting send-off when they die, so their spirits are not forced to walk the earth. Myrna, however, as a freewoman working for a wage, would have had to find a guild of wet nurses to join and pay the fees herself. It was unlikely that she'd made any such provision – and I had never heard of such a women's guild. Marcus would provide at least a proper pyre, with someone to say prayers and offer sacrifice, and a decent resting place for the remains.

He nodded brusquely. 'I ought to ask you, I suppose. What do you make of it?'

I had lowered myself gingerly to my knees beside the girl. It was hard to find a place to kneel where I would not stain my clothes with blood, but I was glad not to be standing up. I steadied myself against a baulk of wood and forced myself to look at her, and think. I had wondered, at one stage, if Myrna herself had somehow been a party to the kidnapping – that was why I had wanted to talk to her so much – but now it seemed she was a victim too. And a pathetic one. The wounds were pitiful.

'It was the deep wound that killed her, almost certainly,' I said, levering myself back to my feet again. 'He used a dagger, by the look of it. You can see the two lips where the knife has been. But these other cuts are just as worrying. They were meant to cause agony, not death – as if her killer had been questioning her first.'

Marcus had turned away, and was gazing determinedly

out of the window space. I guessed that he was struggling with tears. I confess I was a little bit surprised. True, this was not a pretty sight, but Marcus – being a senior magistrate – is required to see that sentences are duly carried out, sometimes in spectacularly grisly ways, and might be expected to be inured to violent scenes like this. Besides, like many Romans, he scarcely considers that servants are human beings at all.

His next words explained his mood. 'So, the kidnappers are killers, as they claim to be,' he said, in the bleakest tone I've ever heard him use. 'Not only killers, but torturers as well. And they still have my wife.'

And very likely mine as well. That was a shocking thought. I was glad that Junio chose this moment to appear, accompanied by Malodius and the page. I forced myself to concentrate on them.

Marcus was doing something similar. The three servants had come in with a piece of sack, and as he barked commands they quickly covered Myrna up with it.

Pulcrus was still looking whiter than a freshly laundered toga, and I said – chiefly to occupy my mind and his – 'You've checked the remainder of the house?'

The question brought a little colour to his cheeks. 'I was doing so when I heard Junio call. I'm sorry, citizen, I should have reported on it earlier – but this had driven it out of my head. There is obviously nobody about – but the place is in an awful mess in there.'

Marcus looked at him sharply. 'What sort of mess?'

The page looked mystified. 'Just a confusion, Excellence. It's clean enough. No . . . blood or anything. Not like in here. But things are overturned and lying everywhere.'

I turned to Marcus. 'Signs of a struggle, by the sound of it.'

'Perhaps we had better go and have a look ourselves,' he said, with such alacrity that I felt he was glad of an excuse to leave the scene. I knew how he felt. 'Malodius, and Junio. Take the body to the cart. Pulcrus, come with us,' Marcus commanded, and strode away. Pulcrus hurried to accompany him. I had to trail after them at a slower pace, back into the lane and down the path towards the cottage door.

This time I followed Marcus and his page inside, and could get a better impression of the place than had been possible from the exterior.

There were two adjoining living spaces, in imitation of the Roman style, each with a brazier rather than a fire. The larger room, which we had caught a glimpse of from the door, was neat and ordered, but as soon as we got into the inner area it was obvious what Pulcrus had been alluding to. A battered table, set against the wall, was somehow still upright but everything else – loom, stools, and benches – had been overturned. Pans and cooking vessels had been tossed aside, their contents emptied roughly out upon the floor, and behind a small partition the sleeping area had been similarly pulled apart – the bedstraw scattered everywhere, and items of women's clothing strewn in untidy heaps.

I righted the smallest of the stools and sank down on it, grateful for a chance to take a rest. This was an offence against my patron's dignity, since he was still on his feet and had not invited me to sit, but my head was spinning so much that I had little choice. Marcus acknowledged my dilemma with a frown, and gestured to the slave to bring a seat for him.

'Rest yourself,' he said, without a smile. He looked around the room. 'A struggle, do you think?'

'More like a search,' I managed. 'Why else turn out the contents of the pots? There's nothing broken here, that I can see.'

The frown deepened. 'Searching for what, do you suppose?'

'Money perhaps. Or something fairly small, in any case. They seem to have been looking under things. Whatever it was,' I was thinking slowly as I spoke, 'it appears that they found it in the end – otherwise they would have hunted in the outer room as well.'

'Unless they were disturbed. By that woman with the children, possibly?'

I shook my head, and wished I hadn't. 'But where could they vanish to? She swears that she saw no one, and we were here immediately afterwards ourselves. Someone might have run out into the garden, I suppose, but that wall surrounding it is far too high to climb. And she didn't rob the place. We both saw she had barely two coins in her purse.'

Marcus seemed unwilling to relinquish his idea. He said, still in that strained voice he had been using more and more, 'I'm sure that she knows more than she's admitting to. And this has all happened very recently – Pulcrus was here yesterday, and there was no murder then.'

'You can't think she had any hand in that?'

'She's withholding information. We know she came round to the back – she must have looked inside. She would have seen the turmoil, if nothing else, but she didn't mention it to us.' Marcus had that grim look on his face again. 'When we get back to the villa, I will send for her and bring her in for questioning again. It won't be hard to find her. It's obvious she can't live far away. If she – or anyone else for that matter – has any information which could lead us to this brutal kidnapper, they'll wish they never . . .' He tailed off, but I understood him perfectly. 'I'll get at the truth. This is no time for gentleness. Julia's life and safety is at stake.'

I said, partly to convince myself, 'We have no actual proof that this was the kidnapper. It does seem very likely, I agree, but there is no solid evidence to link this crime with him.'

Marcus turned to face me, and even in my exhausted state I could see the anguish on his face. 'Oh, but there is. You saw that cord round the nursemaid's wrists? That's Julia's. Her favourite girdle – woven silk and gold – she was wearing it the day she disappeared. And that's her lilac *stola*, over there, lying on the floor. You can see the frayed edge where they tore the strip off it to tie round the scroll. Believe me, Libertus, this was the kidnapper.'

I stared at him. My thoughts were in a whirl. So it was possible that Julia had been here? In that little workshop room, perhaps. Yet who could possibly have brought her there? And why, and how? There was a lock on the outside of the door and it would have made a prison, of a kind. But if that was the case, where was she now? Where were the other inhabitants of the house? And, most importantly for me, where was my Gwellia?

Marcus was struggling for Roman self-control. 'I wonder what he was searching so desperately to find. Was that what the torture was about? Questioning Myrna, to find out where it was – whatever it was that he was looking for?'

'Questioning Myrna!' I exclaimed, struck by a sudden, very different, thought. 'Dear gods! That's what we were hoping to go back and do. But if that is Myrna lying dead there in the stable block, she can't have been arrested outside

Lallius's house today. So who is it that the guards are dragging to the villa as we speak?'

Marcus looked startled, and for the first time since we had come here, he used his normal tone. 'Great Jupiter, I hadn't thought of that. In fact, I'd quite forgotten that the guards were on their way. We'd best be getting back. Pulcrus, assist Libertus to the carriage, and tell the coachman to make all speed home. You stay here with the horse and guard the house. Make sure no one tries to rob the place. It's conceivable Myrna's mother will come back – in which case you can break the news and tell her that funeral arrangements have been made. I'll have someone relieve you as soon as possible – probably some land slaves in the interim, until I can get a proper guard detachment from the garrison.'

Pulcrus looked as though he wanted to protest, but seeing Marcus's face he clearly thought better of it, and the last we saw of him he was standing forlornly at the cottage gate as we lurched and jolted back along the lane towards the villa, where the escort party was by this time no doubt awaiting our return.

Chapter Sixteen

They were. As soon as we drew up at the gate Philades came bustling out to greet us with the news. 'The guards from Glevum have arrived with their prisoner, Excellence. They came some time ago.' There was a sort of suppressed excitement in his tone. He was clearly bursting with importance at having been asked to act on Marcus's behalf, but it was more than that – the air of a man who's staked a fortune on the dice, and knows that he is just about to win. He was smiling fulsomely at my patron as he spoke. He ignored me utterly.

Marcus nodded tetchily. He had summoned Malodius to the carriage door, and was giving instructions about where to put the grisly cargo and the blanket from the cart, and which group of land slaves he was then to transport to Myrna's house as guards. The medicus had all but interrupted him. Anyone else would have earned a sharp rebuke for having spoken out of turn, but the doctor – as usual – seemed immune from reprimand.

Philades seemed oblivious of possible offence. He was still buoyed up by that curious energy. 'I had the girl locked up as you required,' he went on, 'but as soon as I heard that your carriage had arrived, I instructed them to take her to the atrium. I trust that meets with your approval? I thought it would be more convenient for you to question her in there.'

Marcus assented with a dismissive nod. 'We have found Myrna,' he said wearily. 'You'd better have a look at her a little later on – although there's nothing you can do for her just now.' He had descended from the carriage, and Junio was assisting me to do the same.

Philades did not even spare a glance for that pathetic, shrouded figure on the cart. 'I will be extremely glad to, Excellence, whenever you command. But here are your two serving boys to escort you to the house. The prisoner is being taken to the atrium as we speak. I have ordered wine and dates for you, and a folding chair as well.'

Maximus and Minimus had come out to us by now, and my patron – in the absence of his page – allowed them to escort him to the house and bring some perfumed water so we could rinse our hands and faces. 'We'll have a stool for Libertus, too,' he said to Minimus, handing him the linen towel. 'I want him to be present when I interview this girl. With the permission of the medicus, of course.'

I had my own face in the water bowl by now, so I could not see the expression on the doctor's face. I expected him to veto such a plan, and I was so tired that I would not have cared, but to my surprise I heard him say, 'That might be very wise. I think that he should see her. It is possible that there are some interesting questions to be asked.' He paused, and as I straightened up and leaned on Junio, he added, with a curious little smile, 'But obviously, Excellence, that is for you to judge.'

It was clear that this last remark was somehow aimed at me, but in my fuddled state I had no notion what he meant. I did not even know who this famous captive was – since it clearly wasn't the wet nurse after all. I had searched my mind the whole way back and had come to the conclusion that Myrna's sister was the most likely candidate – and I had no association with her of any kind. As far as I was aware, I'd never seen the girl, though I admit to feeling curious to meet her now.

But it wasn't Myrna's sister. I followed Marcus and his little red-haired slaves into the atrium, and saw the girl led in. I was still leaning heavily on Junio's arm, and perhaps it was convenient that I was – I might have fallen otherwise, from shock.

'Cilla?' I could not believe my eyes. It was my own wife's attendant, gagged and bound and looking terrified – as well she might. She was surrounded by four soldiers, all with daggers drawn; and one of them also held a length of heavy chain, which had been secured round her waist and wrists, and by which she had evidently been dragged along. Her forearms and knees were grazed and streaked with dirt, her face was muddy and her new tunic was torn. She looked a sorry sight.

All the same, she was defiant still. Her eyes were flashing and she was struggling to speak. Marcus looked as surprised as I was to see Cilla there, but he evidently intended to conduct things formally. He settled himself magisterially on the carved folding chair which Maximus had brought, gestured for the doctor and myself to sit on either side, and gave the signal to tear away the gag.

They pushed the girl before us, with a shove that made her stagger. 'Master?' the girl said breathlessly to me, as soon as she could speak. 'Tell them to let me go. I'm innocent. They claim that I'm in contact with this Lallius, but I've never seen or spoken to the man, and I haven't been inside the house, I keep on telling them.'

The burliest of the guards gave her a savage shake. 'Be

silent, girl. Speak when you are spoken to, and not until – and when you do, address His Excellence. You've called on his protection, I recall. So why are you now appealing to this citizen?' I saw him exchange a look with Philades.

My patron intervened before I had a chance to speak at all. He sounded weary. 'She was my slave once. I gave her as a gift to this citizen and his wife. I am his patron, so the girl is right to call on both of us. Let her go.'

The burly guard looked almost mutinous. He glanced at Philades again as if in mute appeal, but, finding no assistance there, put away his dagger and signalled to the others to sheathe theirs. 'We'll have to get an ironsmith to strike off that chain,' he muttered, as he dropped his end of it with a deliberate clatter on the floor. 'It isn't my fault, Excellence, if we arrested one of yours. You asked us to detain anyone who visited the coin inspector's house – and she was lurking in the street outside at dawn. And it was not the first time. She was there last night as well.'

'Is this true, Cilla?' Marcus was more severe than I have ever heard him sound. 'What were you doing there?'

'Obeying my mistress's commands,' the slave-girl said, and I felt a shock run down my spine – quickly followed by a shiver of relief. I remembered what the messenger had said. There had been an older woman seen with the prisoner late the night before. I had supposed, at the time, that it was the old woman with the herbs, but suddenly I was delirious with hope.

'Gwellia was with you?' I blurted. It wasn't my place to interrupt, but the words were forced out of me.

Cilla shook her head. 'Not at that moment, master. That was the whole idea . . .' She looked somewhat nervously around her at the guards, and then turned to Marcus. 'May

I speak frankly, Excellence? Without fear of punishment?'

Marcus was unsmiling. 'Your best hope of avoiding punishment is to be as frank as possible. What is it you are wishing to confess? You had some secret reason for visiting the house? Some conspiratorial errand on your mistress's behalf?'

'It was for my master, really,' Cilla said, and despite the fact that I was sitting on a stool I felt as if the ground had given under me. I swayed and felt Junio's supporting hand against my back.

'Some business of your master's? That's what you're telling me?' Marcus didn't look at me but I could sense he felt betrayed.

'Patron, I know nothing of this,' I murmured in despair. I glanced towards him, but he had turned away and refused to meet my eyes. Philades, beside him, was looking flushed and smug.

'Excellence, I don't know how freely I can speak,' Cilla went on. 'My mistress told me the matter was not to be divulged, except in private to my master and yourself. That's why I refused to tell them anything.' She gestured at the guards.

Marcus dismissed her scruples crisply. 'I have no secrets from this company. What have you got to say?'

Cilla took a deep breath. She was still bound and bedraggled, but she spoke with dignity. 'It is about Lallius – the coin inspector's son. You were' – she looked around at her expectant audience and went on – 'obliged to release him yesterday, I understand.'

There was an uncomfortable muttering among the listeners in the room. I suspected that this was news to most of them.

Marcus had turned crimson. 'There was an irregularity in

the formula of the preliminary trials,' he snapped. 'Several cases had to be withdrawn. The high priest of Jupiter himself demanded it.' He glanced around. You could almost feel the tension in the atrium. 'The law is no concern of yours. How dare you speak of that?'

He was impressive in his anger, but Cilla was not cowed. She had been a servant in this house, and she knew Marcus well enough to know that – given time – he would not be deliberately unjust. She knelt before him, forehead to his feet. 'Excellence, forgive me, but I did suggest a private interview,' she ventured, in a humble voice.

Marcus gave a sharp, impatient sigh. 'Oh, very well. Perhaps, after all, I should hear this girl in camera. Slaves, guards, attendants – leave us. Go and wait outside. Libertus – as her owner – you may stay.'

Since, without the help of Junio, I could no more have struggled to my feet and walked than used my arms to fly, this was perhaps a wise decision on his part. However, there was no time to feel relief, because my patron added instantly, 'You too, medicus.'

The servants and the soldiers straggled out until only the burly captain of the guard remained. Then Marcus had the folding screen pulled to – to the chagrin of those now left outside, whose curiosity had clearly been aroused.

'Now!' Marcus said. He sounded furious. 'What is this all about? You have caused me public embarrassment. I hope you have good reason for it, or I shall have you flogged.'

I longed to point out that he'd invited her to speak, but I didn't dare. Instead I ventured to express what I'd deduced. 'Gwellia sent you to the house today to discover what you could about Lallius because she knew His Excellence had sought my help in finding out who sent the ransom note. Is that it, Cilla? Something of the kind?'

She was still kneeling on the floor, but now she raised her head. She looked relieved. 'Master, I knew you'd understand. When . . .'

Philades interrupted scornfully. 'Do not believe it, Excellence,' he said. 'The citizen is putting words into her mouth.'

Marcus quelled him with a look. 'Go on,' he said to Cilla. 'When . . . ?'

She took a deep breath, and the words came in a rush. 'When the oil-delivery man arrived with your message telling the mistress not to come here yesterday, she was upset, of course. She called me to her side. "There's something more to this than my husband's being ill," she said. "He would want me by his side if he was sick, and anyway he was clearly on the mend. And why not send Junio if there was a message for this house? There's something new afoot, I'm sure of it. Well, I can't sit here all night and not attempt to help. What would Libertus do, if he was here?" I said that I supposed he'd go and ask some questions, and she replied, "Exactly, and that's precisely what we're going to do, as well. That oil cart is going to Glevum, so the driver can take us there. We can make a few enquiries in the morning and come back on foot. Perhaps I'll have something to tell them at the villa when I go." ' Cilla paused. 'So that is what we did. The driver didn't mind.'

Philades was derisive. 'And you expect us to believe this tale? She suddenly decides to go to Glevum, all alone, where nobody's expecting her – and in the dusk, as well?'

Cilla looked defiantly at him. 'Well, obviously she didn't go alone. She took me and Kurso with her. She was all prepared to leave the house in any case – because she was intending to come here – and the animals were settled for the night. It didn't take a minute to get on to the cart. And as for anyone expecting us, we hardly needed that. My master has a workshop in the town with a sleeping area over it, where he used to live. Of course, no one has slept there now for a moon or two, but when we got to Glevum my mistress sent Kurso ahead to beg bedstraw and some embers from neighbours round about so he could light a fire and warm the workshop up. You can ask the potter opposite, if you doubt my word. No doubt they would remember, because they gave him some.'

I was almost light-headed with relief by now. Gwellia was safe in Glevum after all. That possibility had not occurred to me, though perhaps it should have done. She has been proud to help with my enquiries before, and has proved herself to be resourceful more than once.

Marcus, however, was impatient with these domestic details. 'What has all this to do with Lallius?'

'I am coming to that, Excellence,' the girl replied. 'Kurso went ahead, as I say, but I stayed with my mistress. "Well, we've got to find out where this Lallius lives," she said. "His father is the coin inspector, as I understand, so let's start with that." So we went into the forum, where he has his niche, but the stalls were closing down, and there was no sign of Numidius at all. Then we found an old man selling pots, and he said that Numidius had not been there for days and a younger man had been working there instead. "The old man's desperately ill, from what I hear," the potman said. "It's not expected that he'll last the night. They're waiting for that boy of his to come, so they can start to make arrangements for the funeral." ' She turned to Marcus. 'You may already know this, Excellence, since they've appointed someone else to take his place. I don't know the new coin inspector's name – we didn't think to ask – but any of the market police will tell you who it is.'

I stared at Marcus. He had bowed his head and was scowling at the mosaic of Neptune on the floor, obviously as startled as he was furious. I should not care to be the commander of the guard, I thought. All his attention had been on finding Lallius at his house, and though his messenger had told us that no one but the slaves had come and gone all day, we had not seen the significance of his words. But of course we should have done – since, by implication, there was no sign of Numidius himself going about his usual business in the forum. Yet his illness was obviously no secret in the town. The briefest of enquiries would have established as much.

'If the old man is too ill for visitors,' I voiced my thoughts aloud, 'he certainly was not sending ransom notes. And it would explain why there have been no callers at the house.'

Marcus frowned. 'Then it's doubly surprising that Lallius has not come home. You would have expected him to come at once, if his father's on his deathbed, wouldn't you – even if they were not on the best of terms?' Because Lallius as the only son would be the heir, he meant. Heirs are expected to do things properly – close the eyes and start off the lament, as well as arranging for elaborate biers, pyres, musicians, and the rest of it – often as a prerequisite of the inheritance.

'Apparently they were always quarrelling,' Cilla supplied, still from her position on the floor. 'Lallius was too fond of gambling and wine, and he was dreadfully in debt, and his father was a very careful man. There were dreadful arguments. They almost came to blows quite recently and

Lallius stormed out in a rage. He did attempt to make amends, as usual – sent his father an amphora of his favourite wine – but this time Numidius refused to pardon him, because Lallius had been charged with fighting in the street. The old man was furious at the disgrace.'

'How do you know all this? I thought you claimed you had never spoken to the man or been into the house?' The doctor barked the question before Marcus could.

'I haven't,' Cilla said. 'I spoke to one of Numidius's slaves, that's all. The potman pointed the woman out to us – she had come into the forum to buy some bread and fish. You know it's always cheaper at the end of the day, and the household was in need of food, she said. Numidius was too ill to order things himself, so she had found a coin and come out to buy a few scraps for the slaves to eat, and meats for the funeral if it came to it. We walked back to the street with her and she showed us the house.'

'So you admit that you were there last evening, and again today!' Marcus had relaxed enough by now to be picking at the dates and wine the doctor had sent for earlier. He made no attempt to share them, but I was reassured. Up until this moment he had been too tense to eat.

'Excellence, I have not denied that I was in the street,' my slave-girl said. 'But I have never been inside the house. It was obvious the place was under guard. There was a group of soldiers on the corner of the road: they had been there all day, the servant said, and it was clearly Numidius's house that they were watching. They questioned all the slaves when they went in and out. The cook-woman we spoke to said they'd stopped and questioned her the minute she left the house, and that was why she'd come to the market so late.'

Marcus was looking furious again – but this time at the

guard. 'Surveillance of a property is not a lot of use if it is obvious to everyone that you're watching it,' he said. 'So, Cilla, you saw the soldiers. What did you do then?'

'Well, naturally we went away again – but not before they'd had a good look at us. It was clear that we'd get stopped if we went there again, so my mistress came up with a plan. I would go to the house, this morning, and make myself conspicuous outside. The guards would stop and question me, she said, and she would take the opportunity to approach the house. It worked, as well. As I was being marched away, I saw a servant let her in.'

Philades had been listening impatiently to this and now he could contain himself no longer. 'This is blatant nonsense, Excellence. The truth is clearly this – Libertus has some connection with Lallius. The girl has just admitted a con- spiracy to avoid the guard, and get her mistress into Numidius's house without their seeing her. Is that the action of an honest citizen?'

I had been thinking that the girl's account did not argue much intelligence on the watchers' part. Obviously the same thing had occurred to the burly soldier, too, because a dull flush was creeping up around his ears and he looked so mortified that I was almost tempted to a smile. Knowing that Gwellia was safe had made that possible.

The doctor's, next words, however, wiped amusement from my face. 'And now we learn that Numidius is ill. Libertus has just been suffering from a fever too. I wonder if that is significant?'

Marcus turned to me and his tone was urgent and intense. 'Libertus. Tell me the truth. Have you ever had dealings of any kind either with Numidius or with his son?'

That was difficult. Naturally, like any tradesman in the

town, I had dealt with the coin inspector once or twice. 'Only with the coin inspector, Excellence,' I said apologetically. 'And only in the normal course of business.'

Philades had sensed my hesitation and he pounced on me at once. 'You see, Excellence? He knew the family. He can't deny the fact, Indeed, his wife has gone to visit them this very day, and his slave-girl was arrested at the house. The same slave-girl that I saw standing at the roundhouse gate talking to the wet nurse, who then disappeared. It is time to stop pretending. I formally accuse this man of criminal complicity in the abduction of your wife. Let's hear what he's got to say to that!'

Chapter Seventeen

For a moment I had nothing to say at all. I was incapable of speech. I could not have been more shocked and terrified if the painted birds and cherubs on the frieze round the wall had suddenly detached themselves and flown across the room.

For this was very serious indeed. A formal accusation of that type, made before a person in authority and in the presence of the man accused, is legally all that is required for an arrest – though Marcus, as a senior magistrate, had discretion to decide whether a prosecution should proceed. I remember thinking that this ordered atrium, with its fine mosaics and gilded sacred niche, was a strange place to find oneself effectively on trial.

Marcus, too, was staring in astonishment. He had been nibbling at a date but now he sat transfixed, as if the words had turned him into stone with his hand halfway to his mouth. There was a pause before he put the remnant down, drew himself magisterially erect and said, in his coldest, most unbending tone, 'I regret, Libertus, that you have chosen not to mention Myrna's visit until now. Cilla, is it true?'

Even the burly guard could see that the tone of questioning had abruptly changed. He stepped forward, seized Cilla by the hair and hauled her roughly to her feet. 'Answer His Excellence,' he snarled, thrusting her forward as he spoke.

Cilla's head was forced backwards by his grasp but through gritted teeth she stammered out, 'I don't know anything about a nurse. Ow, let me go!'

The soldier did not relax his grip.

Philades said coldly, 'Don't tell us lies, girl. Nothing you can say will protect your master now. I saw you with the woman only yesterday, when I came with the litter to escort Libertus here. I saw you talking to her at the gate.'

Cilla said, 'That woman? I remember her – ow! – at least I could do, if I had a chance to think, instead of having my hair pulled out by this man.' She was forced to speak to the ceiling, as she could not look at us.

My patron nodded at the soldier, and he let her go – though not without a spiteful parting yank.

'So now you do admit it?' Marcus barked.

Cilla's eyes had filled with tears of pain. 'I didn't know she was the wet nurse here. She didn't say she worked for you. She certainly wasn't here when I was – Julia had another woman then. Excellence, I swear, I didn't know. I thought she'd come about a pavement. She wanted the mosaic-maker, she said.'

'So you admit that she had business with your master?' That was Philades.

Cilla nodded. 'She asked to see him, as they always do. It has happened several times since he's been ill. So I said what I always say: "It's quite impossible. He's been very ill. He's resting at the moment and can't be disturbed." I asked if it was a commission, and she said it was – "And a very urgent one as well, and nobody but Libertus Flavius will do. He'll want to see me when he knows what it's about." Well, I've heard that before, as well. I was quite stern with her. "If it's about a pavement, it will have to wait. You can come back in a day or two," I said. I didn't want to put her off too much. My master was getting a little better, after all, and I thought he might want the commission, later on – obviously he hasn't earned since he's been ill.'

Marcus had been listening to this narrative with care. 'So you told her to come back later on? And what did Myrna say to that?'

'Myrna, is that her name? She wasn't pleased. In fact, she went quite pale and jumpy suddenly – I thought her master must be very cruel, and that she was expecting to be whipped when she got home for failing to deliver the message properly. I felt quite sorry for her. So I said, "You can leave the details with me. I'll see he gets the message when he's better." But that wasn't good enough. "I have to speak to him myself," she said, as sharp as she could be. "I'll come back a bit later on this afternoon, if there is a chance he'll be awake. I tell you, you'll regret it if you don't let me see him soon." ' Cilla had never been trained in rhetoric but she had a natural sense of theatre: she told this story as if talking to a child, altering her tone for every speaker and acting out each part.

Marcus acknowledged the performance with a nod. 'And?'

'Well, I was a bit annoyed, to tell the truth. Talking to me in that sort of voice, when all I wanted was to help her out. So I went all official. "I'm afraid it won't do you any good at all," I said. "He's going to the villa of his patron later on today." And just to make sure she got the point, I added. "That's His Excellence Marcus Aurelius Septimus. You can see the litter now, just coming down the lane." Well, I could see from her face she was impressed, and she starting backing away from me at once. That'll teach her to have a bit more respect, I thought, and so it did. Next thing I knew she'd scuttled off without a word.'

Philades was visibly impatient. He gave a derisive snort. 'Excellence, how long are you going to listen to these lies? It's quite clear that Myrna went to the pavement-maker's house. Even this slave admits the fact. And an hour afterwards, at most, your son mysteriously reappears. Myrna has always seemed suspicious to me. She was the one servant who was anywhere near Julia the day she disappeared – and she was conveniently in the kitchens at the time. Then, when you send for her again, she can't be found. Do you really believe this is coincidence?'

'But I've never spoken to the wet nurse,' I protested. 'You heard what Cilla said. She didn't get a chance to speak to me, even if she did come to the house.'

'All the more suspicious,' the doctor said, in a most unpleasant tone. 'Clearly some arrangement was already made. Excellence, you heard the maidservant. It's clear the roundhouse was the centre of all this. There have been several people calling there, she says, on the pretence of wanting pavements made. Do you believe that they'd come all that way, when there are other pavement-makers in the town?'

'My master is renowned for miles around,' Cilla said stoutly. It was meant in my defence but it earned her another vicious shove.

'Silence!' Marcus snapped the word. He turned towards me and his eyes were cold. He had slipped on the role of impartial magistrate as certainly as if he were in the courts. 'Libertus, it pains me to have to say so, but this does look bad for you. The doctor's right. Myrna calls at your house, and shortly afterwards my son appears again – with you. Then your slave and your wife are found at Lallius's house, and Lallius is clearly implicated in the kidnapping.'

'But, Excellence . . .' I had half started from my stool, but a gesture from Marcus sent me to my knees, another petitioner alongside Cilla on the floor. 'I swear that I know nothing of any of this.'

'He's lying, Excellence,' Philades said, and his lips twisted into that strange smile again. 'I should warn him that I have other evidence against him, which emerged while you were out. More than enough to have this accusation brought to court.'

'Evidence?' My patron and I exclaimed in chorus.

The medicus gave another of his smiles. 'Excellence, it is more than evidence – it is outright proof. As soon as this girl was brought here by the guard I remembered where I'd seen her earlier. I asked the officer commanding to send two of his mounted escorts back at once to search the mosaic-maker's house again.' He glanced at me. 'And to do it properly this time.'

Marcus looked annoyed at this – it was not the doctor's place to organise the guard – and I was about to make a feeble protest too, but the medicus held up his hand. 'Excellence, I presumed on your authority a little, and I apologise. But hear me out. I know that you were there in person a little while ago, but I knew that you would not go inside the house yourself, and if there was anything to find the pavement-maker would obviously not produce it. And I think you will agree that I was justified. He has been a party to everything – as, Excellence, I hope to prove to you. If I may have a servant . . . ?'

'But . . .' I began.

'Silence, pavement-maker!' my patron barked at me. My heart sank to my sandal-soles. He would never normally address me in that way.

He clapped his hands together, and at once Minimus and

Maximus appeared – so quickly that I was left in little doubt that there'd been listeners in the court with their ears pressed eagerly against the door. News would be round the villa in a trice. My patron took their alacrity for granted, as he always did. He gestured for the medicus to instruct them what to do.

'Fetch the bag that was brought back from the roundhouse earlier.'

'Bag, Excellence?' I echoed stupidly. I might have tried to rise, but a push from the burly guard reminded me that this was not a good idea. 'I noticed that a bag was missing from the house, but I supposed that Gwellia had taken it.'

'A clever answer, citizen, as I might have expected from your lips. But this is no bag of yours,' the doctor said, his pinched face sharp and shrewd.

I was surprised by the wave of helpless fury which washed over me. All this, I was convinced, was his doing in some way. He had set out to undermine my patron's trust in me and he seemed to be succeeding. I wondered what the famous 'proof'would be.

We had not long to wait. The two boys were back in what seemed no time at all. With them was a lanky soldier, in burnished uniform. He carried his helmet underneath one arm, and in the other hand he was holding an enormous leather bag, straight before him at arm's length, as though it were some sort of ceremonial.

He marched up to Marcus and drew smartly to a halt. 'In the name of his most imperial divinity, the emperor . . .' – and so on through Commodus's growing list of names and honorifics (he was even calling himself 'Hercules' these days), finishing breathlessly, 'Cavalryman Rectus, reporting as requested. Excellence!' He held the bag out for inspection. It was a fine drawstring one, of a quality and size that isn't often seen. Not by me, certainly.

Marcus looked levelly at me. 'Well?'

I shook my head. 'Excellence. I swear by all the gods. I have never seen that bag before. It's . . .' And then, of course. I realised what it was. I felt myself go pale. 'Is that the bag you put the ransom in?'

'He's feigning. Excellence. He knows quite well it is.' The doctor had half risen to his feet, and turned triumphantly to Marcus. 'Wait until you see what was found inside. With your permission, Excellence, that is?'

Marcus nodded. The soldier placed his trophy on the ground and took two smart steps backwards. Everybody watched.

Philades took the bag and slowly opened it, and – in the manner of a market conjurer – drew out a small embroided garment. There was a gasp. An infant's long-sleeved tunic. And then a little woollen cap with ties under the chin. I watched with horror as the doctor added to the pile, finishing with a pair of tiny leather shoes and a hooded cape with gold embroidery – the very miniature of Marcus's own. There was a hush until, after what seemed an eternity, Philades spoke again. 'These would belong to Marcellinus, I presume?'

My patron had turned as white as newly fulled cloth, though two angry spots were burning in his cheeks.

'Does this not convince you that this man was part of it?' Philades said.

'Do not believe him,' I begged.

Marcus looked at me. It was clear that he really thought he'd been betrayed. 'I should have listened to him earlier. He warned me that you were in the plot and that a fever could derange the mind. It distresses me to find he was right,

187

though I was loth to think so. I can scarcely believe it even now, but I cannot ignore the evidence of my own two eyes. Yet I cannot comprehend how you could plan all this when you were almost ready for the ferryman to take you across the Styx.' He turned to the soldier 'Where did you find the bag?'

Two steps forward and a swift salute. 'Sir! Stuffed into the woven fence that encircles the roundhouse. Just beside the gate and only half concealed. I dismounted and collected it while my companion went inside and searched the rest of the enclosure and the huts. There appeared to be nothing else to find, though he was very thorough, I believe. Sir!'

Meaning he had ransacked everything. I could not restrain myself any longer. Even before the soldier had moved back to stand beside the burly guard. I was already crying out. 'I swear that it was not there when we were, Excellence!' By now I was pleading for my life. 'Ask Junio . . .' I saw my patron's look of scorn. 'Ask Pulcrus – he was there! Ask your carriage driver. Patron, you were there yourself! If it was as badly hidden as this man suggests, someone would have seen it, wouldn't they?' I could see that my patron was considering my words, and a sudden inspiration struck me. 'Ask Malodius – he was holding the horses the whole time we were in the house – and he was standing right beside the gate.'

Marcus's expression did not change a whit. 'You two pageboys, fetch Malodius. Soldier, you may dismiss. Report to your commander.' All three obeyed at once.

There followed a long and anxious wait – hushed, except that my heart was thumping so I was sure that everyone could hear. I wanted to plead that the medicus had very likely contrived to have the bag and its contents found, but I knew that counter-accusations would do no good. The soldier had obviously found the bag exactly where he claimed. But who had put it there? I could see no way that Philades could have managed it himself. He could not have left the villa without someone seeing him, and doubtless there would be a dozen witnesses to swear that he had been here all day. I was still wrestling with this problem when Philades broke the silence, still arguing his case.

'Forgive me, Excellence, but even if Malodius did not see the bag, it doesn't prove Libertus innocent. It may be that he hid it in the fencing as he left. Ask yourself why he was so keen to call in at the roundhouse at all? Because he knew the bag was there, perhaps?'

'My wife was missing!' I protested.

Philades sneered. 'How convenient! And now the money's missing too. Excellence, consider. We only have this Cilla's word for it that there was no one in that house last night: someone picked up the ransom, after all. And we did find the bag, with your son's clothes inside.'

My patron turned to me. 'Libertus, I want to believe you had no part in this. But I fear that it is difficult to do. First my son is mysteriously returned to you, and not to me; then your wife and maidservant are seen to call at Lallius's house – indeed they scheme to do so and elude the guards; next I learn that Myrna has visited your house, although you swear you never saw her in your life – and now I'm faced with this! The medicus is right. I am forced to draw conclusions, am I not? These facts would be sufficient in a court of law to have you exiled to a barren island for life – if not to something a great deal nastier . . . Ah – slaves, there you are.'

This time it was Maximus who began. 'I regret to inform you, Excellence . . .'

'But Malodius is nowhere to be found . . .'

'They say he's gone out in the cart . . .'

'To take some land slaves out . . .'

'On your own instructions, Excellence,' the older page finished with a gulp, as if apologetic for having failed in his task. And then he added, in a solo rush, 'But he's put the body of the wet nurse where you told him to. It is dressed and ready for the pyre.'

'Never mind Malodius and what he saw or didn't see,' the doctor snapped. 'The point is that the bag was there. It is clear that . . .' He stopped and his face took on a sudden puzzled frown. 'Did you say the body of the wet nurse?'

The two redheads stepped forward. 'They've got her washed . . .'

'And wrapped up in a sheet . . .'

'With a few herbs from the kitchen and a candle at her head . . .'

'She's lying on a piece of board, all ready for the cart.'

'The female house slaves saw to it. They say that Malodius called them in and told them those were your orders, Excellence.' Minimus might have said more but his other half prodded him sharply in the back and he stepped meekly into his place again, beside the gilded pillar on the wall.

Marcus nodded vaguely. Obviously he had more important matters on his mind. 'I had forgotten that I'd ordered the cart out again. Why, what is the problem, Philades?'

The doctor was looking shaken. 'You asked me to have a look at Myrna, not half an hour ago.'

'Of course. It is clear the girl's been stabbed, but I would be interested in your opinion, all the same. She has been tortured, by the look of it. I would like you to examine her and give me your views.'

190

'But . . . ?' Philades was staring at me in that way he had. 'How long has she been dead?'

'You are better qualified than I am to determine that,' Marcus said brusquely. 'Not longer than a day, apparently, since you saw her alive yesterday at Libertus's gate.'

I gained a little courage from this brisk rebuke, and raised my head again. Something of interest had occurred to me. 'With your permission, Excellence, with regard to that. How did the doctor know that it was Myrna he saw? According to the household pages, he was never at the villa while she was working here. By the time he arrived, you had sent her home. So how could he have recognised her, as he says he did? And why didn't he mention it before?'

Philades gave me another of his looks and turned his back on me. He spoke to Marcus. 'With respect, Excellence, I did attempt to tell you. You would hear nothing against this citizen for which I had no solid proof. But now, perhaps, you are prepared to hear. And as to knowing who it was, she fitted the description of Myrna that I'd heard – and a wet nurse has certain features which are obvious, even if one is not a medicus. However, since the girl is lying in your stable block, it will be a simple matter to resolve. If I go and look at her I can tell at once if it is the girl I saw before.'

Marcus nodded. 'Do so,' he said, and the doctor went.

My heart sank. Whether this was the same girl or not I was certain that the medicus would claim it was. However, I summoned the last remnants of my strength and tried to conduct myself with dignity. 'Forgive me, Excellence. I do not trust the medicus to tell the truth. Permit Cilla to go with him and look at the body too. She can confirm his story – either way.'

191

Marcus looked stonily at me. 'You do not think that she would lie for you?'

'Well,' Cilla offered, 'Kurso saw our visitor, as well. He is the one who fetched me when she came – he's far too shy to speak to her himself, but he must have had a proper look at her. If you could send for him, he'd soon tell you the truth. He can't know what has been happening here, so he would have no reason to tell you any lies.'

Marcus considered this. 'And where is Kurso now?'

'I suppose he's in the workshop in the town. Or on his way back from Glevum with my mistress by this time. In any case he won't be hard to find.'

I took a chance and knelt a little more upright. The guard raised his hand, but Marcus bade him stop. 'You see, Excellence,' I urged, 'the girl offers you an impartial witness of her own accord. She knows that what she's telling you is true. Patron – mightiness – I swear by all the gods, I had no part in this. I didn't know the girl had come to me – I didn't know the bag was in my fence. I've never seen those little clothes before, and I have no idea who could have put them there.'

A cloud passed over Marcus's face. 'I wish I could believe you,' he said.

I seized on this tiny scrap of hope. 'Excellence, you said yourself, I have been very ill. How could I possibly have been involved?' I saw that he was weakening, and I said impulsively, 'Give me a day or two – that's all I ask – to prove my innocence.'

He looked at me. 'The doctor thinks I ought to have you in the cells. He has been telling me that ever since you came here yesterday. And certainly the facts look bad for you. But I still find it hard to understand how, when you were so ill . . .' He paused. 'Very well. I accede to your request. You may not leave the villa, unless under guard, but within the walls you may continue free. I will even consent to have you waited on and you may make enquiries of the servants as you wish. I hope you can convince me that my leniency in this is justified. You can do that best by bringing Julia back. Two days, that's all – or I'll be forced to reconsider. You understand?'

I noticed that he still talked about my 'bringing Julia back' as though it were in my power, but I nodded gratefully. 'You are merciful, Excellence.' I bowed my head.

He did not smile, but rose majestically and clapped his hands again. Servants and soldiers crowded in. 'Take the girl away and strike the chains from her. Junio, take this citizen to bed and let him rest. He looks in want of it. Pages, attend me to my bedchamber – I am in need of a little rest myself.'

Chapter Eighteen

Marcus was quite right. I did need to rest – though after what had just happened in the atrium I could see little prospect of a relaxing nap. I might have won a temporary reprieve, but I was shaken to my bones, and I was thankful for Junio's strong arm to lead me to my room. I could tell, from the expression on his face, that my slave needed no explanation of what had occurred.

'You heard?' I said, as we reached the bedchamber and he assisted me to sit down on the bed.

'Well, Maximus and Minimus were listening,' Junio said, stooping to unlatch my sandals, and then slip them off. 'They kept the rest of us more or less informed, until Marcus's chief steward came along and ordered us all over to the servants' room. After that, I think, he took a post outside the atrium door himself.' He helped me to lift my legs and I sank into the blissful comfort of the stretched goatskin mattress and soft feather cushions of the bed. At least I could lie down for a little while.

I pulled the covers over me, aware that my head was thumping and I was shivering and weak. Junio stirred the embers in the brazier, then came and tucked me in. 'I have ordered a cup of something warm for you,' he murmured. 'The kitchens are already making it and Porphyllia will bring it by and by. Now, master, do you wish to sleep, or would you prefer a chance to talk things through, in case I can help to clarify your thoughts?'

Did I wish to sleep? I would have given anything to slide into oblivion, but in my current state of mind it was impossible. 'There are so many unconnected elements in this,' I muttered, leaning back on to my pillows with a sigh. 'And I've just two days to come up with an explanation of it all, or Marcus swears that he will have me in the cells. I may never see Gwellia again – except on a barren island, in exile perhaps.' I did not need to add that if things went badly wrong, I might find my whole estate was forfeit to the state – and that included Junio and both my other slaves.

'There must *be* an explanation,' Junio said, placing my shoes beside the brazier to warm. 'Perhaps between us we can work out what it is.' He was keeping his back to me as much as possible, and I knew that he was afraid to meet my eyes in case he should betray the anxiety he felt. He need not have bothered. I could read the tension in his shoulders and in his sudden nervous business.

'Marcus obviously still thinks that I have contacts and could arrange to free his wife – thanks to that wretched doctor, I believe. That accusation is enough to put me in jail,' I said, with a shiver. I was feeling weak enough in all this luxury: a night in Glevum's draughty cells would be the end of me. 'And what transpired in the atrium today won't change his mind. Why should Myrna come to find me – supposing that she did? Me, of all people? I have never met her in my life.'

Junio, correctly interpreting my question as an invitation to come and talk things through as he'd suggested, abandoned his fretful activities and bustled over to squat down at my bedside on his usual perch. 'Let's start from the beginning, and consider all the facts.' He gave me a disarming grin. 'It is a technique my master taught me once, and I know that it has helped him on more than one occasion. So, Julia and Marcellinus are in the court one afternoon, when suddenly they simply disappear. No one sees them leave the premises, and no one unexpected comes or goes.' He numbered these statements on his fingers as he spoke.

'Only plainly that's nonsensical, unless there is some sorcery afoot,' I said. 'People do not simply vanish. Yet it seems impossible that they passed the gate-keepers.'

Junio nodded. 'But they manifestly did. Marcellinus was returned to you outside the villa walls. So someone knew that you were coming here – which suggests that it was someone in this household, or your own. I think we are agreed so far?'

I nodded. 'I still think it was the doctor. He could easily have left the ransom note that was delivered here.'

'Anyone in the two households could have managed that.'

'But not the scroll which claimed that Julia and the boy would be released,' I said. 'That was left for Marcus at the basilica, after the announcement which set Lallius free. None of the slaves here could have put it there, but the doctor could have arranged it easily. He was with Marcus in Glevum at the time.'

Junio nodded. 'So was the pontifex, I understand. You remember he was staying here in the villa then. And the page – Pulcrus – he was there as well. And there was a carriage-driver too, I suppose.'

I frowned. 'Very well. All these people were in Glevum when that scroll arrived, but they were not outside the orchard when the litter stopped and the last message was thrown over the wall. The doctor was. Why are you so eager to defend him, suddenly?'

'I'm not. But even if he is involved there must be someone else. He can't have done the kidnapping himself – he was not known here in the villa then, and his presence would have infallibly been noticed by the guards. He could not have been the person who returned the child to you, and certainly he wasn't Myrna's murderer. He has been accounted for inside the villa, or in Marcus's company – or yours – ever since you got into that litter yesterday.'

I grunted, unwilling to acknowledge the justice of his argument. 'So where is all this leading?'

'I want to make sure that there is nothing we have missed – nothing that we have failed to put together in our minds.'

I closed my eyes and said ungraciously, 'All right. So the pontifex and Pulcrus were in Glevum too . . . And Malodius perhaps,' I added wearily.

'Not Malodius. He only drives the cart. Marcus has a proper driver for his other vehicles. You know that, master. You were out with him today, and you have driven with Marcus many times before.'

My eyes snapped open and I stared at him. Of course, it was quite true. Marcus was always driven by a special slave on occasions when he was about his personal affairs and did not have a military gig and an official driver from the garrison. I had seen the man myself a hundred times, but I could not have described him in the least – beyond the fact that he was young and strong – though Jove knows that he was eye-catching enough, in the flamboyant crimson tunic, cloak and shoes that told the world his master was a very wealthy man.

How many other people had become invisible like this, I thought, by being so familiar that they were not seen at all? Something was nagging at the corner of my brain – something I should have noticed or enquired – but in my exhausted state I could not capture it. I decided to let Junio think instead.

'Go on,' I said. I permitted myself the phantom of a grin. 'Your master is clearly quite intelligent. There is a lot of sense in thinking systematically.'

He refused to be deflected from his argument. 'So, the scroll set out arrangements for the hostages' return, but suddenly there is a change of plan. Marcellinus is returned to you – alone, but well cared for, it appears.'

'Without his bulla, drugged with poppy juice and hidden in a dark, smelly basket with some filthy cloths?' I muttered. 'That doesn't sound like loving care to me.'

'But he was smeared with grease against the cold and he'd been washed and fed. Even Marcus is admitting that.'

I nodded. 'I have been thinking about that myself. The doctor's right, you know, about Myrna's having opportunity. She was alone with Julia and the child before they disappeared, and even if she didn't kidnap them herself, it's possible she colluded in some way – passed on a message, or something of the kind, so that Julia left the villa of her own accord. That would be much easier than smuggling people out.'

Junio nodded. 'We heard she was so frightened afterwards that she could hardly talk! That would make sense, wouldn't it? And someone had been caring for the child.'

I sighed. 'But then, to complete your little summary of events, Myrna was found this morning stabbed to death, clearly the victim of the kidnappers herself. So that theory doesn't work at all.'

Junio interrupted. 'But perhaps it does!' He was speaking

eagerly. 'Suppose that Myrna *was* involved – but in a different way? Suppose that she worked out where the kidnappers had gone, and somehow managed to extract the child? She hid him somewhere – in that house of hers, perhaps; there was a room which had been cleaned and swept – did her best to care for him, and then came to your roundhouse and tried to speak to you, because she wanted to arrange to send him back.'

I was thinking very slowly still. I closed my eyes. 'All right, I allow that to be possible. So why not come directly to the villa here? Surely that would have been the natural thing to do? She would have earned eternal gratitude and very likely a good reward as well.'

He considered for a moment. 'Maybe the problem was in getting here – if the kidnappers were somewhere nearby. In the woods, perhaps, since that is where they claimed the ransom from. It might explain why she was murdered too, if they found out what she'd done and caught her afterwards.'

I thought about that for a minute. I could see a hundred flaws in it, but it did have a kind of logic – and that had been missing from everything so far. 'There may be an element of truth in what you say,' I murmured. 'But it doesn't prove that Philades was not mixed up in it.'

'On the contrary. It was his arrival with the litter which scared the wet nurse. off. That would fit our theory very well. If Myrna knew that the doctor had planned the kidnapping she would not wish to meet him at your house. Especially not if she was hoping that you would take the boy.'

'But he saw her anyway . . . and we know what happened next. If you are right, she was immensely brave to try to come to me at all. She must have guessed the kind of people she was dealing with.' I shook my head. 'Why would she put her life at risk like that?'

'She would be terrified for Marcellinus, too.'

'So when she couldn't see me face to face, she seized what opportunity she had? Thrusting him at me in the litter to get him safely home? She knew that I was coming here because Cilla told her so.' I nodded. 'There are questions left unanswered, but it makes a lot of sense. Well done, Junio.'

I knew that he was flattered, but he brushed my words aside. 'Of course I realise that it doesn't help us very much, even supposing that any of it's true. Myrna's lying in the stables, dead, and she can't answer any questions now. We don't know who carried out the kidnapping or how. We certainly don't know where Julia is.'

'What could have led Myrna to the kidnappers?' I said. 'Something that she saw in Glevum yesterday, perhaps? I wonder . . .' I was interrupted by a knocking at the door, which opened to reveal a dumpling face and a bowl of something steaming on a tray.

I was about to tell Porphyllia to come in, but she had not waited to be asked. She was already in the room.

'This is for you, citizen,' she said, affording me the briefest curtsey before turning to gaze at Junio with adoring eyes. Perhaps I blinked for an instant because she hurried on. 'Oh, I think your master is asleep. Where shall I put this? I'm allowed to stay. I'm going to be his poison-taster, like he promised yesterday.'

I had indeed intended to speak to Marcus about appointing her, but with all the happenings of the day it had completely slipped my mind. I doubted that he would now permit me such a thing, especially with Cilla on the premises. If I were to have a poison-taster, he'd expect me to use her.

I explained this to Porphyllia, though without regret.

She dimpled. 'Oh, don't worry yourself about that, citizen. Of course, I know you're in disgrace, but I arranged it earlier. I told them yesterday that you wanted me, and the chief steward was instructed, then, that you were to have anything you required. So here I am. I think he was glad to find a job for me, if truth were told. And there's nothing the matter with the broth because I've already tasted it.' She gestured to the tray. 'It's barley soup with chickpeas, lentils, onions, peas and beets, and cabbage leaves on top. It doesn't taste of very much without the fennel seed and cumin, but the cook says that's how it has to be. The medicus has forbidden herbs and spices in your food. They'll put some in this afternoon, of course, before it's served tonight.'

She had passed the tray to Junio as she spoke. It was not the simple painted wooden board which Maximus and Minimus had carried earlier, but a much more grand device, made from beaten metal shaped into a disc and ornamented with designs round the rim.

Porphyllia caught my glance. 'Pretty, isn't it? It was the mistress's favourite. It's the one she used for lunch the day she disappeared. Not that she ever had anything very much. Usually only fruit, or bread and cheese or a plate of cold cooked meat. Or just occasionally a little soup if the weather was particularly cold.'

I nodded. Marcus himself rarely ate more than that in the middle of the day, preferring to save his appetite for the evening meal, which always ran to many courses, even when he did not have guests to dine. This lunchtime broth which Porphyllia had brought had obviously been ordered on my express account, and following the medicus's guidelines, too. I was prepared to be quite heartened by that thought until it occurred to me that, in order for the soup to be cooked in time for lunch, the instructions must have been given shortly after dawn – long before my present troubles had begun.

Junio picked up the bowl and spoon and came to occupy the stool. 'Try to eat some, master,' he implored.

I motioned to Porphyllia to eat a little first. I had no compunction about doing so. Apparently she'd already tasted some, with no effect. Anyway, once a poison-taster is in place it is almost certain that food is safe, since there is no value in its being otherwise. But she was clearly anxious to fulfil her role, so I permitted her to do it and then fell to myself.

It was in fact delicious: warm and nourishing and tasting of nothing but the main ingredients. It appealed to me far more than the highly seasoned version which would appear on my patron's dining table later on that night. The Roman habit of smothering every flavour under spice and herbs has never especially appealed to me – though it was obvious my taster felt otherwise. She kept apologising for the blandness of the meal.

'I'm sorry if that was boring, citizen,' she muttered for at least the twentieth time. 'I could have got you some garum, I suppose, and you could have mixed it in – if we didn't tell the doctor, he would never know. It would have given it a little bit of taste, and I'm sure a tiny drop of garum couldn't hurt.'

I smiled weakly. I knew that she was trying to be kind. Garum, made from sun-fermented fish – and spice, of course – is served at every Roman meal and beloved of every Roman I have ever met – but rotting fish entrails never did appeal to me, even at the best of times. The thought of it at present made my stomach heave.

She saw my expression and misunderstood. 'Well,

liquifrumen, I suppose I ought to say. The mistress always insisted on the most expensive kind – twice-filtered and made with the finest anchovies. She always added it to anything too bland. In fact she put some in her soup the day she disappeared – I remember Myrna coming in for it. Mind you, that was a bad omen too. You shouldn't bring things from another room and add them to a dish after you have started eating it.'

Something slotted slowly into place within my brain. 'Do you mean that she was served with unspiced broth that day? Surely that must have been unusual?' I could not imagine Julia, the epitome of style, choosing to eat unfashionably unseasoned soup, as peasants did.

Porphyllia waved an airy hand. 'Well, she'd ordered soup for dinner, rather than for lunch – but, as I say, the weather was unusually cold. The master was at the *ordo* meeting and not expected back till dark, so she'd ordered a warming dinner to be prepared for him that night – roasted fowl with apricots, and peas with cumin sauce, among other things. All wasted effort, too. When he came home and found his wife was gone, he didn't eat a thing – just sacrificed a little to the gods.'

'And then the servants had to finish up the rest?' I said, realising why Porphyllia had been so certain of the menu. Slaves are not usually fed such splendid fare, but Marcus is frugal in his habits and I knew that he would not have permitted good food to go to waste.

She flashed me a conspiratorial grin. 'And very nice it was. Anyway, the soup was in the kitchens at midday – rather like today – waiting for the cooks to add the herbs, and the mistress sent Myrna down to fetch her some for lunch. And a bit of garum to go with it – though the mistress hardly touched it in the end. Worn out from being in the carriage, I suppose. I know she had a headache and went straight to rest.'

I stared at her. 'Are you telling me that Julia was ill?'

She shook her head. 'Nothing as serious as that. In fact, I helped her dress that morning and she was in the peak of health, but she was very tired when she got home again. I think that it was just because the day was very chill and because she'd got a headache from being in the coach. There's a lot of dust about, this time of year, and it can get in your throat, especially when you're being driven through the countryside and get off the proper roads. That's why Roman matrons often wear a veil – apart from decent modesty, of course. It keeps the dust out of your face and hair, and the mistress was so careful with her looks.'

Modesty? Despite the desperate situation I was in, I almost smiled. Julia was a lot of things – beautiful, charming and intelligent – but modesty was not her greatest attribute. I forced my mind back to the question of the soup.

'So your mistress wasn't following anyone's advice in asking for bland food that afternoon? She wasn't adhering to Celsus's famous scrolls?' I pretended to lie back in the bed and close my eyes, but in fact I was watching her reaction carefully. I had been hoping to learn that the medicus had somehow been an influence in the house even before Julia disappeared. I was disappointed.

My poison-taster laughed. 'We hadn't heard about all that by then. Anyway, she wasn't really ill. A little tired and headachy perhaps, but nothing more. She simply went and had a rest while Myrna fed the child, and after that she seemed to be all right. Certainly, it didn't stop her coming out to the court and playing with the boy – and she would never take a risk where he's concerned.' She flashed another glance at Junio, and added in a soft, suggestive tone, 'He was very precious to her, as you know.'

Junio flushed and turned to me at once, the embodiment of brisk efficency. 'Would you like us to send for more soup, master?' he enquired. 'Otherwise . . .' He put the empty bowl back on the tray, and held it out to her. As a clear hint that she could be dismissed.

But I was thinking about what she'd said. There was something – surely? – that was significant. I was certain of it, but in my current fuddled state I could not place it. 'Just a minute,' I said to Junio. 'Before she goes, I'd like to hear a little more about her memories of what Julia did that day.'

The girl put on a long-suffering face. 'Very well, citizen, since you ask me to I'll say it all again. But really there is nothing new to tell. One minute she was sitting in the court, with Marcellinus crawling at her feet – I saw her there myself – and the next thing I knew, they'd gone. Just as though they had suddenly grown wings – like flying ants or something.'

'I know all that,' I said, trying not to imagine Julia's face if someone compared her to a flying ant. 'That isn't what I meant. Junio was talking a little while ago about thinking logically. Start at the very beginning of the day.'

Porphyllia stole another look at Junio, as if commiserating with him for having a master who was obviously insane, and then said stolidly, 'As you command. Where would you like me to begin?'

Junio returned her glance steadily. 'There is a reason why my master asks you this. We have a theory that Myrna might have seen something – something she didn't think about till afterwards, but which later led her to the kidnappers. And if she noticed it, you might have seen it too, even though you did not realise it. So tell us everything you can about that day – any little detail which occurs to you. Don't worry if it doesn't seem significant.'

Porphyllia looked first doubtful, and then terrified. 'I suppose it's possible. Poor Myrna . . .' She broke off suddenly. 'You think that might be why she met her death?'

'We're considering the possibility,' I said. She hesitated still.

It was Junio who found the way to loosen her tongue. 'So you see why it is important to tell us everything,' he urged. 'You may know something that is dangerous to you, without your knowing it! If you tell us you make it harder for the kidnapper. He'd have to silence all of us to make sure he was safe.'

This logic was too much for her – or, on second thoughts, perhaps it was not the logic after all. I suspect that she would have jumped off the Tarpeian rock if it was Junio who had suggested it. She looked into his eyes. 'In that case . . .' she began.

Chapter Nineteen

Porphyllia was not the most concise of narrators, but like Cilla she told a lively tale and I learned more than I wished to know about Julia's toilette – not only the perfumed water with which she bathed her face ('the chill taken off it, citizen, and fresh rose petals floating in the bowl'), but the ear-scoops, the pointed rod for loosening the wax and the tweezers for removing facial hair. I learned how Porphyllia herself had mixed the white lead and red ochre which gave Marcus's wife her artless pink complexion, helped to pin the curled and braided wig exactly into place to give that effortless look of elegance, and fetched the kohl, the lamp-black and the ash that her mistress used to make her eyes look larger and her eyebrows lustrous. There were a good many diversions and embellishments in the telling, but I had asked for detail and I was getting it, until by the end of it I felt that I could have done the job myself.

Porphyllia broke off and looked earnestly at me. 'Is this the sort of thing you want to know?'

'I find it most informative,' I said. I meant it, too. Julia was beautiful, there was no doubt of that, but I'd never look at her loveliness with quite the same eyes again. I had a sudden memory of my dear Gwellia, rinsing her face and hands in cold water from the stream and content with the natural beauty she was fortunate to have. My lovely wife. Where was she? And what was happening to her?

I was so immersed in my anxiety that I was almost surprised to hear Porphyllia again. 'You want me to tell you any more?'

I had to force myself to concentrate. 'Of course. Go on – so your mistress was washed and clean. What happened next?'

We heard, at length: how Julia had rejected various other gowns ('too hot, too heavy or too short') before she finally selected the lilac *stola* from which we'd seen the strip; how she'd chosen a dramatic blue overtunic to set it off; and how the girdle, which we'd found so tragically, had to be tied and retied a dozen times before the knot was right. Then there was the jewellery to be chosen for the day – a bracelet, necklets, hair ornaments and rings, selected from the boxes which the servants brought – and perfumed oil to be applied behind the ears and on the throat, until finally, with the addition of a pair of pretty leather slippers on the feet, the lady was prepared to face the day.

'She chose her finest woollen *palla* – a pretty blue cloak that would fold to make a hood – and had it put aside for later when she wanted to go out . . .' Porphyllia had just reached this enthralling stage in her narrative when there was a gentle tapping at the door, and a dishevelled Cilla sidled in. She had been given a clean tunic and her arms and legs were washed, but she was still bruised and battered, and my heart went out to her.

She crossed to my bedside and flung herself at my feet. 'Master, forgive me if I did not help your case. I tried to do what my mistress instructed me to do – but I see that I did not assist you much. I seemed, if anything, to make it worse, although I told them nothing but the truth.'

I took her hand and motioned her to rise. 'They struck the irons off?'

She nodded. 'The medicus has given me some balm to rub into the place – apparently your patron ordered that he should. And they told me that I was to come and wait on you. Though I see that you already have a female slave at your command.' She glanced towards Porphyllia, who dragged adoring eyes from Junio long enough to acknowledge this comment with a smirk.

'This is one of Julia's handmaidens,' I explained. 'She has been assigned to me as a poison-taster while her mistress is away, and she was telling us about what Julia did the day she disappeared.'

'We thought it might be useful,' Junio added, with a smile. He made an obvious attempt to look Cilla in the eyes, but she turned away from him and spoke to me.

'Then I must not interrupt you, master,' she observed. 'Though of course I worked for Julia too, for years, before I was given to you. You never know, I may be able to assist.'

Porphyllia, listening, turned pink and scowled. I gave an inward sigh. Dealing with one infatuation was enough, but now there was clearly rivalry abroad. I longed to assure Cilla that Junio's heart was safe, but of course I could do nothing of the kind. Instead, I motioned Cilla to the stool which Junio had left. She looked as if she needed to sit down.

'Master, you are very good,' she said, and sat.

I invited my little poison-taster to go on with her tale. 'As you were saying . . .'

'As I was saying,' Porphyllia spoke rather more loudly than was strictly necessary, 'Julia called for breakfast in her room.'

211

'Bread and fruit and watered wine,' Cilla supplied swiftly, from her perch. 'That's what she always had.'

Porphyllia was scowling, and I tried to mediate. Rivalry for Junio might have one good effect – the two girls were competing as to who could tell me more. 'She ate that alone?' I said, addressing my question to Porphyllia.

'Apart from myself – because I brought it in – and the girl who had been watching Marcellinus through the night. But by the time she'd finished, Myrna had arrived, so that slave could be dismissed. Then the other girls came in, and we were all given our allocated tasks and sent away. And then . . .' The dumpling stopped, and looked a little nonplussed. She thought for a while and then said in a rush, 'I suppose that's all I know. Later on the carriage came for her. I wasn't the one summoned to help put on her cloak and veil, so I didn't see her go, but I knew that she had gone out to visit friends.'

'Taking Marcellinus with her?' I asked.

An enthusiastic nod. 'She was visiting the house where Myrna used to work, and she always took the boy when she went there.' Porphyllia balanced the empty tray against her hip and tossed her head, as if to flaunt the fact that she was the proper centre of attention here. 'And she wanted to buy some teething herbs for him as well.'

'She must have taken an attendant,' Cilla said. 'The mistress wouldn't travel anywhere without a slave.'

'Of course she did. She took the wet nurse with her – as she always did, especially when she went to Grappius's villa. I know some people think she did it purposely, to demonstrate that she had Myrna now, but I don't think she meant to be unkind. She liked to show Marcellinus off, that's all. He was always pretty forward for his age – he could do all the

212

things that Myrna's daughter does and he's younger than her by a moon or more. And if the boy went, Myrna would go too. She was the obvious companion for the mistress then – whatever the other handmaidens may say.'

So Myrna was resented by the other maids, I thought – including, no doubt, Porphyllia herself. I noticed how adeptly the little dumpling had conveyed that impression while carefully distancing herself from any criticism implied. I understood. It is not wise for slaves to court the charge of speaking out against their mistresses.

I nodded. 'So you did not see Julia again till she came back?'

'Not really even then. I just glimpsed them coming in across the court.'

Cilla sniffed. 'Surely there was someone standing by, in case she wanted help with her cloak. In my time there would have been a frightful fuss if there was nobody waiting to attend on her.'

The other girl flushed. 'Well, of course we were ready to attend to her, but she just went straight over to her room.'

'And didn't she want someone on call outside the door? She always used to,' Cilla said.

The younger girl took umbrage at this implied rebuke. 'Two of the girls went over to report, but they were shooed away. The mistress had a headache and she wanted to lie down. She sent a message she was not to be disturbed. The boy was fast asleep in any case and she'd apparently decided that she would rest until he woke to take his feed, and call us later when she wanted us. And that was all. It was not unusual.'

Cilla laughed. 'Leaving you idle for the afternoon?'

'We all had jobs to do.'

I intervened again. 'But did you see Julia and the child again? Yourself?'

Porphyllia frowned with concentration. 'I'm sure I did. A little while after Myrna came over for the soup. I saw them playing in the court.'

'The court?' A thought had just occurred to me. I gestured to the door. 'Could you show Junio and Cilla exactly where they were?'

'But, master . . .' Junio had backed away towards the door, but now he stepped forward in alarm. I thought he was protesting at the idea of being paired off with his plump admirer in that way, but his next words came as a surprise. 'They wouldn't have been over here, would they? It would be the new courtyard, surely, in the private wing – where Marcus and the family have their rooms?'

Porphyllia and Cilla were both nodding now, in a moment of unexpected unanimity. 'That's where she always gave the child his airing after lunch,' the dumpling said. 'It's much more sheltered than the courtyard over here, and they aren't likely to be embarrassed or disturbed by any of the master's official visitors.'

Cilla was not to be outdone. 'Master, that's the very reason why Marcus had the new wing built – to have more privacy. He even had the summer dining room put over there as well, when Julia was expecting Marcellinus and could not generally been seen in company.'

I frowned. I should have thought of that before. Of course, there were now two courtyards in the house. Perhaps it was an indication that my brain was still not working perfectly, but somehow I'd assumed all along that it was the central court from which they'd disappeared. Yet I had been told repeatedly that Julia had just come from her room, and I should have known where that was nowadays. After all, I was enjoying the luxury of her former bedchamber myself! And it did make perfect sense. Julia would obviously prefer to sit out over there, I thought, remembering the pretty little garden, with its arbour and its shrine, sheltered on all sides by walls and full of fragrant plants and scented herbs.

Junio crossed anxiously to stand beside the bed. 'Does that make a difference to your thinking about the kidnapping, master? I should have thought it was more difficult than ever to abduct them from there.'

Porphyllia was still gazing adoringly at him, as though he were the Delphic oracle. She tore her eyes away to say to me, 'That's right. You can only get there from the passageway that leads through from the main part of the house.' Then she clamped her gaze on him again.

Cilla said sharply, 'But surely there's a back way out of there? There is a little gateway, isn't there, leading to the orchard and across the open fields? The path was there before the wing was even built. It's pretty difficult and unfrequented, certainly – it goes across ploughed fields and through the tangled woods – but it is possible to go that way.' She turned to me and grinned. 'Master, I seem to remember that you used it once yourself. Isn't that right, Junio?'

It was a deliberate attempt to exclude the other girl, by drawing on a shared experience. Cilla was quite right, of course: I had once used that path, escaping from hostile soldiers in the dark, though that was moons ago, when the new wing was first built and Marcellinus was only a few days old. However, it was not a story that I wished to amplify in front of one of Marcus's household slaves – especially one who babbled like a brook. I frowned at Cilla as a warning that she should hold her tongue. Junio, who also knew about my ignominious flight, caught my eye and winked con-spiratorially at me. But Porphyllia was not even curious, it seemed.

Instead she assumed a rather lofty air, as the only one who knew the present villa and its ways. 'It must be a long time since you were in that section of the house, then, citizen. The master had that pathway gated off moons and moons ago – certainly before he purchased me. He said that if it was possible for people to get out that way, it was possible for strangers to get in.' She gave the tray a little hoick against her hip, as if to emphasise a point well made.

Cilla was all false silkiness and charm. 'I heard him talk of doing that, even before I left the house. I think he was afraid of robbers at the time – there were reports of thieves and bandits in the forest round about. But the path led to the orchard, didn't it? The mistress used to like to go out there, especially when there was blossom on the trees. Surely the master didn't block that off?'

Porphyllia treated the interruption with disdain. 'There still is a path into the orchard and she still uses it – she used to take the baby there and let him see the geese – but it's had a gate put on it. These days there's no way out on to the farm except past the gate-keeper. The kidnappers could not have come and gone that way, if that was what you were thinking, citizen.'

It had occurred to me, of course. Erroneously, it seemed. 'And the man on duty saw nothing untoward?'

'Only the normal business of the day. Slaves taking laundry in and out, and produce from the farm. The master had him in his study for an hour for questioning – the poor man was quite shaken by the time he was released – but there wasn't anything he could report that afternoon. Not even any omens, like horrible old groping Onions at the front.' She spoke the nickname with disgust, as though it tasted of itself.

'Aulus is still here and at his tricks?' Cilla asked, with a look that said 'Fondling anything that's fool enough to let him?' as clearly as if she'd spoken the words aloud.

Porphyllia turned scarlet to her tunic-hems. 'No one likes that sort of thing.' She flashed a little glance at Junio. 'From Aulus, anyway.'

The boy exhibited such squirming embarrassment at this that I was hard put to it to suppress an inward smile. However, I kept my face as straight as possible, and stolidly pursued my questioning. 'So how is it that so many people say they saw Julia and Marcellinus in the courtyard of that wing? As you say, it was built for privacy. Surely the area isn't overlooked?'

It was Cilla who hastened to reply. 'Not from the main body of the house. But there is a store cupboard, just where the passageway comes out into the court – or there was in my day anyway. That's where the candles and the oil lamps for that wing were kept – fresh bedcovers and sleep herbs and all that sort of thing. Everything that might be needed over there.'

'And the cleaning sponges for the clothes.' Porphyllia was eager to give more information than her rival on the point. 'We maidservants were always in and out, to fetch them or the mending chest, or else the spare spatulas and bowls for mixing facial pastes.' She tossed her head at Cilla. 'And before you ask, there was generally one of us in earshot anyway. The mistress might have sent us all away but she did have a gong to summon us, and she would not have been best pleased if she had wanted something done and there was suddenly no servant to be found.'

'But that afternoon she didn't call on you, not even for the soup? Or the cooked fruit for Marcellinus?' I said.

The girl shrugged. 'She just sent Myrna, as she often did. In fact it was Myrna who persuaded her to introduce the gong – to keep the rest of us away, the others said. Not that I minded very much. It can be cold out in that courtyard, if you're simply standing by, waiting for somebody to find a job for you.'

Cilla raised her eyebrows, as if to say that servants in the villa nowadays were getting soft and self-indulgent. But a small connection was forming in my mind, like two pieces of pavement tile that fit together to form a pleasing shape.

'Cold,' I murmured. 'People keep telling me how cold it was. And yet she took the child into the court.'

'I know what the other girls are saying, citizen, but of course the mistress wouldn't take a risk. Myrna always advocated an outing after lunch. The inner courtyard's sheltered from the wind and the child was properly wrapped up.'

'Wrapped up?' I echoed. I was thinking of those little coverings which Philades had produced with such a flourish from the bag. 'Of course he was. Woollen coverings on his legs and hands, a long-sleeved tunic that must have reached at least to his knees, and a warm cap to cover his head.'

'That's right,' Porphyllia agreed. 'And the dearest little cloak and hood, all made of woollen cloth – I helped to stitch some of it myself. The mistress's very favourite it was – made to match his father's.' She stopped, confused. 'But of course you know that, you've seen it for yourself.' And then, because she was unstoppable, 'And then they took it off him when they sent him back. Poor little mite. It's a wonder he didn't catch his death of cold, despite that stinking grease they put on him.'

But I was hardly listening any more. 'Dear Jupiter!' I cried. 'Of course, you're right. Cold weather, headaches and a carriage ride. How could I be so stupid!' I was sitting upright now, fired with an unexpected energy. The beginnings of an almost incredible idea had just occurred to me. 'Junio, I think I see how it was done. I believe we've been asking the wrong questions all along. In fact, I suspect we were intended to.'

Chapter Twenty

'Master?' Junio was looking concerned and mystified, as though he were afraid that I was feverish again.

I shook my head, unwilling to commit myself any more as yet.

I turned towards Porphyllia, who was still standing with her tray, trying to look at once flirtatious and demure – neither of which were natural attributes of hers. 'Now, listen carefully,' I said. 'You say that you saw Marcellinus take an airing in the court. But are you sure of that? It seems to me that what you saw was just a muffled child. Were you close enough to see his face?'

The girl looked from me to Junio, as if alarmed that I had suddenly gone mad and she might need protection. 'But, citizen, of course it was Marcellinus I saw. Who else could it possibly have been?' She drew her breath in sharply and her eyes got very wide. 'You aren't suggesting that the gods sent some sort of changeling in his place? I've heard about that kind of thing, of course, but I never thought I would live to see . . .'

'Not exactly that,' I interrupted soberly. 'But something not so very different, perhaps. So I'm asking you again. Were you close enough to recognise his face?' I could see that she was ready to burst into speech again, but I prevented her by holding up my hand. 'Think carefully before you answer me. It is very easy to see what you expect.'

I had the satisfaction of seeing her reflect, and the dumpling face furrow into a troubled frown. 'Well, I'm almost sure . . . though, now you come to mention it, I couldn't swear before the gods that it wasn't possibly a changeling that I saw. It certainly looked like Marcellinus, though – that's all I can say. And surely his mother would have noticed it – after all, she was right there at his side.'

I glanced at Junio, and saw that he was following my thoughts, with a look of dawning understanding on his face. He nodded at me, mouth agape, and turned away to add some more fuel to the brazier which was burning down to chilly embers now.

I turned to Porphyllia again. 'And that's another thing,' I said. 'Did you see Julia, or just a woman in a cloak? If it was as chilly as you say, presumably she was wrapped up too?'

Porphyllia stared at me. 'Well, I suppose she had her hood pulled up. But, citizen, I would know the mistress anywhere. It isn't like a baby – the gods don't steal adults for sport. Anyway, she is conspicuous; you would know her in a crowd. From her hair if nothing else – even with her hood on you can always see a little of her hair, and there is no one else I know who has blond hair like that. And I remember distinctly seeing it that day.'

'But it's a wig,' I said. 'You told us that yourself.'

She looked abashed. 'I can't believe that it was anybody else. It was her cloak and *stola*, I am sure of that. I remember thinking that I'd have to clean them afterwards, if she let her hems drag in the mud. The fuller's boy had been the day before, and I didn't fancy taking them myself. It's a long walk at this time of year, when it is cold and windy on the road.'

'But don't I remember you remarking that, while she was

222

in the court, she accidentally let her ankles show? A bad omen, you called it at the time.'

'It wasn't Julia, then! My former mistress was very careful about things like that,' Cilla burst in unexpectedly. 'I remember how she would rehearse the things she had to do each day – clamber into a carriage for example, or climb public stairs – and reject a *stola* as unsuitable if she thought it might reveal immodest glimpses of her feet. We slaves would grumble and make jokes behind her back. Sometimes it would take her ages to decide.'

'And she is no different now – as Porphyllia told us a short time ago.' I felt as if someone had lit a candle in my brain – suddenly the mists had departed from my mind and I could see things clearly as I used to do. 'We know that Julia rejected at least one *stola* on that day because it was too short. And yet when she was in the court, her dress allows a piece of leg to show sufficiently for her maids to notice it. That suggests to me that Cilla may be right, and the second time it wasn't Julia at all.'

Junio had worked out the implications of all this. 'You mean, the kidnapping didn't happen that afternoon at all?' He was standing near the brazier with a piece of wood, ready to put it on the fire, but he was frozen into immobility.

I nodded slowly. 'I think it may have happened earlier, while Julia was out. That's much more likely, isn't it, in every way? Someone stopped her carriage, perhaps, and forced her out of it. And when it returned here, it brought back, not Julia, as everyone supposed, but somebody dressed up to take her place.'

Prophyllia put the tray down on the table with a clang. 'But that's preposterous. A thousand pardons, citizen – I mean . . . impossible. How could an impostor get in past the gate?'

'It seems at first sight to be an enormous risk, I know,' I said. 'But I think it might be possible if it was planned with enough care. Julia was going out for a visit in the morning to see friends. She wore a veil, you say?'

Porphyllia seemed inclined to take this as a personal affront. 'She's done so off and on the whole time I've been here,' she said, in a defensive tone. 'Depended who she was visiting, I think, and where. Though Cilla here will tell you different, I expect.'

Cilla shook her head. 'I have known her wear one, in winter especially. She used to say cold weather chapped her cheeks. Or when she was visiting a Roman home where there was an older woman in the house. It's what the older ones expect, when you are a matron with a child. Julia wouldn't cause gossip in the town – it might reflect on Marcus. Though she resented it. "What's the point of taking pains with how you look if no one's going to see you anyway?" she'd say. But it didn't totally conceal her face, as soon as you got close enough to see.'

'Which explains why Aulus was distracted from his post when the carriage came back through the gate,' I said – and then remembered that Cilla didn't know the tale. 'He was told that there were strangers hiding in the bushes up the lane so naturally he went along to look, while Julia and the carriage came inside – to safety, as he thought. Of course, no one paid much attention at the time, but in the light of what happened afterwards it seemed that there might really have been someone lurking there. But suppose it was a fiction, entirely designed to draw him for a moment from his post? It would allow the still-veiled "Julia" to alight and go inside while his attention was on something else.'

'But wasn't it Julia herself who claimed to see . . . ?' Junio began, and then he worked it out. 'But of course, she would not get down herself and ask Aulus to investigate. She would send the nurse. And, while he was looking down the lane, the impostor could alight and walk inside.' He put the wood into the brazier and stirred the fire, and the room was filled with the sweet smell of burning applewood. He dusted off his hands and turned to me. 'But master, what on earth would be the point of it? It's taking such a risk. There would still be lots of household servants to avoid and if Julia was to be captured anyway, why pretend that it was done at another time?' He paused, and put down the iron bar he'd used to poke the fire. 'Oh, I see. To do exactly what it did, in fact: to cause alarm and draw attention from the truth, and from the obvious conspirator.'

I nodded my approval. 'And that was . . .' I prompted.

'Well, Myrna, clearly,' Junio replied.

'Myrna!' Porphyllia exclaimed. 'But she's been murdered by the kidnapper – everybody in the household is aware of that. And the master is arranging a funeral for her. You can't mean that she was part of this all along?'

'If we have hit on the truth, then she had to be,' I said bleakly, recalling that Myrna had visited my house – and brought many of my present troubles on my head. That, and the memory of that distressing corpse, was enough to sap my feverish energy. I had been buoyed up by the excitement of my own deductions for a time, but suddenly I was weary to my bones. I shut my eyes. 'Junio can explain it to you, I expect.'

I heard his exasperated little gasp, and realised what I had done. I had intended it as simply flattery, but I'd given her the opportunity to make eyes at him again.

'Oh, would you, Junio,' she breathed, and Cilla coughed.
I heard him poke the fire savagely again. 'My master's
right,' he muttered. 'The risk was not so great. Once the
gate-keeper's attention is engaged elsewhere, Myrna escorts
the so-called Julia to her room – that was the most dangerous
moment, I suppose. After that, who sees her close again?
Two maidservants report a little afterwards, you tell us, but
they are sent away because their mistress has a headache and
wants to lie down.'

Cilla's voice – still sharp with jealousy. 'I imagine that if
we enquire, we shall discover that it was Myrna who came to
Julia's door and delivered that message to the slaves.'

'Well, of course she did,' Porphyllia replied. 'There was
nothing new in that. No one would expect the mistress to get
up herself.'

'Exactly!' Junio must have forgotten his embarrassment in
the joy of pursuing an idea. He was speaking with real
enthusiasm now. 'No one would think of questioning her
word. And she made a point of being with the child when it
was fed and was jealous of others being with him. That is the
point, of course: once she and the wet nurse were safely in
the room, there was no risk from anyone outside.'

Porphyllia looked grudging. 'So why go into the court?'

'Because it was part of the routine – and it was important
to the plan that they were seen, so that the alarm was raised
in the wrong time and place. And who brings that about?
Who attends the child and woman in the court, fetches soup,
and sees that all the other slaves have orders to be somewhere
else? Who conveniently comes to get the cooked fruit just at
the moment when the other two disappear? And, in fact,
who raises the alarm? Myrna, Myrna, Myrna every time!'

He was so animated and triumphant that he grinned at

dumpling-face, who flushed beneath her freckles and gave him an adoring smile for his pains.

He turned bright red himself, and turned to speak to me. 'So we must have been mistaken, master, when we thought that she had come to you for help. She was conspiring with the kidnappers all along. She must have been – if our theory is true. And it is the only explanation which makes any sense. Julia and Marcellinus didn't disappear – they weren't there in the first place.'

Cilla frowned. 'But it does not solve the mystery, all the same. Suppose that somebody did take their place. What happened to them then? It would be just as impossible for them to disappear as it would be for Julia and the child. More so, perhaps, because they would have to pass the gate-keepers, who would certainly notice if there were strangers in the house. And above all, if Myrna was conspiring with the kidnappers, who killed her, and why?'

I hung my head. 'I know,' I said. 'I thought of that myself. But all the same, I am convinced that in principle we're right. The child would pose no problem, if there was someone in the lane. If you went into the orchard you could pass it over the wall. And as for the woman, if she took off the cloak and *stola*, and was wearing a servant's uniform underneath, she could probably walk straight out of the gate, especially if she used the orchard path and seemed to have a proper errand to fulfil. Don't I remember hearing that there was a slave taking laundry to the fuller that afternoon? I wouldn't be surprised it that was it. That *stola* got out of the villa somehow – they tore a strip off it – and in a household of this size there must always be a few tunics wanting launder-ing, even if the fuller's boy has collected a load the day before, as Porphyllia says. Who would ever give a slave carrying such a bundle a second glance – especially if the whole household is busily engaged on a very active search for someone else?'

Porphyllia picked up her tray again. 'Well, I still can't believe it. Someone coming into the house and passing herself off as Julia? Who could it possibly have been, in any case?'

Junio met my eye and we replied as one. 'Myrna had a sister, didn't she?'

'It would fit,' I said, finding the strength to struggle up again, now that progress seemed to be in view. 'Marcus told us that she was the taller of the two. Taller than Julia, I think he said. That would explain why the *stola* was too short.'

'And she did come to the villa often, so she'd know her way about,' Junio said.

'And wasn't Myrna's little girl brought up to the villa just later on?' I said. 'She would be the obvious candidate to be the subsitute Marcellinus. She's only a little older than he is, and not a strapping child, apparently, so presumably they're much the same in size. Suppose her grandmother was waiting, outside in the lane. The child is stripped of Marcellinus's clothes – down to an undertunic, anyway – and handed out over the wall. It would be a simple matter then to wrap it up in something else, and come straight to the gates. Clever too, since it would divert attention from the family.'

'The grandmother came up with a herb basket, we heard that too. She could have concealed some clothing for the child in that, until the moment came. And the boy's finery would be carried out of the villa in the fuller's pile.' Junio was grinning with delight. 'It must be the solution, mustn't it? Will you explain to Marcus, master? He could send those guards out to arrest the girl, and then perhaps we'd learn the rest of it.'

I nodded. 'Unless the soldiers have already gone away.'

Surprisingly, it was Porphyllia who spoke. 'They are still here, citizen. They were given some refreshment in the servants' room – and if they'd left we would have heard them go. So they could go and arrest this sister if you wish – if you can persuade the master that there's any sense in it. Personally I don't believe there is. Though there might have been a changeling, I can see.'

'Thank you, Porphyllia,' I said. 'That will be all. You may take the tray back to the kitchens now. And Junio, get a message to my patron if you can. Tell him I have a theory about what happened but need his help to bring some suspects in. Ask if he will accord me a private interview.'

My slave-boy nodded and disappeared at once, whereupon Porphyllia, who up to now had been standing aimlessly with her tray, suddenly sprang into action and bustled out as well.

Cilla stood up from the stool and came to stand beside the bed. 'I could be your poison-taster, master, if you would prefer,' she murmured shyly. 'Now that I am here in any case.'

I smiled. 'Better to use the one I've got,' I said gently. 'Any would-be poisoner will be more deterred by the thought of harming one of Marcus's slaves. Anyway, I am glad to have her here, because she knows about the household and its ways. Besides, I'm hoping your mistress is coming very soon, and you will be wanted to attend to her.' I didn't add that I was longing for that hour.

'As you command, master, though I could do that too,' Cilla said, and I could hear the disappointment in her voice. 'Doubtless Junio wants that girl to be here, anyway.'

This time I laughed aloud. 'I don't think Junio would thank me in the least,' I said. 'But she did know Myrna, and she was here that day – and thanks to her we've made such progress as we have.'

'So, you really feel you've found the answer, master? Or a part of it?'

'I have the glimmering of an idea, at least.' I looked at her. 'You don't seem much convinced.'

She shook her head. 'It's just that . . . with the greatest of respect . . . what has Myrna to do with Lallius? A young man from the city – a spendthrift gambling lout with scarcely any friends, from what the servants say of him – and a wet nurse from the country, who rarely goes to town except to help her mother selling herbs. It seems most unlikely they have even met.'

I had to concede that she was right, of course, but I was too pleased with my reasoning to admit that there were flaws. 'Who knows?' I murmured sleepily. 'Myrna did work near Glevum for a time. Perhaps the two were lovers. There have been stranger things. Or perhaps she owed him money. I don't know. I can't be expected to work everything out at once.' I gave my pillow a disgruntled thump. 'Now,' I murmured, settling myself back on it and closing my eyelids for the second time, 'you take Junio's place till he comes back. Sit there quietly and keep watch and let me have some sleep.'

Chapter Twenty-one

The interview with Marcus did not seem quite such a wonderful idea when I awoke, but naturally by then it had been arranged. He had decreed a time, about mid-afternoon, and on this occasion he expected me to come to him. Junio explained this rather diffidently to me as he roused me and helped me with my shoes.

'I'm sorry that I had to wake you, master, but you see how it is,' he said, latching up my second sandal and assisting me to rise. 'He isn't coming to your room to visit you, the way he did before. I expect he feels that you are much improved – you managed very well this morning, after all.' He rearranged my tunic, which I'd been sleeping in, into a semblance of acceptable attire.

But I understood the message. With a serious accusation still dangling over me I was firmly in disgrace – especially after the doctor had produced that damning piece of so-called 'evidence'. Marcus had stretched his goodwill to the limits as it was, by allowing me two days to try to come up with some defence, and – what is more – to stay here in comfort while I did so, instead of languishing in misery inside Glevum jail. My patron had done everything he could, and I could look for no more friendly concessions from now on.

Junio was still fussing over me. 'I've borrowed this cloak for you from the servants' hall. It's Aulus's. It's rather on the large side, I'm afraid, but it's a very heavy one and it will protect your legs from the cold. Of course we'll be walking beneath the colonnade, but it looks like rain this afternoon and you mustn't catch a chill. Here, let me help you put it on. It must be time to go.' He draped the garment round me as he spoke. Junio was right: it was far too big for me – so much so that it almost brushed the ground – but it was welcome for all that. The courtyard felt extremely cold after the warm snugness of my sleeping room.

'No time to linger, master. There isn't any sun this afternoon, so it is hard to judge the hour, and we must not be late. Marcus was extremely crisp with me. He isn't very pleased with our household as it is.'

I gave an inward groan. I had been hoping to come up with some extra element of proof which would persuade my patron that my theory had some weight. If I was to clear my name, I desperately needed him to be sufficiently convinced to round up Myrna's family and bring them in – I had been forbidden to go out and look for them for myself. Nor did I expect that they'd be easy to find. If they had the ransom money, or any part of it, I reasoned that they would be miles away by now.

Still, I would face those problems when I came to them. My first task was to persuade my patron to accept my views at all. 'Lead the way,' I said to Junio.

Marcus was waiting for us in the winter dining room. He was stretched out on one of his dining couches with a goblet in one hand, languidly picking at a bowl of sugared figs. He had dressed for the occasion in an amber-coloured robe, with a matching over-drape, a sort of *synthesis* – rather like the fashionable combination toga-and-tunic which he wore to entertain. But he was no less intimidating for that.

I knew my patron well. There was no need for him to have changed his clothes, and the fact that he had done so was quite deliberate. He was clearly signalling to me, not merely that he was now a private citizen relaxing at his home and that this meeting was therefore an enormous privilege, but that he had deliberately set aside his civic and imperial offices. His patrician toga was a symbol of his rank, and his consequent position as senior magistrate to which Philades had formally appealed. Marcus was reminding me – as if I could forget – that he was condescending to this private interview because next time I met him in his official role he would be obliged to find that there was a case for me to answer and hand me over to the courts.

He scarcely raised his eyes when I limped in and made a deep obeisance at his feet. I didn't even stop to give Junio my cloak – a slave's garment made me look decently humble, I thought.

'Very well,' my patron said, and motioned me to rise. 'Junio says you wish to speak to me?' His tone was cool and quite impersonal and I realised that he had not extended his ring for me to kiss, as he would normally have done. More signals. That salute was the expected greeting between a patron and his loyal client – and Marcus was pointedly not affording me that status now.

'Excellence!' I murmured, almost in despair. 'Please believe that I had no part in this affair – despite everything the doctor claims. By diverting your attention to arresting me you only give the real culprits more chances to escape. After all, they have your money now. And remember that they still have Julia.'

'Do you imagine that I'd forgotten that? I have thought of nothing else for days and nights.'

I nodded. I knew exactly how he felt. Even now I was worried about where Gwellia was, and I wasn't getting ransom notes from ruthless kidnappers.

He took another fig and held his goblet out for Minimus to fill. Roman custom would usually demand that he should get the slaves to offer me the plate and fetch a drinking cup to pour some wine for me, but of course he did nothing of the kind. He was avoiding even glancing at my face. 'And Philades thinks you are responsible.'

I swallowed. 'The reason that I asked to see you this afternoon is that I have a theory about how it was done.'

'Let's hear it, then,' he said, biting the sugared fruit. 'But don't be long about it. I have a slave-trader coming here a little later on. He's bringing a girl for me to look at.'

I was startled for a moment. This seemed a strange time to be buying slaves. But then I understood. 'A new wet nurse for Marcellinus?'

He paused in mid-nibble to say, 'Of course. I need one as soon as possible, and I heard from the pontifex that he's got one for sale.' He took another bite and went on reflectively, 'I shall buy her, almost certainly, if she looks suitable and clean – she is supposed to have good teeth and no disease. I'm going to get the medicus to examine her for me, but she should be all right. This trader is a specialist – expensive, but he buys all his stock in Rome and only has the best. He deals with the wealthiest families in the capital. I've bought from him before. He sometimes has other commodities as well.'

He seemed to realise that he was chatting to me in the old familiar way. He stopped at once and cleared his throat. 'What is your theory, then?'

I spelt it out to him, exactly as I had thought it through myself – citing the clothes, the supposed strangers in the lane, and all the other suggestive details. My patron seemed surprisingly unmoved, I thought, so I urged the case with extra eloquence.

'So, Excellence,' I finished, 'it seems to me that the kidnapping took place, not from the villa, as we'd been led to think, but while Julia was out in the carriage earlier. That means that the wet nurse was party to the plot, and I think it was her sister who dressed up as Julia and Myrna's child who was playing in the court.' I outlined the theory as to how they got out again. 'Perhaps we should check with your gate-keepers once more.'

He nodded vaguely. I took this as encouragement, although he was still concentrating mostly on his fig.

I took a deep breath. 'So, with your permission, Excellence, I think that we should try to talk to Myrna's family. You may have to institute a search for them. There was no one at the house when we called there earlier, and I suspect they may have fled. It may be difficult to track them down, but it's likely that if we find them we'll find Julia as well.'

I half expected him to disagree with me, and swear that my theory was impossible. I was already marshalling my arguments to reply.

But all he said as he picked out another fruit was, 'It still sounds implausible to me, but I'm reluctantly compelled to think you may be right. You realise that I've heard all this before?'

I gaped at him. 'Excellence? You mean that Junio . . . ?'

He waved that suggestion loftily aside. 'Philades! He was arguing the same thing earlier, when he came to tell me it was definitely Myrna he saw talking to your Cilla yesterday. And then that little freckled girl came in, and he was sure she'd overheard and would report to you. He predicted that

235

you would come and see me and confess the truth – or at least a part of it – pretending that the theory had just occurred to you.'

'*Confess*, Excellence?' I almost squeaked the word.

'That was his expression for it,' my patron said. 'And here you are, exactly as he said.'

There was no possible reply to that, and I made none.

Marcus was deliberating on the choice of figs, as if this were a matter of imperial concern, and still refusing to look in my direction as he spoke. 'And Philades pointed out some other things as well, which you might find significant. Things that unfortunately aren't explained in your account at all.'

'Such as, Excellence?' I could scarcely breathe the words.

'He says that after the initial kidnapping something seems to have gone seriously awry. The kidnappers, for instance, had a sudden change of plan. You recall that they abruptly altered the arrangements for the hostages' return?'

I could only nod.

'And if Myrna was really a conspirator – and since you and Philades both think so, I am prepared to accept that she very probably was – then something had obviously gone very wrong indeed, because we found her murdered body in the barn. I don't suppose that even you could disagree with that?'

I said carefully, 'It does seem that something happened to disrupt their plans.'

He abandoned the fruit and took another sip of wine. 'So what could it have been? What change had occurred between the two events? Only one thing that I can think of – though it took the medicus to point it out to me. You left your roundhouse unexpectedly and came here to stay instead. Can you deny that he is right?'

I was so thunderstruck by this association of ideas that I could make no reply.

He met my glance, at last, and I realised that he had been drinking rather hard. His eyes, which had been red-rimmed with lack of sleep, were glassy now and bleared with wine. Marcus did not often drink too much, he was too mindful of his status and dignity, and that made it the more dreadful when he did.

Even as I looked at him he drained his globlet and held it out again for Minimus to fill.

'Your coming here was all arranged so suddenly. There would have been no time to let anybody know. And – as Philades observed – after that the kidnapping took on a different tone. Almost as if the mastermind was suddenly removed . . .' He trailed off, and gulped the contents of the replenished goblet down without a pause for breath.

'Excellence,' I pleaded. 'I was ill. I had only recently come back to consciousness. You know that yourself. How could I possibly have planned all this?'

He raised his wine-bleared eyes to mine again. 'Perhaps *you* should be explaining that to *me*, Libertus! You cannot possibly deny that your roundhouse was involved. Myrna, the ransom bag, the clothes – it all points to one conclusion, doesn't it? You don't expect me to believe it was coincidence and that some passer-by just happened to select your fence to hide those things in? As the medicus pointed out to me, there must be a thousand better hiding places in the forest round about.'

He had a point, of course, but I had no solution to advance. Unless someone wanted to implicate me, and had arranged everything to that end – in which case I could suggest one obvious candidate. But unsubstantiated counter-claims would do more harm than good. 'Excellence, all that I can say is that it wasn't me.'

'I would like to believe that, Libertus, more than I can express.' He put the goblet down. With great deliberation he picked up a fig and tore it delicately in two. 'There is one other possibility, I suppose, though I have not said this to the medicus. Could it have been one of your household, do you think? Cilla, perhaps – she had connections here? Or . . .' here he raised his eyes and looked me in the face, 'are you quite sure it wasn't Gwellia?'

'Gwellia!' Even as I exclaimed the word, I heard Junio beside me make a swift, incredulous drawing-in of breath. 'Excellence, that's quite impossible!'

Junio gasped again – on my account this time. I was so outraged by the suggestion that I had contradicted Marcus outright.

He did not reprove me. He looked rather sad. 'Libertus, how can you be sure it wasn't her? You were parted from the woman for twenty years or so, and only found her again quite recently. What do you know about those missing years? I'm not suggesting that she would do this willingly – she is not a wicked woman, quite the contrary. But is it not possible, for instance, that someone forced her into it – someone who had some ancient hold on her?'

I wanted to protest that it could not be true – that I knew everything there was to know about my wife – but I could not force the words to pass my lips. Marcus was quite right. There was much about Gwellia's past that was a mystery to me. I had gained some glimpses of her former lifetime as a slave, of course, but there were many hurts and horrors that she'd never talked about and I had never pressed her on the subject, though her occasional nightmares gave me clues. A

female slave is just her owner's chattel, to use as he thinks fit
– and Gwellia had been very beautiful. Clearly there were
things she wanted to forget. Better, I'd always thought, to let
her do so if she could, though they sometimes lay between us
still, like phantoms in our bed.

So all I could say to Marcus now was, 'I cannot believe
that Gwellia would stoop to being involved in anything like
that – whatever the pressures or promises might be.'

'Not even to protect you?' Marcus said. 'Women will do
amazing things to save their families.'

That idea disturbed me, but I shook my head. 'I have
done many things in my life, Excellence, and doubtless I've
made some enemies along the way, but I don't know of
anyone who has information that could really threaten me.' I
gave a bitter little laugh. 'Apart from your medicus, of course.
For some reason he seems intent on causing as much trouble
for me as he can. I think he would like to destroy me if he
could.'

'He saved your life. You should be grateful to him,' Marcus
said.

'Grateful? He hates me!'

'He doesn't seem to like you, certainly. Or doesn't
trust you, anyway. He keeps warning me that fevers are
known to turn the brain and that you may have evil
humours which have changed your mind and heart, however
loyal you used to be before.' He sighed. 'And he may be
right. He sent the soldiers to your roundhouse and they
found that bag.'

'Well, perhaps he knew that it was there for them to find!'
I retorted.

'How could he know anything of the kind? He never left
the house. There are lots of witnesses to that. These two, for

instance.' With a half-eaten fig, he gestured towards Maximus and Minimus who were standing by.

'May I ask them something, Excellence?'

'Certainly.'

I turned to Maximus. 'It isn't possible the doctor put the bag there himself? Or sent another slave to hide it earlier?'

The boy looked quite upset. He shook his head. 'I would like to be able to say so, citizen. You have been kind to us. But I'm afraid it simply isn't possible. The doctor never left the house at all . . .'

'And nobody came here, except the guards . . .' Minimus chimed in, as usual.

'He sent them to your roundhouse to see what they could find . . .'

'And he was gleeful when they came back with the bag . . .'

'Of course they didn't realise what it was. They didn't know it was the bag that had the ransom money in. It was just a bag of baby clothes to them, but because it was hidden in the fence they brought it anyway,' Maximus concluded, in a breathless rush.

'But the doctor knew exactly what it was,' I muttered bitterly. 'Of course.'

'I'm sure he saw the implications instantly,' my patron agreed. 'He has a clever mind. The cleverest man I know, aside from you. He knows about diseases. And he says you may be ill – suffering from bad humours that change your character. Who else but you, he says, could dream up such a plan? You see why I have a problem knowing what to think?' He sighed. 'Perhaps I should have him trepan you after all. I know he wanted to. He says that it would solve the problem instantly.'

I could well believe it! Instantly and permanently, too.

240

Trepanning is a well-respected cure, and it was just possible that Marcus might be persuaded to agree. The idea of the medicus boring holes into my skull – even in order to let supposed humours out – was not one that I could bear to contemplate. I could quite see what Philades would do to me, if Marcus was persuaded to give him the glimmer of a chance – and there would not even be suspicion afterwards. There are always as many accidents as there are cures with a trepan.

'Believe me, there is no question of evil humours, Excellence. I am entirely in my proper senses . . .' I began – but we were interrupted by the arrival of someone at the door.

Chapter Twenty-two

The newcomer was Pulcrus, very pink and out of breath, but smoothing down his hair and uniform, and clearly still conscious of his own good looks. He strode importantly into the *triclinium*, paused theatrically, and made an exaggerated bow. 'Your pardon, Excellence . . .' he began.

Marcus interrupted. 'You have just come from Myrna's house? Is that correct?' He flashed a sharp glance at me, as if inviting me to register that he was already taking action on my immediate request.

Pulcrus was taken visibly aback by being greeted with this brusque salutation, and obviously concluded that he was deemed to be at fault. 'I ask your pardon, Excellence. I'm sorry that I was not here before now, but it was your own command that I should stay until the guard arrived. I rode back as quickly as I could, but . . .'

Marcus made an impatient tutting noise, and cut him off again. 'I did not ask how long it took you to get back. The question is whether you came here straight from Myrna's house. Am I to take it that you did?'

Pulcrus nodded dumbly.

'Then you may have important information, which we need to know. Our views about this kidnapping have changed. It seems that Myrna was not a simple victim, as we thought, after all. It seems she may have been a chief conspirator.'

'Myrn—' the page began, but then thought better of it and turned the exclamation into a sort of cough. Only his eyes spoke his astonishment.

Marcus fixed him with an iron stare. 'Myrna! And not only Myrna, but her sister too, it seems. Both this citizen and the medicus have come to the same conclusion, and I cannot ignore their combined advice. I am about to give orders to the guard to bring the entire family in. But, of course, we don't know where they are. Unless one of them has been back to the house? It didn't look as if any of their possessions had been removed, and presumably someone will have to return for their things. Did anybody come while you were there?'

I thought privately that if I had that ransom money and something had gone wrong, I might well disappear and leave my possessions exactly where they were – especially if I still hoped to extort more payment by and by. However, I knew my patron better than to contradict him again.

It seemed that I was right. The pageboy was already saying, in an injured tone, 'There wasn't anyone at all. In fact I was beginning to wonder when your land slaves would turn up to take my place. I was a bit worried that whoever killed Myrna would come back . . .' He tailed off with a shudder.

'But of course they didn't,' Marcus said unsympathetically, as if he were not the one who had left the boy alone at the scene, without so much as a dagger to defend himself.

Pulcrus managed an unsteady smile. 'The only person I saw at all was that woman who wanted to buy the medicines. She came by on the road, with a pile of kindling on her back and all the children trailing after her. I did wonder for a moment if she had expected Myrna's mother to be back, and was hoping to buy that remedy for the child – I thought she seemed to hover for a moment at the gate – but if so she must have changed her mind. Next thing I knew she was walking on again.'

I glanced at Marcus. It was not my place to intervene in this, but that woman was our best link to Myrna's family. I took a risk and voiced what was in my mind. 'That might be significant in itself. Do you think she saw you?'

Pulcrus looked from me to Marcus. He seemed to hesitate, as if waiting for permission to reply.

To my relief my patron's irritation was directed at his slave. 'Well? Answer the citizen,' he said.

Pulcrus shrugged. It was not important to him to be polite to me. 'I don't know. I suppose she might have done. I was standing where you left me, just beside the door – and of course my horse was in the lane. All I know is that she didn't come up the path at all – in fact she hurried off as fast as possible and never gave the house a second glance.'

'So she slipped through our fingers once again.' Marcus looked vexed. 'I regard her as suspicious. She must at the very least have known that the house was ransacked when she spoke to us, because she'd just been round the back – and yet she didn't say a word. I intended to have her brought in for questioning.'

Pulcrus, who had been looking apologetic until now, suddenly became unutterably smug. 'I knew that, Excellence,' he said. 'I heard you say so when you were at the house. So – forgive me – I told the land slaves so, and Malodius has gone off with two of them to try to pick her up. I hope I did the right thing, Excellence.'

Marcus waved a vague hand. 'Of course you did. Well done, Pulcrus. Remind me to give you a reward – an extra tip or something of the kind.' The page began to preen until

Marcus added, 'Provided that the woman talks, of course. We can expect her shortly?'

The cocksure swaggering disappeared like smoke. 'Of course I don't know exactly where she lives. I pointed out to them the direction that she'd gone, and with all those children she won't be hard to find. They were all carrying firewood, so they weren't moving fast. I left Malodius to look for her and rode on ahead. I thought you would require my services.'

Marcus nodded. 'Then you can wait outside.'

Pulcrus looked almost comically nonplussed. 'Your pardon, Excellence,' he stammered. 'I have a message for you – from the gate-keeper.' His owner looked like thunder, and he went on hastily, 'I would have delivered it before: I was about to do it, but you asked me to report on Myrna's house and obviously my first duty was to answer you.'

'The message?' Marcus did not look convinced. 'I presume it was not urgent?'

'I don't think so, Excellence. There is a man to see you, that is all. Not a citizen or anything. A slave-trader by the look of it. He says that you invited him to come. The chief steward didn't know what to do with him while you were occupied in here, so he's put him in the atrium to wait. He's left his cart of goods outside, with Aulus standing by to keep an eye on it. The chief steward says to ask you if he should provide some food and wine, or wasn't this that kind of visitor?'

Marcus nodded. 'I was expecting him. Tell the slaves to offer hospitality, but not the finest wine. A few dates perhaps and some of that watered Rhenish stuff I didn't really like. But see that he is comfortable – he has come all the way from Rome, and he will have been travelling for days.' He looked down at his amber robe and sighed. 'I suppose I'd better go and change my clothes – I can't conduct business in this informal dress. The trader will take it as a sign that I'm not serious, and either try to sell me inferior goods or charge me double for the girl I want. Minimus, go and tell them that I am on my way. Maximus, see that my second-best toga is prepared.'

The two redheads, who had been patiently standing by against the wall with that glazed immobility of all slaves everywhere, sprang instantly to action at his words. They put down the jug of watered wine they had been holding ready to fill their master's glass again, gave him the linen napkin with which to wipe his lips, and hurried off to do as they were bid.

My patron turned to me with an air of deliberate formality. 'Libertus, that concludes our interview, I think. You wanted me to bring Myrna's family in for questioning, and I agree to do so. And I'll question this other woman too. I would like you to be present when I speak to her. She is obviously more at home in Celtic, and I need your services as interpreter. I imagine that such an arrangement would meet with your approval, too?'

'I am grateful, Excellence,' I said with genuine feeling. He had found a clever way of permitting me to talk to the witnesses. Normally I could expect the rulling on my case to be the first thing he did in his role as magistrate. However, since I was to assist him – in an official capacity – with a questioning, any potential hearing against me could be properly deferred until I had discharged my duties. There were several legal precedents for that sort of amnesty, so even the medicus could not object.

However, Marcus's next words rather modified my joy.

'Of course, I shall want the medicus to attend me too,' he

said. 'I will meet you in the atrium as soon as Malodius gets back and I have finished with the slave-trader. I will send for you. Meanwhile, I have important purchases to make. Pulcrus, when we go from here, get the chief steward to summon Philades. I want him to look over this wet nurse with me. And while we are doing that' – here he turned to me – 'perhaps it would be wise for you to go back and rest a little while. So, if you will excuse me, citizen.'

And accompanied by his page, he swept out of the room, leaving me and Junio staring after him.

Junio turned towards me with a grin and offered me his arm. 'Well, master, it seems I should assist you to your room.'

I grunted. Marcus had not actually ordered me to bed, but he had made his wishes clear, and really I did not have a lot of choice. 'Oh, very well,' I said. 'But you can take me for a short walk round the courtyard first. I want to see exactly where one would have to stand to see the other courtyard from this part of the house.'

'Then put your hood up, master, or you'll catch a chill.' I was still wearing the cloak which Junio had brought me, and he arranged it over my head and shoulders as he spoke. 'It is actually raining now and you'll get wet otherwise, even if you stay underneath the colonnade.'

I submitted to his ministrations and we hobbled round the court, but I found there was little more to learn. It was clear that Porphyllia's description was correct and that the only clear sight of the place where the supposed Julia had sat was from the passageway which led into the private wing.

I walked as far as the storage cupboard Porphyllia had told me about. It was a large walk-in affair and I peeped inside, but there was nothing to be seen but neat piles of linen and baskets of supplies.

I would have liked to go through to the inner court and investigate the path that led out to the orchard and the gate. I was about to do so, when the door of one of the apartments opened from within, and a pair of handmaidens came bustling out with bowls of water and a linen cloth, obviously attending Marcellinus in some way, so I stepped quickly back. I did not want to be observed myself.

I was thinking of all the questions which I ought to ask Myrna's sister, if I got the chance. How long, for instance, did it take a woman to change her clothes? Gwellia could have advised me, perhaps, if she had been here. Where was she? Still at Numidius's house? Thank all the goods that Marcus still had it under guard – at least Lallius was unlikely to return there for a time. In fact, I had been hourly expecting the arrival of soldiers bringing Gwellia back to us in chains. If only they would do so! Though, I reminded myself, in my present situation it was dangerous for her here. She might well be imprisoned as my conspirator. The sooner I could solve this business, the better for us both. I turned my mind back to Myrna's sister and the cloak.

I decided to try a small experiment. I said to Junio, 'I wonder if you could arrange to bring me another cup of mead?'

He looked surprised, and then a slow grin crossed his face. 'I see. You want to see how long an errand of that kind would take. Well, if you are sure that you can manage from here on your own?'

'Of course I can. It's no more than a step or two at most, and Cilla is waiting in the room. She will assist me if I need any help. Anyway, I really want the drink. I'm chilly and the warmth would do me good. I'm sure it would improve my health more than any of the doctor's wretched medicines.'

249

I waved him off, and watched him scuttle over to the kitchen block, which was in a separate building at the far end of the court that we were in. Just time, I thought, for Myrna's sister to slip out of her room, dressed in a servant's tunic and cloak, drop Julia's cloak in the courtyard where it would be seen, and be in the orchard with the pile of washing and the child before Myrna came back with the fruit and raised a well-feigned alarm. A voice rang out behind me.

'You there! Aulus! What are you doing there? Why aren't you on duty at the gate? Who gave you permission to come and get your cloak? You ugly whoring son of a she-bear, I'll have you whipped for this. Just wait until I tell your master that I found you here.'

It took me a moment to realise that this was meant for me, but eventually I whirled round – or as near a whirl as I could manage in my current state of health. The voice belonged to Marcus's chief steward and the man himself was hastening towards me with his baton raised, his plump face puce with fury and his hobnailed sandals ringing on the ground. As I turned to face him, his expression changed. He turned from angry purple to an embarrassed white, his blue eyes almost popping from his head

'Oh, a thousand pardons, citizen! I did not realise that it was you. Only I knew that Aulus didn't have his cloak and I thought for a moment. . .' He tailed off in confusion

'You mean, you didn't think at all,' I said.

That flustered him. 'Of course, I should have looked again before I spoke. I thought you . . . he . . . didn't look quite the same as usual.'

'A Greek understatement, if I ever heard one,' I replied. It was true. I did not look anything like the gate-keeper, even from the back. Aulus was noted for his size and strength and, granted that the cloak perhaps disguised my lack of width and thinning hair, nothing could alter the fact that I was a good hand shorter than him. Besides, I had thin bony ankles. Aulus was stouter and hairier than a bear.

The steward was still burbling. 'Forgive me, citizen. Those things I said to you – the insults – it was unforgivable. Please, if there is anything at all that I can do . . .'

I found that I was grinning for the first time that day. 'I have been tempted to call Aulus a few names myself. You have already been more help than you realise,' I said. 'You have just proved that it is possible to see what you expect and jump to the wrong conclusions about who you are looking at. Are you prepared to tell your master that?' Marcus seemed ready to believe me anyway, but I felt that this testimony would improve my case.

'Of course, citizen, if you insist.' The steward looked chagrined and alarmed. 'I suppose that will be strictly necessary? I am afraid His Excellence will not be pleased with me. I have already earned his displeasure once today, by giving that slave-trader the wrong wine to drink, and to make matters worse he's had another of those wretched ransom notes. And now I have another message which he won't want to hear. He's asking for the medicus to attend him in the atrium and examine the wet nurse that he wants to buy. But I've looked right through the villa and I can't find him anywhere.'

Chapter Twenty-three

I found that I was frowning. 'The medicus has gone?'

The steward ran a hand across his hair. 'Well, I suppose he can't have disappeared. At least not very far. He was in this very courtyard not long ago, when I was bringing the slave-trader into the atrium. I saw him through the open doorway. I thought he'd join us then, but he just waved a hand and went on walking towards the private wing. Of course the master was still occupied with you, so there was no point in intercepting Philades, if he had a job to do. I supposed he was going over to look at the boy again – I know he supervised the feeding earlier.'

'I've just come from that direction,' I observed. 'There are a couple of girls over there, attending to Marcellinus by the look of it. But I didn't see the doctor – though that doesn't prove he wasn't there. He might have gone inside the room, perhaps, to advise the maidservants on what to do?'

The steward shook his head. 'Naturally that was the first place I looked, but the slave-girls hadn't seen him over there. Not since this morning early – though he did say then that he was coming back.' He frowned. 'I thought he might have gone back to his room – to consult those famous scrolls of his perhaps – but I can't find any sign of him at all. That's when I began to be alarmed.'

I was beginning to be more than a little curious myself.

'He hasn't come past me. Have you searched the outer grounds?' I said. 'Up by the *nymphaeum*, possibly?' There was a pleasant walk within the outer walls, up to the little spring and temple in the grounds, much of which was hidden from the house. 'Or even the latrine.'

The steward shook his head. 'I've had two people searching everywhere.' He waved a hand, as if to indicate the wideness of the search. 'They've been right through the house and outbuildings. Even the slaves' sleeping quarters and the winter woodpiles in the storage yard, but there's still no sign of him.' He gave a nervous laugh. 'Unless he's in the cesspit or the well, I can't think where he can possibly have gone.'

'Have you asked the gate-keepers, in case he's left the house?' I was all attention, suddenly. Whatever was the doctor up to now? Of course there was no legal reason why he shouldn't leave the premises, if he decided to – unlike me he was not under arrest – but he must have known that Marcus wanted him. Even if something urgent had cropped up while Marcus had been occupied with me, it took a brave man to leave my patron in the lurch. 'And what was that about a ransom note?'

'I believe it was the slave-trader who brought it in,' he said. 'I don't know any details at all. His Excellence is saying nothing, except "Where's the medicus?" I was on my way to ask them at the gate. Perhaps that why I called out to you like that. I was thinking about Aulus, anyway.'

'Thinking that if there was no keeper at the gate, the doctor might have slipped out unobserved?'

The steward looked uncomfortable at this. 'Perhaps he has simply walked out into the lane. I know that he was working on a theory about the kidnapping. He told me earlier that he thought he knew how it was done. I thought he might have gone outside to test out his ideas.' His brow cleared. 'Perhaps he has. But you would have expected him to say so, wouldn't you? Not just to disappear? You don't think . . .'

'That he has been kidnapped too?' I said. 'I doubt it very much.'

The steward nodded. 'I'm sure I'm worrying for nothing, citizen. It's probable he's just gone for a stroll along the lane. To see where the ransom bag was left, perhaps.'

To plant more so-called evidence in my house, more like, I thought. Or to meet up with his confederates, now that the other ransom note was here? But the steward was clearly in the doctor's confidence and it was not wise to voice my doubts aloud. Instead I murmured, 'Let's go and see what Aulus has to say.'

The steward seemed grateful for my sympathy. 'A good idea,' he said, and fell into step with me. He even offered me his arm to lean upon. 'We won't go through the atrium, perhaps. My master will be there and he'll be furious with me for not finding the doctor when he wanted him. This way.' He opened the small side door from the court, which gave on to a narrow passageway and afforded the servants access to the front. 'I'm sure there's really no mystery at all,' he fretted, allowing me to pass. 'Only, citizen, I went into Philades' room just now, to see if he was there. And, well . . . it looks as if his box and books are gone.'

That stopped me where I stood. 'Then I think you should tell His Excellence at once,' I said, attempting to sound dispassionate, but actually full of unreasonable hope. If the doctor had absconded suddenly, and there was another demand for ransom, even Marcus would be forced to re-examine his ideas. 'At once,' I said again.

Too forceful. The steward was worried on his own account. 'We'll speak to Aulus first,' he said. 'I don't want to alarm the master unnecessarily. Jove only knows what he will say if he discovers that Philades is gone. That I have been neglectful, I expect.' He sighed. 'Well, here we are.'

We had crossed the outer courtyard by this time and reached the little guard-niche by the gate, where the gate-keeper performed his unenviable task of keeping watch on visitors and passers-by from a small spyhole in the wall. It was cramped and airless, even in this wind, but it provided some shelter from the rain and I was glad to follow the steward into it. It smelt of stale sweat and onions.

Aulus was in there, perching on the stone seat and peering idly out into the lane, where the slave-trader's covered cart could just be seen. It was perishingly cold in his little hidey-hole and I wondered that he had not worn his cloak. It seemed the bear-like Aulus scorned such luxuries – though he was wearing several tunics, I observed.

When he saw us he lumbered to his feet, and favoured me with a ferocious glower. Aulus is a powerful, big, bad-tempered man and I began to wish I hadn't borrowed that wretched cape myself.

I was about to stammer an apology for appropriating it, but the steward had forestalled me. 'We are looking for the medicus,' he said, with the peremptory air that chief slaves always reserve for their inferiors. 'Have you seen him pass this way at all?'

Aulus looked surprised. 'Of course. He went out just a little while ago, to look over the slaves that are for sale, I understand.'

'Ah!' the steward said, with undisguised relief. 'That explains it. A small misunderstanding, that is all. The slave he was to examine is in the atrium. The master is awaiting him impatiently. I'll go and fetch him in.' He flashed me a conspiratorial smile. 'You wanted to talk to Aulus, didn't you?'

It was a signal that I was to stay where I was inside the gate. After all, I was officially under house arrest. However, what the steward said was true, although he could not know it. I did want to speak to Aulus. My new theory about the kidnapping had raised new questions for the gate-keeper. But Aulus and I have never seen exactly eye to eye, and I felt at a special disadvantage now that I had used his cloak without consulting him. I seized my unexpected opportunity with some trepidation.

'About the day that Julia disappeared . . .' I began.

Aulus looked more than ordinarily sour. 'I've told you everything I know,' he grumbled sullenly.

'I'm interested in the moment that Julia came back from visiting,' I said, trying to sound as friendly as I could. 'She drew up in the carriage, and complained that she'd seen people in the lane?'

'And I went down there to investigate. That's right.' Aulus gave a theatrical sigh. 'I've been through all this with the medicus. And I'll say the same thing to you as I said to him. It's no good trying to pin any blame on me. I was just obeying orders.'

So Philades had been playing his little games again! What was the doctor up to? There was only one way to find out. 'Of course you were,' I murmured soothingly. 'You hadn't any choice. They were the mistress's instructions, after all?'

He looked a little mollified at this mendacious ploy, but a brusque nod was all the answer I received.

'Except I don't think it was Julia at all,' I said.

'Of course it was.' Aulus was running a thick tongue round his lips, as if it helped him with his powers of recall. 'It's like I told the medicus. I think I saw the mistress through the window space, though I wouldn't swear on Jupiter to that – it was one of those hired carriages with a leather flap that you can raise – but I know I saw her getting down and going inside the house.'

I looked at him intently. 'But you weren't anywhere close by, were you? You were walking down the lane, checking out the movement in the trees?'

He frowned. 'Well, I suppose I was, but I'm sure it was the mistress all the same. I noticed that she had the baby in her arms, and that for once he seemed to be asleep. She gave him to the wet nurse while the driver helped her down.'

'And you are sure that it was Julia you saw?'

He answered in the same way as Porphyllia had done when I asked her about the child. 'Of course it was the mistress. Who else would it have been?' He ran his tongue round his lips again. 'In any case, I recognised the clothes. It was just what she went out in – blue cape, blue hood, and that purply *stola* thing she wears. And Myrna was with her all the time, and she ought to know her mistress, oughtn't she? And it certainly was Myrna. I spoke to her myself. And I was close enough to *her*.'

There was something in the tone in which he said the words and the leering expression on his face which reminded me of what Porphyllia had said about his groping hands. No doubt Myrna had been subjected to his attentions too. Yet it occurred to me that a man whose mind is on a shapely female he's about to pinch may not have his full attention on what's happening elsewhere. A false Julia, for example, might pass him easily. I was about to challenge him on this point when suddenly another piece of the mosaic slotted into place.

'Julia had been to visit friends?' I said.

Aulus stared at me. 'But of course. The Grappius family – or the wife, at least. The master was with the husband in the town. They were at an *ordo* meeting for the day. You knew that, didn't you?'

I made a non-committal sound. It seemed unlikely that the councillor and his wife were any part of this – it was hard to see what they could hope to gain – but I suppose they could not be entirely ruled out. If we learned nothing sensible from Myrna's sister, I would have to suggest to Marcus that he search the Grappius house and ensure that they could account for their actions on that day – though I knew he would not like it, and it was even more certain that his friends would not. But no doubt there would be slaves and witnesses to prove that Julia had really left the premises.

And then, what?

My brain teemed with questions. If she did get into the carriage intending to come home, what happened on the way? Did she ask the carriage-driver to stop and let her out? If so, it would have to be at her own request, unless it was a hold-up – in which case, presumably we should have heard of it, unless the driver was party to the plot as well. To shop, perhaps? That would make sense. And she had wanted to buy some teething remedy. Suppose she went into the house we'd seen, and someone was lying in wait there to strip her clothes from her and take her place. Far easier to do it there than in a public spot. And in that case, would the driver have noticed if the hooded lady who stepped into his carriage was not the same one as got out of it? It was distinctly possible that he would not – especially if her attendant was obviously the same and still had a sleeping infant in her arms. But he would know for certain where he'd stopped the coach!

I needed to trace that driver as soon as possible. I was seven kinds of idiot not to have asked about him before – though until I realised that Julia had not been kidnapped from the house, what happened earlier in the day had not seemed particularly significant.

'Would you recognise the driver?' I said to Aulus. 'Was it the same one every time?'

He furrowed his brow in a parody of concentration. 'I think so, citizen. I hadn't stopped to think. I know there are a pair of them that drive the coach. Now if I just had something to refresh my memory...'

I was wondering whether Marcus would think it worth a bribe when suddenly the steward hurried in. His face was flushed and flustered and he was badly out of breath. He ignored the gate-keeper and came straight to me. 'Citizen?' he panted.

'What is it?' He was puffing so heavily I was concerned for him.

He shook his head as if he couldn't voice the words, but at last he recovered enough to speak. 'It's the medicus, citizen,' he managed finally, although the words came out in little breathless spurts. 'He had his ... box and books with him ... but he didn't stop ... to look at slaves at all. Slave-trader's assistant ... out there with the cart ... doctor told him ... needed urgently in town ... ignored slave-cages ... and went rushing down the lane.'

I looked at his red face and heaving chest. 'So you went running after him?' I prompted. No wonder the poor man was out of breath. He was a senior servant and no longer young. It must have been many moons since he had been required to move at anything other than the most dignified of glides.

He nodded. 'Right down to the corner of the lane,' he gasped. He was sounding a little more coherent now, but he was still pressing a hand against his heart. 'I did see Malodius . . . in the distance with the cart . . . but there was no sign . . . of Philades at all. It rather looks as if he's run away.'

Chapter Twenty-four

'Run away? The doctor? Why, whatever for?' Aulus's open-mouthed expression was almost comical – like the mask the actors put on in a theatre to represent the fool. 'He hasn't upset the master, surely to Jupiter?'

The steward shook his head, still breathless. 'I don't believe so. In fact Marcus is asking for his help – that's why we're looking for him now. I don't know. It's inexplicable. I can't believe he's done a thing like this. Why, only this morning . . .' He broke off and shook his head again.

Aulus gave his snaggled-toothed, ugly grin. 'He's just gone off on some errand or other, steward, you mark what I say. And whatever it is, he'll charge the master high. He's a clever sort of devil. Knows which urn his wine is coming from. He's got himself a really cosy little set-up here: a regular little income and a lot of influence,' he said approvingly. I was just thinking that one could rely on Aulus to see the mercenary angle when he added, with a note of malicious pleasure in his voice, 'In fact, the physician's turned into such a favourite with the master that he's almost taken over from that cloak-thief over there.' He seemed to mean the steward, I was surprised to see. I thought I was the cloak-thief if anybody was!

The steward looked unhappy. 'I know the master was beginning to ask the medicus for advice, but I hardly think . . .'

The gate-keeper interrupted him – when you are as big as Aulus is, you can sometimes afford to take a risk like that with your superiors. 'Oh, come on, steward, you know quite well I'm right,' he said with an unpleasant wink, baring his broken teeth at us again. 'I heard you saying just the same thing last night to the cook. The doctor knows exactly how to get his just rewards – unlike some people round here I could name. I've watched him working his way into the master's favour with his scrolls and his special diets. He's set up for life here, if he plays it right. He wouldn't throw all that away and just run off for good. As I say, he is up to something. He'll be back again, see if he's not.'

The steward looked a little brighter. 'I suppose you're right,' he said. 'I know the master offered him an enormous fee to leave his previous employer and come here instead.'

Aulus was still grinning like an ogre. 'You see? He wouldn't risk throwing a salary like that away unless his life depended on it. I wouldn't, in his place.'

'Not unless he was hoping to gain a greater sum,' I put in soberly. The two slaves boggled at me in astonishment. I had not voiced my suspicions of the doctor up to now, but if I wanted somebody sent after Philades I would have to persuade the steward to do it soon, or it would be too late. I decided that the time had come to express what I had been thinking all along – after all, the medicus had gone off without a word, and there was just a chance that I might be believed.

Well, there was only one way to find out. I took it. 'If he is due to have a share of that ransom money, for example,' I explained.

Aulus muttered, 'But surely . . .' just as the steward cried, 'By all the gods . . .' They both stopped together and stared at me again.

The steward was the first to find his voice. 'Citizen, you can't be serious in this. The medicus is a very learned man. Not at all the sort of person you would expect . . .' He trailed off helplessly.

'Clever?' I suggested. 'And resourceful too? I agree. And he is capable of taking unexpected risks and making quick decisions – we've seen that today.'

'But kidnapping? And ransom? That's quite another thing. And what has he to do with Lallius?'

'It does seem rather out of character,' I allowed. 'But surely, that's the cleverest part of it. He was the very last man you'd suspect – just as Mryna was the last person you'd suspect of taking risks with Marcellinus. That was probably exactly why he used her in his plans. And the doctor did know Lallius's family. We were told that from the start. Perhaps he was promised a very large reward – as Aulus said, he was quite capable of demanding one.'

'But suddenly demanding huge sums of ransom money from the master? Why would he do that? He could make a handsome living anywhere he chose. A man in his position . . .'

'And what was his position, exactly?' I enquired. 'A citizen – with no more independence than a slave, because he has no money of his own? Forced to be in somebody's employ and at his master's beck and call – and yet a person who is very conscious of his worth? Intelligent, quick-thinking and not afraid of risks? I think a man like that is more than capable of mounting such a plot.'

They were still gaping like barbarians for the first time at the games. Obviously they'd never thought of Philades in that way.

I was sympathetic. 'You know, he had me completely

fooled at first. He had persuaded me that he was slow and logical and completely unbending in his thoughts and attitudes. I suppose that only shows how clever and inventive he can really be. Don't underestimate the sharpness of his mind.'

The chief slave looked doubtful. 'He said the same of you – told me that you were the only man round here who had the wits to make a daring plan like this, and then think fast enough to take account of changing circumstances. He even wondered if you were really ill at all: there are herbs that will bring sickness and dreaming-fever on, he said, and he wouldn't put it past you to have taken them, to give yourself a convincing alibi. You had the imagination to think of such a scheme, the cleverness to judge the doses right, and enough cool arrogance to see it through – forgive me, citizen. Those were his very words.' He essayed a feeble smile. 'I suppose it was a sort of compliment.'

If so, it was the most roundabout compliment I have ever heard – I've received more flattering insults in my time. I was still struggling to think of some response when Aulus chimed in with a practical remark.

'Well, whatever he is, he's well and truly down the lane by now. Though I suppose that if Malodius is on his way, you could send him out again to pick the doctor up – tell him the master needs him urgently and it's vital that he brings him back at once. The cart would do that, if a runner can't.'

The steward looked at him with something like respect. 'Aulus, I do believe you're right. And I've not forgotten that you helped us earlier. Remind me to put your duty schedule back to normal, with immediate effect.' He turned to me. 'I had thought of sending Pulcrus on a horse, but he's in the atrium with the master, and I'd have to go in and explain all this before he'd be released – and if this citizen is right about the medicus it wouldn't have been sensible, in any case.'

'You could send Marcus's carriage,' I suggested. 'That's not being used.'

He shook his head. 'It was used this morning and it's being cleaned. I got a couple of the stable boys to make a start on it, since Malodius has been doing something else. Besides, I'd have to send an escort, I suppose, otherwise the doctor might try to clamber out along the way.' He was finding excuses, that was obvious.

'And the master would have to give permission for all that as well?' The gate-keeper was outwardly respectful, but he gave me an exaggerated wink behind the chief slave's back. I knew what he was signalling. It was transparent to the merest idiot that the steward did not want to face his master until the doctor had been found. I could understand that. If Marcus had received another ransom note, he would be more than usually upset.

'It had better be Malodius,' the steward said.

'Well, in that case, you had best be quick,' Aulus said. 'I can see him, through the spyhole, coming now.' Sure enough, a moment later there was the faint clatter of hooves and cartwheels in the lane.

The steward brightened, happy that there was something he could do. 'I'll go out and stop him before he goes round to the back – he can't get past the slave cart anyway.' He bustled off, and a moment later we heard the sound of muffled cursing from the gate and a great deal of snorting as the horses were backed up.

'So,' Aulus said in a grumbling tone, as the commotion died away. 'I'm returned to normal duties. And about time too. That steward's had me standing sentry for so many hours I began to think I'd soon be taking root.' He took a step towards me. 'And if he has quite finished what he's doing with that cloak, perhaps I can have it back sometime, before I freeze to death.'

I was a guest of Marcus's and of course there was no threat, but Aulus is not the sort of man to argue with. I was already in the process of removing the offending article before I took in the force of what he'd said. 'If *who*'s finished with the cloak?' I said, pausing in the act of loosening the ties. 'I thought I was the one who'd borrowed it. Do you mean Junio, my slave?'

Aulus did not have a lot of forehead, but he furrowed what he had. 'I meant that confounded chief slave, naturally. He came here this morning and demanded it. Told me that it was needed to test out an idea. I might have known he wanted it for you.'

'I didn't ask . . .' I began, and stopped. I was going to protest that it was not my doing that he'd lost his cloak, but since I was still actually wearing it, I could see that this was unlikely to convince.

Aulus misinterpreted my comment, anyway. 'I dare say you didn't specify that he should borrow mine, but of course it had to be my cloak he chose to use – he's always had it in for me, that man. I had a niche to shelter in, he said, and I would be all right. He ought to try it sometime, with just a tunic on. But he's the senior steward, so I hadn't any choice. I simply do as I'm told. All the same,' he bent towards me so that his massive face was just an inch from mine, 'if you have quite finished your little experiments, I'd like to have it back.'

I stripped it off and handed it to him – anything to make him straighten up. The whiff of onions and bad breath was overpowering. He didn't move.

'What did the steward want it for, in any case?'

'Why are you asking me? To see if he could be recognised from a distance, when the hood was up, he said.' Aulus's face took on a different look. 'I hope you found it useful?' he said, suggestively.

He was asking for a tip. Now I was really in a fix. I had no money with me – I hadn't brought my purse – but to refuse him was to double my offence. And I could make no sense at all of Aulus's account. Who could have asked the steward to do anything like that? The doctor, perhaps? Pretending to test out his so-called theory – when he must have known the answer all along? I could see that sounded feeble, but it was the only explanation I could find. 'The steward didn't borrow your cloak on my account,' I said. 'My slave found it hanging in the servants' room, and obviously, since you weren't using it . . . But here he is in person. You can ask him for yourself.'

But there was no time for asking questions. Junio was as pink and flustered as the steward had been before, and he made no excuses for addressing me without any of the usual courtesies. 'Master! There you are! Thank Jupiter I've found you and you're safe and sound. You are wanted in the house. We have been looking for you everywhere.'

'We?'

'Myself, and Cilla and Porphyllia and – when we couldn't find you – several of Marcus's household too. There were already servants searching all the outbuildings and grounds, trying to find the doctor. He seems to have disappeared as well.'

'That is what I'm doing here,' I said. 'I came to help the steward look for him.'

Junio ran a hand across his brow. 'Well, thank all the gods

I found you. When I came back with that drink of mead you asked for, and you were nowhere to be found, I thought – well, it doesn't matter what I thought – but you had us all concerned. Then someone suggested looking over here – and there you were. As safe as anything!'

I had to smile at that. He sounded more indignant than relieved, the way worried people do – like a mother when her errant child comes home. 'Meanwhile my cup of mead was going cold, I suppose?' I teased.

He realised that he must have sounded inappropriate. He offered me his arm and added, in a humbler tone of voice, 'I am sincerely glad to find you, master. Do you wish me to assist you to your room?' He was already tugging me into the court, and I was happy that he should. It solved the problem of Aulus and his tip – for the moment anyway.

'I'll talk to you again,' I said to him, and allowed Junio to lead me away. The last I saw of the gate-keeper, he was scowling after us and wrapping his cloak round himself with the air of someone going to meet the beasts.

'You say that I am wanted?' I said to Junio, as he led the way into the house by the servants' corridor again. 'Aren't we going to Marcus in the atrium? I hear there's been another ransom note.'

He shook his head. 'Marcus hasn't asked for you,' he said. 'We are going back to your sleeping room. Marcus said you were to have some rest, and you are more than ready for it, by the look of you. And . . .'

He was right. I had been so interested in the doctor's disappearance that I had forgotten my own ills, but I was much more weary than I had realised. However, I would not admit to that, and I tried to lean less heavily on his arm.

'And?' I enquired. 'There was another thing?'

He nodded. 'There is someone there I know you'll want to see.'

'And that is?' The doctor? Myrna's mother? Her sister? Even Lallius? I was imagining a hundred possibilities, but none was as welcome as the truth turned out to be.

Junio could disguise his glee no longer and he broke into a grin. 'Master, I thought you would have guessed. It's Gwellia – your wife. She came with Kurso through the back gate just a little while ago. They've just got back from Glevum and she wants to talk to you.'

Chapter Twenty-five

Not nearly as much as I longed to talk to her! Relief and gladness knocked the strength from me. I was every bit as weary as Junio thought I was, and it was beyond my capabilities to run, but I did my very best. I hurried through the house and out into the court at an undignified hobble, and did not pause until I reached the doorway of my room.

'Gwellia!'

She was waiting for me, looking as beautiful as it is possible for a lady of almost fifty years to look when she is scowling in obvious concern. It was not possible to sweep her up into my arms, as I would have liked to do – there were servants present, and we were guests in Marcus's house – but I crossed the room and seized her by the hands. 'Gwellia!' I said again. 'I have been so worried about you.'

'Me?' She squeezed my fingers and released herself. Her eyes were fringed with tears. 'It's you that we should be concerned about. Look at you! Out in the courtyard in the rain, without a covering – and after you have been so ill, as well. You'll catch a chill on top of everything, and I'll have to nurse you all over again.' She patted the pillows and the bed. 'Come on, lie down. I know you, husband. You're in need of it.'

I was. I was suddenly overwhelmed with love and weariness. I did as she commanded and reclined, while my servants took off my sandals and pulled the covers over me.

Gwellia was still scolding – I knew it was her way of showing how much she cared for me. 'And what have you been up to while I have been in town? Up to your investigative tricks, I understand? I'm surprised that Marcus has permitted it. Obviously you're very far from well. And it is more than your health that you have put at risk. I hear that doctor has brought a charge against you, and Marcus has you more or less under arrest.'

I heaved a happy sigh. 'But that's all over now. Without an accuser there can be no case. And I don't think he'll be back. You know what happened here?' I began to offer an explanation, but she interrupted me.

'Cilla and Junio have told me everything. Of course Kurso and I already knew that something was amiss. We looked in at the roundhouse on our way here, so that he could see to the animals and pick up any eggs – but we found a soldier standing guard beside the gate. He actually refused to let us go inside.'

I thought privately that perhaps it was as well, since the house would certainly have been ransacked in the search, but I knew how upset Gwellia would have been to come home unexpectedly to that. 'It was because they found the ransom bag . . .'

'Of course, husband, I know that now, but at the time the soldier wouldn't tell us anything at all – and we very nearly got arrested too. If that cart-driver hadn't come along and agreed to bring us to the villa in the cart, I believe we would have been tied up and locked in the dye house until reinforcements came.' She had waved the slaves aside by now, and was plumping up my pillows with her own hand as she spoke

274

– with a vigour which left me in no doubt as to what a shock all this had been.

'You came here with Malodius?' I said foolishly, as I snuggled luxuriously back into the bed.

She gave a short laugh. 'Malodius – the evil-smelling one! Is that his name? I never heard it mentioned, but he deserved it, certainly. I've rarely had a more smelly and uncomfortable ride. I was forced to sit quite close behind him at the front. He already had that poor woman and her children on the cart – though goodness knows how anyone can think she was involved in any kidnapping. I've never seen a woman so frightened in my life.'

I was sufficiently interested to struggle up again. 'He found her, then? Where is she? I ought to question her.'

She urged me back on to my cushions with a firm and wifely hand. 'Then, husband, you will have to wait your turn. Marcus is proposing to speak to her himself. I saw her led away to wait for him.' She shook her head. 'Though I doubt that he will get very much from her. Poor lady, she is too frightened to tell him anything. I spoke to her a little in Celtic on the way – in the hope that old Smelly wouldn't understand. She says that you found her at a house earlier today – someone had turned the whole place upside down and most of the valuables were gone. She is sure that she has been arrested in connection with the thefts – though she swears she hasn't taken anything herself.'

'It's more serious than robbery,' I said. 'There was a woman murdered in that house.'

My wife was not as startled as I expected her to be. She shook her head. 'I'm sure the woman in the cart didn't know anything about a death. It was the missing items she was concerned about. She said there was a wooden money chest and some pretty silverware which were usually kept in a recess beside the fire, and she noticed that both were gone. She was sure that you would suspect her of taking them, unless the owner of the house came back and told you otherwise. An old woman who made herbal remedies, I understand, and made quite a little living out of them?'

'She was the mother of the wet nurse who worked here,' I said. 'Myrna – the girl whose corpse we discovered in the house. I'm almost certain that she was involved in Julia's kidnapping, and that her murder was somehow a result of that.'

Gwellia frowned. 'But why would a wet nurse want to ransom Lallius?' she asked. She gave a little smile. 'In fact, when you listen to what I've got to tell, you might wonder why anybody would. I've been talking to his household servants for a while, and I can tell you this: his father would not have done anything to help – bribed the girl or anything like that – if that was what you had supposed. He has been far too ill in any case – but he would not have chosen to. He'd made it clear he would not speak to Lallius again, and even told the servants not to lend him cash.'

I had propped myself up on my elbow once again, but this time she made no move to force me to lie down. 'Perhaps Myrna was a secret lover of Lallius?'

Gwellia gave a derisive snort. 'Not according to the servants. Lallius's interests did not lie that way. He preferred the company of boys, and even then he had to purchase them. He was not the sort of person who had many friends at all. In fact, it seems that he had only one – and that was another rather feckless youth, with tastes that the old man thought were equally depraved – a good deal too much wine, and gambling, and a fondness for hiring pretty slave-boys for the night and indulging in the most exotic food – peacocks' tongues, and gilded swans, and all that sort of thing. The other boy could afford it – he'd recently inherited estates – but Lallius could not. He borrowed from the money-lenders. It scandalised Numidius, of course.'

I could imagine that from what I knew of the old man. He was the personification of cautious respectability: famously careful where money was concerned – he would walk a mile to save a *quadrans*, people said – and his hawk-like face and bony frame suggested that he was equally frugal with his meals. It was rumoured that he'd never held a banquet in his life – or been a guest at one.

'So he was tired of paying Lallius's debts? The boy did have an allowance from his father, I suppose?' I said. The leisured sons of Roman citizens were usually given one. It was called a *peculium*, like the allowance of a slave, and it wasn't very different from that in some respects. Unless a son was legally emancipated by a court, any who lived at home, of whatever age, was still under the legal power of the paterfamilias. And apart from anything he earned from military service, a son legally owned nothing of his own. Most young men married dowried women and set up households of their own, but Lallius had never done that. And no doubt his father gave him the minimum. Numidius was anxious to appear as like a Roman citizen as possible, but being generous to an idle son would not come easily to a man like that – especially when the youth had been born inside the walls and had the privileged status which he himself coveted.

Gwellia seemed to read my thoughts. She smiled. 'An allowance, certainly, though not a very large one, I believe. Even then Numidius had threatened several times to cut it off, because his son was always running into debt and "bringing the family name into disrepute" he said. There was even talk of sending Lallius to the legions for a spell in the hope that a bit of army discipline would help to sort him out – Numidius knew an officer who was prepared to act as patron to the boy – but Lallius simply went on a drinking bout for days before he was supposed to meet the man. Of course, he would have failed to pass the physical examination and that would have disgraced the family even more. Numidius had to put it off – he was angrier than ever about that.'

'The idea of gaining money of his own did not attract Lallius, then?'

'Apparently he was furious about the whole idea, raging that he'd never had to lift a finger in his life, except to summon a slave to bring more wine, and that route marches in full kit would kill him in a week. He had the whole household completely terrified – they all say he is very nasty when he's drunk.'

'This friend is a bad influence, perhaps?' I said.

'Quite the opposite!' my wife exclaimed. 'It seems that Lallius was the leader in all their exploits from the start. They went to school together at the *paedagogus* in the town and Lallius was always getting his comrade into scrapes. Lallius was unpleasant even as a child – he modelled himself on the young Caligula. He was almost banished from the house when he was six years old, for deliberately setting fire to a dog. The sort of boy who pulls the legs off flies, and pulls fish from the water just to see them squirm. And he frightened this Cassius into following his lead. Anyway, even that friendship didn't last, it seems. Cassius is the person who had Lallius brought to court – there was a fight about a gambling debt they owed, and Lallius took his money and knocked him down, he said.'

'So no chance that Cassius is behind the ransom plot?' I frowned. For a moment I'd thought I'd found the first plausible explanation for the whole affair. I was reluctant to abandon it.

Gwellia shook her head. 'Nor any of the household servants, either, husband, I'm afraid.' She had been rearranging the covers over me, but now she turned towards me with a little smile. 'I had been hoping to find out something useful of that kind for you – some loyal slave who might have taken risks on Lallius's account – but I cannot find a single servant in the house who has anything but hatred and contempt for him. They think it is disgraceful that he stayed away when his father was so desperately ill. True, he had been banished from the house, but they sent a message to him in the jail before he was released. Of course, they didn't know about the kidnapping, and no doubt the soldiers frightened him away. But there was almost a feeling of relief that he has not come home. Good riddance to him, seems to be the general attitude. I wonder if he'll come back for the funeral, now that Numidius is dead.'

'Dead?' The word was startled out of me. 'I didn't know that he was dead. I knew that he was dangerously ill . . .'

'Numidius died this morning, in the early hours. That is one reason why they let me in. They thought I was an anointing woman come to prepare the corpse. The servants were in quite a quandary what to do, in fact, since Lallius had not come home. Numidius would have wanted a Roman-style funeral, and it is properly the duty of the eldest son to close the eyes and start up the lament. So they'd sent out for the undertaker to arrange a pyre, and started the rituals themselves. The women did come round, a little afterwards, and I helped to wash the body and wrap it up in herbs and oil and lay it in the atrium on a bier. Quite pathetic, really. I don't suppose there will be many visitors to mourn. Oh, don't look at me like that – I've done the job before, and Numidius was not a lengthy task. The poor man had gone to skin and bone.' She grinned. 'Anyway, it was useful in the end. How do you suppose that I got past the soldiers and escaped the house?'

'How did you?' She clearly wanted to me to ask.

'I simply walked out with the anointing women when they left. One ageing female with a basket looks very much like another, and I kept well to the middle of the group.'

I found that I was grinning back. 'Pretending to be someone else has been the theme of this affair. But I'm so relieved it worked for you. You are resourceful, Gwellia.'

She was delighted by my praise, but all she said was, 'Kurso was waiting at the workshop all this time. I knew that he would be concerned for me.'

The mention of attendants raised a question in my mind. 'Lallius didn't have a personal slave at all?' I said. 'Someone who might have tried to ransom him? It has been known for some servants to be foolishly attached – even to the most unlikely men.' I winked at Junio.

This time she laughed aloud. 'Well, he did have a servant, before he went to jail, but it seems that the slave took advantage of the imprisonment to throw himself on the mercy of the temple priests.'

'Great Jupiter!' I murmured, in genuine surprise. The punishment for a runaway is usually death, but there is one possible defence in law. If he can prove that his former owner was unnaturally cruel, he can appeal to another master who he hopes will be less unkind, pleading jeopardy in mitigation of his crime. But it is a desperate gamble, and not always justified.

'No doubt he had the scars to prove his case – the other servants say that he was often cruelly whipped – because the priests found in his favour straight away and arranged to sell him on. So the boy is no longer in the town, and certainly he would not have worked to get his master free. Quite the contrary. The longer Lallius was locked up in jail, the more certain the slave was of escaping into sanctuary this time. Apparently he'd twice attempted to run away before, but his master dragged him back, and took delight in seeing he was punished savagely. Numidius rebuked Lallius for that as well, but the boy said he was only doing what Commodus did, and was his father going to criticise the Emperor? So Numidius was helpless. You know what would have happened if Lalllius had denounced him publicly?'

I did. 'This Lallius sounds a most unpleasant character,' I said. 'No wonder his father had no time for him.'

Gwellia put down the oil lamp she was trimming, and came over to sit on Junio's stool beside the bed. 'That was probably the trouble, so the female servants say. The boy was never wanted from the start. His father blamed him for his mother's death and would not even look at him for weeks. His wet nurse had to insist he came and picked him up.'

I nodded. It was a ceremony in every Roman home, and signified acceptance into the family. Without it the child had no claim at all.

'All his life it has been much the same,' my wife went on. 'That nurse seems to have been the only one who cared – she seemed genuinely to be quite fond of him – but Numidius

281

dismissed her as soon as the boy was old enough to wean and brought in tutors to "make a man of him". He never bothered with the child himself, except to criticise. He saw the boy was not in want, of course – in fact when the boy was young he was more than generous, as if in that way he was doing his duty by the child. Lallius has never wanted for a single thing – except a little human company. His father did give him a puppy once, but I think I told you what became of that. It was a little better with his horse – Lallius learned to ride before he learned to walk, and the servants say that was the only time they ever heard him laugh.'

'You would make me feel almost sorry for the youth, if it were not for that murdered girl I told you of.' I began to give her an edited account of the horrors we had found.

She interrupted me. 'I know,' she said. 'Old Smelly-boots was telling us. He gave us all the details. No wonder that poor woman was so terrified.' She looked at me. 'Husband, do you really want to question her about the death?'

I shook my head. 'She knew Myrna's family, and that's what interests me,' I said. 'I am quite sure that they were involved in this kidnapping somehow, and for some reason they seem to have wanted to suggest that it was me.' I shook my head. 'I still cannot understand it. To the best of my knowledge I've never spoken to the girl. Or to the mother either. Not even to buy her herbal remedies. I always get mine from the kindling-seller's wife.'

It was Junio who spoke up from his post beside the door. 'Don't forget the doctor had a hand in all this, as well. Perhaps he had some dealing with the mother, over herbs.'

Gwellia stared at him. 'The medicus? Oh, Junio, don't be so absurd. The physician is a very clever man. He saved your master's life, I'm sure of it, and . . .' She trailed into silence as she saw my face. 'Husband, surely you don't believe what Junio says?'

'There was something odd about the doctor from the start,' I said. 'He was so secretive – and he clearly hated me. Because he knew I was suspicious, I believe. And now that he has disappeared without a word, I am more than ever sure that I was right.'

Gwellia was still frowning. 'Disappeared? I thought that he had simply changed his mind about the charge.'

'He left here without warning and never said a word,' I replied. 'Took all his books and scrolls and simply fled – and at the same time another ransom note turned up. Does that sound like a mere coincidence? The steward has sent the cart out after him, but I'm afraid he'll get away. And we don't even know where he was going.'

Gwellia stared. 'But I do,' she said, unexpectedly. 'He took the carriage that had brought me back from town. He went back to Glevum in it.'

She must have seen my startled face. 'You hired a carriage back?'

'I'm sorry, husband. I know it was extravagant, but I was still worried about your state of health, especially since they wouldn't let me come here yesterday. I could have had a litter, but there was Kurso too, and it was cheaper just to take a hiring-coach. Fortunately I had a little money with me. The driver had just dropped me at the roundhouse gate, and I was having an argument with the soldier – as I told you earlier – when the medicus came scuttling down the lane. He was hot and breathless, and when he saw the carriage he called out to it – said he was wanted urgently in town. The last I saw of him, he was climbing into it and swearing at the driver to be quick.'

I pushed the covers back and swung my feet on to the ground. 'Then I must speak to Marcus urgently,' I said. 'I know he's busy and he hasn't summoned me, but we must find out who owns that carriage and ask questions of the man.'

Junio stepped obediently forward with my sandals ready to kneel down and face them on my feet. Gwellia rose too, as though to order him away and insist that I lie down on the bed again, but I forestalled her with a gesture of my hand. A sudden inspiration had just come to me.

'Wait!' I said. 'I think I know who owns it. Great Minerva! How could I be such an idiot? I have had the answer all along. That woman with the children. She told us that Myrna's sister had taken all the carts her father built as a dowry when she wed – to a man who owned a little business on this side of town. Was it a hiring-stables, do you think?'

Chapter Twenty-six

Everyone was staring at me. Cilla, Porphyllia, my wife, and Junio who was kneeling at my feet by now. Even little Kurso, whom I now perceived loitering timidly in the rain outside the door, had obviously been listening and was watching goggle-eyed.

'Don't you see?' I said. 'This is the part of the pattern that was missing up till now. When Julia went out visiting that day, she didn't take a carriage of her own, because it had taken Marcus to the *ordo* meeting in the town. We know she sent out for a hiring-coach. And Myrna, of course, knew someone who would serve them beautifully! I wondered how the coachman noticed nothing when the kidnapping took place. But the answer is more simple than I thought. He was a part of the whole conspiracy. And now he has contrived to pick the doctor up, as well. We need to find out where these stables are, and bring this man in as soon as possible.'

'Well, I can tell you where it is,' my wife remarked. 'I picked up the carriage at the gates, of course, where it was waiting for custom as they always do, but the driver pointed out the stables as we passed. It is a little off the military road, a mile or so this side of Glevum – just before the *terratorium* begins. I could show you, if you were only well enough to walk that far. It is not difficult to find.'

I nodded. 'I think I've seen the signs for it.' I was not given to hiring vehicles myself, but I thought I knew the place she was referring to. Almost all the farmland bordering the main road on this side of the town had been purchased or appropriated by the state to supply the army with its food (the *territorium* that Gwellia had spoken of), but up the ancient tracks there were still areas – more infertile or less convenient – which the former owners had managed to retain. I recalled a sort of placard at the side of such a lane – an inexpert picture of a horse and cart, and a finger pointing to a gaggle of buildings up behind an inn. 'It must be a successful enterprise, if the likes of Julia hired a coach from them,' I said.

'It's the biggest hiring-stables in the area, or so that driver boasted. They've got everything from carts to carriages – or if you want an animal to ride, they rent out those as well. They've even got a handcart you can hire.'

I stretched out my other foot to Junio, who latched the second sandal on then helped me to my feet. A few moments earlier I had been weak and faint, but now I was buoyed up by sudden hope. Of course Marcus would not be in his most forgiving mood; the arrival of the ransom note alone would see to that. But now that the doctor had abruptly disappeared. I was no longer under threat – unless my patron chose to accuse and charge me on his own account. Of course, with the so-called evidence against me, that was always possible, but I would take a chance on that. I had been promised a day or two to prove my innocence. 'If Marcus will take me to those stables unannounced, I am confident that we will find the doctor on the premises,' I said.

'And Lallius?' my slave said hopefully. He had finished with my sandal strips by now. 'And possibly even Julia as well?'

'Perhaps,' I answered shortly. The truth was that I really did not know. I was certain that Philades and Lallius were linked somehow, but I still could not see what the connection was, or how Myrna and her family had got caught up in it. However, I hoped that we would soon find out. I saw the cup of mead that Junio had brought, which was now cooling rapidly on the chest beside the door. I gestured to Cilla that she should give it me.

'Master, it will be cold by now.' Junio almost let go of my arm. 'If you want a drink of mead, I'll get a proper one. Or Kurso can. The kitchens know exactly how to do it right, by now.'

I nodded. 'Kurso can go and fetch me one,' I said, but I drained the goblet before I gave it back. Even tepid mead is better than no mead at all, and as usual it seemed to give me energy. It gave me courage too. 'You can take me to see Marcus in the atrium, and the girls can stay here and attend my wife.'

Gwellia snorted, 'Husband, of course I am subject to your will, but I remind you that you have been ill. My place is close beside you in such circumstances, and if you are going to see your patron I am coming too. Besides,' she went on in a gentler tone, 'if you want to tell him about the hiring-carriages, perhaps I am the one with most to tell.'

I was about to reply that, in his present mood, Marcus was unlikely to be sympathetic to a delegation of that kind, but she forestalled me with a hand upon my arm.

'Husband, I have been kept away from you for what seems like days. Please allow me to accompany you now.'

There was an expression in her tone and eyes which I could not resist. I sighed. 'Oh, very well,' I muttered, not very graciously. I was afraid that Marcus might be very cross by now, and I wanted to protect her from his wrath.

Gwellia had more practical considerations in mind. 'Here, wait. It's raining in the court. You can't go out like that.' She picked up the battered leather bag – the one which had been missing from the roundhouse earlier, and which she had obviously taken with her into town. She opened it and pulled out a length of cloth. 'I brought your toga with me – I'd had it at the fuller's while you were so ill. Here, wrap it round you; it will help to keep you warm. And I've brought you a proper cloak, as well. A plaid one which I wove while you were sick. I meant it as a surprise for you when you were well again, but I can't think of a better moment than the present one.'

Junio was grinning like a maniac, but he wound my toga round me and arranged its folds, and when he'd finished Gwellia draped the cloak.

It look a little while, but my wife was right. The toga made me feel more like a man again, and home-made cloth was warm and comforting, without the weight of Aulus's heavy cloak. 'Thank you, Gwellia,' I said, and met her eyes. No words were spoken, but a great deal was said, and I went out into the courtyard warmed by more than plaid.

I was glad of my small procession when we reached the atrium. I was in the lead, on Junio's arm, with my wife a formal step or two behind, and the two female attendants bringing up the rear. The folding door which led into the atrium was shut, and Maximus and Minimus were standing guard outside. They looked at us apprehensively.

'The master is much occupied . . .' the older one began.

'He told us he was not to be disturbed . . .'

'And he's in a dreadful mood,' Maximus observed. 'With

that note and everything. He's – uh – got a flask of wine in there, as well. And he insists on pouring it himself.'

'He will want to see me, and hear what I have got to say,' I said, in my most formal voice, trying to convince myself that this was the case.

Maximus looked uncomfortable and shifted on his feet, 'Of course, citizen, if you command, we will go in and tell him you are here. Only, when the steward came, a little while ago . . .' he began, and paused. He was obviously nervous about saying any more, but his colleague interrupted in a rush.

'The master was so angry, you could hear him shout from here. Threatened to have him whipped – the senior slave!' He looked at me. 'So, be very careful, citizen. That ransom note disturbed him terribly.'

I nodded. 'Tell him I have news about the doctor's whereabouts,' I said. 'And an idea that might lead us to where Julia is, as well.' That was an overstatement, I was well aware, but I could think of nothing that was more likely to win my patron's ear.

I was right. Minimus departed, with another furtive glance, but he was quickly back again. He looked relieved. 'The master will see you straight away,' he said, and pulled the door ajar.

Marcus was sitting in his accustomed wicker chair. There was a jug of wine beside him, and from his flushed face and dishevelled air, it looked as though he'd emptied most of it. There was no sign of Pulcrus, but to my surprise the slave-trader was still in evidence.

He was a swarthy fellow in a rust-coloured tunic with a sort of greenish turban round his head, and had obviously been exhibiting his wares: not only the chubby female, who was standing naked in the centre of the room with her hands tied behind her so that her professional attributes were distinctly on display, but also several lengths of costly coloured silk – crimson, yellow, pink, emerald and blue – which had been laid out like rivers of vibrant colour on the floor. Silken treasures to take your breath away. Literally treasures – such fabrics were worth three times their weight in gold, if you were able to lay hands on them.

Marcus was ignoring all of this and gazing at a writing tablet in his hands. He wasn't angry, as I thought he might have been. His face was anguished and there was perspiration on his brow.

Another man might have realised that there was no chance of a sale, but the trader was persisting with his wheedling talk. 'Very rare, Excellence. Very fine. A special price for you.' His Latin was fluent but ungrammatical, and he was wringing his hands as if he could somehow squeeze a bargain out of them. 'I traded a whole cart of slaves for them. You remember last time that I come . . .'

Marcus looked up and interrupted, in a weary tone. 'I bought all you had, I know, and asked for more. But things are different now. Ah, Libertus. You have news for me?' This time he did stretch out his hand to me.

I stumbled to my knees and kissed it thankfully. 'I believe so, Excellence.'

'Very well.' He motioned me to rise, then snapped his fingers at the visitor. 'I'll take the girl. Put all the rest away. Speak to my steward for your money when you have finished packing up.' He turned to me, paying no attention to my little retinue. 'Now, what is it that you have to say? I warn you, it had better be significant. I am in no mood for trivialities. You have heard that I received another note?'

I nodded and rose slowly to my feet, trying to ignore the turbaned man who was now snatching up his precious wares almost from underneath our feet and placing them carefully in a lined wooden chest. 'The slave-trader brought it in, I understand?'

The fellow had been listening, for he stopped in the act of winding up a bale of damson silk, and came to bow before me as though I were a person of some consequence. Perhaps my small crowd of followers had led to that mistake. 'It was give me as I drive up to the door. A man on horseback, that is all I know. He wear a toga, so I know he wealthy man. I take the packet, and I bring it in. I no idea what it contains, I swear by Isis and all the gods of Nile.'

'He paid you to take it, I suppose?' I said. It was not an accusation, I was merely thinking aloud, but the trader was instantly afraid.

'Only a *denarius*, most gracious citizen. My cart is standing in the road, across the gate, and he cannot get past. He say "No answer is required" and gallop off. I am a poor man, citizen. I not turn down an honest chance to earn.'

Of course the fellow was unfortunate. He obviously could not know about the kidnapping – Marcus had succeeded in keeping his misfortune from the gossips in the town. But a *denarius* was such a handsome tip that I would have thought twice before accepting it. I'd have known at once that something was amiss, and the errand was likely to prove rather dangerous.

Marcus, however, had waved all this aside. 'Of course, of course, I am not blaming you. It's obvious this person, whoever he might be, did not wish to come up to the gate. If you had not been there, he would most likely just have thrown the tablet in over the wall, like the last time. The problem is not who brought it in, but that it came at all. So, when you have finshed with your cloths . . .'

He waited pointedly until the trader had first bundled up his goods, and then – walking backwards and clasping the box of fabrics against his chest – bowed himself and the naked wet nurse out.

Only then did Marcus burst out, bitterly, 'You know how much they are demanding now?'

I shook my head, and he named a sum which made me whistle in surprise. My patron is a very wealthy man, but even he would have some trouble in amassing it.

'By tomorrow, at the lastest, that is the demand. Or else they will return Julia to me, a little at a time.' His voice was slurred with wine, but there was no mistaking the raw anguish in his tone. 'And to show that they are serious, they have sent me this.' He handed me a little leather bag, whose drawstrings had been used to hold the tablet closed. It held what looked like a bloodstained fingertip, a woman's, neatly severed at the joint.

Shock and numbing horror made me speak before I thought. 'Of course, that might not be Julia's at all . . .' and then I stumbled to a stop. That was no solace, in the circumstances. If the man who sent it was capable of doing this to anyone at all, he was capable of doing it to Julia.

'I cannot take the chance,' Marcus murmured in despair. 'We've seen what these people did to Myrna, too. I'm to leave the money in the woods tomorrow night, close to where we left the bag before.' He sighed. 'The guards are to be withdrawn from Lallius's street as well, at least until after the father's funeral. Julia will be returned to us next day.' He frowned. 'I didn't know that he was even dead.'

I was wondering whether to urge him to attempt a

compromise and point out that the kidnappers had not honoured their promises so far, when my wife moved swiftly to my side, and made a deep obeisance of her own.

'With your permission, Excellence?' Her voice was low and sweet.

My patron gave her the phantom of a smile. 'Well?'

Gwellia, with a dignity which made me proud of her, told Marcus everything that she'd told me about the situation in the coin inspector's house. 'I can tell you this of my own knowledge, Excellence,' she finished, dropping him a bob.

'So Lallius needs to come back for the funeral,' he said, 'to take possession of his father's goods – and wants to ensure we don't arrest him on the way. Well, let him try. I'll have to withdraw the soldiers from the streets, for Julia's sake, but once she is safely back to me, I'll search the Empire till I find him out. The fact that he's inherited a large estate won't help him then: there's no sum large enough to bribe my private guards. Or the army either, when I have done with them.'

My patron obviously meant that he would bribe them himself – but I wondered if he would have any fortune left, if those demands were met. And he had no guarantee that he would ever see his wife again alive. But there was no point in saying any of that. 'That letter talks about the funeral,' I said. 'So the writer must have known Numidius was dead. Does that suggest that Lallius is in Glevum, do you think?'

'He knew the death was imminent.' Marcus was dismissive of such trivialities. 'They sent a message to the prison, after all.'

I was aware that I was frowning. 'But it is odd,' I said. 'If he knew he was about to inherit everything, why would he need to set up a kidnapping to ensure you set him free? Even if his father cut off his allowance, as he was always threatening, Lallius would have been able to pay the fine a thousandfold as soon as Numidius was dead. He must have been aware of that.'

Gwellia nodded. 'And why choose Julia and Marcellinus to abduct? There are other women in the town who would be easier targets, I am sure, and with less risk as well – though perhaps their husbands did not have judicial power or could not be relied upon to pay. Certainly not as handsomely as you.'

I stared at her. I had been over the same thoughts in my mind a hundred times, but suddenly the pattern took a different form. It was too early to say anything to Marcus yet – I would seem too foolish if it proved that I was wrong – but a visit to the stables might show if I was right.

'And there is the question of the hiring-stables, Excellence,' I said, and told him what I knew. 'The man who drove the carriage when Julia disappeared. I believe that he's a member of Myrna's family. And Philades used one of their vehicles to get away from here.' I did not add that I had always had suspicions of the man, but I could see by my patron's face that he had not forgotten that.

'Then I suppose we must go after him,' he acknowledged slowly. The admission pained him, I could see.

It was Gwellia who changed the subject. 'Talking of Myrna's family, by the way, whatever happened to her little girl?'

I stared at her. I had not asked myself the question, though I should have done.

Marcus was animated, all at once, though he could not entirely overcome the wine. 'No doubt she is with her grandmother – and probably at the hiring-stables too. Where else would the family have gone? And of course the sister will be there.' He was on his feet. 'Very well, Libertus, you shall have your way. We'll pay a visit to these stables and see what we can find. Maximus! Minimus!' He clapped his hands, and two anxious faces peered round the door. 'See that the carriage is prepared for me. As soon as possible.'

Maximus obediently disappeared at once, but Minimus lingered long enough to say, 'Master, that woman you brought in for questioning . . . ?'

Marcus sighed. 'Leave her under lock and key. I'm certain she can wait.' He glimpsed Gwellia's anguished face, and said impatiently, 'Oh, and send some bread and water in – for the children anyway. Now go, and do as you are bid. And send Pulcrus to attend me – I am going to get ready to go out.'

Chapter Twenty-seven

Even then, it seemed to take for ever before we were on our way. As the steward had predicted, it took some time for the carriage to be readied for the trip. Marcus was back in the atrium by now, tapping his baton on his leg – a sure sign that he was getting restless – and attempting to explain to Gwellia why there was no room in the carriage for her to come with us.

'But you will have to take attendants, surely, Excellence?' Her tone was humble, and she looked demurely up at him from under downcast lids.

He looked at her impatiently, but she gave him her most appealing smile. 'And supposing that you want to make arrests?'

Marcus was susceptible to female wiles, and she managed to persuade him, where I could never have. So when we set off down the lane at last, after the slave-trader and his lumbering wagon had been paid off and moved along, we were accompanied by Pulcrus and a contingent of the mounted guard and also, remarkably, by the military cart – with Gwellia, Cilla and Junio in the back of it. Malodius, having returned empty-handed from his search for Philades, watched us go, muttering discontentedly at being left behind, though he had been driving constantly since shortly after dawn and his horses were ready for a rest.

The journey was less jolting than it had seemed before. For one thing Gwellia had fussed over me with cushions for my back and a blanket to tuck round my knees, and for another I was feeling so relieved at my reprieve that I could have withstood far harsher journeys without too much complaint. Though there was an unpleasant moment as we passed the roundhouse, and I saw the soldier at the gate. He recognised the escort and raised his fist in a salute.

The driver took us to the Roman road, and we bowled along the wide paved thoroughfare which led all the way to the southern gate of town. It was not a route I very often used – it is a military highway and other travellers are forced to hug the muddy edges if a legion marches by, or an imperial messenger comes galloping along to bring sealed reports and orders from other garrisons. Today, however, we had military rights, and for once it was other people who had to huddle into ditches as our entourage swept through.

Marcus, though, was accustomed to such dignities, and was clearly getting restless and concerned. He pushed back the leather curtain, and demanded for the sixth or seventh time, 'Where is this famous hiring-stables, then? We shall have arrived in Glevum very soon.' Then, to the driver, 'Faster! Or I shall have you whipped.' It was not like my patron to be pointlessly unjust, but the danger to Julia weighed very hard on him.

'There it is, patron.' I was glad to see the sign. I gestured to the painted finger, but Marcus was already thumping on the roof, a signal to the driver that he wished to stop. Pulcrus cantered to the window space and Marcus relayed his orders through his page.

'Tell the man to drive a little up the lane but stop the

carriage just short of the inn. Libertus and I will walk the rest. You and Junio can follow us on foot, but the soldiers are to keep out of sight and to the rear, and guard the women till we give the sign. We don't want to rouse suspicions. But tell the guards to keep their sword arms free and their blades unsheathed. We may need them to move up quickly in support. A whistle will be the signal to attack.'

Pulcrus nodded and moved away to pass the orders on, and a moment later we were jolting up the track. It was not very long, however, before we stopped and the driver came round to help us down.

'Excellence, you are sure that you will be all right on foot from here? It is still raining and the lane is muddy.'

Marcus silenced him with one ferocious look. He stepped down, and stood waiting for me to do the same, tapping his baton on his hand this time. I clambered after him with as much haste as I could.'

'Very well, Libertus, you can lead the way. This visit was your idea, I think.'

He spoke as if I had come for entertainment's sake, but I knew him well enough to hold my tongue. This was my responsibility, he meant. I was not out of danger yet. However, I was content to lead the way – Marcus, with that patrician toga-band, did not look like a potential customer – unless some mishap had befallen his carriage wheels, perhaps? I was inventing some such story in my mind, to account for our appearance, when the owner of the hiring-stables hurried out and came towards us of his own accord.

He was an enormous, portly man, with a fringe of reddish hair and a look of greedy glee which told me that he had seen my patron's purple stripe, and was already hearing the chink of silver coins in his mind. He rubbed his huge hands in his leather apron and addressed himself to me. 'May I be of service, citizens?'

I was about to begin some tale about the carriage wheels when Marcus cut in with an abrupt, 'You hire out carriages and drivers, I believe?'

The man looked shifty. 'We do have a splendid carriage, citizens' – he clearly did not want to risk offence by not according Marcus the correct title of respect, so he took refuge in addressing both of us – 'and another, heavier vehicle which plies outside the town for trade. But both are out at present, I regret. I could offer you each a splendid mount, it that is any help. Or . . .' he glanced meaningfully at me, 'one of you might prefer to ride a mule? Other than that we only have a donkey cart or two. Of course, if you don't mind taking one of those . . .'

'Do I look like the kind of man who rides in a donkey cart?' Marcus had no need to say the words aloud. The contempt on his face expressed them perfectly.

I hastened to cover the embarrassed pause. 'I believe you had a recent passenger. A medicus who is a citizen. We are very anxious to have news of him.'

I had expected him to flinch, or to show some signs of guilt, but the man brightened, and his air of hopeful cupidity came back. 'A private medicus? I shouldn't be surprised. We have some most distinguished customers in town, members of the *ordo* and all sorts of wealthy men: some of them are quite regular customers of ours, the ones who don't keep horses or transport of their own. I will consult our records. Come with me.' He led the way into the stable opposite, where there were a number of crude columns scratched up on the wall. These were his 'records', clearly. 'When did this doctor use our services?' He spoke as if he were an advocate

300

or medicus himself, instead of a tradesman hiring out his goods.

'I think he hailed the carriage on the road,' I said.

The fellow shook his head. 'Those journeys are paid for by the mile,' he said. 'There's a device between the wheels which keeps account. But everything that's hired by the hour is noted up here on the wall – it tells us when things are due to be returned, and ensures that all the time is paid for properly.'

'And you note if people arrange a hiring in advance, I suppose, so you don't let it out to someone else?'

He took it as a compliment to his efficiency and turned his massive face towards me with a smile. 'Exactly, citizen.'

'Like when you used to go to Grappius's house?' I said. 'And take a certain lady back to her country home?'

This time there was no doubt of the effect. The sickly smile faded and his face grew pale. All the same, he tried to bluff it out. 'I don't know what you mean.' But his eyes were flickering to Marcus's stripe, and it was clear that it was dawning on him who the wearer was. He gnawed his upper lip and swallowed hard.

'I think you understand me very well,' I said. 'You sent a carriage round to Grappius's house not seven days ago. It was a fixed arrangement. If you can't find the record of the hiring on the wall, I've no doubt there is someone else who can. One of your drivers or stable boys perhaps. Though I suspect you drove that day yourself, since the lady and the child that you delivered at the end were not the ones you picked up at the start. It appears that they were kidnapped, and impostors took their place. And yet the coachman had nothing to report. Now how would you account for that?'

He was still looking desperately from Marcus to myself.

'So you know all that?' he muttered. 'She was sure . . .' He trailed off, breathing heavily, and ran a tongue round his lips.

'She?' Marcus could contain himself no longer. He stepped forward, and his face was black with rage. 'Do you mean that wretched wet nurse?'

The man was twice the size that he was but I think my patron might have tried to throttle him all the same, if I'd not intervened. 'I think he means her mother,' I observed. 'His mother-in-law, if I understand aright.'

I had glanced towards Marcus as I spoke, so the violent lunge towards me took me by surprise. Strong hands pushed me fiercely in the chest and I found myself sprawling on the ground, narrowly avoiding taking Marcus with me as I fell. Fortunately he stepped aside in time. His fury if I'd knocked him over would have rivalled Nero's own.

In the meantime, our man had got away. By the time we'd gathered our collective wits and I'd sat up again, he was already racing to the inn. Our slaves were rushing to our aid, but before anyone could stop him our quarry had run in and shut the door. As I scrambled to my feet, I heard the bolt slam to.

'We were listening to all that,' Junio panted. 'What do we do now?' But Pulcrus had already placed his fingers on his lips and was whistling between them: a single, long, high, piercing note. Almost before the sound had died out on the air, there was the clatter of hobnails storming up the lane, and six armoured soldiers were beside us with their daggers drawn.

Their leader had already seized an unlit torch brand from its bracket on the wall. 'Permission to set fire to the inn, Excellence? We are equipped with tinder and a flint. One flame against the thatch and it will all catch very fast. We'll smoke them out; it won't take very long. Or do you want us to kick down the door?'

Marcus nodded, and in no time at all three of the soldiers had formed into a line, and on the leader's signal they rushed up to the door and thrust the weight of their mailed shoulders on to it, followed by three heavy hobnailed feet.

The door was old but massive and it held, but there was a dreadful creaking from the lock. The soldiers were making ready to have another try when suddenly the door was opened from within and a youngish woman stood there, with two small children at her heels. I noticed that she had a heavily bloodstained bandage round the fingers of one hand.

'All right,' she said, in a voice which trembled so that it was hard to hear the words. 'Take me. But let the children go.'

The leader took her at her word. 'Seize her!' he called, and she was quickly bound with rope. The children looked on with terrified eyes, until Junio and Pulcrus look one each and led them off in the direction of the cart. The soldiers looked at Marcus.

'Search the house,' he ordered, and the three door-stormers disappeared inside. 'We want the husband – and the mother too, or so Libertus says.'

The captive shook her head. 'It is too late to do anything to her,' she said. Her voice was shaking and expressionless, like someone drugged. 'She's dead. Took a rope and hanged herself a little while ago. We had to put her in the paupers' pit. She couldn't live with it, you see, that he could do such things.'

I looked at her. 'Because of what he had done to Myrna – and to you?'

She nodded. 'My finger was the final stone that broke the bridge.' Her face was ashen. 'I told her I'd done it with a knife, by accident – but she knew it was a lie. Up to then, I think, she'd tried to convince herself that he was not responsible for Myrna's death, but in the end she had to face the truth. She felt that he'd betrayed her.'

'After all that she had done for him, through all these years?' I prompted.

Another nod. 'Exactly.' She was close to tears. 'It's destroyed the family, you know. She felt she'd brought this on us – and she did. We used to be so happy, just the three of us.'

'Before you knew your half-brother was alive? And who and where he was?'

Beside me, I glimpsed Marcus's puzzled frown, but she didn't even look surprised that I had guessed. 'We should have known, I suppose. Mother was always so anxious for gossip from the town. Anything concerning Numidius or Lallius at all. And she'd talk about the boy for hours, till we were tired of it: how he was faring at the school, and how the servants said how big he'd grown and how rich and famous he was going to be. Oh, we knew she'd been his nursemaid once, of course we did. We even knew she'd been the midwife who delivered him, but we thought she was attached to him because she'd wet-nursed him. He was a sickly baby and she suckled him to health. It never dawned on us to guess the truth.'

'That when Lallia died in childbirth, her baby had died too – and your mother saw a chance to make a future for her son?'

Marcus pushed the guard aside and came to stare at me. 'Her son? Nobody told us that she had a son. You mean that Lallius was illegitimate?'

'Excellence, he was perfectly legitimate,' I said. 'But he was not Numidius's son.' I could see that he was going to question me again, and I was becoming unsteady on my feet. I said humbly. 'Patron, I think I can explain it to you now. But perhaps, if I might crave permission to sit down while the guards complete their search?'

Marcus scowled, but he nodded and led the way inside. The inn was a long building, and the room that we went into took up almost all the lower floor. Like many small civilian inns it was an uninviting place: a dark, low-ceilinged area, thick with grime and dust, with battered jugs and tankards hung from hooks, and a shelf of ancient platters near the inner door. There were a pair of large bare tables, half a dozen stools – mere sawn-up tree trunks – and a sort of bench affair beside a huge and smoking fire. A huge amphora, presumably of wine, was set into the floor, and there was a battered cooking pot beside the fire. Aside from this, and the accumulated litter on the beaten earth of the floor, there was very little comfort to be had, although a steepish ladder led upstairs at the back to what was clearly an equally uninviting sleeping space above, from which a series of muffled thumps and oaths could now be heard.

Marcus took possession of the bench, while I sank thankfully on the most stable of the stools. The girl was pushed towards us, with the three remaining soldiers at her back and sides. 'You were explaining about Lallius,' Marcus said to me. 'I hope that your account is plausible.'

'I believe so, Excellence. Remember that woman we were questioning? She told us that Myrna's mother was widowed when she was very young and had been forced to work as a midwife and a wet nurse to survive, because her husband left her destitute. We should have seen the implications then – to be a wet nurse she must have had a child. No doubt it was small and sickly – as Secunda said just now – and since Numidius refused to see his son it was not difficult for her to make a swift exchange.'

Secunda could have kept silence, but she chose to help my case. 'Pardon me, Excellence, but the citizen is right. Mother is dead, and there's no need to protect her any more. And who was hurt by it? Lallia's child was dead. It did outlive its mother by an hour or two, long enough for Mother to get it swaddled up – and since she had so lately given birth herself she made an honest effort to give the child the breast. But it was too weak to suckle and it died. She thought of her own child, frail and sick and forced to stay with strangers in a hovel at the gate, because she had no means to keep it otherwise. She put the baby in its cradle and went out then and there, apparently to "get some strengthening herbs" – she was famous for her remedies even then – placed her son in her basket underneath a cloth, smuggled him in and exchanged the dead child for the living one. No one asked what happened to her infant, naturally – she just threw the little corpse into the river later on.'

Marcus looked startled. 'And none of the attendants noticed anything?'

'The other maids were busy with their mistress's corpse: they paid very little heed to what she did. And Numidius was too upset to care.' She looked at us, and suddenly tears were streaming down her face; but since her arms were bound she could not raise her hand to wipe them off. 'Was it so very dreadful, gentlemen? She gave a grieving father the comfort of a child, and saved her own baby from a hungry death.'

I said softly, 'For a time it must have seemed as if she'd found a perfect answer to her needs – she was caring for her child and being paid for it – but Numidius did not like to have reminders of his wife. He had her wean the child as fast as possible and then dismissed her from the house. It must have been an awful blow to her.'

The faintest smile illuminated Secunda's strained face. 'Fortunately she met my father while she was working there. He built a cart for someone who lived close nearby. He married her immediately she was dismissed – and she took in nurslings till she had children of her own. Myself and Myrna. She was very good to us. But still she went to Glevum every single week. She used to sell her herbs there and seek news of her son. And she called me Secunda, though I was the older one. I always wondered why.'

Marcus was looking totally appalled. He had just worked out one implication of all this. 'So Lallius is not a citizen at all?'

Secunda said, 'But of course he didn't know that, Excellence. My mother kept her secret to herself. She didn't even tell the family, until very recently, when she needed our help to get him out of jail – and then she swore us all to secrecy on the oath of Jove.'

'Then how did Libertus come to know of it?' He sounded quite aggrieved.

'I didn't know it, Excellence. I worked it out. It had to be something of the kind. Lallius could not have done the kidnapping himself or sent the ransom note, since he was under lock and key; and we know that no one in Numidius's household did. And it couldn't be his friend – he put him into jail. It seemed a mystery. But once we were convinced that Myrna was party to the plot, and how the deed was done, it was not hard to see who else might have been involved. So I asked myself, why would Myrna's family take such awful risks? You gave me the answer, Excellence, when you said that families will do extraordinary things to help their own. When I put the parts together I began to see. And impersonating Julia was not so strange a plan – substituting one person for another as they did. It was a trick that Myrna's mother had used successfully before . . .'

I was interrupted by the arrival of the soldiers from upstairs. They had Secunda's husband roped between them like a temple sacrifice and were prodding him forward with their dagger-points, one steep step at a time. He was looking bruised and shaken and it was obvious that he'd put up a fight. He was a strong man, but the guards were armed and fit, and there were three of them.

'We found him in the sleeping space upstairs,' the leader said. I noticed he was panting heavily. 'I believe there was someone else as well – but he jumped out of the upper window space and ran away. Permission to go after him, Excellence?'

Marcus scowled impatiently. 'Of course!' he snapped, and the soldier departed at a run. 'And you two,' Marcus added, 'take this fellow to the cart. Tie him to the rear frame and make sure he doesn't get away.'

I saw the fellow flinch. Being dragged behind a cart was an appalling way to die – forced to run until your heart was fit to burst and when you stumbled – as you inevitably did – being slowly battered into pieces on the stony road.

Secunda looked at the huge figure with affection in her eyes, and flung herself at once upon her knees. 'Don't be too harsh with him,' she begged. 'It was we women who carried out the plan. I'll tell you everything. Myrna had pressed her mistress to buy a teething potion for the child, and so persuaded her to come into our house. She'd been there several times before, in fact. She liked to buy a potion that my mother made, a secret recipe to help her keep her youth, and she didn't want her husband to suspect – forgive me, Excellence.'

Marcus made a strange hurrumphing sound. 'So she had the potion?'

'But this time we slipped in a sleeping draught. It was a very strong one, and while she was asleep we slipped off her wig and *palla* and I went in her place. In fact, I had to take her *stola* too, though we had not intended that at first – her cloak was so short that it showed my legs. The infant was no problem. Marcellinus thought it was a splendid joke to take off all his clothes – but none of my niece's things would fit him properly. My mother had to grease him thoroughly to ensure he didn't take a chill. And then we wrote the note out on that piece of bark, and one of my children dropped it at your door. We even used a piece of Julia's dress to tie it up and put in a little snippet of their hair, to make it look as threatening as possible – though of course we never meant them any harm. But it was all our doing, Excellence. My husband really had no part in it. He only drove the carriage. Brought Julia and her baby and my sister to the house – and didn't look too hard at who came out of it.'

'And he dropped those logs across the lane,' I said. 'I recognise him now.'

She nodded. 'He had a load of timber to deliver at the time, and he was close nearby. I couldn't think how else to block the road.' She glanced towards her husband. 'But he didn't want to do it. I had to weep and beg.'

'Waste of a good load of wood,' her husband grumbled. 'I had to leave it there, and they took it into the villa later on. I had to stand by and watch them bear it off. Cost me a whole day's work and more. And the hire of the cart as well. I'm lucky no one caught me in the act. I'd just managed to unload the logs when your litter came in sight.'

'So you stood by with your cart and cursed at the delay? And even helped the litter-bearers move the logs away? I should have asked questions at the time – loads of wood don't just appear from nowhere, and when there is an empty cart nearby . . .'

Secunda still had her arms bound tight behind her back, but she tried to turn to me. 'We had to do something, don't you see. Our plans had gone awry. We meant to keep them just a day or two at most – just long enough to frighten everyone – and then, when Lallius was free, we'd let them go. We knew we'd have to flee, of course, but we had the carriages and we could have made a living somewhere else. And it meant so much to Mother. She even foolishly supposed that Lallius might give us a reward – that's why she went to tell him what we'd done. And then it all went wrong. Myrna was desperate to save the child, at least. She even talked to Julia, through the window space. It was Julia who suggested that we came to you. Myrna would have let Julia go as well, by then, but she didn't have the key to let her out. Julia passed the child out through the window.'

'And she came out to my roundhouse to try to talk to me?'

She nodded. 'But they wouldn't let her in, so we tried to think of some way she could get the child to you. I was holding Marcellinus in the basket close nearby – we didn't dare let anybody see him in our care. Your maid said you were being carried to the villa later on – so we stopped the litter and I pushed him in. It was the best that we could do. We hadn't got much time.' Tears were shining in her eyes again. 'Myrna paid dearly for that act of kindness – with her life.'

That hit its mark with Marcus. He cleared his throat, and said, a little more kindly than he had so far, 'None the less you kidnapped them. You confess to that. Now, get up to your feet, and if you hope that I will spare your life – and that of your wretched husband over there – you'll answer this. What have you done with Julia? And where is the money you extorted yesterday?'

She shook her head and began to weep, helplessly this time, in great gulping sobs. 'I'm sorry, Excellence, I swear I do not know. I don't know what is happening any more – and Mother didn't either in the end. He just took over and altered everything, and all our plans went hopelessly astray.'

'Who took over? I don't know what you mean.' Marcus was instantly severe.

This was my moment and I seized it gleefully. 'I think I can explain it, Excellence,' I said, trying to keep the triumph from my voice. 'This is where the medicus comes into the affair.'

Chapter Twenty-eight

There was a terrible hush. I knew that I had their attention. I could feel all eyes on me, and I hastened to tell them what I had deduced.

'I don't know how he knew Secunda's family – an interest in buying herbs, perhaps – but Philades had met Numidius all right. You remember he was invited to inspect the girl when the coin inspector was looking for a new bride? Presumably he was working with Lallius all along, and once Lallius was free, he persuaded the kidnappers to change their mind and demand a ransom for Julia's release. Maybe he even promised them a share – though it is doubtful that he would have honoured that. Or perhaps he simply worked out how the kidnapping was done, and threatened to betray the family. He was capable of that. Clever too, pretending to work out all the business with the cloak, and persuading Lallius to hide the bag and clothing at my house so that he could arrange to find it. He was determined to persuade you that I had a hand in it – perhaps because he knew that I suspected him throughout.'

I finished with a flourish, and looked expectantly about.

Marcus was looking doubtful. 'It still seems highly implausible to me – though I suppose the fellow did disappear the moment that the final ransom note appeared. And you have been proved right in every other way,' he muttered grudgingly. 'I suppose I must concede the truth of what you say.'

Secunda had been watching this in open disbelief, and suddenly she could no longer hold her tongue. She was still in her beseeching posture on the floor, but she shook herself free from the soldier who was guarding her and shuffled over to me on her knees.

'Citizen, I know nothing of any medicus. It was Lallius entirely who brought this grief on us.' She turned to Marcus. 'My mother went to him so proud, you know, the day that you made the announcement in the town. She and Myrna were in the forum listening – as you know, because they left the scroll – and afterwards she went directly to the jail, and let Lallius know exactly what we'd done. And instead of being grateful, he was simply furious. Seized her by the throat and shook her savagely – if there had not been a jailer just outside the door, I believe there might have been a tragedy. Perhaps there was. He demanded to know why she had dared to interfere, and in the end he dragged the truth from her – that he was her son. And then it all got ugly. We had Julia and Marcellinus in our outhouse then: we'd swept it out and made it comfortable, with blankets and fresh straw and everything, and we were keeping Julia more or less asleep. The less she knew of what was happening, the better, Mother said.'

I did not dare to look at Marcus's face. The thought of his beloved wife reduced to sleeping on straw, and locked into a ruined stable, was almost more than I could contemplate. How he must feel about it, only Pluto knew. 'And Lallius changed all that?' I managed, in a strangled voice.

She nodded. 'He stole the key and said that he would take charge of the matter himself. Of course, Mother realised then that things were desperate. He sent her for a horse to get him out of town as soon as the order for his release came through, and naturally she thought of one of ours. She found our driver just outside the gate, and got him to bring Myrna here. Out of harm's way, she said. Then we attached an animal behind the vehicle, and took it back to wait for Lallius.'

'But you expected Lallius to go straight to his home?'

'He wasn't going to do that. He'd made that very clear. There'd been some argument with his father – or his supposed father, I should say – and he was barred, he said, so he would stay with us, since we had cast him out upon the street. Anyway, it rather suited him. An inn on the outskirts of the town was the last place his creditors would look for him, and since we were family, he said, he did not expect to pay. And we were not to take any other visitors while he was here, he made that clear as well. He even started threatening my mother over it.'

'And Julia?' Marcus was clearly impatient now. 'She was at Myrna's all this time?'

Secunda nodded. 'My husband had the donkey cart set up – he was starting off to get that load of logs – and he took Myrna back to Mother's house at once: I was there already, looking after all the children for the day. When my sister told me what had happened, I was horrified. We couldn't do anything to help Julia, of course, because Lallius had the key, but she passed the baby to us through the window space – and the rest I think you know.'

'And what did Lallius say when he arrived and found the child was gone?' Marcus was clearly following all this.

Another frantic nod. 'He was beside himself with rage, but there was nothing he could do. Marcellinus was already safe. We knew that because just before Lallius arrived your page turned up and asked for Myrna back – I thought that I would die of fright. We hadn't catered for that possibility. Luckily Myrna had gone to the neighbour's with her child – she didn't want her daughter there when Lallius turned up. But Julia was still hidden in the stable at the time.'

'And when Lallius came?'

'He decided he would turn our stupid plans to some effect, he said. He wrote the ransom note – he'd brought a writing tablet with him from the jail, from some friend of his who'd written to him there. Of course we begged and pleaded but he paid no heed to us. He even went in to see Julia and gloated over her. The ransom was all his idea, he said, and he was going to take her somewhere else – and then she'd learn what being a prisoner meant. But he could not take her with him then, because he only had a horse. He lurked around the woods near the villa until he saw your carriage leave and threw the tablet in over the wall. There were watch-geese in the orchard, he told us afterwards, and he knew that they would soon be fed. He rode back to the inn and drank all the wine we had, then went out later on. I suppose he picked the money up.'

'He didn't bring it here?' I gestured at the inn.

'Said it was safer where it was – and he'd put Julia somewhere safe as well. He went out again this morning, shortly after dawn, with a writing tablet that my husband had, and I knew he was going to do it all again. He said he'd teach us to let Marcellinus go, and he now knew exactly where to hide the ransom bag. And he took our best horse with him as well.'

'But he has been back here? Someone leaped out of the window space upstairs.'

'I hope he broke his neck,' she muttered bitterly. 'But of course he won't. It's always others who suffer for his deeds. And he wouldn't even tell us where he'd been.'

'I think we know that anyway,' I said. 'He put Marcellinus's garments in the ransom bag and left it my home. I think we even passed him on the way. Latter he wrote the other ransom note and got the slave-trader to bring it in. Obviously he had money with him then – he gave the fellow a *denarius* for doing it.'

'I doubt that any money would last him very long. He talked about the ransom and all the things that he was going to do with it. I could see how he had got himself so terribly in debt. That was why my mother hatched this plot, you know – she was afraid that Numidius would disinherit him. He had threatened to do it several times before, but last time she went to Glevum she was convinced he would. The servants told her so. This legal hearing was the final straw. If the magistrates decided that it should come to trial, and Lallius was fined, his father was about to change his will. She'd saved him from all that. You would have thought that Lallius would be grateful, wouldn't you?'

'Let him tell you that himself.' The voice came from the door, and there was Gwellia, dripping in the rain, holding a soaking child in either hand. 'We have someone here that you might like to meet.' She hurried in and let the soldiers pass. They had another captive, a short, dark, fleshy youth, whose handsome face was petulant and slack and veined with wine.

Gwellia turned to me and Marcus. 'This is Lallius, of course. I would have recognised him anyway from what the servants said – fat face, slack jaw, small eyes, and twisted mouth – but when I saw that he was sneaking out of here,

317

and that he had a toga, I guessed who it must be. He started limping down the road towards the carriage first – I think he hoped to bribe the driver for a lift – but when he saw the military cart behind it he turned round and hobbled off. I sent the slaves to catch him. He wasn't moving very fast – he's hurt his ankle in some way – so it wasn't very hard, and he's not the sort of man to fight. You would have been proud of Junio, though – he tackled him round the knees and threw him to the ground, then held him till the guards arrived to take control.'

Lallius bore the marks of a scuffle. His toga looked as though no fuller would ever get it clean, he was smeared from head to foot with blood and grime, and one ankle was hugely swollen, with the sandal dangling from a broken strap. But he had received a Roman education and it showed.

'I am Lallius Numidius,' he said. 'What is the meaning of this outrage, citizens? I have been set on unprovoked and arrested without cause. If I am to be charged, I demand an advocate.'

Marcus looked contemptuous. 'Demand? You have no right to demand anything. You're not a citizen. We have witnesses to swear that you're the midwife's son.'

Lallius was collected. 'You can't prove anything. And I have rights in law. My father picked me up when I was laid before him; there are witnesses to that. I believe that makes me legally his son. And I was born free in Glevum, whoever sired me. That makes me legally a citizen, I think.'

I am not an expert on the niceties of law, but Marcus is a senior magistrate. 'You'll lose that status fast enough, if you are tried for this. It will be slavery in the mines for you, at least.'

'And what will I be charged with? Kidnapping?'

'The death of Myrna,' I exclaimed. 'We found her stabbed to death.'

'Indeed. It's most unfortunate. I heard of it myself. A robbery, by the sound of it. I hear the place was ransacked, and the treasures gone.'

Secunda struggled forward in her bonds. 'Don't believe him, Excellence. It was him for sure. He killed her because she had been to see you at the roundhouse earlier. Lallius was convinced that she'd betrayed us then. She pleaded that she'd simply smuggled out the child – and she was in as much danger as the rest of us. But he did not believe her. He obviously wanted to find out what she'd said – no doubt that's why he tortured her before she died.'

I looked at her keenly. 'And how do you know that? No member of the family has been near the place since we discovered her. Marcus has had the cottage under guard.'

Secunda seemed to crumple, like an empty water sack. 'My mother told me, citizen. She went back that night – after she'd been to Glevum, as she always did. It nearly broke her heart. The house was empty, and my sister dead. Julia was gone, and all our treasures too. She could not stay there with that dreadful sight. She left it as it was and walked all the way to us, though it was dark by that time and the roads were dangerous. She was in a kind of nightmare. I don't think she even gave a thought to thieves and wolves and bears. That's why she . . .' She trailed off into silence.

I shuddered, trying to imagine how it must have felt, finding your daughter murdered in that way. It had been bad enough for us.

Lallius interrupted with a sneer. 'You can't prove any part of that,' he said. 'I have a witness who will swear that I was with him all evening.'

'Wait a minute!' I said suddenly. Another fragment of the mosaic fell neatly into place. 'A witness? Would this be Cassius, by any chance? The man who insisted that you should be in jail?'

Lallius shot me a look that would have withered iron. 'And supposing that it is? It's not unknown for friends to reconcile.'

Gwellia glanced at me. 'Especially when a man can pay his debts? Is that why you were interested in money all along? Why, what's the matter, husband?'

I had leaped up from my makeshift stool again. 'It all makes perfect sense. Of course it was the money. His father was intending to get married, wasn't he? That's what Philades told us – that he wanted to get another heir. And that's it, don't you see? He really was intending to disinherit his son. But Lallius goes to prison, and his father's taken ill. Drinking bad water, everybody says. And who is quite above suspicion, because he isn't there? Why, Master Lallius, of course – who is in jail because his closest friend conspired to put him there. Didn't Cilla tell us that he sent his father an amphora of his favourite vintage, in an attempt to make peace between them. Poisoned water? More likely poisoned wine.'

Lallius was defiant still. 'You can't prove any part of that.'

'That latest note – it mentioned Numidius's funeral.' Marcus was joining the inquisition now. 'You were obviously confident that he would soon be dead – and your servants merely told you he was ill.'

Lallius said, 'But I've . . .' and stopped.

'You've been receiving letters from Cassius, perhaps? The man who is supposed to be your enemy? Who more likely than a fellow pupil to send you a letter in the jail – on an old writing tablet which you used at school. You daubed it red and used it to scratch the ransom note. Fortunately, we still have it at the villa – we'll ask his servants whether it is his.'

Lallius was losing much of his bluster now. 'You can't prove anything,' he muttered. 'Not that I murdered Myrna, or Numidius. And even by your own account I am not guilty of the kidnapping.'

I gestured to Secunda. 'You chopped the top joint of her finger off,' I said.

He flushed, but then recovered. 'Who accuses me? I heard her say, in front of witnesses, that she had done it accidentally with a knife.'

'I accuse you,' I said with sudden emphasis. Formally, before this magistrate, of that, of Myrna's murder, and of parricide as well.'

He looked at me rebelliously. Murder of your father is one of the most severely punished of all crimes. 'But he was not my father – you have said as much yourself.'

'So you are not entitled to inherit his estate?'

Too late, he realised his mistake. He gave a cry of protest and launched himself on me.

'And you can add the charge of physical assault upon a citizen,' I said. 'In front of a magistrate, as well.'

He turned and spat at Marcus, like a beast at bay. 'You won't arrest me, Roman. Not if you want to see your wife alive.'

'So you have got her captive.' Marcus clenched his fists. It was obvious to all of us what he would like to do.

Lallius gave his twisted smile. 'But I won't tell you where – not unless you set me free, and give me safe conduct from the province too. There are several boats in Glevum, at the river dock. Let me get on one and your wife goes free.'

I could see that Marcus was wavering again. 'You cannot trust him, Excellence,' I said.

Marcus had come to that conclusion for himself. 'I think I'll have you taken to the public jail. There are people there with ways to jog your memory. I think you'll tell me where she is, and fairly quickly too.'

He was right. Lallius had suddenly paled and there was perspiration on his upper lip.

'Perhaps we should pay a visit to this Cassius,' I said. 'That seems the likely place to look for her.' I saw at once from Lallius's face that I had guessed aright and I pressed my advantage ruthlessly. 'We know that Cassius placed an accusation with the court, and was recently the subject of a will. No doubt the authorities can tell us where he lives – unless Lallius prefers to do it and save himself the pain?'

'Well?' One of the soldiers pressed his sword-point under Lallius's throat, forcing him to stretch his neck till he could hardly breathe. 'Are you going to tell us? Or shall I have a little accident?'

Lallius's eyes were bulging from his head. 'She's . . . at his villa . . . at the back . . . in the . . . disused pig-house . . . on the farm.' He was terrified to speak the words and more afraid to stop. 'It's . . . just outside . . . the city gates . . . the west side . . .' He stammered the directions one by one.

Marcus nodded, and the soldier took the sword away. 'Very well, take him into the cart. Tell the commander he's my prisoner and I want him questioned till he squeaks. And if he attempts to run away again, you have my permission to kill him there and then, though a clean death is probably too good for him. I'd prefer to see him given to the beasts.' He spoke brutally, but I could see relief and hope already lifting the worry from his face.

As the soldiers dragged Lallius away, Secunda gave a cry

of anguish. 'Excellence, my husband! They have tied him to the cart. I beg you . . .'

Gwellia had the children, one under either arm, like a mother hen protecting chickens with her wing. 'Excellence,' she murmured, 'let me add my plea to hers. For the children's sake. She did her best for your son, after all.'

I would not have dared to utter such a thing, but she was clearly moved and Marcus seemed to be considering her words. There was a long moment, and then he gave a sigh.

'Gwellia, what you say is true.' He turned to Secunda. 'Very well, woman, for my son's sake I consent to spare his life – at least for now. I am going to send this villain on his way to the Glevum garrison and drive across myself to find my wife. Libertus and my page will come with me. Your husband can provide a carriage to take Gwellia and her slaves to the guard-house at the south gate of the town. They can await us there. But I shall send tomorrow, and if we find you here, you and your whole family will be sold as slaves, and your property forfeit to the state.'

Secunda looked dumbstruck, but this was merciful – and not entirely without precedent. Citizens are often sentenced to something similar – banished, interdicted from fire and water (which means that nobody can harbour them), and given a day to make good their escape, after which they may be killed if they are found. The difference here was that this was not a court, and Secunda was not a citizen.

When she said, 'Thank you, Excellence,' she meant it from her heart.

It was all over fairly quickly after that. Lallius's directions were accurate, and we found Cassius and his villa without difficulty. For a moment the gate-keeper refused to let us in, but one glimpse of Marcus's seal ring and he quickly changed his mind.

Cassius came out to meet us. He was not as I expected. He was tall and thin, and nervous-looking, and he stuttered when he spoke. It was clear that even now he was more afraid of Lallius than of us: the very mention of his name made the stammer worse.

'I d-d-d-don't know what you're w-w-w-wanting, citizens. You'd b-b-b-best ask L-L-L-Lallius himself. I'm exp-p-p-pecting him in just a little while.'

'Then you will wait for him in vain,' my patron said. 'He's on his way to jail – and you will be joining him quite soon. In the meantime I have come here to collect my wife – I believe that you have locked her in the sty.'

I have never seen anyone collapse as Cassius did. He wept, he grovelled, and he wrung his hands and had to be half carried out towards the farm, and the ancient pig-house at the back of it. But the knowledge that Lallius was safely under guard had made him almost eager to comply.

Even then he dithered with the key, and it was Pulcrus in the end who picked it up, and turned it with difficulty in the lock. It was a larger building than I had rather feared, more like a little barn in size, but stone-built, cold and draughty and smelling dreadfully of pigs. We stood there, blinking in the gloom. For a moment it seemed that there was no one there. Then there was a muffled whimper from the other side, and what had looked like just a pile of filthy straw proved to be a sort of makeshift bed, with something long and struggling in the midst of it.

It was Julia, of course, though she was gagged and bound, and dressed in a wretched tunic like a slave. Her hair was lank and dark and straggling – her own hair, since she had lost her wig – and her face and arms were smeared with mud, or worse. I had to look more than once before I was sure that it was really Marcus's wife.

My patron had no doubts. He was already at her side, and tugging off the gag, and pulling out his dagger to cut away her bonds.

'Husband!' I heard her whisper, and he said 'Julia!'

'Marcellinus?'

'He's safe.' Marcus clasped her to him, and she began to sob.

So, thinking that discretion was the better part of sense, I motioned to the slaves and Cassius, and we tiptoed out and left them together for a while.

Chapter Twenty-nine

When they emerged a little afterwards, it was all activity. Cassius, who kept swearing by all the gods there were that 'I d-d-d-didn't know she was a s-s-s-citzen. I th-th-thought she was a s-s-slave-girl he wanted to s-sell on', was concerned to offer us every luxury – as though that might somehow limit his guilt in this affair. The discovery of a sum of money hidden in the straw – almost but not quite the amount which had been put into the ransom bag – and a pile of Myrna's treasures in a trough, did suggest that Lallius had not kept him fully informed.

'He said he'd b-b-break my arms for m-m-me, if I refused to help,' Cassius pleaded, producing his own cloak to wrap Julia in, after the slaves had brought fresh water, sweet oils and linen cloths for her to clean herself. He had offered figs and dates and almond cakes as well, but all she wanted was a sip of wine. 'Honestly, Excellence, I had n-n-no idea.'

'Well, you can tell that to the courts.' Marcus was abrupt. 'In the meantime, have your servants go and fetch a litter here to take us home. My wife is obviously not well enough to face a carriage drive. If only I still had the medicus. I wonder where he's gone.'

The medicus! I had forgotten him, and his sudden disappearance – was it just hours ago? 'I think he's gone to

Glevum,' I supplied. 'Gwellia heard him tell the carriage-driver to take him to the gates.'

Marcus turned sharply. 'Could you find him, do you think, and bring him back to me? I know that he went off without a word, but I'm prepared to overlook that if he'll care for Julia. Here.' He stripped off his ring and handed it to me. 'Take this seal as my authority. You can have the carriage – I'll stay with Julia. When you get to the city, tell the carriage-driver to meet you at the guard-house where Gwellia and her slaves are waiting. He can bring you home when you are ready.'

I nodded. 'I will try to find him, Excellence. I would like to see him, on my own account. From something Lallius said, I have a notion where to look.'

I was right in my surmise. I found him on a ship in Glevum dock. It was a scruffy wool-ship bound for Gaul, and clearly almost ready to be off. The captain was a surly fellow, and refused at first to let me board at all, but a glimpse of Marcus's seal soon changed his mind on that.

'I'm just an honest trader, citizen,' he whined. 'If someone asks me for a passage – and a citizen at that – am I to refuse him, when he pays me handsomely? Not my business to ask him why he wants to go. If he's offended someone in high places, it's no affair of mine.' He let me up the gangplank – a wobbly piece of wood – but he didn't offer to accompany me.

I hate being on the water – even a ferry on the river makes me sweat. Those few days aboard the slave-ship had seen to that. The boat was shifting on the river, and lurched beneath my feet, and I clutched desperately at the cargo to keep myself upright. The smell of wool and skins was over-powering, and it was already very warm and stuffy in the hold. But there was an unexpected space along the side and I forced myself to inch along it to the front.

The medicus was cowering in a space up at the prow. He had made a sort of nest among the sheepskins for his body and his scrolls and there was a flask of something at his side and a chunk of bread as well. All the same he looked as wretched as I would have been myself, and I felt an unexpected sympathy.

He had pulled his toga up around his head to form a hood, and closed his eyes as if to shut out the sight of wool. He did not seem to notice my approach.

'Thersis?' I murmured, and he answered to his name. He shot upright at once.

He looked at me, and groaned. 'The pavement-maker. I might have known. I suppose there's no point in a struggle. You'll have guards outside – and they will arrest me anyway. Well, you'll have your wish. They'll take me back to Rome and into slavery again. No doubt my owner will brand me and keep me all my life in chains – if they do not execute me first. I almost wish they would. But he's offered such a huge reward for my return that I expect they'll be intent on claiming that. No doubt you'll get a handsome share of it.'

I said nothing. He looked very old and sad, but he had lost his lofty manner and was speaking man to man. I liked him much the better, suddenly.

He began to struggle to his feet and pick up his belongings one by one. 'Well, come on. You have been very clever, citizen. I really thought that I was safe this time. You can't imagine what it's like, you know – being for ever on the run. Every time I think that I have found myself a niche, someone turns up who knew me once in Rome and I'm obliged to run away again – move on and start another life elsewhere.'

'It was the slave-trader that frightened you?' I ventured.

'Of course. He knew who I was. He supplied me to my owner at the start – I went to him because he had a reputation for dealing in the best. I thought he would find me the best price for myself and I could afford the Celsus scrolls – I'd always wanted them. I paid him a good commission too. It proved a big mistake. Not only did he sell me to an owner who refused to let me go, but he has dealings with people throughout the Empire. It's not the first time I've come close to running into him, and naturally he'd know my face at once. So every time he's forced me to move on. Fortunately, I have managed up till now. I have talents, as you know. I made a living everywhere I went. I might have done again, if it were not for you. No use to remind you that I saved your life.'

It wasn't self-conceit: it was the truth. 'I owe you an apology,' I said. 'I really thought you'd planned the kidnapping.'

He paused in the act of picking up a scroll which had escaped its ties and half unrolled itself. 'And how could I do that? I wasn't even there when Julia disappeared. And what possible advantage would it be to me? I was looking for a quiet place away from town where I could earn an honest coin and not be recognised. I really thought I'd found it – I told Aulus so, though of course I didn't tell him why I needed it. Anyway,' he had retrieved his scroll by now and was busy tucking it beneath his arm, 'you must have known I had no part in it. You were surely involved in it yourself – the maid, the bag, the infant's clothes, the cleverness – everything pointed to the fact that it was you. I thought you were trying to raise questions about me in order to divert attention from yourself.'

I found that I was smiling. 'And I thought the same of

you. It was Myrna and her family all along, as you deduced, but there was a brother she didn't know she had.' I gave him a brief outline of the Lallius affair.

He was so astonished he let slip his scrolls again. 'Great Hermes! Well, I must admit it, pavement-maker, you are most astute. It seems you worked it out. With the assistance of your wife and slave of course – and my little contribution with the cloak. Doubtless His Excellence will reward you handsomely.'

I didn't argue. Julia would be grateful, and that was good enough. I did not even bother to point out that I had come to my conclusions about the cloak without his help.

He took my silence as assent. 'Well, I'd better gather up my books. Though whether I shall ever have need of them again is quite another thing.' He sighed. 'I'll hand it to you, pavement-maker, you have bested me. But there is one thing that still puzzles me – if you had worked out who I was, why did you not denounce me to your patron earlier? You had chance enough – although I tried to come between you and make sure that you did not. Because you were not certain – was that it – until you spoke to the slave-trader today?'

I shook my head. 'It did not occur to me to wonder who you were. I did try to make enquiries about your background at one time, but only because I thought you'd planned the ransom notes and I was doubtful about taking any of your cures. And when I could learn nothing, of course that made it worse. I had no notion that you were Thersis, and therefore no longer a citizen at all.'

He glanced down at his toga. It was a capital offence, of course, to impersonate a citizen when you were not entitled to the role. 'As no doubt you've pointed out to them,' he said, with bitterness. 'And of course you had worked out

331

who I was. You mentioned it the day the baby was returned, and when you came here you called me by my name.'

'I swear that it did not occur to me until today,' I said. 'But when I discovered that you were not part of the plot, I asked myself why you would run away. I thought it was the ransom note, but when it wasn't that, it had to be the slave-trader himself, or possibly the wet nurse that he'd brought with him. Then I remembered that the trader came from Rome and the likely explanation came to me. A doctor who refuses to be subservient, has enormous talents, has disappeared and would be about your age by now? You have become famous throughout the Empire, you know. And I remembered how you reacted when I mentioned the affair.'

He bent, as though to pick up the flask and bread, and then seemed to think better of the plan. 'Well,' he said again, 'it seems you've caught me now. If you had not caught me dozing, I might have slipped from you yet. But I must not make the guards impatient. They will be harsh enough with me when they discover that I am – legally – just a slave.'

I shook my head. 'There are no guards outside,' I said.

He gaped at me. 'You didn't come only to apologise?'

'More to satisfy my curiosity.' I didn't mention Marcus. There was no question of Thersis' agreeing to go back. 'I thought that I'd worked it out at last, but I wanted to be sure that I was right.'

There was sudden amusement in his tired eyes. 'I can imagine I might feel the same myself. We are alike in some ways, you and I.'

There was a moment's silence, broken by the captain's voice bellowing above. 'Hey, citizen! Are you finished yet? The wind and tide are turning and we're wanting to set off.'

I turned to Thersis – or Philades, as he would always be to

me. 'You saved my life once – as you pointed out. Now I'm going to do the same for you. I shall tell Marcus that you have gone to Gaul – but only after the boat has safely left.' My patron had done the same thing earlier – I told myself – allowed the culprits a day to get away. I was only following his example. I hoped that if he ever learned what I had done, he would see it the same way.

The medicus could not disguise his disbelief. He grasped my hand – letting the scrolls go scattering again. 'Thank you, citizen. I shall not forget.'

And I would not forget him either, easily, I thought, as I made my slippery passage back and clambered to the deck. The captain had spoken of the wind, but there were men with heavy sweeps already standing by, ready to propel the vessel down the river with the tide. The heavy sail was looped up on the mast, and the master was pacing the deck impatiently.

He looked surprised when I emerged alone. 'You did not take the man?' he muttered, handing me ashore.

'He gave me the information I required,' I said, and turned away. Behind me I could hear the dock slaves struggling with ropes and the creak and swish as the sweeps got under way. I thought of the doctor, already sweltering in that stinking hold.

In another life, I thought, he might have been a friend.

I turned quickly and walked back to the city gates where Gwellia and the carriage were awaiting me.

Epilogue

We were back in the roundhouse once again. I was happy to be home. The central fire was giving off a glow and tomorrow's oatbread was baking on the hearth. I was seated on a little stool, with a cup of hot mead in my hand. The bed of reeds and straw awaiting me was not imperial comfort, but it smelt sweet and fresh, and the woman at my side was Gwellia, contentedly working at her loom. My slaves were chattering peacefully in their new sleeping room next door, and the chickens and the cattle murmured softly from their coops.

No Roman villa had ever offered half such happiness, I thought.

I turned to Gwellia, and saw that she had let her wool-stick drop, and was staring at the wall. She saw me looking and she smiled at once. But I had learned to know my wife.

'What is it, Gwellia?'

She shook her head. 'It's nothing, husband. Everything has worked out splendidly. Julia is fully back to health, and so are you – or almost – even without the medicus to help. And Secunda and her family got away – I was a little worried about that. Especially the little girls.'

I grinned. 'Even Cassius found an advocate to plead his cause and persuade the court that he was not to blame – he escaped with just a heavy fine, I understand, for unwitting *injuria* to Julia's dignity, and bringing a false claim into the court. Of course, Lallius's confession helped with that.'

Gwellia said nothing. She knew as well as I did how that confession had been obtained.

'At least he saw sense and bribed the guards to bring him hemlock before he came to trial,' I said. Marcus was a just man in many ways, but he would have found it difficult to be impartial in this case.

Gwellia nodded. 'I'm sure that it was best.'

'So?'

She gave me a deprecating smile. 'It's that poor woman with the children. I do feel bad for her – she had done nothing except mind Myrna's daughter for her when Lallius was there, and Marcus kept her locked away for hours.'

'She didn't tell us that she had the girl. I might have guessed, I suppose. She talked about five children, and then said that she had another four at home.'

'She was terrified, poor woman, when she found you at the gate,' Gwellia said. 'She was sure that you'd charge her with robbing Myrna's house.'

'But her hands were empty,' I protested. 'How could she be a thief?'

Gwellia laughed, a low delighted sound. 'Oh, husband, you are such an innocent. The girl was pregnant, wasn't she? I think she may have taken something from the house – a blanket probably – and hidden it underneath her dress. And I don't think Myrna would begrudge it to her – she was finding it hard to manage with five children as it was. And now she had Myrna's child as well.'

'Well, there was no problem in the end,' I said. 'When we came back from Glevum, Marcus let her go. He didn't even ask her anything.'

Gwellia looked at me. 'Not even what was to happen to the child?'

And then I understood. It has been a source of grief to both of us that we were reunited too late to hope for a family of our own. Gwellia felt it very much. I remembered how she had stood there in the doorway of the inn, protecting the two children, and I felt a surge of love.

'We had thought about adopting Junio,' I said, 'when he was old enough to manumit.' Freeing slaves before a certain age is very difficult, requiring an expensive case at law.

'So you know what I was thinking,' she said sheepishly.

I reached out and gave her hand a loving squeeze.

She could not let go of the idea. 'But Myrna was free-born,' she murmured. 'The child is not a citizen, of course, but if we applied to Marcus, don't you think . . . ?' She pressed my fingers. 'Julia would speak up for us, I'm sure.'

I said, gently, so as not to cause her hurt, 'But that would not be fair. I can't have anyone take precedence over Junio.'

She grinned at me. 'Then ask Marcus about both of them,' she said. 'He'd make a dispensation for you, I am sure. Julia would make very sure he did. The boy for you, a little girl for me. We have got other slaves. We'd manage perfectly.'

I looked at her. Still my beloved Gwellia, though the dark hair was streaked with grey these days and the lovely face was strained and tired. We were too old, I thought, for tiny children now. And yet . . .

'I'll speak to him tomorrow,' I agreed. 'In the meantime, come and sit by me. We make a splendid duo, you and I.'